Red Death

Red Death

Claude M. Jonnard

iUniverse, Inc.
New York   Bloomington

Red Death

Publisher's Note: This is a work of fiction. The characters, incidents, and dialogues are products of the author's imagination and are not to be construed as real. Any resemblance to actual events and persons, living or dead, is entirely coincidental.

iUniverse books may be ordered through booksellers or by contacting:

iUniverse
1663 Liberty Drive
Bloomington, IN 47403
www.iuniverse.com
1-800-Authors (1-800-288-4677)

Because of the dynamic nature of the Internet, any Web addresses or links contained in this book may have changed since publication and may no longer be valid. The views expressed in this work are solely those of the author and do not necessarily reflect the views of the publisher, and the publisher hereby disclaims any responsibility for them.

ISBN: 978-1-4401-8703-2 (sc)
ISBN: 978-1-4401-8705-6 (hc)
ISBN: 978-1-4401-8704-9 (ebook)

Printed in the United States of America

iUniverse rev. date: 10/20/2009

To my family and friends

Whose understanding

Made possible this book

Attributions

The author is pleased to acknowledge paraphrasing and/or quotations from the following sources:

Gates of Repentance, Central Conference of American Rabbis, 1978. (See Red Death page 131)

Gilgamesh, David Ferry, The Noonday Press; Farrar, Straus and Giroux, New York, 1999. (See Red Death pages 266-267 and 335 -336.

Contents

PART ONE

In The Wake Of The Angelina

1

North of Cancer

Once upon a time there was an island upon which stood a volcano. It erupted and rivers of blood red molten lava poured down its sides into the sea and swamped the Angelina. The old freighter broke up and Eldridge went down with the ship. Hands grabbed at his shoulders and shook him until he awoke in a cold sweat with Milton hovering over him.

"Wake up, man!" Milton yelled, shaking him. "You dozed off."

Eldridge was on his back and his shirt was soaked with perspiration. He opened his eyes and took a deep breath. It was that damn dream again. The big Jamaican lay still under the Christmas tree, a small ornament clutched in one hand, until the accountant helped him to his feet.

"Let's finish re-wiring this thing," said Milton.

The ornament Eldridge held in his hand was a bride and groom statuette from the Sloane wedding twenty years ago and was always at the base of the Christmas tree in the dining room. Eldridge suspected that it might have graced the couple's first wedding cake six years before, but neither Jack nor Doreen ever said a word about their earlier relationship and he wasn't about to ask.

He needed to hang a winged angel on top of the tree, but there was a snag. The tree lights should have gone on together and the trouble was that nothing went on when the wall switch was pulled. Eldridge and Milton felt they had no choice but to take everything down and start from scratch. Night would be falling soon and they had to get the lights going before the start of the New Year's Eve festivities.

The winged angel reminded Eldridge of the bronze wings on the Angelina's bow, the old rust bucket he and his brother Hugo had skippered from the eastern end of the Mediterranean twenty five years ago. The ship

3

became tangled in the thick sea grass of the Sargasso northeast of the Bahamas and had to be abandoned. That was the official story; Eldridge knew what really happened but right now he was having a memory lapse, being unable to recall the number of lifeboats it carried.

"Is everyone here yet?" Eldridge asked, rubbing his eyes.

"Yes," answered Milton. "Jake's kids and grandkids are here with Alexandra and Rebecca. So are the Doyle's, the Tully's, the Sinclair's, Virgil and Clovis and their families..." And he went on with an almost endless list of names."

"The tree should have been on the lawn facing the waterway," said Eldridge. "It would have given everyone a better view of the inlet and the yachts going by when the fireworks start at midnight."

"What about rain?" Milton asked. "It rained on Christmas Day."

The big gray bearded Jamaican could not argue against Milton's logic.

"And it rained on and off almost every Christmas holiday since Jake has been having these parties," Milton went on."

"How about when we got here twenty years ago, did it rain? Eldridge asked.

Milton shook his head, saying, "We found a torched wasteland and rotting bodies in the middle of a rainstorm. There was nothing, and half of the people here and in the world were dead. But it didn't rain that first Christmas."

Eldridge looked out the floor-to-ceiling windows at the manicured lawn and at the waterway beyond where gleaming white yachts were passing by.

"Who would believe we are standing on what was once rubble?"

"Kids don't know and adults don't want to remember," remarked Milton. "And lucky for us and everyone, the plague never returned, and it's been twenty years."

A big broad smile crossed Eldridge's face and he nodded towards the tree.

"I bet you can't remember the first Christmas tree Jack made us put up, Milt."

"You're wrong, old friend; the scene is forever etched in my mind," said Milton.

"It was October and our three little sailboats barreled through the inlet with a fast incoming tide in a blinding downpour. We tied up not far from here, and a couple of months later, to celebrate Christmas, Jake stuck a palm tree branch in the ground and we decorated it with whatever doodads were on hand."

"At least we didn't need to light it up," remarked Eldridge.

"That's because we had no power."

A radio at the foot of the tree was playing an old tape of Kenny Rogers singing the refrain from 'The Gambler,' and Eldridge hummed the tune in synch with the mournful wail of the singer's soft velvety voice.

"You got to know when to hold 'em, know how to fold 'em; know when to walk away and know when to run. You never count your money when you're sitting at the table; there'll be time enough for countin' when the dealins' done."

The radio announcer broke to announce that it was New Year's in Paris.

Eldridge could hear Jack's voice when they landed as if it was yesterday.

"We need luck," he had said in his gravelly voice. "And luck is what we got."

He was older now but his voice was the about the same. It betrayed his Louisiana roots, and he still had that toothy grin and slight lisp.

What was with those lights? Eldridge and Milton were scrambling to re-arrange the wiring when Jack's old cronies suddenly barged into the dining room, most likely to aggravate them. They were about to start cracking jokes when a noise came from the kitchen. It was Dennis Sinclair coming in with a tray of cups and saucers.

"Does Jake know yet?" Gordon Tully asked the doctor.

"I told him," replied Dennis.

"You did right," agreed Hugo. "He had to be told."

"How old would you say the old man was?" Eldridge asked.

"Maybe ninety," the physician answered. Jake's mom died last year at eighty nine, and they were the same age. So he must have been ninety. It's a good age."

"I got it!" Eldridge yelled, catching everyone by surprise. He hit the switch and the tree came alive. "We have a short somewhere in the system, but it will hold."

He and Milton were given a standing ovation and a round of applause.

"No age is good," said Dennis when the applause faded. "A doctor hates to lose his patients, any patient, young or old."

His wife Jane came out of the kitchen with Angela Doyle, Pattie Tully, Cynthia Cooper and Jack's wife Doreen with coffee and tea. They were followed by Jack carrying a platter of pastries. He had overheard Dennis.

"Switch to obstetrics or pediatrics, Dennis. You'll lose fewer patients that way."

He set the pastry tray on a table in time for his wife to admonish him.

"Shelly, you're talking about your parents!"

"That's men for you," said Pattie. "They have a weird sense of humor." And she gave Gordon a peck on his bald head.

Jack in turn kissed his wife on the cheek. "They had seventy years together," he explained in his flat, growly drawl. "Dad wanted to go find Ma."

"How do you know he wanted to die, Jake?" Frank asked, wiping his mouth with a napkin. "I don't want to die."

"My husband thinks everyone wants to live forever," said Angela.

Frank shrugged, saying, "I'm not against dying," he said. "It's just that I'm in no hurry to go."

"I need to know how I'm going to write this party off as a business expense," said Milton, looking around in exasperation.

"You're the numbers man," said Jack. "You'll figure it out."

"That's all I'm good for," complained Milton. "I figure things out."

"That's good," said Jack's wife. "We're here today because of you."

"Amen," Cynthia murmured in agreement.

Hugo Johnson raised a glass of soda, saying, "To life and tax deductions."

"I'd drink to that if I was a drinking man," Jack agreed.

Eldridge echoed the word 'life' and started munching on a pastry.

"How long have you been off the booze, Jake?" Hugo asked. "I know you never touched it once you got back to the islands."

"Well, let's see. I stopped smoking twenty years ago," Jack said, scratching his head. "So I must have stopped drinking twenty five years ago."

"Well, you're healthy. You'll see your grandkids marry," Dennis predicted.

"You think?" Jack gave Doreen another kiss as she took him aside to say that someone from the FBI's Miami office was on his way to make an off-duty visit.

Jack smiled, shrugged his shoulders and said, "I'm here."

"Are you going to be doing Auld Lang Syne on your horn for us again tonight?" Gordon asked.

"You bet," Jack replied, squinting slightly and rubbing his head. He couldn't put a finger on it but his vision was blurred and he felt out of sorts.

"I need to tune up for tonight," he said, leaning against a table for support.

Doreen sensed that something was wrong.

"Are you ok, Shelly?"

Jack placed his arm around her waist and gave her a squeeze.

"It's just that I'm out of practice and I want to sound good tonight." Turning to everyone else, he said, "You folks all enjoy yourselves, you hear."

Once in the privacy of his study, Jack took the shiny brass trumpet off his desk and stopped in front of the full length mirror on the wall under the charred Yin-Yang engraving. Oh well, it had been a good run. Doreen was a beautiful woman, as beautiful as she was when they met a long time ago. He smiled into the mirror and the Doreen he knew many years ago smiled back. He blinked. Next to her was Ginny Malone. They were blowing him kisses and waving as he sailed away on Archangel. And then they were gone and he was alone at sea.

Out on the lawn by the water, a pig was roasting on a spit over a fire in an open pit under the dying light of day and the Sloane home reflected the festive noises of the holiday season that would end with the county fireworks at midnight. Children and teenagers shared the lawn with young adults chasing their squealing toddlers. It was a multi-generational party bracing for the roast, the feast, the fireworks and Jack's rendition of Auld Lang Syne.

Jack's two kids from his first marriage were at the party with their spouses. Ron was a history teacher and Eve was a nurse and in their twenties and married. They had four children between them who were all at the party. His two daughters from a second marriage were also home for the holidays. Alexandra was twenty two years old and a graduate student. Rebecca was twenty and a college senior. He had two more children through his third wife who was actually once his first wife; they were teenagers. His total was therefore six children and four grandchildren.

Ron supplemented his income by writing family biographies and was putting the Sloane family history together. He was now at his dad's home determined this time to find out what secrets about their lives they were withholding. Jack and Doreen would ever discuss the past with anyone, and Ron thought that perhaps Eldridge or Milton might help him out.

It was the sound Doreen dreaded to hear; the sound of a sack of potatoes falling to the ground, and Doreen knew who it was. She dropped what she was doing and ran to the study followed by Dennis where Jack was face down and out cold on the floor, his trumpet at his side.

She knelt down to cushion Jack's head and began rocking back and forth.

"Do something," she sobbed hysterically. "Oh, God, don't let him die."

"It's his heart," Dennis told her, checking his vital signs. "I've called 911 and the hospital. His heart needs a jump start and I don't have enough tricks in my black bag to keep it going."

Two police cars and an EMS vehicle, lights flashing and sirens blaring, pulled up in front of the house within minutes and medical technicians began stabilizing Jack and moving him on to a gurney. He was already being taken outside when the FBI man showed up at the door with an attaché case in hand, and his bewilderment was easy to understand. The Sloane house was filled with bedlam and confusion; Jack was being rushed away to the hospital and people were piling into cars to follow. He didn't know what was going on and to whom he should talk. To complicate things, one of the children began coughing and shaking and was obviously coming down with something.

"I'm looking for a Jack Shelby Sloane," said the FBI agent, trying desperately to get someone to listen. "Where can I find him?"

A young woman, about to leave for the hospital with a male companion heard him, caught her breath and stopped long enough to reply.

"Hi, my name is Alexandra, and this is my brother Ron. Can we help you?"

Blonde and soft featured as was Alexandra, the FBI man, also young but slightly older than she, had dark hair and had a firm, determined jaw. But their respective chemistries must have mixed well because they made eye contact right away and Alexandra seemed quite sensitive to the young man's plight.

"Yes," replied the FBI man, pointing to the attaché case in his hand. "I need to see him about something belonging to a naval officer named Robert Byrne who died about twenty years ago. I was told they were friends and that Mr. Sloane lives here. I'm being re-assigned to Los Angeles so this is the only time I can see him."

"He lives here," said Ron, impatiently answering for Alexandra. "But right now he's on the way to the hospital. Can this wait?"

"We need to go," Alexandra went on, tears welling up in her eyes. "But you can ride with us if you wish. My dad needs luck and you might be his lucky charm."

"That'll be the day," the FBI man muttered under his breath.

Dennis Sinclair and Doreen sped away in one car behind the EMS van. Eldridge Johnson and Milton Cooper took Gordon Tully and followed in another car while Alexandra, Ron and the FBI man brought up the rear in a third car. Everyone else stayed behind with the children. It was just as well. No hospital is ever cheery, let alone on a New Year's Eve when hospitals are nearly deserted.

Life and death cast perpendicular shadows over nearly comatose patients being pushed in their transport gurneys down empty hallways. Voices are barely audible but their whispers are magnified as they echo off walls. Medical types, suited from the neck down in polyester cotton color coded pajamas, make deep muffled sounds and hover ominously over operating tables in surgery rooms deep in the bowels of the hospital where the stars never shine and the sun never enters.

And so they sat around a table, Alexandra, Ron, the FBI man, Eldridge, Milton and Gordon Tully, so buried in their own inner thoughts that they never bothered to ask the FBI man for his name or for any form of identification. Now and then they looked down the long corridor in front of them on either side of which were banks of operating rooms, doors shut to prying eyes. They didn't know where Jack was and could only guess that Doreen and Dennis were waiting nearby.

"It's not fair," said Eldridge. "Jake can't die."

The FBI man looked up, asking, "Jake? I thought his name was Jack."

"Guys call him Jake," Gordon said. "Women call him Shelly."

"He must be a great guy," noted the FBI man.

"He is," said Gordon. "He is the glue that keeps us together."

"How did that Yin-Yang engraving end up in the house?" Ron asked, sensing an opening to learn more about his parents. "Didn't it come from the Bahamas?"

"Yes," answered Milton. "It came from my dad's rectory that burned down. My dad died in that fire. As a matter of fact, I also lost my brothers, my wife and my kids. But Plague took them."

"And I lost my sister and my folks," Eldridge added, heaving a sigh.

"We all left flesh behind," said Gordon. "My entire family was wiped out in that damn epidemic."

"I remember my dad telling me about it. I was a kid in Washington D.C., but we were given shots, so we never got sick."

"Well, most of us weren't that lucky," said Eldridge.

"What I don't understand," Ron interjected, "is how my mom and dad ended up in the Bahamas to begin with."

The FBI man asked, "Wasn't this Robert Byrne involved somehow?"

"Well, it's a long story, but we have time," Milton sighed. "It began when the sun began moving north of the Tropic of Cancer. I was told that the last time that it happened was a thousand years ago."

2

The Angelina

Jack was a sea captain who skippered large container ships across oceans for a living, Milton began. He also had a part interest in a boat repair yard in Boynton Beach. The problem was that he had a bad temper, drank a lot and killed a man. That last act of indiscretion was twenty five years ago and was a career stopping move. He lost his license, his marriage and his kids who were not yet born.

That was when he stopped drinking and began paying closer attention to his boatyard business in Florida and to another yard he eventually opened in Agnes Town on North Border Island in the Bahamas. His Florida partners were Bob Byrne with forty percent and Emile Honoree with twenty percent. Emile was a mechanic and Bob was a career naval officer. Jack's partners in Agnes Town at first were Tom Kennedy with fifty percent and Fred Hawk with ten percent. But the two businesses were on land owned by Louie Gold, a retired salesman, and he had planned to leave it to Bob Byrne, his adopted son.

Bob, Fred, Jack and Tom were boyhood chums, but Jack was closer to Bob than to the others. He therefore accepted Louie's wish to protect his son's interest in good cheer, figuring he could always take care of himself. And take care of himself he did. He rebuilt his life and career and had plenty of money to spare. But he was having nightmares. Some included his ex-wife, and some had to do with Emile's prediction of a cosmic disturbance pushing Capricorn north and forcing a temporary change in the earth's tilt that would bring the sun north of the tropic of Cancer to a point over the North and South Border islands of the Bahamas.

It was a bad omen that came only once every thousand years, according to Emile, and could spell doom for North and South Border islands. Now,

Jack knew that Emile was high strung about such things, and it wasn't that Jack was the suspicious type, but he decided to visit his Agnes Town business anyway and check things out for himself.

"You're nothing but a drunk, a goddamn drunk and a homicidal maniac!"

"And you're a whore, Doreen! I never would have married you if I knew you were screwing Fred behind my back."

"Get out," Doreen screamed. "Get out or I'll call the cops!"

A bottle of whisky was thrown. A gun was fired and Jack woke up in a sweat.

It was a lousy nightmare. The office phone light on the desk next to his cot was on, prompting him to check for messages. There was only one from Doreen, and it was a reminder about the child support money. So, it was a dream after all and she was alive and well, and by now he figured that Bob Byrne would have given her the envelope.

Jack laughed. Bob had married her first; he married her when she dumped Bob; and then Doreen dumped him for Fred. He tapped the trumpet standing upright by the phone and thanked his lucky star that she only wanted full custody of their yet unborn twins and did not ask for a stake in his business. But he would have been happy giving her everything for joint custody. Man, was that only five years ago?

There was a second message. It was from Louie Gold, the Cross Island Air agent in the islands. Louie had no phone and Jack guessed he must have either gone to the telephone center or patched the call through on Tom Kennedy's ham radio. It was a reminder from Louie that he had filed a new will in Nassau and Florida that made Jack the sole beneficiary of his estate and forgave any monies that Jack may have owed him. That was good news, but he knew Bob would be pissed.

The message was anticlimactic; he had already received and signed off on the official papers. Bob Byrne always thought that his claim to Jack's Boynton Beach business also applied to the Bahamian operation and Jack expected Bob to contest the will but it hadn't happened, at least not yet. He felt sorry for Bob but he also felt good. He grabbed the horn from the top of his desk and blew out a few loud dissonant notes. Oh well, he and Emile had work to do. They needed to get Ned Baron's yacht ready for a day of fishing outside the inlet.

Emile Honoree was a dark skinned Haitian with big eyes behind horn rimmed glasses and had a big wide grin that exposed two rows of shiny white teeth. He was in the engine room and Frank Doyle was busy checking the weather fax. His sister Pattie, a pretty, perky brunette, was with Jack at the helm of Ned Baron's new yacht. He focused on steadying it in the gathering swells and she focused on him.

It was a one sided infatuation Jack wanted to ignore. Pattie was a bit of a flirt; she also liked Gordon Tully, South Border's police chief, even though she hardly knew him and he was married with kids. On the yacht with her was Angela Baron, Ned's niece. She was the daughter of Nigel Baron, Ned's brother who lived in the Bahamas. Angela moved to Florida to attend college and never moved back. She had a thing for Frank but he wasn't biting, at least not yet.

"Doreen," Jack mused to himself. "How did you turn out to be such a whore? Hell! How did I turn out to be such a drunk? Why did things turn out so badly?"

He steered the yacht past the sea buoy outside Palm Beach's Lake Worth inlet under gray skies, a worn skipper's cap hiding his thinning gray speckled brown hair. The swells under the vessel did not faze him. He stood loose, his legs and body swaying with their motion, whistling a Kenny Rogers tune as he worked the throttles.

Jack listened to the news on the marine band radio on the consol of the bridge over the main cabin and kept an eye on the weather deteriorating around him. At a full six feet he was tall enough to see over the tinted spray shield and could watch the rising seas around the yacht. One ear was trained on the gong of the sea buoy bell in the gathering fog while the other ear listened to news on the radio about a measles outbreak in Riviera Beach and North Palm Beach.

It was an unknown strain, said the report, combining flu or pneumonia symptoms with an angry red rash that tended to blister. Jack thought he had heard of a similar outbreak several years ago. When he and Doreen discussed it in terms of it being a threat to their children with Cyrus Cooper and his colleague Henry Alden, the two physicians suggested that it was a form of Rubella or "rougeole," or "scarlatina."

Jack had to look up the words; loosely translated they meant a "red rash." But it was not chicken pox, which was of concern to all parents of all young children. Scarlatina was in fact Scarlet Fever and that did not sound fatal. No one knew for sure what it was and Cyrus gave them all measles and chicken pox shots to be on the safe side,

Whatever; how could flu or measles strike in May? It reminded Jack of another brief outbreak five years ago that reportedly came from a contaminated chemicals leak into the air from a failed experiment. Victims also developed a red rash. Some said it was a combination of "walking pneumonia" and measles.

Jack recalled that Cyrus, Henry and Ben Alden, Henry's brother, were involved in a project to find a cure for the bubonic plague, but the project was supposedly shelved. Henry returned to his patients in the Bahamas; Ben dropped out of sight, and Cyrus resumed his medical practice.

Doreen routinely used Cyrus Cooper for the children but she was rarely at his office with Jack. She and the kids lived in a development tract house with Fred Hawk in Wellington twenty miles west of Palm Beach and communicated with her ex-husband mainly through Bob Byrne. The twins would be five years old the end of June and Jack had never seen them. Doreen was pregnant when they divorced and because of his murder conviction the court denied him visitation rights. Lucky Fred, he had gotten himself a wife and instant family without even trying.

The sea buoy's gong grew weaker and fog moved in, meaning that the yacht was past the marker and that it was time to start keeping an eye on the instrument panel. Jack turned off the radio during a piece about a new flare up in Asia. Boring; wars were always raging and people never learn. That's what happens when people have strong convictions or no convictions at all. Compromise becomes impossible. They should all die.

Jack was in this foul mood when Ned Baron climbed up to the bridge to take the helm. Ned hated the sea and used the yacht for business entertainment, hiring Jack to run the vessel. Yesterday, Sunday, was his daughter Jane's engagement party at the Delray Yacht Club, and today he was treating Bob Byrne, Larry Fisher, Jimmy Wales and the Cooper brothers, Milton and Cyrus, all of whom were guests at the party, to a day of fishing.

Jimmy Wales was Bob's friend from Washington DC. He had a wife and young son and worked as a cop for the Capitol police. He once borrowed Bob's revolver and flew in to return it and spend quality time with his buddy. He was not a boater and tagged along for the ride. Bob was busy so Jimmy gave Jack the weapon for safekeeping, and Jack promptly forgot to return it to Bob.

Milton, being born and bred in the islands, was used to boats and was perched on the foredeck fiddling with a pocket GPS. An accountant by trade, he too was not very social although he basked in the financial success of his peers.

"I appraised your business and Ginny's club in Agnes Town for the Bahamian government," he said with a chuckle when Jack passed by him on the way to check the fishing gear in the bow lockers. "Those two properties are worth $3.5 million each, Jake. You and Ginny will need to pay more real estate taxes. Will you pass the word to Ginny and her dad? You may see them before I get there."

Jack groaned. Milton was well connected in the islands and Jack knew he could not be bribed to keep his mouth shut. He would end up paying more taxes. Such was life.

Contrary to Milton, Cyrus was a landlubber like Ned and had come along to be with his brother. Cyrus specialized in tropical and rare and exotic diseases and was s consultant for the Centers for Disease Control (CDC) in Atlanta when he was not treating his patients. It was there that he was temporarily teamed up with Ben and Henry Alden.

Bob Byrne and Larry Fisher were also experienced seamen. Bob was with the Navy and Larry was chief of the Palm Beach marine police. They were retirement eligible, but Bob was staying on in the hope of becoming a rear Admiral. Larry wanted to leave police work for the private sector.

Jack surrendered the helm to Ned and climbed off the bridge, encountering Bob Byrne and Larry Fisher in the after cockpit who were readying their fishing gear.

"Congratulations, old buddy," said Jack. "But why so glum?"

"Congratulations for what?" Bob scowled.

"Bob may be a big Navy man" said Larry ruefully. "But Louie cut him loose."

Bob Byrne managed to give Jack a smile anyway.

"Thanks, Jake. It took me ten years to get this naval intelligence post. The money is good but it stinks in comparison to the value of Louie's holdings. What gets me even more is the fact that Louie is leaving you everything."

"Don't lose sleep over it," Jack said. "I'll safeguard your end. I owe you that."

Bob Byrne smiled. "Thanks," he said. "You're a good friend."

"You and I should sit down and talk," suggested Jack.

"He's in Naval Intelligence, no less," added Frank Doyle who overheard them.

"Yeah, if I'm so smart, why aren't I rich?" Bob asked rhetorically. "I make more money partnering with Jake than on what the Navy pays me. Oh, by the way, Jake. I gave Doreen the money like you wanted. I also took care of her meds. I bought them at a deep discount from Vernon Peters' pharmacy on South Border."

"Thanks," said Jack. "Well, someday you might decide to quit your government job and go full time into my business since you own part of it."

"What about Emile Honoree, Frank Doyle and Tom Kennedy?"

"Frank will ride your coat tails. He'll join us full time if you do. Emile is a great mechanic and we need him. Tom likes the islands and is in tight with Thelma. But he needs an operation for a bum ticker in the States. That's why I bought him out. When Tom and Thelma leave, I'll either sell the Agnes Town yard or take on new partners. The two businesses are growing so a new partnership arrangement here or there could work. The only possible snag could be Louie since he still owns the land."

"The guy will probably live forever," Bob moaned.

"That's not our call," said Jack. "And as I said, you and I should talk."

The smile on Bob's face vanished and his lips curled.

"I made two mistakes with Louie. The first was when I refused to be converted to Judaism. That's what Louie wanted from the day he and his wife adopted me. The second mistake was when I had my Coast Guard guys stop him for running drugs. That son-of-a-bitch never forgot and has had it in for me all these years."

Jack nodded in agreement although his face registered a question.

"How come you put a collar on him anyway?" he asked.

"He never paid me or Larry for protection, like you, Eldridge and Hugo did."

"That's right," Larry Fisher added smugly. "People need to pay to play."

"We never pay shit, guys," corrected Jack. "Our deal is with Ed Baron, and he takes care of that. I assume he is still is."

"Well, Louie should have cut himself into that deal," said Larry.

"Maybe he still can," Jack suggested.

Bob shook his head.

"No. I don't want anything from him. You can have it all. You deserve it."

Jack enjoyed Bob Byrne's company and could never understand why Doreen had dumped him.

"Listen Robert, I owe you my life. But tell me, how come you gave me a hand when I was out on my back?"

Bob shrugged his shoulders, saying, "I thought it was a good idea." He put his gear in place and looked squarely at Jack. "And we should see about your business when your probation ends in July. It's been five years, hasn't it?"

"Just about," Jack confirmed. "But it wasn't that bad. Thanks to you and Larry, the judge let me run my businesses here and in the Bahamas."

"Are you thinking of settling down?" Larry asked.

Jack winked.

"Who knows, I might even try marriage again."

"I'm available if anyone is interested," said Pattie Doyle under her breath.

"Are you thinking of Ginny Malone in the Borders?" Bob asked.

"I don't know," said Jack. "I got scalded with Doreen."

"She took me too," said Bob, "in case you don't remember. That's not the issue. Doreen still likes you, and she's White. Ginny is mixed."

Jack sighed.

"Most of the world is not Anglo, Robert."

"That's why it's important for us to stick together," said Bob. "And why we need to be careful. Whites have fewer diseases and live longer. Ginny is Jamaican, isn't she?"

Jack protested.

"No way; Ginny doesn't even look Jamaican. Her dad and his brother Dale and their and their families lived in the South for generations. Somewhere in the past, one of their grandparents married a Jamaican gal. Hell, Robert, Ginny, Kyle and Dale look more Irish than Jamaican. Besides, Ginny may not want to marry me, and even if she does, she might not want to leave her home."

Bob nodded, saying, "You'll make the right decision, I'm sure. But I bet Doreen now regrets ditching you for Fred Hawk. You've done much better than him."

"Well, that's not my fault. He's her problem and she's his problem."

"That is the thing, Jake," Bob persisted. "He's away on sales trips most of the time. That leaves her alone with the kids and she isn't feeling well these days. For that matter, neither is he."

Jack looked at his watch and changed the subject.

"Listen, you guys hold the fort here. I want to see how Cyrus is doing."

"He's below in the cabin," Bob pointed. Then he nodded at the fog surrounding the boat. "It doesn't look so good out there, Jake."

"No, it doesn't," Jack agreed. "We may need to head back."

Jack made his way to the cabin with Frank Doyle following. He was about to go in when Frank said, "I thought you always knew why Bob put up that money."

"He was being a good friend," said Jack.

Frank shook his head.

"I got the real story from Patricia and she got it from Doreen. They were friends, you know."

"What was the story?"

"Pattie told me that Doreen made Bob put up the money."

"Doreen?" The conversation was interrupted by the sound of a groan from inside the cabin. "Listen," said Jack. "I think Cyrus is seasick. Check the bridge. I want to look in on the doctor. We'll talk later."

Frank left and Jack opened the door where he found Cyrus checking the supplies in his medical bag and groaning at no one in particular.

"What's up, doctor?"

Cyrus looked up anxiously and asked, "My belly says a storm is coming."

Jack put his fears to rest, saying, "No, this is just normally lousy weather."

"I wouldn't be here if my brother wasn't. But Milton has to fly back tomorrow for his new job and we wanted to have face time together."

"What new job?"

"He was promoted from tax reviewer to tax assessor for the northern Bahamas," answered Cyrus. "Our brother Lance arranged it with Malcolm Harding and with the regional commissioner."

Jack whistled.

"You mean Hamilton Graves? Man, He's the big shot in the northern Bahamas."   "He sure is," said Cyrus. "Our family knows people, you know."

That was an understatement. The Cooper family was indeed influential. Cyrus's brother, Lancelot, was the regional commander of the Bahamian Defense Force (the BDF as it was called in the islands) and its fleet of cutters. Hiram Cooper, the family patriarch, was the minister at the Church of Christ, the principal house of worship in the Border islands. Hiram, in particular, was a good friend of Malcolm Harding and Hamilton Graves.

Jack gave Cyrus some pills to control his queasiness and went back on deck and looked out to sea. The weather was bad and getting worse. Why Ned picked this day to go out was beyond him.

Jack was sorry he missed the engagement party. Weekends were busy at Jack's Marine and he and Emile Honoree had to work. They had to keep an eye on the fuel pumps that fed the thirsty tanks of mega yachts whose skippers often paid in hundred dollar bills. Mondays were different. Business was dead and he had plenty of time.

Jack regretted not seeing Jane Baron more often. He had seen her last as a baby when he was a teenage mechanic at the yard he eventually bought. She was raised by nannies and brought up in out-of-state boarding schools.

He made his way back to the bridge where Frank was trying to get Ned to leave the helm. He stepped aside only when Jack appeared, meekly moving his corpulent body away from the consol.

"My brother Nigel was at the party yesterday, "he said, trying to make small talk. "He told me that Tom Kennedy filed the papers last week transferring his share of the boat yard to you. Anyway, Nigel sends his regards."

"I'll see him soon," said Jack. "How was the food?"

"The club served the usual meat and fish dishes, but you got to hear this, Jake. A trawler from Riviera Beach that caught the fish snagged some wooden crates filled with opium. Some were broken and water logged but about a dozen were sealed."

"That's right," said Frank. "Good, pure, semi-processed heroin; the crew left the fish but stole a truck and skipped town with the heroin one step ahead of the cops."

Jack was not sure he believed the story and asked, "Who said it was heroin?"

"The cops tested the stuff in one of the crates," Frank replied. "They also figured out the markings on the crate. They read 'Angelina,' like the name of a ship. Isn't that the freighter you were once supposed to skipper?

Jack recollected vaguely, nodded and turned to Ned. "Say, you're an insurance guy. Hear anything recent on the Angelina? It got lost five or six years ago."

"Gee, we do life and casualty, Jake. We don't do boats."

Ned Baron was older than Jack. Middle aged, good natured, pot bellied and bald, he looked every bit like the successful businessman he was. His insurance agency in Palm Beach sold insurance policies through Jonathan Hall in the Border islands who happened to be Doreen's father, making him Jack's ex father-in-law. He was also the mayor of South Border Island and owned the Ocean View hotel. Both men respected Jack's street smarts, especially Jonathan. In April, when a few cruise ship passengers died while it was anchored for the day in the bay near his hotel, he went to Jack for advice, being concerned that bad publicity might harm tourism in the islands.

"Let the boat go with the bodies, and don't make a big deal over it," Jack urged. "They may have had food poisoning. But call Dan Schulman. Let him decide. He owns a good piece of the cruise line."

Jonathan never called Dan. He asked Cynthia, his other daughter, to call Dan since she was originally married to him before ditching him for Henry Alden, her current husband. It was unclear what conversation transpired between Cynthia and Dan, if any. What was clear was that it was Henry who finally talked Jonathan into sending the cruise ship on its way without detention and inspection. It was almost as if it was good riddance to bad rubbish.

"Any of you guys ever hear of a steamer called the Angelina?"

They shook their heads.

"Ask Ned," Larry yelled back. "He's in the insurance business."

"Not me," Ned kept insisting. "I don't do boats."

Jack turned on the auto-helm and scampered down to the after-deck.

Larry Fisher and Ned Baron had a deal. Ned had Larry's chase boats maintained at Jack's yard at his regular price in return for which Jack kicked back money to Ned that was split with Larry who then kept his police chasers away from Ned's yacht when Emile Honoree periodically took it to the Bahamas with cash and returned with cocaine. Larry was as trim as Ned was overweight and his dark hair was slicked back with a gel like pomade that made it stick in wind and rain.

"May I ask how much you paid for Tom Kennedy's stake, Jake?" Larry asked.

Jack grinned, keeping an eye on the darkening sky.

"The price was right," he answered. "Tom needs an operation here. I gave him cash and put him on my Boynton payroll as manager to give him health insurance coverage for his medical bills."

Larry Fisher and Ned Baron agreed it was a "real sweet deal."

Ned Baron liked cash deals and respected people who dealt in cash. Bahamian by birth, he had moved to Florida and opened an agency that sold casualty, life and liability insurance in the Border islands. Nigel Baron, his brother, was the mayor of North Border and owned the North Border Hotel in Agnes Town, the island's main hamlet. They too had a special arrangement. Nigel sent leads to Jonathan Hall, his sales rep in the Borders; Jonathan followed up and sold policies created by Ned's insurance underwriters. It was never clear to Jack if the policies in fact existed, but the premium revenues were substantial and Jonathan Ned and Nigel split all the profits. It also helped that Jonathan also owned the Island Trust, the only bank for the Border islands. Everyone banked at Island Trust, a cozy, convenient offshore tax haven close to Florida. That is, everyone banked there except Jack who kept his money in Florida.

"I don't trust local banks," he said once. "They have no accountability."

To guard against piracy once out of the sight of Larry Fisher's police chasers and Bob Byrne's Coast Guard cutters, Jack hired the armed escort services of two drug traffickers, the Johnson brothers, Hugo and Eldridge. They owned the Zebra club on North Border Island, dealt in cocaine and sold liquor to Cheetah's, a night club owned by Ginny Malone next to Jack's boatyard. They had a sister named Thelma who had a romantic interest in Tom Kennedy.

Emile, his usual grin and laughing eyes now dead serious, came up from below to warn that the weather fax had just reported a rapidly approaching storm.

"Incidentally, when are you heading for the Borders?" Ned asked.

"I'm leaving in a few days; any messages?"

"Tell Jonathan his customers' policies aren't being renewed. I got an e-mail from our underwriters first thing this morning cancelling all policies."

Rain began falling, but before Jack could turn the vessel about, Larry Fisher saw something bobbing in the water near the sea buoy.

"Boat," he bellowed, pointing to the object in the water.

Jack brought the yacht closer. It was a lifeboat. On its hull letters spelled out the name, Angelina, and in the open lifeboat their eyes were greeted by a strange and grotesque sight. Two freshly decomposing bodies lay twisted on the floorboards. What was left of their skin surfaces was covered with red crusts of blood and the smell of death was heavy in the air. Bob Byrne gagged and went below.

"So, there is an Angelina after all," Larry exclaimed.

Milton and Ned said nothing but Cyrus muttered under his breath, "That damn ship was supposed to be history. Someone has opened Pandora's Box."

"The big question for me is how fresh bodies ended up on a lifeboat from a ship that fell off the radar years ago," said Jack.

"I'm glad I'm going back to Washington," Jimmy Wales concluded.

3

The Mystery Lifeboats

Ned Baron never reported the incident and Jack made no entries on the ship's log. Bob Byrne left the matter to Larry Fisher to handle but he went on vacation without doing anything. Jack was fearful of somehow jeopardizing the last few months of his probation and decided to keep his mouth shut. Still, that aborted fishing trip stirred up memories. The ghost of the Angelina had risen from the deep with a curse for those it touched. Something rooted in the past had surfaced and he was at a loss to explain what it was. One thing for sure, he was now glad he had declined Dan Schulman's offer to skipper the vessel to and from Lebanon to meet a prior commitment to skipper a container ship from Fort Lauderdale to Buenos Aires when the regular captain got sick.

The barroom fight and killing that almost ruined his life and career happened when he returned from Buenos Aires. It was with a six-pack captain, one of those guys who had a mail order license to run charters with a maximum of six passengers. He had been hired by Jack and Fred Hawk to run their yacht, End Run, on weekend charters from Florida to the Bahamas. Jack left the details of the charter business to Fred, an arrangement that worked well until End Run was intercepted with a load of cocaine by the DEA. His life started unraveling at that point.

Against the advice of Bob Byrne's attorney, he and Jimmy Wales met with the charter skipper at a bar to get his side of the story. It just so happened that Jack had Bob's revolver that he borrowed for the firing range earlier in the day. They were drinking and words turned to blows. Jack struck the skipper's head with the revolver and then hid it in Jimmy's pocket. According to the coroner, the man died of a heart attack and the revolver was never produced as evidence.

Jack plead guilty to manslaughter and received a suspended sentence with five years' probation, thanks to good character testimonies by Bob Byrne and Larry Fisher. That was the low point of his life. But that was then and this was now.

Ned wanted to pay Jack for his time, but Jack refused. He figured that the trip to and from the sea buoy had cost Ned over two hundred gallons of fuel for the four hours under power in the rain without catching a single fish. Ned deserved a break.

Tired and wet, Jack returned to his boatyard. He wanted to reach Tom Kennedy and give him the particulars about a medical exam he was booking on his behalf with a cardiologist. And here was another one of those small headaches in life. The Border islands existed in a time warp. Phone calls needed to be placed through the local telephone center and patched the States and elsewhere through Nassau. There wee no cell towers and therefore cell phones were useless. There were also very few street lights and no traffic lights.

Many families had computers, but internet access was spotty even for those with satellite dishes; manual typewriters trumped laptops. Airmail and courier services were reliable, but the fastest way to speak to anyone in the Borders was to fly over in person unless one had wireless transmitting and receiving radios like the ones used on ships, and most people did. These were vintage citizens band (CB) radios once popular with truckers, dependable VHF marine radios and the powerful single side band units used by ham radio aficionados.

Jack and Tom were ham radio hobbyists and kept a ham radio on their sailboat, Archangel, in the Borders. Another radio was in Jack's Boynton Beach boatyard but it was missing a part. Emile Honoree was also a ham operator and kept an SSB radio at his home. He used the radio to reach his uncle, Father Francis Honoree, a priest at All Souls Church at Sanctuary Village on North Border Island and with family and friends in Haiti.

Jack decided to pay Emile a visit and hopped a cab, hoping to find him home. It was dinner time and his wife, Juliette, greeted him at the door with a hug and a kiss and pointed to the back. From the yard outside of the house came the sounds of small children squealing and laughing.

"You will stay for dinner?" Juliette asked.

"I don't want to intrude. I need to call Tom Kennedy."

"You cannot see Emile and not stay for dinner," she insisted as Emile showed up at her side. "We are having an early dinner."

"Oh?"

"Yes. We and the children are getting flu shots tomorrow so we need to go turn in early."

"You're getting flu shots? But this is May."

"This is a different flu," Juliette explained. "It turns into a bad rash, like measles or chicken pox. My sister, Renee, is a nurse for Dr. Cooper who says special shots are needed and that he has enough for a few families. The shots are free so we are going. I hope we are doing the right thing."

"I hope so too," said Jack.

"But why do you want to call Tom?" Emile asked in his French patois accent, ushering Jack into the room behind the kitchen.

"I want to make sure that I have a place to sleep when I get to the Borders. Tom may not have enough room for me on Archangel if he has company."

Emile grinned broadly.

"I understand," he said with a big grin. But Juliette shot him a dirty look.

Emile had nothing more to say. He turned on the crank operated transmitter on the corner table. Next to a half full bottle of rum was a notebook filled with soiled pages of call numbers and names. He carefully turned pages until he came to the name, Thomas Kennedy. Next to the name, he had written the numbers, 25-0-72.5. The notations in his notebook were carefully arranged in two sections. In the first, were listed alphabetically arranged names with their call numbers on the right; the second section was filled with the call numbers with the names on the right.

"Latitudes and longitudes," explained Emile happily, anticipating the question on Jack's mind. "This way, I pick any place in the world and I speak to a friend. See the numbers next to Tom's name? That is the northernmost tropic of cancer latitude line this year. Tom's island is at the intersection of 72.5 north longitude."

He went to a laptop computer connected to the radio and began tapping on the keys with the flourish of a pianist.

"I keep all call numbers on my laptop," he said. "I type his name or call number, et voila!"

And sure enough, within seconds, a green light on the instrument board filling the face of the radio consol lit up.

Emile was now all business.

"Emile Honoree at Palm Radio," he said. "Emile Honoree at Palm Radio," he repeated into the mike. "Come in, Thomas, over."

He looked at his watch.

"He is usually on his boat having dinner with Chico now."

We heard a crackling sound and Emile beamed.

"A connection," Emile exclaimed jubilantly. "We have a connection."

"This is Archangel," a disembodied voice announced over the speaker. "How are you, Emile, over?"

"I am fine, Thomas."

"Your family is good?"

"The family is good, Thomas. Juliette has a job as copy editor at the Courier and our two children are starting school in September. Our friend Jake wishes to speak with you."

"That's a welcome surprise. Put him on."

Jack grabbed the mike.

"How are you doing, Tom?"

"Fine, Jake. When are you returning?"

"In a few days; the reason I'm calling is to find out when you want to fly over to see that heart doctor."

"That's up to you and the doctor, Jake. I can go anytime."

"Great. Is Ginny around?"

"She flew to Jamaica to hire some girls for Cheetah's."

"How are you doing with Thelma Johnson?"

"She's fine. We're thinking of getting married once I get my ticker fixed and we settle down in Florida."

"Oh yeah; how are her brothers taking it?"

"You mean Eldridge and Hugo? You know how they are; they haven't killed me yet so they may like me. Is anything else going on in Florida?"

"Oh, there's one thing. Ned Baron wants me to spread the word to his customers that their insurance policies are being cancelled."

"That's odd. Did he give a reason?"

"No, and I didn't ask. Besides, we're not insured with him."

"Well, that's interesting," said Tom. "I just received a form letter from our own carrier. We're cancelled as we speak, even though our premiums are paid up to the end of the year."

"Are we getting a refund?"

"We are, but we still need another carrier." The suggestion was met by silence.

"I had a feeling this was going to happen," he went on. "So I've been looking for another carrier. Long story short; I can't find one."

"Well, keep trying," Jack urged. "I want to make sure that Chico, Mel and Otis have coverage. How are they doing?"

"They're here with Louie. We're having dinner on board. Do you hear anything from Fred Hawk and Dan Schulman?"

"Say 'hello' and 'thanks' to Louie. And no, I haven't seen those guys in a while. I did hear Dan's got the green light from Nassau to sell prescription drugs in the Bahamas. I imagine that Fred did the footwork."

"That figures," said Tom. "I wonder how much Dan paid Hamilton Graves for the exclusive distributorship"

"The commissioner is too smart to be involved," Jack answered. "Dan or Fred worked it out with Malcolm Harding with a nod from Graves. He wouldn't sign anything with Schulman."

"You may be right," said Tom. "Incidentally, Emile should move here. You need a good electronics and radio man."

Jack was quick to reject the idea.

"He owns part of the business here. It's growing and I need him, and we're going to need you to keep the place going. I want someone local to run the business in the Borders when you're gone. Have you spoken to anyone?"

"I spoke to Clarence Cox and Gordon Tully. They plan to retire from their police work soon and want to meet with you."

"That might work. I also like Hugo Johnson. He's the best around when it comes to boats, and he's smart as a fox," Jack suggested.

"Hugo? That's a super idea, but he may not go for it. His thing is drug trafficking and he's happy with his way of life for the time being."

It was agreed that Jack would take the first available flight to the Borders and that Tom Kennedy would meet him upon his arrival.

"You might need to take the seaplane," said Tom. "The Bahamas Air pilots want to strike."

"There's always a little something," Jack said.

The conversation ended and at Emile's insistence, he decided to accept Juliette's supper invitation. Emile overheard their conversation and wanted to know how Jack was going to run two businesses in two different places. So, over dinner, he gave them a thumbnail sketch of his ideas.

"Tom will join us here when he gets better," Jack said to Emile. "I'll replace him with local partners who I know and can trust. Once I get that place under control, I'll run it from here and commute."

"I hope the political situation stays stable in the Bahamas," said Juliet. "Our poor Haiti used to be such a wonderful place. Look at it now. Our country is in such a mess."

"This is different," Jack explained. "We are a constitutional democracy here, and so is the Bahamian republic. These are two very civilized societies."

Emile folded his hands behind his neck, leaned back and looked at the ceiling.

"How true," he said. "Civilization keeps the human animal under control, at least for a little while. And then something punches a hole through the delicate fabric of civilization and, poof! No more civilization! We become pure animals."

He unfolded his arms and for a moment he lost his smile.

"All things end, Jake, and good things end too. I hope you know what you are doing. We and many people depend on you."

"I think we'll do well," said Jack.

Emile shrugged and looked at his wife.

"Your success is our success, my friend," he said. "We trust you. But while I live, I must keep my family safe, and Florida is safer than the Bahamas. I am not sure how safe the Bahamas will be if something happens. You must be careful."

Juliette agreed.

"We lost our home in Haiti, Shelly. America is our new home. Emile works with you and I have a good job at the newspaper. Our children were born here and their friends are here. You are still looking for your true home. You cannot have more than one home, but I am not sure it should be in the Bahamas."

"Where should it be?"

Juliet smiled and replied, "You need a wife and children. Then you will have a home and a chance for immortality."

"Children will make me immortal?"

"Yes. In Haiti, we say that he who has children is blessed, and he who has grand children is doubly blessed; but he who has great grandchildren shall live forever in the memory of future generations."

"Who said that?"

"My grandfather," laughed Juliet. "He lived to see his great grand children."

Jack thought it was time to change the subject.

"Say, you're with the Courier," said Jack. "Do you have any gossip or exiting news before I leave Florida?"

"I did have something," said Juliette. "It was supposed to be my first byline."

"What was it?"

"It was a story about a life boat with the name Angelina that ran aground on a beach on Singer Island a week ago. It supposedly was from a ship marooned in the Sargasso near the Borders. Bodies were reportedly seen on the lifeboat but the boat and bodies were gone when the police arrived. Unfortunately, the Courier did not run my piece. I think there is a cover up."

Jack and Emile exchanged glances.

"That is news," Jack said, not wishing to tell her what happened to them earlier. "How would anyone know that the life boat came from a vessel in the Sargasso?"

"My sources say the mother ship, Angelina, was photographed from the air by a pilot in a small plane that flew out of either Marsh Harbor or South Border Island," answered Juliet. "The photo ended up in Nassau and Freeport but was never picked up by the Bahamian papers and the papers here decided to ignore the story."

"That could have been an oversight," Jack said. "Who discovered the boat?"

Emile lost his smile for the first time that evening and he had his wife send their children out of the room.

"My friends found it," he said when the children were gone and Juliet returned to the table. "They were fishing from the beach at dawn when the boat washed up and the bodies were in very bad shape. I have seen death many times in Haiti, and they died from something terrible. Satan killed them before the sun did. They were like the bodies we found today."

"Who reported the incident?" Jack asked.

"They called the police and then ran away," said Emile. "They want no trouble."

They had no choice at this point but to tell Juliette of their day at the sea buoy.

"It is crazy," she cried. "How can a boat with bodies evaporate in plain sight?"

"I have another," said Jack. "Ned Baron said some fishermen found crates with the Angelina's markings filled with heroin a week ago, and two Angelina lifeboats have surfaced within days of each other with fresh bodies aboard. How does that work?"

"It is as I prophesied. The sun is moving north of Cancer to the Border islands and that is a very bad omen," said Emile. "Terrible things are going to happen and this will be a very bad time for the world."

"There must be a more reasonable explanation," sighed Jack.

4

Amazing Grace

A more reasonable explanation would have been good and Jack tried calling Ned, Cyrus and Milton, exercises in futility. Angela said Ned was away for a few days; Cyrus was suddenly called back by the CDC; and Milton was on the way to Nassau. Bob Byrne, however, was around and called Jack and asked to meet him for lunch.

They met at an outdoor café under a bright blue sky on Biscayne Bay in Miami. The Navy man was in his dress whites and was deep in thought and concerned with Jack's forthcoming trip and with the weather. He was looking at the sky when Jack arrived.

"Did you know that it hasn't rained in almost a month?"

"I've been noticing," Jack replied, settling down at the table. "I got a notice the other way at the office about conserving water. We're in a drought period, and the islands are dry too, I hear, but it'll pass, I'm sure."

"I'm sure," repeated Bob vacantly. A waiter came over and he ordered a martini and a salad while Jack ordered water and an open face steak sandwich. "Talking about the Bahamas, Jake, are you serious about keeping the two businesses?"

"We'll see what happens," Jack responded. "But you needn't worry, old buddy.

Nothing changes between you and me. What Louie did in his will doesn't affect the Boynton yard. The equity splits stay the same, and if you're worried about the land, you and I can own the land jointly; I'm not greedy."

"What about the Agnes Town operation?"

"I own that thing outright, and I want to keep it that way. If you want half of the land it's on, that's works for me too. Just don't forget that you'll

28

be in for half of the real estate taxes on both properties. Milton says that the Agnes Town property has been re-appraised for $3 million and the Boynton Beach operation is due for a re-appraisal this summer. I'm paying now on an assessed value of $5 million; it's bound to go up, but I don't know."

"Yes," murmured Bob. "Life is filled with uncertainty and unknowns." He sat back and took a sip from his martini. "Tell you what, Jake," he said finally. "I'll wait a while before making a decision. You don't mind, do you? I didn't factor in the cash outlays for the taxes."

"You should also plug the estate and inheritance taxes into your adding machine if you're planning to cut yourself into Louie's estate," said Jack. "That's a lot of money and uncertainly to deal with. I don't even know how I'm going to come up with the cash to pay those bills either in the Bahamas or here in the States."

"We have many unknowns here," Bob agreed.

"Talking about unknowns, old buddy, I'm curious about that lifeboat we found and about Ned's story about the opium that those fishermen hauled in from another lifeboat. Both boats seem to have come from the Angelina. Has anyone come up with anything?"

Bob Byrne shook his head.

"Not yet; we're working on it. You don't want to go there right now."

Jack took the hint, backed off and tried another approach.

"There's another thing," he said. "I had dinner last night with Emile and his wife and they say another lifeboat from the Angelina with two more bodies aboard was found at Singer Island but that it and the bodies vanished before the police arrived. That makes three lifeboats and four bodies in all. The Angelina went off the radar east of the Borders and somehow I feel that's where the answer lies. I'm going to look into it while I'm there."

"Is this trip really necessary for that?" Bob asked. "It seems to me that you can just as easily wrap everything up from here, and our government here is looking into that Angelina matter. We're pretty competent, you know."

"Oh, I know that, Robert. I guess I'm being curious, that's all."

Bob leaned forward and eyed Jack carefully.

"I wouldn't get involved with it if I were you, Jake. You have two businesses and a great future. Let the feds do their work. Something bad is brewing and you don't need to get involved."

Jack threw up his arms in mock surrender.

"You're probably right, old buddy. But I do want to square things with Ginny."

"That's a good idea so long as she's on the same page you are," said Bob. "Just keep in mind that she is pretty well set without you. She has a going business as do her dad and uncle, and that may cause complications. She might not want to leave the Bahamas."

Jack shrugged his shoulders.

"Well, I'm going to find out real soon, aren't I? Meanwhile, can you and Frank help Emile at the boatyard while I'm away?"

"You bet," said Bob, returning to the task of finishing his salad. "Frank and I can drop by before and after work, and Emile can count on us on weekends."

Jack finished his water.

"Still not drinking?" Bob noted.

"I haven't had a drop in five years. But thanks for giving up your weekends. I hope it doesn't cramp your style as a single guy."

"I don't socialize much. It's safer that way," said Bob. "He downed his martini and wiped his mouth. "And that's what I wanted to talk about. It's about your folks up in West Virginia. That's where they live, I understand."

"That's right," said Jack. "My folks left Louisiana when my dad retired from the pulpit. We have a bunch of uncles, aunts and cousins up in the hill country to keep them company. What are you driving at?"

Bob picked his words carefully.

"West Virginia should be safe."

Jack sat up.

"It's safe from what, Bob?"

"I'm talking about this outbreak that's in the news, Jake. It's going to get nasty. That's why may be safer in the mountains. The region is remote and isolated."

He bent forward more to catch Jack's eye. "I'm suggesting you send your kids to stay with your folks until this thing blows over."

"My ex-wife and Fred Hawk can take care of them. She has custody anyway."

Bob kept pressing his point.

"That's the problem, Jake. Doreen isn't well and neither is Fred. I visited with them last week and they agree that the twins should be moved. Doreen and Fred worry me, but the twins worry me more."

Jack took a deep breath.

"I don't have custody over them," he said. "I don't even get visitation rights until my probation is over. It's best for me to stay quiet, lie low and not rock the boat."

"I know," agreed Bob. "But they're your kids even if you never saw them. If you recall, the court gave me power of attorney to act in your absence in the event that Doreen and Fred fell ill or became incapacitated."

"Will the courts need to rule on that?" Jack asked. I don't want to go to court."

"They don't have to," Bob continued. "Doreen and Fred signed a document for me that was witnessed by Larry Fisher. They agreed that it was in the best interest of the kids to be sent away in my custody until the flu outbreak is over. All I need from you is your written permission to send them to your folks."

"You're serious, aren't you?"

Bob looked around to make sure he was not being overheard.

"Dead serious," he replied in low voice. "Give a listen here, Jake. This transfer I received is to a special operations unit, Sidewinder. I head it up. Our job is to stop trouble before it happens. It's a global network of intelligence agents. Larry is with us as an independent contractor. So is Lance Cooper's paymaster, Manny Silvester, in the Bahamas. Matter of fact, you may care to join us."

"Not my bag," said Jack, shaking his head. "But what are you saying, Bob?"

"What I'm saying stays here, Jake. It's this outbreak; it's going to be a killer but it didn't start here. It was brought here by a cruise ship that docked in Charleston where a few sick passengers died. Whatever they had has spread and hit Florida and other states. I spoke with Cyrus and he thinks this outbreak is for real. He was so worried that he even called Henry in the Bahamas to warn him."

"Why?" Jack asked. "Henry is a general practitioner, not an epidemiologist."

"Cyrus is afraid the epidemic might spread to the Bahamas," answered Bob. "It might even go global."

"That's a long shot, isn't it?" Jack began wondering if that cruise ship was the same one that Jonathan Hall had called him about in April.

"This is strictly confidential, Jake, but the Navy, Coast Guard, U.S. Customs, the DEA and Immigration have orders to screen everyone entering the country. Every person suspected of having a contagious disease is to be quarantined."

Jack's eyes narrowed.

"Is that why you're not telling me anything about those lifeboats and bodies?"

"It's a classified matter and I can't talk about it, Jake," replied Bob tersely. "Are you getting the message?"

Jack folded his arms as Bob Byrne peeled a written statement from the inside of his uniform jacket and placed it on the table with a pen.

"Think about it, Jake," suggested Bob. "Then come over to my pad tonight and we can talk about it some more."

Jack did not seem to hear.

"Am I doing the right thing?"

"You need to trust me on this," answered Bob. "I don't like breaking up families, but it will only be for a short time and the kids will be fine. But I need your written consent."

"I hope this is the right thing," he said, signing the paper. "The kids are my life."

"It is," said Bob. "That's why I'm offering you a chance to join my outfit, Jake. It would be good for all of us, and you'll also be doing your country a service."

"Thanks," Jack replied. "I'll get back to you on that. But right now, I have other things on my plate."

An enigmatic smile crossed Bob Byrne's lips.

"I understand," he said. "You do what you need to do. And don't worry; I'll make sure Doreen keeps getting her meds while you're gone."

He took a business card from his pocket, jotted down some numbers and thrust it in front of Jack.

"These are my radio call numbers. Use them in an emergency; you'll reach Frank who's my contact man and he'll call me. What else do you need?"

Jack took the card. Then as an afterthought, he said, "Call Tom Kennedy and tell him I'll be flying in tomorrow on the seaplane. And you look in on Doreen and make sure she takes her meds and gets better, you hear?"

Lunch with Bob Byrne left him jittery, but he calmed his nerves by concluding that his friend was over-reacting and posturing with his newly discovered power and self-importance. Jack called West Virginia early that evening and spoke to his mother who confirmed that she spoke to Bob Byrne and was happy at the prospects of spending time with the twins who she and her husband had also never seen. In her mind, she also saw this as an opportunity of seeing her son reconciled with Doreen irrespective of the fact that she was already married to Fred Hawk. His father was more suspicious.

"Why is Bob being so generous," he asked. "What's in it for him?"

"Nothing," replied Jack. "He's being a good friend."

"Didn't you recently make him executor, trustee and beneficiary of your estate after the kids?"

"Whatever there is of it," Jack chuckled. "I'm guaranteed that he'll take care of the twins if they're left alone before adulthood this way."

"That's the problem," said his father. "You're not stupid and your estate is only going to grow. Are you sure you're doing the right thing?"

"Why do you ask?"

"Well, don't you think you should be with your family during this outbreak? I know your thing with Doreen went sour, but if she's sick and this Fred Hawk guy is making himself scarce, shouldn't you stick close to home? She might need your help. When you were a kid, many bad things happened and we always saw them through together as a family, no matter what."

Jack was stubborn and was clearly not accepting his father's argument.

"I have business in the Bahamas," Jack said. "The kids will be safer with you and mom, and Doreen isn't that sick. She can take care of herself. Besides, she's Fred's problem. He married her. Let him take care of her."

Jack's father made one last attempt to convince his son.

"Well, that's a copout if I ever heard one. I still think Bob's advice is bad. He's not a real friend. He's cut from the same cloth as Fred Hawk. Neither of them were real bargains. They were always out to get you."

"What about Louie Gold, dad, is he a friend?"

Jack heard his father laugh.

"Louie and his wife were neighbors when you, Bob, Fred and Tom were kids down in Louisiana. When his wife took ill, you kids did their errands. Bob and Fred took tips and wouldn't budge unless they got paid but you and Tom never took tips. You and Tom got along with the other kids and played ball but Bob and Fred never participated; they stayed off by themselves.

"Louie may have adopted Bob, but he sees in you the son he never had. That's why you're in his new will. And that's why I don't trust Bob. He wants what you have. And Fred Hawk, he's a sneak. But hey, life is a crapshoot, you know. You roll the dice and you take your chances."

"Thanks, dad; you and mom stay well, you hear."

"And, best of luck whatever you do, young guy. Mom and I will take care of the kids, and you take care of yourself and watch your back, you hear?"

Jack called Doreen later in the evening and sure enough, she was in. She seemed glad to hear from him. But when he asked about Fred, she replied with a sigh of resignation that he had left for the Bahamas.

"He took End Run and went fishing," she explained.

Jack winced. That explained why the yacht was brought to the Boynton boatyard to have its engines checked. Emile did the work but Fred left without paying. The saving grace was that Dan Schulman brought in Kitten, his personal mega yacht, and few days later. He paid his and Fred's bill in cash when he fueled up.

"Anyway," said Jack after telling her the story. "I can send you more money for your medical bills if you want."

"Thanks, Shelly. You're sweet, but I'm ok. The doctor says I have a bronchial infection and it's got to run its course. Bob has been sending me my meds so I'm saving money. But say, you sound great. How are you doing?"

Jack could not see Doreen, and yet, he could see her blond hair in a pony tail and her shapely body and dancer's legs in the slinky black dress she always wore when they went out for an evening of dinner and dancing.

"I get dirty finger nails but it's a living," he said. He then went on to tell her of his conversation with Bob Byrne.

"I signed some papers for him," he said. "Are you sure you want the twins to stay with my folks for a while?"

He could feel her hesitate over the phone. Finally, she answered.

"It will only be for a short while, won't it, Shelly?"

"I guess."

"Will you pray for me, Shelly?"

Jack bristled at the request.

"Damn you, Doreen," he complained. "If you want me to pray for you, why the hell did you divorce me?"

She asked again, "Pray for me?"

"I'm not into praying," insisted Jack. "But okay, okay. I'll pray for you."

"Your probation will be over soon, babe, and we'll be able to get together again, this time with you having visitation rights. We could even work out a joint custody agreement for the kids. Wouldn't that be wonderful?"

"What about Fred?"

"We could work something out, Shelly. That would be nice, wouldn't it."

"It sure would be nice," said Jack lamely. "It's a great idea, Doreen, a real great idea and I can hardly wait."

"You'll be back soon, won't you, Shelly?"

"I will, Doreen. I will."

"I miss you, Shelly. Maybe we can even date again," she said. "I don't think my marriage with Fred is going to last much longer."

"I'm sorry to hear that, Doreen," said Jack with nervous impatience. "We'll talk about it when I get back."

"I need you, Shelly."

"Don't worry. I'll see you soon, probably sooner than you think."

Jack had a lump in his throat. He closed the windows, took the horn in his hands, lifted it to his lips and played the solemn notes of Taps.

He was done in Florida, at least for a while. He had no home; his only address was the boatyard where sleeping on a cot every night was not the way he wanted to live. Even his berth on Archangel was more spacious.

Late that night, satisfied that the business was in good shape and in good hands, he stuffed a few things into a duffel, including his trumpet and service revolver and lay down to sleep.

The next day, Jack was at Cross Island Air's seaplane terminal on the banks of the long inlet connecting the harbor of Miami to the Straits of Florida and the open sea beyond, waiting patiently in the departure lounge with a roomful of passengers. Every few minutes a wall mounted loudspeaker announced that the old seaplane being prepped outside on the tarmac for the shuttle flight to the Bahamas was ready for boarding.

Two aging puddle jumper seaplanes stood on the tarmac near the ramp leading into the water. One was bound for Paradise Island via the Biminis; the other was flying to Agnes Town via Freeport and Marsh Harbor. Cross Island Air now had the only commercial flights to the Bahamas with the grounding of Bahamas Air and the tiny departure lounge was crowded. An ad on the wall by the loudspeaker read, "When you have time to spare, fly Bahamas Air."

"Hey, Jake, what are you doing here?"

It was Reginald Mayhew, a North Border Island police officer. When he was not working for Clarence Cox, the island's police chief, he moonlighted as a part time navigator, pilot and radio man for Cross Island. He lived with his wife, Eunice, and their kids in Patrick City, a village north of Agnes Town. Jack and Ginny came to their home frequently for dinner where Reggie and Jack played chess while Eunice and Ginny chatted late into the night.

Reginald was tall, thin, deadpan serious and loved playing chess despite the fact that he played poorly. They played for money and Jack often let him win as a way to kick money back to him for the patrol boat repair business that Clarence sent to Jack's boatyard. Reginald kept some of the money for himself and turned to rest over to Clarence. He also had a charter flight business consisting of a small plane that Jack had leased from Louie Gold. It was parked at an airstrip on South Border and Reggie paid for its expenses. However, his only customer so far was Vernon Peters, the local druggist on South Border, who had a pilot's license and flew the craft himself.

"Reggie," exclaimed Jack. "What a surprise. Doesn't Clarence have enough work for you these days?"

"It's an emergency," said Reggie. "The pilot died yesterday, a real shocker. He was young and getting started with his wife at their new home in Marsh Harbor."

"What did he die of?"

"We don't know. He had a fever and broke out in sores. The poor guy literally hemorrhaged to death. Even Henry couldn't say what it was. He was able to give the guy's wife a shot and she got better. Are you ticketed for the Borders?"

"Yes," said Jack. "I bought Tom Kennedy out and need to see what's what. Has Ginny been around?"

"She's in Jamaica from what I hear," replied Reggie. "Listen. I'll catch you later; I have to check on my co-pilot. He's also from Marsh Harbor."

Reggie exited through the door leading to the tarmac, leaving Jack alone to wade through old newspapers and listen to religious music being piped in from a local radio station through the intercom mikes. The hymn 'Amazing Grace' was being played.

He began silently to hum the tune and his mind wandered back in time to one of Hiram Cooper's after dinner discussion groups in the library of the air conditioned rectory at his Church of Christ in Agnes Town. Aside from the cool air, the rectory had another interesting feature, a wood burning fireplace framed by a mantle over which hung a lithograph of Yin and Yang.

Those rectory discussions attracted such diverse sorts as Tom Kennedy, Terrence Moore, Jonathan Hall, Nigel Baron, Gordon Tully, Clarence Cox, Kyle and Dale Malone. They were the regulars. Lancelot Cooper and his brother, Milton, often dropped in with Malcolm Harding, Hamilton Graves and Henry Alden. They used to meet at Bea's Market Diner, or Bea's Diner as it was called by the locals, but Hiram had a falling out with Terrence Moore who managed the diner's retail food sales annex for Bea Norris who owned the diner and the market. It was a minor spat over Terrence's practice of reserving his fresh produce for local Bahamians and selling the rest to everyone else. Hiram felt that all customers should be treated equally as Christians but Terrence argued that only those who were born and bred in the Bahamas were true Christians.

Without comment Hiram promptly moved his discussion group to the rectory and made sure that the atmosphere was laidback and congenial if not as collegial as he would have desired. He allowed cognac to flow and cigars to glow, and in short order, the rectory filled with smoke and alcohol laced dialogue about anything and everything. If it was hot outside, it was cool inside.

"Do you know the story of Amazing Grace?" Hiram had asked.

"It's a funeral hymn?" Jonathan Hall ventured to answer.

"Oh, it's more than a hymn, my friends," said Hiram. "It describes the human condition. Listen, it describes the human condition on its path through life."

He turned on a CD player and the sound of bagpipes could be heard through the speakers as he began to read slowly from a worn book of hymns.

"Amazing grace, how sweet the sound that saved a wretch like me.
I once was lost, but now I'm found, was blind, but now I see.
"It was grace that taught my heart to fear, and grace my fears relieved.
How precious did that grace appear the hour I first believed.
"Through many dangers, toils and snares, I have already come.
Grace has brought me safe thus far, and grace will lead me home.
"The Lord has promised good to me, his word my hope secures.
He will my shield and portion be, as long as life endures.
"Yes, when this flesh and heart shall fail and mortal life shall cease.
I shall possess, within the veil, a life of joy and peace.
"The earth shall soon dissolve like snow and the sun forbear to shine;
But God who called me here below, will be forever mine."

"A slave ship captain wrote those words in a storm. When he thought his ship might sink, he released the slaves who made it back to land. He became a preacher when he returned to England and never went out to sea again."

"I guess the moral is that he who does right dies right," said Gordon Tully.

But what was the right thing? Hiram Cooper never said.

Jack's cell phone rang. It was Ned Baron.

"Jake, I got trouble. You remember Jane's engagement party? Half of the guests who ate fish got sick and died, and I've been quarantined. What do I do, Jake?"

"Call Bob Byrne," replied Jack. "He'll get you out of quarantine."

"That's a great idea; I'll do that, and Jake?"

"What?"

"Cyrus says it was Plague. How does one get Plague in the twenty first century?"

5

The Face of Death

News travels fast and bad news travels faster. Milton made a pit stop in Nassau on the way to the Border islands and was in Agnes Town when Jack arrived. By then word of what happened at Ned Baron's party had spread and rumor of the Cross Island Air's pilot's death in Marsh Harbor was raising anxiety levels and adding to the general angst caused by the extended drought. As for Jack up to now, the face of death was faceless and impersonal. It was something that befell strangers and casual acquaintances and bypassed friends and loved ones. It was unimaginable that the face of death could belong to someone close like a sister or brother, a spouse or parent or even a close business associate. What was the face of Death? Jack remembered pieces of an old poem on the subject that he had been required to read in school many years ago.

Have you seen somewhere the face of Death? I have seen somewhere the face of Death. What was it you saw in the face of Death? I have seen somewhere in the face of Death a leaf falling in the setting sun. That was the face of Death I saw somewhere.

Have you seen over there the face of Death? I have seen over there the face of Death. What was it you saw there in the face of Death? I have seen over there in the face of Death barren fields in the rising sun. That was the face of Death I saw over there.

Have you seen over here the face of Death? I have seen over here the face of Death. What did you see here in the face of Death? I have seen over here in the face of Death dreams destroyed and lives denied. This is the face of Death I have seen over here.

Do you see now the face of Death? I can see now the face of Death. What do you see now as the face of Death? I can see now as the face of Death a land drowned by tears of sorrow. This is the face of Death I see right now.

Jack wracked his brain. Who the hell wrote this thing? Before he could come up with an answer, a voice over the loudspeaker announced that the Cross Island Air seaplane was about to take off. Jack grabbed his duffel and made his way to the tarmac. He hoped the early morning flight would reach Agnes Town in time for lunch or at least for dinner if it was running late.

This seaplane was much like a big fat bird and Jack had flown in them before. Even the growls from its engines could raise eyebrows. Its propellers would start turning slowly, engines belching, snorting and trembling until a throaty, deafening thunder filled the air, and the birds on the tarmac would flap their wings and fly off to safer perches.

Jack strapped himself into a weathered leather window seat and peered through the scratchy porthole to catch the action of the plane preparing for takeoff. His eyes were fixed on the propellers. An engine sputtered and a prop began to turn, slowly at first. Then the engine growled and the prop began racing until its blades blurred in the air. The engine on the other wing soon kicked up and soon the two propellers were in full motion.

The plane shook, lurched forward and slowly rolled down the ramp until its two pontoons hit the water with a jolt. With a long roar, the seaplane turned its stubby nose to the mouth of the inlet, picking up forward momentum. Loudly as it roared, it never seemed to have enough speed for lift it up into the air. Children cried and adults gripped their armrests until it reached the mouth of the inlet where it finally left the water and rose slowly, ever so slowly, into the sky.

The Miami skyline fell behind and Freeport lay one hundred miles due northeast beneath the crimson glow of the rising sun. Belly cramps seized Jack briefly when it occurred to him that he might never return home again. What a dumb thought. Of course, he would get back to Florida, by July at the latest. He watched Miami sink slowly below the horizon and grit his teeth, staring at the bulkhead in front of him. The cramps went away.

Next to Jack on the aisle seat was someone in a safari jacket, white slacks, a tee shirt and deck shoes. He was talking to a woman seated across the narrow aisle. She had long brown hair and was in a designer boutique pink and blue jump suit.

They were in their late twenties or early thirties and appeared as if they had never worked a day for a living.

"Getting off in Freeport?" The man asked.

"I'm going to the Borders," answered Jack.

"Oh? That's where we're going," said the woman from across the aisle.

Jack turned his head to the porthole window to discourage further conversation but the young man was insistent.

"I'm Martin Wilson. And this is my fiancée, Jane."

"Hi," she said, waving.

"We're going to a nice tropical island to get married in," Martin told him.

"Congratulations, and good luck," said Jack.

"So, how long is this flight? Do you know?"

"We should be there before noon."

Jack began calculating out loud.

"Freeport is about one hundred miles east of Palm Beach. We make a pit shop there and one in Marsh Harbor one hundred miles further east. The Border islands are another fifty miles northeast of Marsh Harbor. So, I'd say the Borders are about two hundred fifty miles from Palm Beach...."

Martin seemed bored with Jack's long winded response

"I didn't get your name," he interrupted.

"Jack Sloane."

"The name sounds familiar," said Jane.

Martin looked at Jack's clothes, an off-the-rack blue blazer and tan slacks combo and a pair of unquestionably worn boat loafers.

"Is this a vacation?"

"Sure seems that way."

"You married?"

"Nope; I'm in between wives."

Jack considered the prospects of marrying Ginny Malone, his island girlfriend. Her father Kyle owned Pirates' Cove marina on Buccaneer Point on South Border Island where Archangel was docked. He also owned the adjoining tank farm where diesel and gasoline were stored. Kyle was getting on in years and left Ginny to sell fuel and run the marina when she was not busy running her nightclub, Cheetah's. Unfortunately, Kyle disliked Jack and did not want him around his daughter.

The plane landed briefly in Freeport. Some passengers left and others boarded.

It was the same routine in Marsh Harbor. But now it was the home stretch and that biting sensation returned to the pit of Jack's stomach. He found an antacid pill in a pocket, popped it into his mouth. It worked; the pain eased.

"Do you guys work?" Jack asked as the seaplane left for Agnes Town on North Border Island.

Jane admitted that she had never worked full time, but Martin indicated that he was with the government, although he was vague about the work he did.

"Tell me. Why did you pick the Borders?"

Martin's wife heard my question and poked her head into the aisle.

"My uncle, Nigel Baron, owns the North Border Hotel. So our stay is free."

Jack sat up.

"That's neat," he said. 'I know Nigel. You must be Ned's daughter."

Jane beamed at the recognition and asked, "How did you know?"

"Your dad keeps his yacht at my boat yard. I'm sorry I missed your engagement party."

"Now I know who you are," laughed Jane. "You're Shelly, the guy who fixes boats. Everyone talks about you."

"I don't know if that's good or bad," said Jack.

Martin seemed miffed at being ignored and took a closer look at Jack.

"Jack Sloane," he repeated. "Funny. I don't know the name. Are you from Palm Beach? Jane never mentioned your name."

"I wouldn't expect that she would," answered Jack. "She was a baby the last time I saw her. We also don't run in the same circles. Ned sells insurance and I'm just a lousy mechanic with a boat yard."

"You look more like a ship captain," said Jane.

Jack gulped.

"No; I fix boats. But tell me, is the fact that your uncle has a hotel in the Borders the only reason you guys are vacationing there?"

"No," replied Jane. "Martin wants to go scuba diving and deep sea fishing. He's looking for a sunken ship filled with pirates' treasure, and...."

Martin stopped her short.

"Jane has a vivid imagination," he said. "Game fishing is my thing. I also like deep sea scuba diving, but I don't really think we'll find a pirate ship."

Jane threw Martin her prettiest smile.

"Whatever you say, dear; you go fishing and I'll go shopping."

Jack laughed, saying, "Good luck. We don't have that many shops and much of what you'll find is cheaper stateside." Turning to Martin, he asked, "What kind of equipment did you bring?"

"What do you mean?"

"You know, diving equipment, fishing gear and all that," he elaborated. "What kind of rigs...?"

"What kind of rigs? I don't follow."

"Yeah, man, what kind of rods and reels are you carrying?" And he rattled off the different types and brands of heavy duty equipment used for game fishing.

"Oh, that. I'm having all that stuff shipped separately."

Jack let the subject go, turning his attention to Jane Baron who was actually quite nice looking, tall, slim but well built. He was now sorry he had never bothered to try running into her in the past few years.

"Good luck on your shopping spree," Jack told Jane.

He pulled a portable GPS out of his pocket. The seaplane normally flew at an altitude of about one thousand feet. It now went down to eight hundred feet and in accordance with the GPS's compass reading, it was nearing its final destination.   Jack checked the time on his wrist watch. 11:45 A.M. It was right on schedule.

The amphibian's landing depended on several variables, not the least of which was the direction of the tidal current. If it flowed west to east, the plane barreled through the dog eared inlet between North and South Border islands, make a quick left past the cut into the harbor and quickly climb the ramp onto the tarmac outside the customs office at the south end of town. If the current ran east to west, it would circle counter-clockwise around the islands and come in for a landing through the wider channel from the Atlantic and make a bee-line for Agnes Town through the hidden shoals and submerged reefs. Today the current flowed from the east.

The plane banked left to start the semi-circle, giving him a panoramic view of the Borders. Directly under the plane was South Border, a five mile long pizza shaped wedge facing east inhabited by about eight thousand people. Its western shore ran north-south from Buccaneer Point to Jonathan Hall's Ocean View hotel on Ocean Point that lay between Canal Pond and the sea. Canal Pond was actually a deep bay that accommodated cruise ships who often dropped anchor and discharged their passengers for a day of sun and fun at the island's many beaches.

Most of South Border's residents were Bahamians whose families, like Terrence Moore and his kin, had lived on the island for generations. They shopped mostly at

Junction City, a community of shops and churches on Bluff Road situated halfway between Buccaneer Point and Ocean Point. They rarely ventured across the cut to North Border unless they owned a business or worked in Agnes Town.

The western crust of South Border was actually a spine of bluffs that rose above a narrow palm tree lined beach of white sand Ocean Point to Buccaneer Point and was visible as the seaplane banked and began making its counter-clockwise turn. Bluff Road paralleled the bluffs on the inside and was filled with noonday traffic. On Buccaneer Point's underside lay Pirates' Cove with Archangel in plain sight.

The marina was a helter-skelter cluster of trailers, shacks, rental cottages, picnic tables and boat slips protected by the bluffs of Buccaneer Point on South Border's northwest corner. Archangel was the only sailboat among several big yachts and its tall mast stood high among the palms. Six fuel storage tanks occupied a lot near a dock used by a barge that ferried people and vehicles to and from North Border; a chain link fence around the tanks reflected the noonday sun. Most of the residents lived on Division Avenue, an east-west road connecting a small airstrip and beach on the island's eastern tip to Junction City.

North Border was a narrow twenty mile long island shaped like an 'A' without the cross piece. Its western leg, aptly called West Leg, extended a half mile south past Buccaneer Point to create the narrow channel that emptied into Sanctuary Bay, a shallow wide bay filling the void between North and South Border islands. The deepest water was at Agnes Town near the south end of West Leg.

About five thousand people lived in towns, fishing villages and farms on North Border Island, with half residing in Agnes Town, the island's chief hamlet. Two roads circled the municipality. King's Road started at the south end of town at the seaplane landing and curled around to the west and turned north to follow the west shore of the island.

Queen's Road started at the same point, cutting through town past the Church of Christ to the police barracks across the way from Nigel Baron's hotel on Sanctuary Bay. There, it merged with King's Road, becoming the King's Highway, a bumpy, potholed road that ran up West Leg to Patrick City and on to the All Souls Church at Sanctuary Village at the top of the 'A' before turning down East Leg past Bitter End Bay to Sugar Pond at the southeast end of the 'A.'

The Church of Christ in Agnes Town and All Souls Church in Sanctuary Village were more than landmarks. Their tall white spires rose like beacons high above the island that could be seen for miles and were used as land marks by mariners at sea.

Immigrants from the Dominican Republic favored Patrick City and most of them lived in shanties on the south edge of town and fished for a living. Haitians lived Between Patrick City and Sanctuary Village and shared the fishing grounds with the Dominicans. Jamaicans lived between Sanctuary Village and Bitter End Bay.

The small farms on East Leg were owned mostly by Jamaicans, including the Johnson farm, owned by the parents of Eldridge, Hugo and

Thelma. Dan Malone's North Border Treacle Company, a sugar refining and rum producing factory stood at Sugar Pond.

The twenty mile long island was a half mile wide along West Leg and two miles across on East Leg which was mainly farm land, dunes and mangrove. The shallow channel entrance into Sanctuary Bay separating the tip of East Leg from South Border was three miles wide and was the longest distance between the two islands.

The seaplane made one last turn as it descended, giving Jack a chance to look out the cabin window at the boats leaving and entering through the wide channel. He recognized Avalon, the funeral ship or death ship, as locals called it. Avalon was returning to Agnes Town. Someone must have died and was buried at sea earlier in the day. Jack wondered who it was and hoped it was no one he knew.

Sanctuary Bay was protected by the two islands, and a line of barrier reefs from Bitter End Bay to Hermit's Cay five miles to the northeast kept out the harbor clear of the thick invasive Sargasso eel grass. This made the Sanctuary Bay a hurricane hole and a harbor of refuge when weather turned foul.

The cockpit door opened suddenly and Reginald Mayhew stepped out and went directly to Jack. He leaned over Martin's head, messing his carefully coiffed hair, and whispered into Jack's ear. Martin was miffed but he also sensed trouble and demanded to know what was wrong.

"I'm with the government," he declared. "You need to tell me what's going on."

Jack ignored him and stepped over his legs. He followed Reggie to the cockpit and locked the door behind him. The plane was on auto-pilot and was in no danger of crashing, but Reggie was taking no chances. He climbed into the co-pilot's seat and took over the controls, leaving Jack to care for the pilot who had passed out.

He was propped up in his seat, held in place by a safety harness. His eyes were open, his face was filled with bursting blisters and blood trickled out of his nostrils and down the corners of his mouth. Jack checked his hands and the exposed back of his neck where several nasty open sores oozed blood.

"Holy shit, what happened?"

"I haven't a clue," said Reggie. "Give him air while I handle this tub. I'm going to circle around again, slow it down and bring it in through the cut.

Jack pulled an oxygen mask from the cockpit bulkhead and pressed it against the pilot's face as Reggie worked the intercom to calm the nervous passengers and the old seaplane began its final descent.

Reginald Mayhew was at the controls a world away from Jack who was studying the copilot's features partially concealed by the oxygen mask in the now strange tranquility of the cockpit. He was still, and his eyes were searching the heavens with a quiet serenity.

Jack heard a gurgle and then it hit him. It was a death rattle. The pilot was gone and the face he saw in the co-pilot was the face of Death.

6

Yin and Yang

The seaplane panted up the ramp from the water and came to a dripping stop on the tarmac outside the small Bahamian customs office. An electric sign on the high chain link fence separating the tiny terminal from the street welcomed visitors to Agnes Town and announced the time and date as noon of Thursday, May 17. Another sign on a pole between a tank farm and Madame Lamar's Gift Shop across the street read, "The wage of sin is death!" Hiram Cooper must have had it put up.

Jack expected the de-boarding to go smoothly and quickly, especially since a dead body was on board. He was wrong. A bolt of hot air and incredible humidity struck him in the face as he stepped off the amphibian.

The tarmac resembled home coming day and it seemed that the whole town had turned out. Milton was there with his father, Hiram, to help Henry Alden hand out surgical face masks and to inject arriving passengers with a special vaccine he had on hand. Indeed, the blue masks were everywhere. Henry wore no mask, perhaps because he could not find one to fit around his Santa Claus beard. And of course he was unmistakable in his red suspenders.

The big surprise was Hiram Cooper. He usually shunned gatherings of this sort and Jack never expected to see him. The last time he saw him was at one of his Thursday evening meetings by the fireplace under the Yin and Yang picture at the rectory library. Hiram had said that the glyph was a symbol for the constellation Cancer as shown by the two opposing looped lines. He said the pictogram stood for Cancer, the Latin word for Crab, a creature in the stars representing the "tried and true." Cancer was armored on the outside but its center was soft and vulnerable and in a broader sense it emphasized the duality of human nature, the light and the dark or the good and the bad.

Henry saw Jack and Reggie and waved them over.

"Get in line for your shots, Jake; you too, Reggie."

Jack begged off and Reggie also declined, claiming it was against his religion to accept any medication or treatment.

An ambulance jeep was standing by when the seaplane came to a halt. The body was eased off the plane into a body bag and quickly wheeled to the ambulance that stood in the shade of the seaplane's wings not far from where the passengers were being given their shots. That was when the snag began and the arguments started, and all during that time the body lay next to the ambulance, slowly ripening in the midday heat.

Reggie wanted the copilot's body sent to the police barracks at the north end of town across road from Bea's Diner, the North Border Hotel and the telephone center. It had an icehouse in back which served as a morgue and Reggie thought the copilot's body could stay there until the next of kin could be contacted.

A baggage handler reminded him that the custom in the Borders was to have the dead immediately cremated or buried at sea or both. Chancing to look out into the bay, Jack saw Avalon, the trawler run by Virgil and Clovis that carried the dead to sea. He wanted to ask who had died when someone opined that nothing should be done until the medical examiner arrived. That was Malcolm Harding and he was not around, and Henry said he could not do autopsies without authorization.

Jack and Reggie stayed by the ambulance as the arguments went on until all the seaplane's passengers had received their shots, cleared customs and left.

"What do these shots do?" Jack asked Henry.

"I'm not sure," answered the physician. "Cyrus gave me some serum when I was in Florida. He said it might work on bubonic plague. But what the co-pilot caught may be a mutant form."

"Does this mutant have a name, Henry?"

"Red Death," the doctor replied. "Let's hope this thing doesn't spread."

"Amen," said Hiram Cooper.

"You really should get a shot, Jake," warned Milton.

"Maybe later, but thanks anyway."

"Well, don't wait too long," said Henry, packing up his black medical bag.

Hiram and Milton also prepared to leave.

"Will we see you tonight?" Hiram asked.

Jack suddenly remembered. This was Thursday and Hiram would be hosting his usual group chat at the rectory library.

"I'll try to be there," he said.

Henry, Hiram and Milton left as Tom Kennedy and Clarence Cox appeared with Louie Gold, the Cross Island Air agent. Giving Reggie a stack of incident report forms to fill out, he and Jack exchanged high fives.

"Hey, Jake; you got your bugle?" Louie asked.

"You bet!"

Louie Gold was a small wizened man in his early eighties who wore his pants high, keeping them up with a pair of wide suspenders over a white short sleeve shirt. Moving quickly in jerking motions, poking about here and there, he seemed to be everywhere at once. Louie lived in a rental cottage at a small trailer park on Pirates' Cove marina and had worked part time for Cross Island ever since moving to the Borders. He looked poor but the frugality of his life style camouflaged a life of wealth creation. Cross Island paid him a modest salary, and that was enough to pay for his expenses and rent. He was rich in his own right and never hesitated to help Jack, who he thought had been dealt a bad hand of cards.

Jack gave Louie a hearty backslap and waved at Tom Kennedy as he approached.

"Hey, Tom, you look like a million bucks after taxes. Are you making sure old Clarence stays off the juice?"

They were close enough to embrace with Clarence Cox snorting out a retort.

"I don't drink," responded Clarence.

"That's because you're too busy taking drunks from one side of the street to the other."

"The trouble with you Jake is that you know us too well," Clarence laughed.

Jack did know Agnes Town well. It was originally planned as a god fearing, bible thumping town, but it surrendered partially to the pull of human nature. Bars and restaurants with their backs to the docks on the harbor were on one side of the street, facing churches and shops on the other side. The bars and clubs kept vampire hours from sundown to sunup and the churches, schools and businesses opened in the morning. The churches were always filled on Sundays. There were

many restaurants but regulars went to Bea's Diner for lunch. Special occasions like weddings were celebrated at Nigel's North Border Hotel or at Jonathan's Ocean View Hotel at Ocean Point on South Border. Next to the seaplane landing was the public dock where the jitney ferry was on a run to Pirates' Cove. Past the public dock was Jack's Marine, and on its far side stood Cheetah's, Ginny Malone's shocking pink and purple night club.

Madame Lamar's gift shop faced the terminal on the other side of the street. It was a stand alone store with a wooden walk and overhang to protect against the sun and rain. It was empty except for Nigel Baron who ran to meet the plane when its passengers began filling the customs house. Neat and trim in his usual pressed white shirt, tie and dark slacks, he was slim and well put together, his slicked back hair and pencil thin moustache giving him an air of importance. He saw Jack and waved as he passed by to greet his niece and her new fiancé inside the customs office.

Looking through customs' large open windows, Jack could see Nigel rushing his two charges past Bradford and Charleen Douglass, the man and wife team that ran the customs and immigration process. They too waved when they saw Jack.

By now, Avalon had reached the public dock. Virgil and Clovis Charon jumped off the funeral ship, secured it to the dock and made their way to the tarmac. Back from taking a body out to sea that morning, they had heard about the dead copilot and were standing by for instructions. Styx, their big black dog with the long tail and red tongue stood next to them, tongue hanging and tail wagging. It was being petted and fed tidbits by a musician from the Castaways, the reggae band that did birthdays, weddings, wakes and funerals and was always ready to perform another funeral dirge on demand.

Virgil and a drummer from the Castaways came over to greet Jack.

"How's our horn man?" The drummer asked.

"I'm ready," said Jack, shaking hands.

"That's good," Virgil noted. "Our bugle man died suddenly last week. We have plenty of work nowadays."

"Wasn't he too young to die? What did he have?" Jack asked.

"He died too fast for us to find out. He had small pox or measles or something. It was pretty ugly."

They were interrupted by Winthrop Foote, Gladys Lamar's common-law mate, who ran over from her store to announce he had a coffin that fit the copilot. Reggie wanted to make a comment but he was corralled by Louie Gold to fly the seaplane back to Florida with Louie as co-pilot.

"I hope you guys settle this thing," he said as he boarded the seaplane. "I'd sure hate to see him melt on the tarmac."

And so the arguing started anew until Jack suggested that the first thing was to move the body to the ice house. Weighing in on Jack's side were Nigel Baron and Jonathan Hall, both of whom suddenly appeared. Nigel had just sent off Jane and her fiancé to the hotel with his driver and was waiting for Jonathan so they could do lunch at Bea's Diner. The arguments had new energy.

Virgil and Clovis wanted the body buried at sea. Winthrop Foote didn't care so long as he sold a casket. Nigel sided with Winthrop while continuing to agree with Jack and then told Jonathan he would join him for lunch at Bea's. The Castaways had no opinion so long as they had a gig and Jonathan had no opinion, being more interested in asking Jack about Doreen. He was somewhat relieved when told that she was sick but hanging in.

"Let's do lunch one of these days," said Jonathan.

Jack smiled.

"You pick the day and time, old buddy. By the way, how's Cynthia?"

"Thank God, she's in good health. But she has her hands full too. She takes care of Henry when he's home, and she also manages his hotel over in Marsh Harbor."

They shook hands and Jonathan with Nigel took off for Bea's Diner followed in short order by Henry, Hiram and Milton.

"We're meeting tonight," said Hiram as they were leaving. "Join us."

The final decision was to put the body while the next of kin were contacted. That would leave time for an examination. After a week the body would be buried at sea in keeping with tradition.

Clarence Cox was short and squat with a bald spot surrounded by a halo of frizzy graying hair. A slightly lopsided Groucho Marx moustache gave him a quizzically comic appearance. His jurisdiction was North Border until now. Each island once had its own police force and chief until the two jurisdictions merged with Clarence as overall chief. His South Border predecessor, Gordon Tully, was promoted to the post of Marsh Harbor police chief with jurisdiction over the entire Abaco chain of out islands and their outlying cays. It worked out well for him since he had a condo in Marsh Harbor where he spent his working days, returning on his off time to stay with his family at their Junction City home. Gordon was still in transit from Marsh Harbor when Jack landed.

Clarence, Tom and Jack were studies in contrast. Short and compact as Clarence was, Jack and Tom were much taller. Tom was slim, pale and had a studious face while Jack was more sturdily built.

The midday sun was bearing down and Jack pulled an old crumpled straw hat from a duffel pocket and slapped it on his head as a sun shield. Looking around, he said, "Well, gang, it's great to be back."

Clarence and Tom circled around him.

"Now that you're a big hero, will you remember the little people? Tom asked.   Jack gave him a short horse laugh.

"I won't shake your hand," he quipped, handing him his duffel to carry. "But I'll shake hands with Clarence because he's the law around here."

"I won't ask you how the flight was," said Clarence. "You're alive and well and so are the passengers. The Borders owes you and Reggie an eternity of thanks. It could have been a disaster."

Jack agreed. "Give Reggie the credit; he brought the plane in." Turning to Tom, he asked, "Where am I staying?" He could not help noticing that Tom looked tired.

"On Archangel," replied Tom. "It's your sailboat and the price is right."

"By the way," asked Clarence. "Who was the couple with Nigel?"

Jack explained the relationship.

"This guy Martin Wilson says he's with the government and wants to spend his vacation fishing and looking for buried treasure."

"I hope he's luckier than the twenty thousand tourists who came this season for sun and fun," laughed Tom. "They found sun and fun, and Hugo Johnson ran his daily sunken treasure charters to Hermit Cay, but they found no gold except the drugs that the good captain sold them."

Clarence rolled his eyes.

"We don't talk about these things here," he noted.

Tom was going to slap Jack's back when he was stopped short by a coughing fit. He was about to drop the duffel when Virgil, who was still standing on the tarmac waiting with his brother to help move the copilot's body, scooped it up and placed it on a luggage cart, giving Tom a chance to catch his breath.

Virgil was a sinewy six footer with a strong, bony face, deep set eyes and dirty blond hair tied in a ponytail behind his head. Clovis was short and stout and had a crew cut. They were lifelong mariners who moved to the Borders from Louisiana to take over Avalon, the funeral ship, whose owner had died. They had a deal with Winthrop Foote, the local carpenter. Winthrop made the coffins for the dead and Virgil and Clovis took them out on Avalon, even when the bodies were cremated beforehand. There was no official crematorium in the Borders, but the Johnson brothers owned an incinerator in Sanctuary Village that was used to burn rubbish, and they did cremations.

"So, what happens to the copilot's body?" Jack finally asked.

"One thing for sure, it's going to end up in the drink," said Clovis.

"That's the custom here," Virgil reminded him. "It hasn't changed since we ran out of cemetery space."

"Besides," Winthrop added. "I have a casket that should fit him, and it's not very expensive."

Winthrop Foote was short, skinny and had dark porcupine hair. Carpentry was his stock and trade and he was Gladys Lamar's constant companion. Together they had a son, Otis, who worked for Jack and was a spitting younger image of his dad.

"All that stuff is great," agreed Jack, "But I think we should try to find out what he died of. Some nasty stuff is going around and killing people."

Clarence nodded.

"We know; we've been seeing some problems here. That/'s why Henry, Milton and Hiram were here giving out shots and why a lot of folks have face masks. My instinct tells me to get rid of the body now, but Nigel wants us to wait."

"We could ship him back to Florida on a later flight since he got sick there," Jack suggested.

The police chief shook his head.

"We missed our chance, Jake. Cross Island cut back their flights in sympathy for the Bahamas Air slowdown. What's more, the deceased was from Marsh Harbor and his entire family died last week. No one is around to claim the body. There is no next of kin. This talk is all bullshit."

"That's doesn't sound good" said Jack.

"It's true," insisted Clarence. "Some sort of bug has hit the Bahamas from what Henry says. We're in for something bad and I don't know what it is."

Clarence picked up Jack's duffel and with Jack and Tom following, took it to an inflatable dinghy tied to a piling and threw it in while Jack drew a cigarette from a pack in his pocket and lit it.

"We also have a mystery," said Clarence. Does the name 'Angelina' ring a bell?"

"It dropped out of sight about years ago," said Jack.

"Someone from Marsh Harbor claimed to have spotted the vessel on the edge of the Sargasso. So we asked Vernon to do a fly-by on Reggie's plane. He did so but says he saw anything."

"We see many derelict boats," Tom added. "They go off course and get stuck in the grass. We rescue the crew, salvage the cargo and then leave the boats to rot."

"That's interesting," said Jack. "Three of its lifeboats ended up in Palm Beach a week ago, and two of them had fresh bodies on board."

"That's a new twist on things," said Tom. "Fresh bodies usually don't end up on old lifeboats."

"Anyone remember the number of lifeboats the Angelina carried?" Jack asked.

"I think it carried four," answered Clarence. "We heard about what happened in Florida," he continued. "And we also heard that some of Ned's guests who ate the fish from the trawler caught got sick and died."

Jack extinguished his cigarette.

"Say, didn't the Nassau Clipper take over for the Angelina?"

"It was due yesterday with a load of sugar for Dale Malone," said Tom. "But we have another mystery, and this one is financial. It's the Island Trust bank. It hasn't been meeting depositor claims. Jonathan says it's a bad foreign exchange market."

"And I need money now for my son's college tuition," Clarence added.

"We all need money," Jack conceded. "Anyway, what else is new?"

"Lance Cooper called from Hole-in-the-Wall on the VHF on his way to see his brother Cyrus in Florida," replied Clarence. "You have a salvage Satan's Rock."

"Jake can handle it," said Tom. "The business is his now."

"I hope it's a good salvage," Clarence said. "With my cash tied up with Jonathan, your kickbacks are all I have besides my lousy salary."

"We'll fix that," agreed Jack. "Salvage is the real money around here. One good salvage job and we'll all be fine. I guarantee it."

He looked closely at Clarence, asking. "How's the family otherwise?"

"Great. Jason is in your Navy and George is graduating high school and wants to go to the University of the West Indies in Nassau. Doris and I will probably retire when he finishes college. What about you?"

"I'm thinking of popping the question to Ginny," he answered. Turning to Tom, he asked in turn, "How are you doing with Thelma?"

"We went sailing last week and got caught in the only rain we had in a month. I proposed while we were stuck in the bay. But I'm sure you're more interested in Ginny," said Tom. "The good news is that she still loves you. The bad news is that she's not back from Jamaica yet."

"Oh, well, I can wait; and congratulations on your engagement. I'll be your best man. Now, how are Chico, Mel and Otis?"

"They're good," said Tom. "They move slowly, but so does the Bahamas."

"The world moves around us," Clarence said as Jack put out his cigarette. "Are you going to hear Hiram tonight?"

"I like Hiram's bullshit," said Jack. He looked at Tom. "What about you?"

"I don't like religion," Tom snickered. "I'm told that natives once owned all the land. Then missionaries came and taught them to memorize the bible with their eyes closed. When the natives opened their eyes, they owned all the bibles and the missionaries owned all the land."

"So, Tom, you'll join us tonight?"

"Of course," Tom replied.

7

The Preacher's Flock

Hiram Cooper was a preacher known as the Shepherd of the Borders. He was tall, thin, hook nosed and bespectacled and had a mane of white hair. He was descended from a long line of Anglican ministers and was revered not only by the Church of Christ congregation but by everyone in the Borders. He believed that anyone who lived a life of piety and altruism could achieve salvation and find eternal life in heaven. Unfortunately these ideals needed to be tempered by the fact that his three sons had to deal with the urgent issues of the mortal world for which God had no immediate solutions. His wife died when Milton, his youngest, was born and he never remarried. Cyrus, his oldest, left soon after the funeral to study medicine in the States, leaving only Lance and Milton to look after their father. Both had homes and families on South Border near Junction City. Hiram also lived on South Border but as a widower he preferred the small apartment in the rectory behind his church.

There were many churches; however Hiram's Church of Christ and All Souls enjoyed the largest congregations. Protestants in Agnes Town attended Hiram's church and Catholics worshiped at All Souls presided over by Father Francois Honoree. It also had the only cemetery. Under a surface calm of tolerance lay the frictions of diversity with all the usual mutual hatreds. Hiram stayed neutral and focused on his goals of increasing the size of his congregation and building a faith based college. That meant forever chasing down money.

He needed the local Jamaicans because they were cash rich. They dealt drugs, sold fuel and the other essentials of life. They also owned bars, sleaze joints and whorehouses on the bay side of Queen's Road and were heavy contributors to all houses of worship. The Jamaicans were Anglican and yet they attended All Souls a stone's throw from Hugo Johnson's Zebra Club. He also needed Jack who was financially flush from his boat repair business, but so far Jack was not biting.

Jack's first act when he was once again on Archangel was to call his folks to find out if his children arrived. His father assured him that they had been delivered safe and sound and inquired about the trip to the Borders. That gave Jack a chance to give him an up-date.

His father's comment was brief.

"You're in a sea of shit, son," he drawled. "So, watch your back."

"What do you mean, dad?"

"If there is an epidemic, the government is working hard to hide or deny it. Now, about this Wilson feller," he ranted on. "He's no fisherman. Anglers travel like big game hunters; they know their gear and carry it with them. And Bob Byrne, I never trusted him and I still don't. If I was your ex-wife, I wouldn't take an aspirin from him, let alone have him supply her with meds from that Vernon Peters. What the hell do you know about him?"

Jack attributed his father's observations to paternal concern and a slight case of paranoia, and let them slide by. Thanking his dad for the advice and wishing him well, he went off to see Tom Kennedy who had vacated Archangel and moved to a small cabin on the grounds of Pirates' Cove. He found Tom in the cabin, packing and taking stock of his possessions. Jack began with small talk about the business and Tom kept reassuring him that it was going well and that all bills were paid to date.

"If business is that good, then what was Clarence bitching about?" Jack asked.

"It's the salvage operation," replied Tom. "Hiram put pressure on Lance to keep those jobs for the cutters under his command."

"Who put the squeeze on Hiram?"

Gladys Lamar is making noise, and she's got a lot of support. She keeps telling everyone that all the good businesses and jobs are being taken over by foreigners like us, and she wants that to stop. She wants businesses here to be run by the folks born and bred in the Borders."

"The locals could buy us out for a price, I guess," Jack noted.

Tom nodded, saying, "They may be trying to do that, A few business owners are being hassled by some of the old line residents who want to buy them out. It began when Vernon approached Clovis and Virgil with an offer for their barbershop and hardware businesses."

Jack smiled wryly.

"What's wrong with that? They started those gigs when they weren't that busy moving bodies on Avalon."

"That's what's interesting. They're being pushed by Terrence Moore. He had the nerve to tell them they didn't more than one business."

"You're kidding."

"No, Jake. I'm serious. And you know Thelma Johnson's beauty parlor? She got an offer from Bea Norris."

"How did this thing get started?" Jack asked.

"Vernon held a meeting at his home right after you left for Florida," replied Tom. "Bea and Terrence were there. So were Jonathan, Nigel, Gladys and Winthrop and about a dozen other people. They talked about buying Pirates' Cove, your business, Cheetah's and Dale Malone's factory over on East Leg."

"It sure sounds like the old timers want us out," Jack noted. "How did you find out about the meeting?"

"Oh, Otis told me. He said he looked forward to the day when he would own his own place. He said Vernon was going to put a plan together and that Jonathan Hall was going to fund it."

"But that's crazy. Vernon Peters isn't even a Bahamian. He's from Florida, and Jonathan may be broke."

"Vernon is a fake, a phony and a fraud," asserted Tom. "He keeps bringing up his Bahamian ancestry. He's says his ancestors settled Sanctuary Village hundreds of years ago and that there's a gravestone at the old cemetery at All Souls Church that proves it.

"Now, I don't know about Jonathan, Jake, but I'm telling you that big trouble is brewing. I'm too sick to get involved, but you should watch your back, you hear."

"You take care of your health and don't worry about me," said Jack. "If what you say is true, I might have a chance to sell my place at a good price."

"Well, let me give you my take on things since I'm on my way out and don't have a horse in this race anymore. Bea Norris is a good woman, but she's a born again Big Mama. She'll do business with the devil but she knows who's going to Heaven and who's going to Hell, and you and I are not on her good guy short list.

"And Terrence Moore is a real piece of work. He hates everyone except pure blood African Bahamians who are true Christians. He even hates Hiram because he's White. But he depends on Bea for his keep. I think he's a closet queer. Gladys Lamar has a neat little business but she's a holy roller like Winthrop and Bea and is basically stupid. They think their son Otis is an unrecognized genius and should be the Bahamian prime minister. The trouble is that he's too dumb and lazy. But you never know in politics around here."

His was becoming agitated and his voice was rising.

"Nigel Baron is Gladys's son from an earlier marriage. He's a nice guy, totally clueless and does what his mom says. He goes with the flow and that's why he's North Border's mayor. He's on the take and turns over a piece over every action to Hiram Cooper.

"And finally, we have Jonathan Hall. That guy is a thief who likes the slots and the ponies. If he's not careful, he'll bankrupt the islands.

"To sum it up, we're not dealing with great intelligence here. And that's why we need to be careful. Those guys can destroy the world without ever knowing what they're doing."

Jack did his best to calm his old friend down.

"That's old news, Thomas, and you can't let it get to you. You're going to find that shit going on anywhere you go." He took a half empty bottle of rum that was standing on top of a carton, found a shot glass and filled it. "Here, try this. Drink it slowly and take your pills. You'll feel better." He raised an empty glass to make a toast. "Here's to the future; may it be longer than the past."

His next move that afternoon when he finally settled in on Archangel was to call Hole-in-the-Wall on his VHF. He was put through to Manuel Sylvester, Lance Cooper's deputy, who told him that Lance was away but left word that Tom was needed for a salvage job at Satan's Rock. Jack responded by saying that he now owned the business outright and that he would sail down in the next few days.

"Cooper is shorthanded, so this is a bounty job," Manny said.

"That's fine with me if the bounty terms are the same," Jack noted.

"Speak to Lance," Manny retorted. "He makes the decisions."

"Why? Has the deal changed now that I own the whole business?"

"You need to speak to Lance," Manny repeated.

"Listen, friend. The deal stays the same or I stay home, you hear?"

Manny did not reply. Fuming, Jack did the next best thing: he called Clarence on the VHF and complained. The police chief said he would call Hiram or Milton who often spoke for Lance when he was away. Clarence agreed that no one in the local food chain wanted to see a change how Jack's boatyard did business. There were too many mouths to feed.

The afternoon was spent ferrying between Archangel and the boatyard in Agnes Town where Tom was trying to fix an outboard engine that had to be ready for the weekend. Jack's Marine was hardly more than an open hangar. It was open to the street and back where a travel lift lay over a concrete ramp to move boats in and out of the water. Inside were boats of varying sizes in different stages of repair on jacks and hauling cables surrounded by machinery and tools. Outside, two shacks leaning against the hangar faced Cheetah's in an alley with a second travel lift over another ramp next to a long dock to which a dozen skiffs with raised motors were tied. Otis Foot, Melvin Stoop and Chico Gomez were not around and Jack had to help Tom do their jobs.

Tom's current fixation was the outboard, an old ten horsepower job. Hooked up to its fuel tank, it stubbornly refused to start no matter how much it was coaxed. In desperation, Jack drained the motor and connected it directly to the tank from an inflatable dinghy which had been filled at Kyle Malone's fuel dock.

Lo and behold! The motor started up instantly.

"Odd," Tom observed. "Kyle supplies our fuel and it's always fresh. He buys it from Hugo who hauls it weekly from Marsh Harbor."

"Maybe," Jack said. "But not the gas in the red can. Where is it from?"

"It beats me, Jake."

"Gasoline has a half life in the tropics," Jack said. "If it's not used right away, even with fixatives, it goes bad."

Jack stepped away, lit a cigarette, grinned and stood up.

"Let's find out where it comes from."

They had not long to wait for an answer. Clarence Cox came in from the street, looked around and saw the source of their problem.

"Otis and Melvin say they siphoned the fuel from an abandoned motor launch they towed in a few days ago," he explained. "They hid it in the swamps on South Border and have been giving away the gas. They dropped some off for us to use in our chase boats but it's no damn good. It fouled an engine before we figured it out. You must teach your guys the difference between good and bad petrol."

Jack made a mental note to follow up on Clarence's explanation.

The engine fixed and running, they called it a day. They powered back to Pirates' Cove. The jitney shuttle was bobbing quietly in the water at the ferry dock and no other boats were in the marina. Behind a dozen picnic tables and barbeque grills were two trailers. One belonged to Kyle who was having dinner at his brother's East Leg home. Ginny lived in the other, the one with a flower garden in front. Tall trees cast their shadows over the marina and made the grounds appear darker than it really was. Chico Gomez showed up in time to prepare dinner in the catamaran's galley. He seemed glad about Jack being his only boss and wanted to know when Tom would be leaving.

"Not soon enough," said Tom happily. "I'll be gone by the weekend. And now to celebrate, I'm going to have a real drink, a gin and tonic, and heavy on the gin."

"You sure you want to drink, Tom? You already had a shot of rum."

Tom sighed.

"It's time for a good, stiff drink, Jake. I'm going under the knife soon and I want to enjoy a few good drinks in case I don't come through."

Jack said nothing. They were about finished with dinner when he brought up the subject of Ned Baron's insurance policies being cancelled.

"What's that all about?"

"I can't get a handle on this one," said Tom. "All policies issued in the islands by all insurance companies have been cancelled. Has this place been redlined?"

"I'll check with Jonathan," said Jack. "He might know something. And you call the Florida Insurance Commission when you get back."

"What I don't get is why Ned has you delivering the news in person. Cancelations are usually done in writing," said Tom.

"That could be bad public relations," said Jack. "A form cancellation letter, or even an e-mail, assuming one could get through, can get a bad press. A visit adds a personal touch and softens the blow." He looked at his watch, saying, "It's time to go, old buddy. The good shepherd is waiting."

They left together for Agnes Town in the dinghy and docked at the Blue Moon marina behind Nigel's hotel. From there it was a short walk to the Church of Christ where they found Clarence waiting for them at the rectory door with Jonathan Hall, Nigel Baron and Gordon Tully.

Jonathan's dull gray suit over an open collar white short sleeve shirt accented his ungainly appearance and made him look portlier than he was. It also conveyed the image of someone who worked hard for a living, which was probably why he was trusted as a banker.

Gordon Tully, big and bald and built like a bouncer with a thin moustache and a toothy Cheshire cat smile, had just flown in from Abaco and decided to stop at the rectory before going home to see his wife who was Jonathan Hall's sister. Gordon was a West Indian Catholic from Martinique via Georgia; Jonathan was Lutheran turned Anglican, and the rumor was that Gordon married Jonathan's sister because he had gotten her pregnant.

Henry Alden and Milton Cooper stood off to the side with Louie Gold arguing about property values. The three men owned land in the Borders and on Abaco but Henry was the most mobile, having to cover patients all over the northern islands as their only circuit doctor. Since he was getting on in years, Louie and Milton loaned him a large speedboat and the use of a skipper for his inter-island hops.

Terrence Moore arrived last, sweaty and out of breath, his Afro hairdo badly in need of a brushing. He apologized profusely, saying he had been busy with Hugo Johnson at the dock behind the diner with a shipload of fresh fish.

"Those damn Jamaican niggers charge more for fish than they do for drugs."

Everyone, including Jack, chuckled, mainly because Terrence was as black as a Bahamian of purely African descent could be. He resented all the lighter skinned Jamaicans who supplied the islands with all sorts of goods through their monopoly of inter-island shipping. The Jamaicans were accepted for their craftiness and their ability to do business but were otherwise ostracized.

The rectory buzzed with talk about the insurance policy cancellations that Jack announced on behalf of Ned Baron. No fingers were pointed at Ned who seemed to have sold the policies in good faith. Nigel said nothing and Jonathan's comment was a resigned, "you did what you had to do, Jake. Thanks."

Terrence was not so accepting and was adamant about how important it was to have insurance.

"We need a law forcing these companies to deal with us," he said. "Who's going to insure Bea's Diner?"

"We could start our own insurance cooperative," Nigel suggested.

"I have another solution," added Jack. "We can have Hugo sell us insurance. He sells everything else."

Jack intended his statement as a joke but it was taken seriously by Clarence and Gordon who thought it might be a good idea.

Hiram raised his arms, saying, "Gentlemen, gentlemen, we must start."

Jack thought that Hiram would have been happier at Yale or Harvard.

The protocol was simple. Hiram would pick a subject and over fine cigars, finger foods, brandy or cognac, he would start an open debate by uttering a single phrase or a word. Tonight he had two words, "Gilgamesh and Socrates. Does anyone remember when and where the Gilgamesh story takes place?"

"In Iraq," said Clarence, lighting a cigar. "My Jason is there now.""

"What do you think, Jake?" Hiram asked out of the blue.

Jack was only half listening. He was now desperately digging into his memory bank. Damn! Why couldn't he have had more education or be smart like Hiram? He could only blurt out the words, "It's a five thousand year old story."

"Correct," said Hiram. "Now, let's throw out five words, genial, piety, altruism, hubris and greed," Hiram went on. "They're all about Gilgamesh and Socrates."

"Socrates, I know, but Gilgamesh, I don't know," Jonathan lamented.

"Well, let's start with the word, genial," said Hiram, taking a sip of brandy and leafing through the pages of a thick dictionary lying on a table. "It means a warm, friendly and pleasantly cheerful person."

Jack detected a faint grin on Tully's face.

"If we're not congenial, we can't tolerate. If we can't tolerate, we can't work together; if we can't cooperate, we can't function; and if we can't function, then we can't survive in organized society. To conclude, we need to be congenial to live as individuals in an organized society."

Hiram always liked to end his arguments with the words, "to conclude."

"Next," he said. "We have the word, piety."

"That's a pious person," broke in Jonathan. "A church going person has piety."

Hiram puffed on his pipe and shook his head.

"Not always. A pious person may be religious and pray a lot but it might all be for show. People can pray and make sure to leave money in the collection box, and even make sure they're seen leaving money. Piety is more than piousness. It means doing the right thing, like praying not for oneself but for someone else. It means giving for its own sake and not to attract public notice. It means fulfilling one's responsibility to family, society and God.

"This brings us to the word, altruism." Hiram was really on a roll, thought Jack.

"Generosity," said Clarence.

"Close enough," agreed Hiram. "An altruistic person gives to those less fortunate who may benefit from the gift without asking for anything in return. Quid pro quos are absent in acts of altruism. A good example is the person who donates a kidney to a loved one. That's an act of altruism. It is also a sacrifice for the greater good."

"Or, it's a person who donates a kidney to someone he doesn't like," Jack added.

"That'll work," said Nigel.

"What about hubris and greed?" Hiram asked, relishing the participation of his audience.

"False pride," answered Henry.

"Right," Hiram confirmed. "One who performs deeds for personal glory is filled with hubris. That person will also be filled with greed and maybe even envy. These are the opposites of geniality, piety and altruism."

More cigars were lit and smoke rings rose toward the ceiling.

"Now, we can talk about our two friends, Gilgamesh and Socrates. Gilgamesh was the king of a city. He sought immortality once realizing that eternal life would evade him. Everything he did for his city was focused to achieve immortality. He killed a monster after it begged for its life; he insulted the goddess Ishtar when she offered him her body in marriage; and he spent a good part of his life trying to find the secret of eternal life. In short, his failings were his lack of congeniality, piety and altruism. He did for himself and not for his people. His false pride, love of self and greed were his undoing."

"What about Socrates?" Jonathan asked.

"Now, here was an interesting fellow," went on Hiram. "He lived in Athens and was condemned to death for the crime of impiety. He became prickly as he aged and antagonized many Athenians. But the mainstay of his beliefs was that, and I quote, 'the unexamined life is not worth living.' He believed that the way to the way to the good life was through the pursuit of those truths of nature that reposed outside the current mind of man. The important thing to remember about Socrates is that he was willing to die for his beliefs. He was offered a chance to escape and refused. He had lived in Athens all his life where he raised his family, prospered and even fought as a soldier in his younger years. Athens had cared for him and so he decided to die an Athenian in accordance with its law and judgment."

The flames in the fireplace began dying.

"It's interesting. Socrates, philosophically agnostic, and Jesus Christ, devoutly religious, both of whom never wrote down a word, achieved immortality by dying for their ideas. Socrates died for Truth Absolute and Jesus Christ died for God and humanity."

Nigel yawned and helped himself to a snifter of cognac.

"So, what does this all have to do with us?"

Hiram's eyes lit up and his voice turned more urgent.

"Are we prepared to make the supreme sacrifice to ward off some unimaginable catastrophe that could strike at us right here and now?"

Jonathan laughed.

"Nothing happens in our islands," he said. "The worst we face are the tourists and snowbirds that invade our shores from November to April, and they bring us money. So, that's a good thing. But thank God they leave when they do."

"Supposing something happened that would divide us?"

"We would stand together," declared Nigel. "We always have."

Hiram spread his arms out as if making a call to prayer.

"I like your answers, gentlemen. We stand united under God. If there is one way to be saved, gentlemen, it is to accept God. That is the way to beat the Devil."

"Whose God are we talking about?" Gordon asked.

"The God of Jesus Christ of course," answered Hiram quietly.

Hiram finished his drink, knocked the ashes from his pipe and turned to Jack.

"Welcome home, Jake."

"Thanks," said Jack. "It's good to be back."

"By the way, Jake, will you be doing the Devil's work for us at Satan's Rock?"

Jack gave Hiram a friendly smile.

"We're going to give it a whirl, reverend. Do you need anything?"

"My son Lance has a carton of bibles for me that you need to pick up. You'll be doing the Lord's work, and I'll put in a good word for you and your chariot so that your voyage may be safe and successful."

"Is it okay to bless the one who does the Devil's work for pay, reverend?"

"It is a good cause, and therefore you work for the Lord," said Hiram. "We will not forget you as I am sure you will remember us. And don't worry. I will square your situation with Manny. You will get your ten percent blood money."

8

Bitter End Bay

Self sufficiency was sheer bullshit. Interdependence within the Borders and dependence on the outside world were the keys to survival. The problem was that when trouble surfaced, the old line families relied on the help of newcomers like Jack. And so, when dead bodies suddenly began surfacing along the beaches, a rip tide of fear rippled across the islands. Calls flooded the police barracks but Clarence could not reach the few officers in his command. There was a call to the barracks from Sanctuary Village reporting a body on the beach near the cemetery. It was followed by another call saying that a lifeboat and skiff were found adrift between North Border and Hermit Cay. Two decomposing bodies lay in the skiff and the skeletal remains of two more bodies were in the lifeboat whose markings were those of the Angelina. The skiff was towed to Bitter End Bay on East Leg and left on the beach. The lifeboat was left anchored in the bay. Clarence promptly contacted Jack on Archangel.

It was actually Father Francois Honoree who discovered the first body. He was scouting the cemetery grounds with two workers for available burial space when a noise from the beach caught his attention. Offshore, invisible game fish deep under the ocean's waters were being chased by party boats which in turn were followed by seagulls looking for a meal. Far off in the distance, a sailboat slipped over the northern horizon. But the noise on the beach came from children walking home from school. A group of them had gathered around something that had washed up with the tide and now lay with the dead shells and debris at the high water line. It was the body of a man laying face down in the wet sand.

The priest and the two workers ran down to the beach, shooed away the children, and took a closer look. The partially naked man's body was riddled by sores that had blistered and burst and was beginning to decompose. The workers fled in fear, leaving it to the priest to call the police. The slightly later sighting of the skiff and lifeboat was anonymously reported to the police barracks. A few minutes later, a call came in through the VHF radio in Archangel's main cabin where Jack and Tom were sorting out the vessel's marine charts and setting course waypoints on the GPS. Chico was in the galley, mixing soft drinks.

Jack did not respond when told about the body on the beach but his jaw dropped when told that the lifeboat at Bitter End was from the Angelina.

"That's the fourth lifeboat," he said.

"The fourth what, you say?"

"The fourth lifeboat; the Angelina had four lifeboats when it disappeared five years ago. They are all accounted for now."

Clarence did a fast count before asking, "Then what about the motor launch that Melvin and Otis found?"

"I don't know," said Jack. "Maybe it's from another ship. I'll see you first thing in the morning."

He hung up and turned to Tom.

"Some bodies ended up at Sanctuary Village and Bitter End," he said somewhat tentatively. "Clarence wants us to go with him tomorrow."

Clarence's call was followed by one on the ham radio from Emile Honoree in Florida relaying a message that Cyrus Cooper had just given his brother Lance a parcel to be delivered to Hiram. Lance was expected to arrive at Hole-in-the-Wall via Nassau later in the day and wanted to confirm that Jack was going to pick it up on his next trip to Hole-in-the-Wall.

"No problem." Jack assured him. "I won't forget. By the way, did you and your family get those shots?"

"No, Jake," answered Emile. "The kids caught a cold and we had to make a new appointment. Is everything good with you in the Borders? My uncle called to say that some people have died."

"They have, Emile. It seems that these strange deaths in Florida have followed us here."

"I do not follow, Jake."

"I met Reginald Mayhew on the flight. You remember him, don't you? He took over for the regular pilot who died suddenly. That alone wouldn't bother me much, Emile. The problem is that as we were landing, Reggie's co-pilot passed out and died. I could swear he caught whatever got those guys in Florida."

"That is not good, Jake."

"I know that. And now I just hung up on Clarence Cox. He's telling me that more bodies have been found."

"You should speak to my uncle, Father Honoree. He knows things no one else knows. Have you seen him yet?"

"No, and I'll make a point of paying him a visit tomorrow."

Chico Gomez poked his head out of the galley just as Jack hung up on Emile.

"I heard you talking, boss. Is it about what Otis found, boss?"

Jack raised his head from the GPS.

"Yes. How did you know?"

"Otis. He called this afternoon. He mucho scared, boss. I too, mucho scared."

Jack scratched his head.

"Why didn't you say anything?"

"I scared, boss," repeated Chico. "And you were busy."

Chico Gomez was normally cheerful, but now he was subdued. A native of the Dominican Republic, he had met Jack and Tom five years ago when he hooked up with them as a mechanic and first mate. And since Archangel was a big, blue water cruising boat and Chico had nowhere to live, he traded his services in exchange for a hammock slung between bulkheads in the port pontoon forward of the engine and fuel tank. The boat had shore and generator powered central air-conditioning. Hence, it was comfortable during hot spells. For Chico this was first class living.

The Dominican was of medium height and was somewhat chunky with a round face and head of dark curly hair that made him attractive to women. He had a wife and kids back home but he had no lack of female companionship in the Borders.

"What else happened this afternoon, Chico?" Tom asked. "Any calls?"

Chico's good humor returned and he smiled broadly.

"Si, boss, el senor Baron called. So did la senora Lamar."

"And did they say or want anything?"

He sensed a tone of exasperation in Jack's voice.

"Si, it was something about a boat engine, but I forget. I no remember."

Tom excused himself to return their calls while Chico led Jack to a small cabin forward of his quarters in the port pontoon where he found his duffel tucked away in one of the two lower berths. There, Chico told Jack more about Otis's call.

"The captain and Otis found the boats, boss," said Chico.

"Hugo Johnson?"

"Si, the captain was at the farm where his mama was trimming his beard when Otis came to see him."

Big, black bearded Captain Hugo, as he was known in the islands, was the head of the Johnson family that included his older brother Eldridge, their sister Thelma and their aging parents. The family moved from Jamaica to the Borders and took up farming on land they bought in the flats of East Leg near Bitter End Bay. Hugo became a commercial fisherman and went into drug trafficking with Eldridge, and when they made enough money they staked Thelma to a beauty parlor in the center of Agnes Town. Getting his hands on a small tanker, Hugo bought fuel, food and water in from Nassau and Florida for resale in the Borders. To make more money, he formed a gang and moved cocaine from Jamaica to the Bahamas and Florida with the Zebra Club as command center. The Zebra and Cheetah's once belonged to Nigel Baron who sold them to Hugo and Ginny to preserve his clean reputation when he was elected mayor.

The gossip was that people went to the Zebra for drugs and to Cheetah's for sex. The gossip was also that Ginny Malone was a Black woman and had crossed over to White. Her dad, Kyle, was a light, brown skinned Jamaican, as was Dale. They had left for the States as small children, grew up and married White. Kyle married an Irish-American. That may have explained why Ginny was ruddy faced with long, thick curly brown hair and could have passed for a Dublin pub bar girl.

Jack thought Hugo was one of the smartest men in the islands. Otis had worked for Hugo before going to Jack's Marine. Hugo thought Otis was stupid and sneaky and was glad to see him leave but sad to see him land on Jack. Now, according to Chico, Hugo and Otis went bottom fishing off North Border Thursday afternoon when they came upon a fishing skiff with a red and yellow hull. Its bow line was secured to a larger lifeboat that bore the markings of the Angelina.

The lifeboat was too heavy and its draft too deep for beaching That explained why it was left anchored in the bay. The skiff was pulled up on the beach and left in the high dune grass. It was then that they took their first close-up look inside the skiff. The faces on the two dead men were gray and their mouths were gaping and coated with dried blood as if they had strangled or choked to death, and dried rust colored blisters, sores and boils covered their bodies.

The skiff was well known to the islanders. Skiffs belonged to marinas who rented them on a per diem basis to fishermen who could not afford their own. Each fleet and therefore its marina of origin could be identified by the colors of its hull and keel. The skiff's screaming red and yellow hull belonged to Kyle Malone's fleet at Pirates' Cove.

Hugo and Otis thought one of the bodies was Gordon Tully's younger son. Hugo did not wait to find out. He panicked and ran off, leaving Otis behind to radio his grisly find. Clarence first tried to reach Gordon, but he and his wife had left on a private plane for a police conference in Nassau.

The police chief called Jack again later that night when he was about to turn in to ask him to be Gladys Lamar's gift shop first thing in the morning,

But now there was a new wrinkle. Tom woke up at dawn, Friday, May 19, with chest pains and fever. Jack gave him medicine, made sure he was comfortable and left alone for Nigel Baron's hotel to pick up Martin. He found him without Jane on the road who he explained was going to pass up the morning's activities. He went back with Jack to Madame Lamar's where the old woman, her long gray hair tied loosely behind her head, broom in her hands, was sweeping the planks of the raised wooden walk outside her door and tidying up and getting ready to open.

Multi-colored glass crystals dangled on strings from the sidewalk overhang and more hung down inside from the top of the store window.

"Good morning, Gladys," Jack greeted her. "You're up early today."

"Good morning, Shelly. It's great to see you again. I'm a little busy, so don't mind me. I want to be open when the seaplane gets here. What about you? Your place usually doesn't get started before nine."

"I'm waiting for Clarence so I thought I'd stop by to say that Winthrop's motor is ready. It's as good as new. I'll have Mel send it over when he gets in."

She smiled at the young man with Jack.

"How are you? You must be Martin Wilson, Nigel's soon-to-be nephew.

"How did you know?" Martin asked.

"Nigel is my son," she replied. "He pointed you and Jane out to me when you landed yesterday. I hope Jane invites Winthrop and me to the wedding."

Martin ignored her plea and took a whiff of the air.

"I smell something," he said.

The old lady laughed.

"Heroin," she indicated rapidly.

"I thought you use cocaine," said Jack, breaking into the conversation. He was all of a sudden reminded of Ned Baron's story about the heroin that was in the crates those Riviera Beach fishermen had found along the coast.

"It's heroin," she confirmed. "That's all Otis has been bringing home to his dad these days."

"Heroin; well, you take care of your self, Gladys. You sure you're not too old to be taking that stuff?"

The hint of that Louisiana drawl was in his voice whenever he was engaged in an informal conversation.

The old lady gave him her trademark cackle.

"If I knew I was going to make it this long, I would have taken better care of myself."

Jack gave her a peck on the cheek.

"You're not old. Just think of yourself as fine wine that improves with age."

Mrs. Lamar broke out laughing.

"You're good with women, Shelly. Too bad you're not older and a Bahamian."

"Oh, I am a Bahamian at heart; you know that. I'm a real Conch. But you don't want me at any age, Gladys. I'm no bargain. Besides, you have Winthrop. How's his casket business?"

"All right, I guess. The Foote Funeral Home has been around forever, but things are a little slow. Winthrop says people aren't dying much any more. They're living too long. So, we're thinking of helping Otis start a business or maybe buy one here in town. Do you have any ideas, Shelly?"

Jack chuckled.

"I got plenty of ideas, Gladys, and as a Bahamian at heart, I'll certainly think of Otis if I decide to sell or take on new partners."

Gladys cackled under her breath.

"Bahamian at heart, he says, Hah!"

Jack was about to make a comment when the window crystals began chiming.

"Is that the incoming flight?" he asked.

Gladys put down the broom and looked at the window clock.

"No," she answered. "It's too early. It's not due for another half hour. I keep time by those flights."

The chiming stopped and a look of relief fell over their faces.

"Must have been the wind," said Jack.

"Oh, I don't know," she countered. "It could be waste water from the houses up on King's Road coming down the sewer pipe under us. It gets my crystals shaking. Listen, when you see Otis, tell him that his dad and I prefer cocaine to heroin."

Jack looked down at the open sewer in front of the store into which the pipe from King's Road would have drained. It was dry.

"Do many people do drugs here?" Martin asked.

Jack gave him a friendly pat on the back.

"Cocaine is the drug of choice," he replied. "It's a dirty little secret here and it's shared by everyone. I don't care for it but what folks do in none of my business. What gets me, though, is this thing about heroin. It's new around here."

Clarence came out of the Cross Island Air customs office at that moment with a long box wrapped in gray duct tape in his arms.

"Morning, Jake, Martin, Thomas," he panted. "Package for you, Martin; came in a week ago and was misplaced. It's heavy, man. So watch it."

He gave the box to Martin, asking, "What's in the box?"

"Fishing reels," answered Martin. "I like using my own gear."

Clarence had other things on his mind and was scarcely listening,

"There's a service at Hiram's church now for one of the passengers on the flight you came in," he told Jack. "He fell ill at Nigel's hotel last night and died before Henry could help him."

"What did he die of?"

"Henry didn't say. The only thing he did was to call Winthrop for a casket. And oh, we can forget about the body at Sanctuary Village. Locals torched it last night."

Madame Lamar overheard them and said, "That's right. He building one now; matter of fact, Winthrop is readying more caskets."

"Are they needed?" Martin asked.

"Just in case," she answered, again with that piercing cackle. And she continued with her sweeping.

Clarence shivered, but he nodded anyway and said, "Let's go."

"Where are we going?" Martin wanted to know.

"To see dead bodies on a beach," answered Jack.

Martin placed the box carefully in the back of the jeep and said nothing,

They climbed into the jeep and drove off, passing the Church of Christ on the left. The service must have ended early and no mourners were in sight. In the space between two bars on their right facing the bay, they saw Avalon in the distance, the mournful wail of its siren breaking the watery silence at thirty second intervals as the Castaways on board sang funeral hymns.

Jack found binoculars under the dashboard and pressed them to his eyes. Sure enough, Virgil was at the helm, motioning to Clovis who was on deck positioning iron pigs into the casket to make sure it sank when dropped overboard. The pigs came from Hugo's junkyard behind the Zebra Club. Hugo kept a small smelter on the grounds where his Jamaicans shaped scrap iron into coffin weights that were sold for fifty dollars apiece.

"How come people are buried at sea?" Martin Wilson asked when Jack put down the glasses. "It seems like denying a person a final resting place."

"Not really," said Tom. "One's final resting place is in the sky."

. "We ran out of space a century ago," added Clarence. "The cemetery at All Souls has a few lots left and that's it."

"At least, burial at sea saves money," Martin observed.

"You'd think," said Jack. "Winthrop charges five hundred to a thousand dollars for a casket; the weights cost fifty bucks each and Virgil gets five hundred dollars for the day. And then there's the cost of the horse and wagon from the church to the dock, the cost of the service, the church contribution and the Castaways fee. Dying isn't free even here in the islands."

They finally took off for Bitter End Bay, a bone jarring drive that took an hour, up West Leg through Patrick City to Sanctuary Village and then halfway down East Leg. Small honking cars and pickup trucks competed for space on the narrow dusty road with donkeys and mules pulling carts but the traffic was light for what should ordinarily be a work day. Very few people were out and about in Patrick City on the way up to Sanctuary Village where the cluster of small homes hugged the road seemed almost deserted except for wandering chickens, pigs and goats. The Zebra Club was closed of course but the door to All Souls Church was open to worshippers. Between the club and the church was the cemetery. Two caretakers were tending the grounds.

They finally reached a flat stretch of land and made a left turn into a path that led through two dunes until it ended at a beach on a wide half-moon lagoon. This was Bitter End Bay.

They found the skiff in the dune grass. The morning heat was setting in and their clothes were turning into wet dishrags. Jack and Clarence were savvy to the humid heat; they were fully clothed and wore hats. But Martin, in shorts and thin tee-shirt, had to endure the heat and bugs. Their incessant buzz and hiss was worse than the silence of the dunes. And then there was the stench that had made its way to them.

They left the jeep, shuffled through the sand to the skiff and took a peek over the gunwales where they were met by the smell of death that met them. It was hard to keep from gagging.

The two bodies in the skiff were grotesquely decomposed and no longer human; their carcasses open and gutted, eyes hanging out of their sockets and part of their skulls exposed. Martin took one look, grew misty eyed and ran back to the jeep to vomit. Bugs of every size and description swarmed and crawled over and in and out of the skiff. Clarence held his nose and leaned over to have a closer look.

"It's Tully's boy," he gasped, fighting tears. "Now he's down to one son."

"He was a good kid," said Jack. "He worked weekends for Vernon Peters to save money for college when he wasn't in school." He searched the mouth of the lagoon with his eyes. "There's that lifeboat," he pointed. "What do we tell Gordon?"

"Nothing," said Clarence. "He and his wife are in Nassau and won't be back for days. We need to put the bodies on ice. Will you be lodging salvage rights, Jake?"

Jack shook his head vigorously, replying, "No way, man!"

Clarence sighed and called the barracks on his portable VHF.

"Well, let's go on to Dale's and pick up animal feed for the Johnson couple. It will give us time to think. He may know something we don't."

Martin was sitting quietly in the jeep and had recovered his composure enough when they returned to ask, "How many were there?"

Clarence held up four fingers, saying, "Two in the skiff and two in the lifeboat, and we may have more out there."

Friday, May 19, was not off to a good start.

9

Action and Reaction

Every action had a ripple effect that invited reaction. Henry Alden often said: when one person sneezed everyone caught cold. Gordon Tully may have said it better. "Either we hang together or we hang separately." To Jack this meant not rocking the boat of life, and it was becoming clear that it was being rocked hard by an unknown force and drawn into the rapids of disaster.

Gordon Tully once put it all in sharper perspective.

"In the belly of a White man lurks a Black man and conversely."

Jack had laughed at the suggestion.

"Let's say that many of us share a common gene pool," said Gordon. "I hate to think what would happen if the right epidemic hit us. It could kill us all."

Clarence's dark Bahamian features seemed darker against his white short sleeved police officer's shirt tucked neatly into a pair of dark slacks supported at the waist by a gun belt holding a holstered service pistol. He was usually a friendly sort, full of smiles and jokes, but his mood was now subdued.

The jeep continued south on the bumpy road until East Leg became a narrow ribbon of land surrounded by flat, slate colored water. Just as it seemed that the road was going to sink into the sea, a squat concrete building with smoke stacks suddenly appeared. This was the North Border Treacle Company owned by Dale Malone by Sugar Pond on East Leg's southern tip.

One loading platform faced the road with cars and bicycles parked alongside and another in back was connected to a pier that reached like a long finger into Sugar Pond, a lagoon extension of Sanctuary Bay. At the building's north end, workers were completing the shell of a factory addition.

Clarence stopped the jeep stopped by the roadside loading platform and honked for someone to come help load feed bags into the jeep's open back while Jack sat quietly next to him, puffing away on a cigarette. Martin Wilson, with nothing to do in the rear seat, fondled the box at his side. Jack was curious about its contents but figured he would find out in time.

They jumped out of the vehicle as Dale Malone, square jawed and bald, came out to greet them, saying to Jack, "Welcome back, Jake. I hear you bought Tom out."

"Tom needs an operation. It had to be," said Jack.

"I'll miss him," Dale nodded. "It's usually him I see from the office window."

"You'll need to get used my face now," said Jack. "How's the family?"

Dale knocked twice on the jeep's fender.

"Everyone's good," he said. "My wife is away visiting the kids and grandkids in Florida. I wanted to go too, but I got busy." He swept his hand in the direction of the plant extension. How are things at your end, Clarence?"

"Can't complain," replied Clarence.

"Oh, by the way, Jake, my brother was over for dinner last night when Ginny called from Nassau," Dale continued. "She's getting back on one of Lance's boats. I thought you'd like to know."

"Oh? How come she's not flying?"

"It's that Bahamas Air slowdown," explained Dale. "It's backing up traffic in all the islands. What do you hear, Clarence?"

"We haven't seen a Bahamas Air flight touch down on the South Border airstrip in days," replied the police chief.

"Well, I'm glad she's safe," said Jack.

Dale returned to the subject of Jack's business.

"I hear tell that you might want to sell your business or take on new partners now that you own it outright. I know people who might want to make an investment."

Clarence coughed and Jack made a wry face.

"I may need partners, Dale. But I need younger, working partners. But I'll talk to anyone you suggest."

"Thanks, Jake." He looked at Martin Wilson. "I don't think we've met."

"Oh, I'm sorry," said Clarence. "This is Martin Wilson, Ned Baron's soon to be son-in-law."

They exchanged hand shakes.

"Martin and Jane are vacationing here. You remember Jane. She's Nigel's niece and Ned's daughter."

Dale nodded, saying, "I saw her when she was a baby. Well, is anything else new in our island paradise?"

"Nothing much," replied Clarence, "Has the Nassau Clipper been here yet?"

Dale Malone shook his head.

"It overdue and I'm running short on stocks. It brings us cane from Haiti and the Dominican Republic and if it doesn't get here soon, I'll be out of business."

Jack nudged Clarence in the ribs.

"That means we're going to run low on rum. If we run out, we'll have to go back to making babies."

"Well, we could use a bit of population pressure," Dale observed seriously. "I got a copy of the new Bahamian census," he went on. "Thirteen thousand residents live in the Borders, five thousand here and eight thousand in South Border. Same as it was ten years ago."

"I saw that too," replied Clarence. "How's business otherwise?"

Dale sounded indifferent.

"Same O, same O. We can't grow if our islands don't grow, and our exports are limited because today molasses is too easily synthesized. We have the local market because folks like our animal feed with a mixture of cane, corn and molasses as an additive. Right now, we're developing new uses for our high test molasses and are starting to ship some of it to Dan Schulman's outfit."

"Are you making a better brand of rum?"

"No. We already produce one of the best. It's almost like a sweet cognac laced liqueur. It's better straight than as a mixer, but how much rum can we drink, Jake? If every man, woman and child drank rum in the Borders, we still wouldn't have much of a market. How many drunks do you round up these days, Clarence?"

Clarence laughed.

"We still get a few. We bag Mel and Otis regularly. And we get Hugo and a few Jamaicans, and maybe a few tourists in season. That's about it."

"Well, we're not playing dead. My brother Kyle has a deal with Dan Schulman's South Florida Pharmaceuticals. They're buying our high test molasses for their gel caps and we're going to produce some of their products under license and sell them in the Bahamas and the West Indies. We got new equipment a few months ago that Hugo bought for us in Miami and it's going to put us on the map."

"Is Kyle going into business with you or will he still keep the marina at Pirates' Cove?" Jack asked.

"Oh. He won't give it up," said Dale. "He wants the place for Ginny. You're safe, Jake. You won't have to move your boat. You might even end up with that damn place if you play your cards right with Ginny."

Jack grinned.

"I'm glad. I like having a steady address."

Clarence pointed to the new extension at the end of the old factory.

"Is that why you built that expansion, Dale?

Dale nodded.

"It's a warehouse. We have two hundred people working for us right now. We're also out of Hermit Cay. When the new system goes on stream we hope to hire fifty more people."

Clarence whistled.

"That makes you the Borders' largest single employer, Dale. But why would you give up Hermit Cay?"

"Producing there was a good idea at first. Nigel Baron and Jonathan Hall got us a long term tax free lease with Hamilton Graves. Hermit Cay was better for us. It has deep water on its west side. The trouble is that it gets those quakes that scare away our workers. Anyway, are you guys here for anything special?"

"Feed for the Johnson farm," replied Clarence.

"Not a problem."

Dale left and returned a few minutes later with Marvell Sullivan, his foreman. Winslow Bates, his warehouse man, followed on a fork lift truck holding a skid filled with bags of animal feed. He maneuvered the lift against the jeep and Dale and Marvell eased the bags into its open back.

"Great," said Jack. "Cows and chickens don't like waiting for breakfast. What's the tab, Dale?"

"I'll bill you and you can collect from Thelma or Hugo."

Dale shuffled off while Marvell and Winslow finished arranging the feed bags in the jeep.

"That's it," said Marvell, panting. "Ten fifty pound bags." How are you doing in Florida, Jake?"

"Business could always be better."

Winslow laughed.

"We know," and he winked at Marvel. "That's why Marvel offered your guys, Chico, Mel and Otis, jobs when we saw them at Bea's. Didn't we, Marvel?"

"If they go work for you," Jack retorted good naturedly. "I'll go bankrupt. They work cheap and I can't afford to replace them. I'm too poor."

"Your problem, Jake," said Marvell, "is that your assets are all tied up in cash."

"That's enough," Clarence interrupted. "We need to go."

They waved their goodbyes and took off up the dusty road.

"Why did Dale built his factory and dock at the bottom of North Border's right leg instead of on the outskirts of Agnes Town?" Martin asked aloud as they drove off.

"It's the tidal current," replied Jack. "It runs in and out of Sugar Pond every six hours. That's easy in and out for inter-island steamers. They come in with the tide, off load, reload and leave in time to catch the ebb. Hermit's Cay would have been better since tides aren't an issue there. The Nassau Clipper was always able to get in and out anytime."

"So was the Angelina before it disappeared," Clarence observed.

Jack's eyes lit up.

"I know where the Angelina is stuck," he said.

"I don't follow," said Martin.

"I'm talking about that skiff. It was where it was supposed to be, in the shallows outside Hermit Cay. But the lifeboat's position bothered me until now. Listen, the Gulf Stream runs a northerly course and normally flotsam breaking off from the Sargasso would eventually drift west to Florida. But between the Borders and the Sargasso the Stream has a spinoff counter current eddy pushing south."

"So?"

"So, it means that the Angelina is somewhere in the Sargasso's northwest sector. That's the only way the lifeboat could have drifted to where it was found. It drifted west a few miles and then rode the eddy south to Bitter End. I bet the Angelina is not more than fifty to a hundred miles from where we stand, maybe less. What's even stranger is that if all we have north of us is ocean, the Angelina would have been way off course by heading west to Florida or getting stuck in the Sargasso."

No one had a satisfactory explanation. Marine navigation was not their forte.

They headed back up East Leg and past Bitter End Bay where black smoke was rising over the dunes. Deep in conversation and paying it no mind, they drove on until they stopped at a roadside farm next to a car parked out back by an open barn. Jack though it looked like Nigel Baron's sedan.

"Have you thought about partners, Jake? Clarence asked when they stopped.

Jack gave him a quick response.

"Clarence, you and Gordon will have the first right of refusal if I decide to do anything. But I'd like us to consider one more person."

"Who's that?" Clarence asked.

"I want us to talk to Hugo Johnson as a possible partner. He's younger, smarter, and knows more about boats than any of us."

"But he's a thief," protested the police chief.

"Let's give him a hearing," said Jack. "It's the Christian way, isn't it? I think it's called Redemption. He might be right for us if we want to expand."

He held up an open hand.

Clarence smiled, saying, "I can't fault your reasoning, Jake. You're a good man."

"Come, let's unload the bags," said Jack.

Henry Alden came out of the barn at that moment. He started walking to the car as they started to unload the bags of feed. His black medical bag was in one hand, his car keys in another and he was mumbling to himself.

"Hey, Henry, what's up?"

The physician looked up and blinked.

"Clarence, Jake. Good to see you this morning. And who's this young man?"

Martin introduced himself.

"Martin Wilson. I'm with the government."

"I hope you find something to govern, young feller."

"How's the Johnson couple, doctor?" Clarence asked.

"Oh, they're fine. I'm not here for them. It's one of their goats."

"A goat, you say?"

"Yes. We have a sick goat," said Henry. "I have no idea what it has but I gave it something anyway. Ma Johnson is milking one of her cows if you need her."

He climbed into his car.

"Is that Nigel's car, Henry?"

"He loaned it to me. I'm getting too old for my bike."

"You're not old, Henry," Jack said. "You're just smart."

"Thanks, Jake. That's what I tell my weary bones. Well, I have to take off and see the rest of my patients before returning to Hope Town."

"See anything unusual?" Clarence asked.

"A few sprains, a bruised pig, a case of measles, and a few people with flu and measles like symptoms. I think that's what brought down that pilot and the other passenger."

"But this is May, Henry."

The doctor stroked his beard.

"Yes. It is strange. It's a virus or bacterial infection and may be contagious. It's hard to tell without tests. I gave them shots from a cocktail of experimental drugs that Cyrus developed. Dan Schulman sent them to me for testing. I used that same vaccine in Marsh Harbor on a few patients and they recovered, and I also used it on the passengers when you landed, Jake."

He patted his black medical bag.

"I have specimen. I'll know in a few days when I get to my lab at home."

"Can you examine a couple of bodies before leaving?" Clarence asked. "They died of something awful, and one of them is Gordon Tully's kid."

Henry stopped in his tracks.

"Where are they?"

"They'll be on ice at the police barracks later."

The doctor mumbled something and sped off. Martin looked puzzled.

"Is he always in such a rush?" He asked.

"Not usually," answered Clarence.

They dropped the subject to concentrate on dragging the bags of feed to the barn where an old woman was milking one of two cows with her gnarled hands under the watchful eyes of two black and white spotted cats.

Outside, several pigs, goats and chickens roamed about.

"Is that you, Clarence?"

The woman never bothered to turn and the cats refused to budge.

"Yes, Ma," he said loudly so that she could hear him.

"We're putting the feed in the corner. Okay?"

"Did you see Dr. Alden?"

She obviously never heard him. She knew the doctor had been around and that she had company. She continued to milk the cow.

Jack went over and gave the woman a peck on the head. She pressed her head against his lips, moved her body slightly, and they started stacking the bags.

"Shelly?" she said. "Don't you pay for the feed; Pa will take care of it."

"Where's Pa?" Jack asked.

"He went fishing."

"Fishing, alone?"

"Oh, he stays on the beach."

Jack heaved a sigh of relief.

They finished with the bags and Jack asked the old lady if she needed anything.

"I thought I needed rat poison from Vernon's store, but I don't need any now. Something else is killing the rats," she said, struggling to her feet.

"Where are the dead rats now?"

"Pa burned them before leaving this morning."

The old lady took the leftover milk and poured it into a bowl on the ground. The cats needed no invitation. They scurried over and began lapping up the milk.

10

Of Bugs, Cats and Dogs

The irony was that Vernon, who Jack thought looked like a rodent, was the islands' single supply source for rat poison. And the Borders sure did have rats.

The consensus was that rodents far outnumbered the human population. There were rats and mice of all species and sizes. Many were local, and some came in on planes and boats, periodically infesting homes and entire neighborhoods.

Cats kept these unwelcome guests in check but could not eradicate them. Dogs skillfully sniffed out the rodents and bugs but they never killed them. And so life went on and rats and bugs continued to thrive. .

Vernon had the rat poison and insecticide monopoly and that with his regular pharmacy business should have made him happy. A question that nagged Jack who never dwelt much on his own mortality was if Vernon wanted to establish himself as the descendent of an old-line Borders family to reserve a space in the Borders' only cemetery to avoid that final voyage on Virgil's death ship.

Jack gave Ma Johnson another kiss and they left, driving to the top of the island where at the cemetery East Leg Road became West Leg Road. Martin pointed to the white cottages with green shutters behind All Souls Church whose steeple rose high above the island at that point.

"Who lives there?" he asked.

"That's Sanctuary Village," said Clarence. "Mostly Jamaicans and a few Haitians and Dominicans live here. One of Jake's guys, Chico Gomez, has a room near the church. Many of them work for Dale. A few fish for a living and many work at our restaurants and shops or at the two hotels, the

North Border or the Ocean View on South Border. Folks aren't rich, but everyone is working, even the immigrants."

Clarence stopped the jeep when he saw Francois Honoree talking to one of his parishioners outside his church. The man was standing, holding his hat in his hands and shifting nervously from one foot to another. Jack waved, and the priest waved back. He left the parishioner standing in front of the church and came over to the jeep.

"Jake, I am glad to see you. How is Emile, Juliette and their children?"

"They're fine, Father. I'm sure they called since I left Florida," said Jack.

"They have. They have," Francois acknowledged. "And that has me worried, my friend. Is there an epidemic in Florida?"

Jack shook his head.

"A few people are coming down with the flu, or so it seems," replied Jack.

"And there are the Angelina bodies you found," the priest continued.

"It's a weird situation," Jack admitted.

"Why are you asking?" Clarence wanted to know.

Francois Honoree pointed to the man in front of the church door.

"This poor soul just lost his wife, may she rest in peace, and his children are very ill. I must call Virgil to make arrangements. I would have another man whose body was swept in by the sea. He may have been a sailor from the Nassau Clipper, but his body was burned by some of our people."

Clarence sighed.

"Well, Virgil is on Avalon and we'll tell him when he gets back."

The priest smiled in appreciation.

"God bless you, my sons. I am grateful."

"Tell me," said Jack. "Does Vernon Peters have an ancestor buried here?"

Francois Honoree rolled his eyes and laughed.

"He has claimed that," he said, "but it cannot be proven. However, my church accepted his claim and gave him a dispensation to put a small monument in our cemetery. I found a discarded grave stone behind the church and had Hugo age it and carve inscriptions on it. Vernon paid ten thousand dollars for the dispensation. We used the money for school books for our children and to fix our fishing boats. Some of that money went to you, Jake, for the boat repairs."

"Vernon must have been desperate to prove his heritage," noted Jack, "at least enough to fake his family history."

"We are all vainglorious sinners," said Father Francois Honoree. "But I gave him something more that I found in an old house."

"What was that?"

"It was an old copy of a royal charter dating back to the seventeenth century. He said it was an antique and wanted it for his personal collection."

"Is it genuine?"

Father Francois laughed, replying, "Of course not. It took Eldridge one year to produce it. No one has ever seen the original document if indeed it exists."

The priest returned to his waiting parishioner and Clarence began driving down the road.

"See what I mean," said Clarence. "Almost everyone has a boat needing repair. Your business is a gold mine. You should stay and take on partners."

Clarence, in his own oblique way, was trying to convince Jack to settle in the islands. They drove past the Zebra Club where a battered panel truck was parked in front. A sign on a panel read, 'Captain John's Deep Sea Charters & Ventures."

This meant that Hugo was in. He made a mental note to see him later.

They drove past Patrick City whose predominantly Dominican population was enjoying a market fair on the town square. They stopped briefly for lunch at one of the stands and finally returned to the police barracks.

"What bothers me is the isolation of this place," Martin observed. "If something happened, who would know?"

"It's like the joke," Jack reminded him. "If a tree falls in the forest and no one knows, did the tree really fall in the forest?"

"Well, listen, Jake. I'd like to find out more about what's going on. Would you mind if I tag along for a while?"

"Suit yourself. Just make sure to touch base with Clarence."

"I'll do that," he said, removing the box from the back of the jeep. "But now I'm going to the hotel to see how Jane is doing. I'll catch up with you guys later."

He left with his box as a constable came out of the barracks to tell Clarence that Bahamas Air was now officially on strike.

"This will kill us if it lasts more than a few days," moaned Clarence.

"We're ok if we have the seaplanes," Jack noted.

"And Hugo's tanker," Clarence added. "We're dead in the water without gas and diesel."

The constable saw Jack and added, "Oh. Lance called to say that he needs you at Hole-in-the-Wall for a salvage job at Satan's Rock."

"It must be a really great job if Coop keeps reminding us," said Jack.

"It's a drug boat," said the constable.

"There's always a little something," Jack remarked.

"I'm going in to check on things," said Clarence. "I'll be right out."

"Listen," said Jack. "Lend me the jeep. I want to see Hugo."

"Don't be long, Jake," said Clarence testily. "I have things to do."

He jumped out of the jeep and disappeared inside the barracks.

Jack took the jeep and drove back to Sanctuary Village. Seeing Hugo's truck still in front of the club, he parked next to it and walked through the batwing doors into the dimly lit room.

It was a typical island bar with ceiling fans slowly turning over plastic chairs and tables arranged around a dance floor in front of a long bar that extended the length of the back wall. Someone on the dance floor was moving about with a broom and dust pan sweeping up a pile of dead bugs and the carcasses of a half eaten mouse and cat. A barstool by the door was filled by Eldridge Johnson, a huge mountain of a man with side whiskers and a handlebar moustache and heavy dark beard.

Reggae music would ordinarily be filling the air but now the jukebox was quiet and the place was dark. Eldridge placed a hand on Jack's neck and stopped him inside the swinging batwing doors.

"We're closed, mate," he said without cracking a smile.

"I'm here to see Hugo," Jack explained.

A deep voice from the bar asked, "Who's that?"

Jack looked into the room and saw Hugo seated on another barstool at the far corner of the bar near the back door. He was wearing glasses and poring over an open book, but he seemed sad and was having trouble concentrating. He looked over his glasses at the door and recognized Jack.

"I heard you were back in town, Jake. What's up?" He nodded to Eldridge who grunted and let Jack in.

Jack pointed to the dance floor as the sweeper carefully dropped his grisly haul into a plastic bag.

"What's with your guests, Hugo?"

"We found those things all over the place when we opened," Hugo said, stroking his thick black beard. "I don't know where they hell they came from and how the hell they died. Anyway, how are you doing?"

Jack stepped gingerly around the dance floor and sauntered up to the bar and sat down next to Hugo who, though seated, still towered over him.

"I'm hanging in, Hugo. I thought I'd drop by and touch base." He pointed to the book on the bar counter. "Have you taken up reading in your old age?"

"It's a trigonometry text," said Hugo, taking off his glasses. "I've been taking distance learning courses at Las Olas University in Fort Lauderdale."

Jack's voice registered surprise as he examined the book cover.

"When did you start this?"

"Two years ago. They have a neat program. I take six, one-week seminars on site in Florida and do the rest on my laptop from my boat when I'm at sea between here and Florida. That's the only place I can pick up a signal."

"How come you decided to go to college?"

"Eldridge convinced me," replied Hugo. "He got his degree last year. It's a good move for us. We can't keep doing what we're doing forever. Eldridge graduated as a business major. I like numbers so I'm a math major. I'm finishing my last course and graduating."

"That's neat. You guys will become college professors yet."

Hugo laughed sarcastically.

"Fat chance; Now, boy, what's on your mind. I know you want something."

Jack wanted to ask about the bodies at Bitter End Bay but held back, thinking it was best to leave the matter to Clarence. He chose instead a circuitous approach.

"My buddy, Tom Kennedy sold out to me because he has a bad ticker and needs out to get medical attention in the States. That leaves me without a partner…." And he went on to explain the ideas he had laid out to Clarence.

"I need more than one partner," concluded Jack. "Since you're a college graduate now, you may be planning a career move."

Hugo nodded.

"I'll keep it mind," he said. "What else you got?"

"It's what Gladys Lamar told me early this morning when I ran into her. She says she's been using heroin lately. I thought you dealt in cocaine."

Hugo's smile disappeared.

"I got a good price on heroin and started peddling it."

"What's your source?"

Hugo's toothy smile reappeared.

"You make me a partner; I'll make you a partner and tell you my sources."

"I'll keep that under advisement, Hugo," said Jack. "By the way, Tom Kennedy was asking about Thelma."

The big Jamaican's face drooped. Still, he managed a sarcastic laugh.

"Why? Is he going to marry her?"

Jack was taken aback.

"Shit, man. I don't know. He's not feeling good and he asked about her."

Hugo's lips curled as he responded. "You guys are all the same. You spend time with black women and you think you own them."

"Listen, big guy, I'm not here to fight. I'm relaying a message, that's all. Tom is seeing Thelma like I'm seeing Ginny."

Hugo snorted.

"That's different. Ginny's a single woman; Thelma is my sister."

Jack got off the barstool and tapped the Jamaican on the chest with his finger.

"I understand, but you need to do is give Thelma two messages. The first is from Tom; the second is about a cosmetics line she wanted. Tell her that Dan Schulman carries beauty products and will be here soon. She could make a deal with him."

"Oh?"

Jack raised his hands, palms outward.

"That's all, old buddy. That's all."

He left Hugo at the bar and walked past Eldridge, tipping his hat on the way out of the club.

"You have a good day, college grad, you hear."

Eldridge's voice trailed Jack out the door.

"I'm sorry, Jake. My brother doesn't mean to be so short. We're very upset here and we weren't expecting visitors."

Jack turned around and was about to walk back into the bar, but Eldridge laid a hand softly on his shoulder and stopped him at the door.

"It's Thelma, Jake," explained Eldridge. "She passed away."

Jack's mouth dropped and his felt his legs shake under him.

"How did that happen?"

"She got sick the day before you returned, Jake and couldn't make it. It was nasty, man, real nasty. She lasted maybe three or four hours."

"I guess Tom doesn't know," said Jack.

"No one knows," said Hugo from the bar. "We didn't want our folks to know and we didn't want anyone making a grab for her beauty parlor. Virgil took Thelma's body out to sea when you landed. I hope you keep your mouth shut too, Jake."

Jack left the club quietly. Outside, the sun bore down, forcing him to squint, and he drove slowly, almost aimlessly, back to Agnes Town where on impulse he made a pit stop at his boatyard to see if Melvin Stoop and Otis Foote had surfaced. And sure enough, they were furiously working away to make up for lost time.

Jack did not bother looking at Otis, aiming his ire at Mel.

"Where you been, man? Does Tom pay you to goof off?"

Otis tried to hide behind the cover of a milling machine but Jack caught him.

"Don't hide, Otis." He turned his attention back to Mel. "Where you been, man?"

Mel stood up. He was a big, ungainly, helpless hulk, his long arms dangling at his side and his hands hanging with their palms out.

"I guess I been away, boss," he said slowly in a deep, slow monotone.

Jack allowed a faint smile to leave his lips.

"I know you been away, Mel; where at?"

He could hear Otis whispering, "Tell him the truth, Mel; you been fishing."

"Shut up, Otis," barked Jack. "Let Mel speak for himself."

"Otis is right," said Mel, a little more confident now. "I've been fishing."

"Where, Mel?"

"Down at Canal Pond."

Jack decided not to pursue the matter and turned his attention to Otis.

"Come on, Otis. Tell me what happened at Bitter End Bay. How come Hugo ran away?"

Otis came out from behind the milling machine and began to shake.

"We were scared, boss."

"Why is that, Otis?"

"Because Hugo knows about an old steamer stuck in the weeds and told some his Jamaicans at the Zebra. One of them went out there on one of Kyle's skiff with the Tully boy, and we went looking for them when they didn't get back."

"Did you tell anyone besides Clarence about what you found?"

Otis shook his head.

"I just told you. I dunno who Hugo told. I also told Kyle."

The puzzle was falling in place. Otis told Kyle and Kyle sent word to Hugo who got his men to torch the boats. That explained the smoke he saw when he, Clarence Cox and Martin Wilson drove up East Leg earlier.

Jack pointed to the fading hand painted sign hanging from the fence in front of his shop and ordered, "I need your help. Paint the sign and change the name from 'Jack's Marine' to 'Jake's Marine.' Everyone here calls me 'Jake' so we might as well go with the flow."

"You mad at us, boss?" Mel asked anxiously.

Jack smiled at last.

"No. I don't want you to get hurt, that's all. Now, get to work."

Jack drove back to the barracks and was about to go in when he saw Chico who was standing with Clarence, Hiram and Jonathan and seemed very agitated. The few words Jack caught as he approached concerned Louie and Reggie.

"Are they back?" Jack asked innocently.

"Yes, this morning," said Clarence. "Louie wasn't well and went home and I sent Reggie to Bitter End with some men, but the skiff, lifeboat and bodies were gone."

"Not good," said Jack. "Hear anything from Lance?"

"His cutters found the Angelina on the edge of the Sargasso," Clarence replied. But something else was bothering them and Jack braced himself. Clarence was choking his words and Hiram and Jonathan had their arms around Chico. Finally, the police chief burst out crying, "Tom died this morning," he sobbed.

"I'm sorry, Jake," said Hiram Cooper, trying hard to keep his eyes steady. "Tom was a good man, even for a Catholic."

11

The Red Pail

Bad luck for some is good for others. Tom Kennedy was dead so that money and anything else of value he would have received for his half of the Borders boat business would now stay in Jack's pockets along with a free and clear title to the entire enterprise. He was now also the full owner of Archangel. Last but not least, he owned Tom's bank account and vault in Florida and all else that he owned on the planet. Like it or not, he was a wealthy man.

Friday, May 19, ended poorly. Jack was in the Borders one full day. Tom was gone and so was Thelma.

Jack tried his best to keep his cool.

"What did he die of, Clarence?" Jack asked.

"His was shaking like he was freezing and then he stopped shaking,"

"Where's Tom now?"

Jonathan pointed to the barracks behind him.

"We had him brought here. I also took the liberty of checking Archangel. As you know, Jake, I am the elected mayor of South Border and have the people's interest to protect. I should quarantine Archangel. There could be a public health hazard."

Clarence became uncharacteristically, retorting, "You do that and I'll shoot you. We need Jake and his boat. He needs to do a job for Lance."

"It is a delicate matter, as you can imagine," Hiram added.

Jack shrugged his shoulders,

"I'm sorry, Jonathan. Archangel is off limits right now. Now since Tom was a Catholic, a service at All Souls will do fine and then Virgil and Clovis can take over. Let's do it when I'm back from Hole-in-the-Wall."

Jonathan pulled some folded sheets of printed matter from his inside pocket and gave them to Jack.

"This is Tom's will. He filed signed originals in Florida and in Junction City so I'm familiar with it. It leaves all his worldly possessions to you, Jake."

Jack took the papers and shoved them into his trouser pocket.

"Thanks," he said. Uncomfortable with talking further about Tom, he changed the subject to Doreen and asked. "Has she contacted you?"

Jonathan nodded and replied, "She has, and wants to come here."

"If that's what she wants, that's what we'll do," Jack agreed.

"It's that lousy husband of hers," said Jonathan. "Fred gave her whatever she has. He should go to Hell! I curse the ground he walks on." Jonathan spit on the ground and started raving. "You should never have allowed your marriage to Doreen to end. Your divorce was her downfall."

"It wasn't my call," responded Jack defensively. "She kicked me out. But if you want me to get her out of Florida, let me know and I'll do it."

Jonathan began stalking away.

"Thanks, but I don't need your help. Dan Schulman will take care of that."

"Come, I'll drive you and Chico," said Clarence, climbing aboard the jeep. "You must forgive Jonathan," he continued. "He's under a lot of stress."

Clarence dropped them off at the pier where the jitney ferry was preparing to make its run to Buccaneer Point and Pirates' Cove.

Jack took a deep breath and stared at the ripples in the water.

"I'm no doctor," he said, "but it doesn't sound like Tom had a heart attack."

"Chico nodded in agreement.

"He no look good, boss; maybe the heart gave up, but something made the heart give up."

"I'm with Chico," said Clarence. "I saw Tom before he died. I could swear he had the measles or chicken pox or something."

Jack looked up at the puffy clouds in the sky.

"We need rain," he observed. "I remember Tom saying when I got here that the only time rain fell was when he proposed marriage to Thelma."

"Did Hugo mention his sister when you saw him?" Clarence asked out of nowhere, perhaps out of idle curiosity and to make conversation. "Her shop has been closed for days."

"She died, old buddy. She died."

Clarence looked as if he had been shot.

"Dead, you say? Eldridge and Hugo never said a word."

"Hugo told me. He didn't say anything because he and Eldridge didn't want to upset their parents. Virgil had just come back from dropping her body off at sea when I landed. So, try to keep it quiet for a while."

"I can't believe it," exclaimed Clarence.

"Believe it, and don't forget we still have to account to Tully for his kid."

Clarence sounded exasperated.

"Damn it, Jake. I'm being hammered; I don't know what to do."

"It's not you alone, Clarence," said Jack. "We're all being hammered. I think the rumors we're getting are right; some sort of killer epidemic is closing in on us."

"I don't want to believe it," said Clarence. "It's got to be coincidence."

"Maybe, but boats and bodies don't disappear or get torched for nothing. I saw Hugo at the Zebra and couldn't get anything out of him. But I figured it out when I spoke to Otis and Melvin. Otis told Kyle because his skiff was out there, and Kyle told Hugo who had his guys go out and burn the evidence."

"What the hell for?"

"Well, the Angelina is not far off and its four lifeboats have been fully accounted for. I'll bet that Hugo got to the ship found the ship before Lance's cutter found it. Heroin was on board and Hugo is selling it. I know he's peddling the stuff because he told me and because it's all over the islands. Even the Lamar woman is on it."

"You have a point," agreed Clarence. "Should he be picked up for questioning?"

Jack shook his head.

"He'd only clam up and we don't need that. Besides, Lance's people will keep Hugo away from the boat. Our goal is to find out what's killing people. It may end up being that it's the stuff from the Angelina."

Clarence laughed, saying, "That's a long shot, isn't it? What about the Angelina lifeboats in Florida? How are they connected?"

"The ones with skeletal remains drifted over that five year period; the ones with the fresh bodies were more recently eased into the water from the Angelina when it was found. That damn ship is leaving a bloody wake, Clarence."

Clarence shook his head, exclaiming, "What a mess."

"You bet, and it's going to get worse if we don't get a handle on it. We need to find out how Tully's kid got mixed up with the Jamaicans. He's usually in school during the week and at Vernon's pharmacy on weekends."

Clarence was totally unnerved by now.

"Gordon and his wife will be home soon. What should I do?"

They were interrupted by the roar of engines coming from the cut. It was the Cross Island Air seaplane which had just departed and was now circling overhead.

"I'm heading to Hole-in-the-Wall," Jack replied after the noise abated. "You need to contact Gordon and cushion the blow before he gets home. As it is, his wife is a basket case. She'll be totally unwrapped when she finds out and I don't know how Jonathan will take it. She's his sister and Tully's kid is his nephew."

Jack bid Clarence goodbye and jumped aboard the ferry with Chico as it left the dock. They were alone except for one other passenger who was arguing with the jitney skipper. The shrill high pitched voice was unmistakable. It belonged to a small fat man with beady eyes who tried hard to avoid Jack.

"Vernon Peters, what a surprise. You don't usually hang around Agnes Town."

Vernon gave Jack a limp handshake, saying, "It was business."

"Was it anything good?" Jack asked.

"If you must know, Jake, I'm opening a pharmacy in town. I hear that Thelma's place may be for sale."

So much for secrets; Jack couldn't decide if Vernon was a rat or weasel and he only half-listened when the pharmacist told him he had something for Chico.

"Is it cocaine or heroin?" Jack asked without much thought.

"Heroin; I may get cocaine later."

"I'll tell Chico, Vernon. How are things in Junction Village? You must be busy."

"I am. And now I'll have two stores to run; Vernon Drugs in Junction Village and Vernon Drugs in Agnes Town. I may also be opening outlets elsewhere."

"That takes money, Vernon. Are you robbing a bank?"

Vernon smiled.

"Better. Fred Hawk is on his way from Florida with Dan Schulman to meet with me and Jonathan. They want to make an investment.""

"Oh yeah, when are they due?"

Vernon was evasive.

"It might be a week more or less. Why are you asking?"

"I'm curious, Vernon. "I thought Doreen might be with them."

A snicker escaped Vernon's lips.

"I wouldn't worry about Doreen. She's in good hands. If you took care of her as well as you take care of your business, you'd still be married.

Anyway, to get back to Fred and Dan, they want to make some heavy investments in businesses that will be owned by us old line Bahamian families. We must stick together, you know."

Jack didn't know whether to laugh or cry. He knew that Vernon was a Florida native who owned a drug store chain until he was accused of Medicare fraud and had to leave the state. He surfaced a year later in the Mediterranean before ending up in the Bahamas. That was when Jack was having his legal problems.

"Are you thinking of selling your business now that Tom is dead?" Vernon was asking.

"I might," said Jack. "Or I might take on new partners."

"Well, if you do decide, I'm interested. Dan and Jonathan want to back me."

Jack smiled and flicked an imaginary speck off the collar of Vernon's shirt.

"It's good to know, Vernon. You stay out of trouble, you hear."

The ferry dropped them off and they went their separate ways.

Jack and Chico spent the afternoon getting Archangel ready for its trip and by the time the sun went down and the air cooled they were physically spent. After a light dinner they were ready to turn in.

Reginald Mayhew learned from Clarence that Archangel was sailing at dawn for Hole-in-the-Wall and asked Jack Friday night if he could tag along. His explained that he wanted to try out an SSB radio Louie had loaned him. Jack acquiesced so long as he agreed to stay out of the way if things got out of hand.

That evening, Jack pulled out an old dog eared mariner's handbook and to while the time away they went over the color coded signal flags and buoy types, many of which were never in use in unmarked Bahamian waters and no longer in use either in U.S. coastal areas.

"Colors fascinate me," said Reggie after perusing the signal flag pictures. "Take Black for example. It absorbs all light and colors. Does it also absorb all facts and knowledge about the Universe?"

"It means being solvent and not broke," said Jack. "And it's the color Avalon flies when it takes bodies out to sea, so it can mean Death or the absence of Life."

"I prefer White," Reggie stated. "It reflects light. It's also a blank slate; it denies facts and holds no history, memory or knowledge."

"You must be a philosopher," Chico noted.

Reggie burst out laughing, saying, "You like this stuff, huh?"

"What about the white heat of summer?" Jack asked.

"White heat can be deadly and lead to the total blackness of eternal night."

"What about the color Red?".

"It is the color of debt," replied Reggie. "A Red sun at dawn, as in a crimson dawn, could mean a white hot day. Blood is red and Red can be the color of lust and love. It can also stand for anger. In some cultures, it is also the color of Death. I hear that Tom Kennedy's body was splotchy and bluish black when he died, and that he had blistered boils that burst and covered him with blood."

It was enough. They decided to call it day and went to sleep.

Archangel left at dawn, Saturday, May 20, at slack tide. Jack threaded the big catamaran through the cut between the two islands and sailed southwest in open water to the Abaco cays. They bore south along the barrier islands until the made a landfall at Hole-in-the-Wall at the bottom of Abaco at dusk, tying up at the end of the town's long customs dock. By then the night had fallen and there was little to do but to tinker around Archangel.

Jack called Manny Silvester on the VHF but the BDF office was closed and there was no answer. Manny called later to concede that the old salvage terms would be honored. It was good to be connected, thought Jack.

In the meantime, Reggie began tinkering with the ham radio while Chico busied himself with preparing a dinner of spiced up leftovers. Later, Jack and Chico went about the grim business of arranging boarding tackle and cleaning their weapons.

"Take this, boss," said Chico asked, handing him his service revolver.

Jack examined the weapon.

"I don't like guns," he declared. "Besides, this belongs to Bob Byrne."

"Si, but it is just in case."

In the meantime, Lance Cooper called on the VHF, informing Jack that he was back and gave him the coordinates of a small vessel that was reported abandoned at Satan's Rock in the vicinity of the Berry Islands in Providence Channel. He was quick to add that he was respecting the same salvage contract terms as in the past, ten percent of the salvage value for Jack plus whatever inventory the government rejected.

The next morning, Sunday, May 21, Archangel edged away from the dock under a hot morning sun and ghosted up along a white sandy beach on the way to open water. Jack was busy with the main sheet halyard at the base of the mast on the cabin top behind the wheelhouse and Chico was at the helm. Reggie had finished raising the mainsail and took the first watch on the bow of the starboard pontoon.

He had hardly settled into his shift when he spotted a toddler playing alone with a red pail and shovel on the beach. He pointed to the beach and yelled to Chico in the wheelhouse. Chico looked and saw the same infant shaking a tiny shovel at the red pail. He called out to Jack and drew his attention.

Jack nodded and darted into the wheelhouse where he radioed Lance to report the sighting.

"Coop is sending a detail," said Jack, grabbing a pair of binoculars from the top of the consol to pan the beach.

Chico motioned with his head.

"Look over there, boss."

"I'm looking for her folks," Jack explained. "Coop says they must be there."

"Si," replied the deck hand. "But I see no people."

They were about to sail in for a closer look when two uniformed men appeared on the beach. They waved, scooped up the toddler and carried it away.

"The baby's parents must have fallen asleep," Jack thought aloud.

"No se," replied Chico, shrugging. "I no sleep when my baby play."

The catamaran pulled away and made for the open sea. The mainsail was already up and within minutes the cat's big white and red cruising spinnaker was raised to catch the wind. A short time later, a signal came over the VHF radio.

"This is BDF Station Ten hailing Archangel. Come in Archangel, over."

Jack recognized the voice. He grabbed the receiver and answered.

"This is Archangel."

"Is that you, Jake?"

"You got him. Where are you, Clarence?"

"Agnes Town. How long will it take you to get back to Hole-in-the-Wall?"

"Overnight. With luck, we'll be back tomorrow afternoon. Why?"

"We're going to need you and your boat. So don't get lost."

"I won't," Jack laughed. "By the way, did you speak to Lance?"

"We just got off the phone. He told me about the baby on the beach. He says the baby wandered off from her parents. It's a girl, about two years old. Her name is Alexandra, at least according to plane tickets and passports left lying around."

"What about her folks?"

"They were found dead in a rental cottage near the beach. Their names are Amy and Robert Cole from New York. They were on vacation and flew in from Nassau last week. Lance thinks they died during the night. It's too bad. They were young."

"Any idea as to how they died?"

"No, but Malcolm Harding is in Hole-in-the-Wall with Dennis Sinclair, Henry's covering doctor. Malcolm will probably do an autopsy."

"It looks like Henry is taking a breather. That's seems odd right now," said Jack.

Archangel sailed past a small church and an old sign that Hiram Cooper had put up long ago and which mariners used it as a marker to keep them away from the shallows. The rule was that it was safe sailing when the words, "The Wage of Sin is Death," could no longer be read.

Reggie Mayhew also saw the sign, as he had many times before, but this time it reminded him of something he had wanted to tell Jack.

"I did some star gazing last night, Jake. Did you know that the sun is moving north of the Tropic of Cancer?"

"I didn't know that," replied Jack. "Does it mean anything?"

"It will be over the Borders by the third week of June. They say it happens every thousand years and that a pale horse is unleashed to ride the heavens until the sun moves back to its cycle between Cancer and Capricorn and the balance between Yin and Yang is restored."

"Does the pale horse have a rider?"

"No. It has no rider. Death has no rider. The Pale Horse rides alone."

PART TWO

Behold A Pale Horse Riding

12

Satan's Rock

There was a story that when Satan left Heaven he planted a big black rock in the middle of the ocean. It was guarded by an army of demons that beckoned the damned the rest of the way to the gates of Hell. In reality, Satan's Rock was a high ledge at the end of a limestone spine that was an extension of one of the local Berry islands and was surrounded by a circular line of reefs submerged at high tide. Satan's Rock could be seen from a distance on nice days, but no bell or buoy warned of its presence and it was invisible in haze and at night. Satan's Rock was a hazard to navigation and its reefs were accidents waiting to happen and explained why they were called Satan's Rock by a 17th century captain who discovered them the hard way.

Jack had been there many times. He would have normally run a compass course at night or on a haze filled day, but now under a perfectly blue sky the picture in his mind's eye of the infant with the red pail and shovel guided him like a beacon to his destination. The rhythmic creaks and groans of Archangel's hull and sailing gear as it raced over the flat motionless sea in the silent white hot heat of the day dulled the senses, and a melancholy torpor set in that became a feeling of fear and foreboding as Satan's Rock drew nearer.

And finally there it was, tall and black against the sky, the breaking sound of waves leaping over submerged reefs warning all to turn or die. It was easy to understand why Lance Cooper wanted Jack for this mission. Lance's cutters easily drew eight to ten feet while Archangel drew three feet with its retractable dagger boards up. The big cat's shorter draft made negotiating shallows simple and uneventful.

The stranded yacht was exactly where it was supposed to be, adrift about a quarter of a mile from Satan's Rock and still free of the reefs. But they found more than they bargained for. Two men were aboard and were very much alive. It seemed to Jack from their accent that they were Jamaican and not Bahamian and probably from a rival gang that had invaded Hugo's turf.

One bled from a shoulder wound and had bloodshot eyes. The other was feverish and moved sluggishly. They glared defiantly at the business end of the revolver in Jack's hand, lesions streaking their faces and open sores all over their arms. Jack made sure to keep them at a safe distance in the cockpit while Reggie kept the cat steady and braced against the yacht's hull to allow Chico to jump aboard the larger vessel. He kept his weapon trained on the Jamaicans while Chico went below to check the inside cabin.

"What do we have?" Jack asked Chico.

"Plenty, boss," came the reply first in exited rapid fire Spanish. "Pesos, hashish y ratones; cash, heroin and rats," he added in English.

"You say heroin? It's usually cocaine in these parts."

Chico stuck his head out of the cabin and smacked his lips.

"Si, we have heroin but no cocaine. But the rats no look so good; they dead."

Jack drew another gun, a pistol this time, from a holster tucked inside the back of his pants. Chico was a drama queen, but figuring out what to do with the Jamaicans was more important than worrying about dead rats.

He ordered Chico back from the cabin and handed him the pistol. The Jamaicans stood sullenly in the yacht's cockpit and he was sure they were up to something.

"Can you guys swim?"

Defiance melted into fear when the Jamaicans realized that they were going to be thrown overboard. Chico came to their defense.

"Blood will bring sharks, boss. Give them a chance."

Jack agreed and waved his gun at a dingy mounted on the yacht's davits.

"Thirty seconds," he said.

The Jamaicans wasted no time. They ran for the davits, jumped into the raft and began lowering themselves into the water. As they did so, they reached into its floor boards and spun around with pistols in their hands. But they were too slow.

Jack fired, followed by Chico, and the two West Indians collapsed. One was not quite dead and made an attempt to get off a shot, but Chico drew a knife from his waist band and threw it into his chest. The Jamaican dropped his gun and fell over his partner.

Jack turned to Chico.

"Thanks," he remarked drily.

"You shoot nice," said Chico. "I thought you no like guns."

"I don't," Jack admitted. "I only know how to use them."

Chico went over to the dead Jamaican with a self-satisfied grin on his face. He retrieved the knife and wiped off the blood on his slacks.

"What now, boss?"

"Sink the dingy with the bodies," Jack ordered.

Chico shot two holes into the raft and lowered it the rest of way into the water where it quickly sank.

"Neat. Now, take the cash and put it on Archangel. Then we'll tow the vessel to Hole-in-the-Wall."

"What about the heroin, boss?"

Jack shook his head.

"It stays on the boat with the rats. Lance can deal with the mess."

Jack thought of the cottage where the baby girl's parents died. It was a vacation hut, one of several in the woods away from the beach, and he had stayed in one of them with Ginny a year ago. It was white with green shutters on a flowering patch of land of red, pink and blue flowering shrubs enclosed by a white picket fence. It was worlds away from Satan's Rock, but it too had been visited by the pale horse.

Reggie had a book in hand and opened it at random about halfway. He wanted to read a passage that hit his eyes to memorialize the dead. Jack understood what he wanted to do and signaled his consent with a nod and gathered around him with Chico. Reggie cleared his throat and read from the lines touched by his finger.

"Life and death alike are mysteries. We journey through a country dimly seen by the uncertain light of thought and feeling, and death is an undiscovered territory, a land without report."

When he was finished, he looked down at the water where the dinghy had sunk.

"They were bad but must also have had some good," he said. Then he went on to read, "They have faded from our sight, but they live on in God's presence, where nothing good can perish. In the Eternal, all good and beauty shines forever."

"What kind of book is that?" Jack asked Reggie when he was done.

"I don't know," he replied. "Louie Gold gave it to me when he got sick."

The yacht was under tow Sunday night and they were back at Hole-in-the-Wall early Monday morning, May the twenty second. Within minutes, a call came in on Archangel's radio from Manuel asking Jack to bring the yacht to the customs dock.

Hole-in-the-Wall was a tiny seafaring town that hosted the local BDF command center. It was home to several aging cutters donated by the U.S. Coast Guard and to a half dozen smaller chase boats. Several large sailboats whose owners belonged to a yacht club at the far end of the harbor were anchored a short distance from the cutters. This flotilla of government and private boats and their live-aboard male and female crew kept the town's marine maintenance facilities and tank farm busy. On the outskirts of town were another two dozen small homes and trailers occupied by families that made their livings in town or from farming and fishing. The town was quiet by day and jumping at night. Lights filtered through the foliage and palm trees and bounced across the still bay waters. Behind their glare, shadows danced to the hot calypso beat of reggae music until dawn when Hole-in-the-Wall was fast asleep in the gray damp mist of the coming day. And when the sun came up, the town was all business again.

Manny was on his best behavior when he greeted Jack as he and Chico tied up at the customs dock. .

"Nice haul," said the adjutant, admiring the imposing yacht.

"One of the latest models afloat," said Jack. "It's has great electronics and the best communications package money can buy."

"Are you selling yachts? What's in it?"

"Heroin and dead rats; the crew is gone."

"Heroin; there's no heroin in the Bahamas."

"Well, there is now, Manny. Check it out."

Manny was big, black and broad shouldered with a bearing suggesting a military past, and his deep resonating voice seemed more American than West Indian. The close cropped salt and pepper hair peeking out of his officer's cap suggested that he might be fortyish. One thing he knew was that Bob Byrne mentioned Manny as one of his Sidewinders.

Manny said something to two officers standing with clipboards in their hands and they quickly climbed aboard the vessel and started taking inventory.

"Come by the office later," he said. "We have money for you."

He was about to walk away when Jack called out.

"Do you have anything on Alexandra's parents?"

Manuel stopped turned around.

"You mean the Cole couple? They died of natural causes."

"Why? How old were they, a hundred?"

The adjutant threw Jack a dirty look.

"Don't be a wise ass, Jake. I'm telling you what I'm being told to say."

Jack tried again, asking, "What about the girl?"

"She's with Lance's family until her next of kin can be contacted. Do you want to adopt her?"

Jack shook his head.

"I need a wife first. There's one more thing, Manny; that old sign by the church as we go out to sea; I've often wondered about it."

"What about it?"

"Shouldn't it read, 'the wages of sin is death' and not 'the wage of sin is death?' Besides, it needs a fresh coat of paint."

"Speak to Hiram," said Manny. "He put the sign up years ago. His point was that Sin can only have one wage, and that is Death without redemption."

"That's fierce, Manny," Jack noted.

The adjutant chuckled.

"You can always be saved, Jake. The Lord's door is open twenty four-seven."

Manny left. Jack and Chico unhooked the tow line and powered the cat back to the end of the customs dock. That night, Lancelot Cooper called to tell Jack that he would receive fifty thousand dollars spot cash for the yacht. The BDF chief was by nature tight and Jack could grudgingly accept that. What was unacceptable was the power failure that darkened Hole-in-the-Wall. It was the night the music stopped.

"No power, no light, no juice for music, no ice for rum, no party tonight."

So said Chico as Archangel's occupants sweltered in the airless cabin. It was hot inside but the biting bugs were worse outside. And so Jack woke up early Tuesday morning with a curse on his lips. It was the twenty third day of May with no relief in sight from the oppressive heat and humidity. It was wet dishrag time again.

He had time to contemplate Lance's reward. The money was short to his way of thinking. The consolation prize was better; Cooper had offered him ten thousand dollars flat for whatever else was on board. Nothing was mentioned about the cash that Archangel's crew had already removed from the yacht. All in all, it had been a good mission.

"Ten percent," Lancelot had said. "You get ten percent. That's what we pay for salvage around here. The yacht is worth five hundred thousand and you get fifty thousand. That was the deal you made five years ago, if you remember?"

Jack grumbled a bit but kept his peace. He and Lance had a side deal. He gave the BDF commander a ten percent kick-back on all salvage revenues in order to secure his support and it made no sense to argue.

To keep Reggie and Chico happy, Jack split his share with them after deducting what he would need to kick back to Clarence. Friends were more loyal when spoils were shared. There was more than enough money to go around and Jack should have been very happy. But this was not about the money. It was about the heat and power failure. Jack's bunk and the entire boat beaded up with perspiration due to the power failure and he knew they were in for a long hot day.

The sun rose and staying below decks was unbearable. Chico and Reggie fled for the shade of the sun cover over the after cockpit to capture what little breeze there was and tried to ignore Jack's ranting below. He was in a foul mood. He cursed his state of being about being holed up in a boat in the middle of nowhere a million miles from anywhere. There were other islands, to be sure, more than seven hundred in the archipelago. Every island was within a day's sail of the other. But each one would be the same, a barren hell of sand and scrub with boredom broken by storms and gales. Never in a lifetime would he have thought of ending up in this armpit of the world. He could have been an accountant or something else. Perhaps Hugo and Eldridge had it right. They were going to do something else with their lives somewhere else. Jack kept brooding and as he brooded the heat and humidity rose. A light breeze came up but it died, leaving everyone dripping wet and tired.

"I have an idea," said Jack suddenly from the companionway hatch.

"What is it?" Reggie asked

"How much fuel do we have on this tub?"

Chico did a fast mental calculation and replied, "Half full, boss."

"Why don't we top off the tanks and run the air conditioner from the generator?"

"The land power is out. That means the pumps are out," Reggie explained

"We have ten gallon belly drums," Chico said. "We can roll them over to the fuel pumps on the dock, fill them manually and roll them back."

The fuel tank pumps had to be hand primed. The process was smelly, sweaty and long, but by noon it was done and Archangel was fueled up. Chico switched on the generator and the air conditioning the vessel immediately began cooling down. It was one of life's little victories that lifted the human spirit. Jack showered and put on fresh clothes, and over coffee and a hearty lunch, he was in a much improved frame of mind and went over to help Reggie operate Louie's ham radio.

The radio emitted a loud buzzing noise. It was working. He jumped up from joy and did a quick short jig to celebrate his success.

"Okay," said Jack. "Call someone. Call Emile. Do you need his call numbers?"

"No. I have them."

Reggie called Emile who happened to be home. They took turns with the usual small talk until Jack asked if he and his family had a reaction to the shots Cyrus gave them.

"No shots," said Emile. His voice seemed hollow. "The doctor is dead."

"What happened?"

"People are dying where we live and there is rioting. It is so bad that the good doctor's home was broken into by thieves who stole his medicines. Some people say it was a mob. The doctor was killed."

Jack felt the blood drain down from his head.

"We hear the screams of the dying all night long. At dawn, trucks come to pick up the dead. Jake?"

Yes?"

"We may need your help, Jake. Will you help us?"

"Of course," Jack replied hoarsely.

And then the radio went dead. The Pale Horse was on the move.

13

The City of God

Jack was once at one of Hiram Cooper's meetings when the reverend discussed Saint Augustine's City of God to demonstrate who went to Heaven and who went to Hell. Hiram made nine points that Jack could never forget.

1- A city is a group of people joined together by their love of one object.

2- There are only two objects of human love: God and Self.

3- There are only two "cities:" a City of God that requires a communal interest to a higher calling in Life, and a City of Man which is dominated by self-interest.

4- In the City of Man, self-interest makes every sinner an enemy of every other. 5- In the City of God, the bonds of charity form a community of the faithful.

6- Sinners and the faithful form a crowd in the City of Man which is in reality a symbol for Hell on Earth where sinners and the faithful coexist.

7- On the Judgment Day, the City of Man is destroyed.

8- The faithful go to Heaven.

9- Sinners go to Hell where there is no forgiveness but only different forms of eternal punishment.

What city could Hiram have been thinking of? Was it Agnes Town? Or was the City of Man a metaphor for the world as it was and where it was headed?

Jack had no firm opinion, but he did recall Tom Kennedy's quip under his breath when Hiram had finished talking.

"The problem is that everyone wants to go to heaven but nobody wants to die."

Now Jack could never really follow the reverend's reasoning and was not sure if it made any sense. He grew even more skeptical when Hiram admonished him later for not regularly attending church services.

"We may believe in freedom of religion, but we do not believe in freedom from religion," Hiram had said.

Jack had stared at him incredulously, remarking, "You're kidding."

"No, Jake. Religion is no joke. Only a person with no soul has no religion, and a person without a soul cannot be saved. Now, you may be a Hindu or a Moslem or even a Jew, and that's okay. Jews believe in a God Almighty but with a different name. They're redeemable because they are smart and human enough to be taught to see the light and to accept God and Jesus Christ the Savior. There can be hope for their kind but only if they embrace the Savior with open arms. If not, they rot in Hell, forever."

Of course, Hiram was slightly tipsy during that conversation and Jack did not take him seriously. However, Jack needed to concede that Hiram stood for and by a belief system. Hiram had a moral compass and Jack wondered sometimes if his own was that well tuned, if indeed he had one.

The wake from a passing fishing boat and a buzz from the VHF radio in Jack's quarters woke him up at dawn. It was now Wednesday, May the twenty fourth.

He picked up the receiver, answering, "Sherwood Forest, Robin Hood speaking!"

"Hey, Jake, You up?"

Jack couldn't help grinning despite the bad news from Florida the day before.

"I am now, Clarence."

"Where the hell are you?"

"Hole-in-the-Wall; I'm docked at the customs dock." Where are you?"

"I'm here also, at the customs office."

"What are you doing here?" Jack asked.

"I like the weather down here. I hear you cashed in yesterday. Where exactly are you?"

"Look at the end of the dock."

There was a short pause.

"I think I see your boat's mast."

There was no avoiding him.

"Yes, and you can recognize me. I'm tall, dark and handsome."

"I know what you look like," said Clarence tartly. "Don't leave."

"I won't. I just woke up. What's going on?"

"I hitched a ride on one of Lance's cutters with Otis Foote to pick up a batch of death certificate forms from the printer here in town. Henry thinks we're going to need a whole bunch. Otis is going the rest of the way to Nassau."

"What about Louie Gold? He has a print shop."

A long moment of silence followed. Finally, Clarence said in a tone hardly above a whisper, "Louie died soon after you left, Jake."

This was not what Jack needed to hear so early in the morning. But Clarence was a bulldog that would keep charging no matter what. And maybe that was the type of jolt Jack needed.

"Listen to me, Jake, and listen good." Clarence pressed on. "I'm real sorry about Louie. We all are. He was one of us; you're one of us, and we have problems. Fred Hawk went on a sales trip to Nassau from Florida on End Run and got sick. So, I sent Otis down to bring him back here on his yacht. He's too sick to make it out on his own. And that's part of the reason I'm calling. We need you and your boat. We also need Reggie. We're short handed; Milton is in Agnes Town and has to go to Marsh Harbor, and Henry is in Hope Town and needs to get to Marsh Harbor to cover his patients. Can you help us out?"

"Shit, man, I'm in the marine repair and salvage business. I'm not a water taxi. What happened to Henry's transportation? I thought he had a skipper." Clarence's voice was insistent.

"The boat is fine, Jake, but the guy died while he was visiting his family. I think he caught the same bug that hit Tully's boy."

"Too many people are dying too soon," Jack observed.

"I know. But Bahamas Air isn't flying and the two water taxis are down with bad engines and Otis hasn't fixed them yet. So, I'm asking you to help out."

"Well, I have more bad news, Clarence," said Jack. "We just spoke to Emile in Florida. Cyrus was shot dead."

Clarence cursed.

"What the hell are we going to tell Lance?"

Jack related Emile's story and when he was done, he could hear Clarence taking a deep breath before saying, "Listen, I'll handle Lance, but I need you, your boat and crew. We have health issues to address here in town, but we'll get to you by tomorrow. So, stick around. I'd also stay on board if I were you. It's safer."

"We'll do that," said Jack. "But getting back to Cyrus; you better handle Hiram and Milton too."

It was a minor and convenient trade. Jack never liked being a bearer of bad news, especially when it came to dealing with Lancelot Cooper.

Clarence was piling up the excuses about why he needed Jack when Archangel's generator stopped and the air conditioning whirred to a halt. In seconds, the vessel began heating up again.

"Inter-island traffic is backed up, so we need anything that flies or floats. And since I have no ride, you're my ticket back to Agnes Town. We also need to take Dennis Sinclair and Malcolm Harding with us."

"What's Malcolm doing around here? He's usually in Nassau."

"See that big white yacht moored near the yacht club? It belongs to Hamilton Graves, our regional commissioner. Harding is with him."

"Tell Graves to turn the power back on."

"Enjoy our tropical air. It's good and healthy for you," Clarence replied. Then he added, "And stay out of town. We have an epidemic and it's a killer."

And so Jack had his new marching orders. He hung up and on his situation for a few moments. He was rich, but if he was rich, why was he unhappy?

He asked Chico and Reggie about the air conditioning and Chico explained that the generator needed oil and overheated. It was fixed a few minutes later; the cool air began circulating inside the boat and Jack was happy again. He took a shower, and to celebrate the new found wealth that was no his from Louie's untimely death he put on a multi-colored tropical shirt and a pair of sunglasses. It was the outfit he had on four years earlier when he showed up with Tom Kennedy at a Nassau boat auction held by the Bahamian government to unload abandoned and seized vessels. It was there that they met Chico who was trying to buy back his boat after it had been seized for non-payment of registration fees and dockage charges.

He had just finished a prison term for manslaughter and ran into Jack and Tom at a local eatery where he explained his tale of woe. Chico said that he was too broke to fix an old catamaran he had left at a local marina when he went to prison and needed help. Jack and Tom had money; they also needed cheap labor for their new business in the Borders; and Chico needed work. It was a convergence of mutual interests. They paid off the boat charges, refitted it, had it re-titled in the name of the business, paid to make it seaworthy and hired Chico as a deckhand, mechanic and cook.

"Do you trust me?" Chico had asked.

"We can always throw you overboard," said Jack.

"How did you guys end up here?"

"Here in Nassau?"

"No. I mean, what happened in Florida?"

"I was a ship captain," said Jack. "And Tom and I also ran a boatyard. But I had a problem. I drank a lot and killed someone."

Chico's eyes lit up in admiration.

"Man! Did you start it?"

"That's what the court said."

"Man! So, what happened?"

"I got a suspended sentence, five years' probation and my best buddy stole my wife."

Chico had nodded sympathetically, remarking, "No justice in the world."

Fred Hawk and Doreen Hall's affair surfaced after Jack's trial when he went to a diner with Fred, Doreen and Dan Schulman. He had to be with them because the court, in giving him probation with permission to keep working so he could afford to make alimony payments, placed him temporarily in Dan's custody. He knew at that moment that the fix was in and he was powerless to prevent the hit.

If there was ever an odd couple it was Fred Hawk and Dan Schulman. Fred was all smiles, ruddy faced and sturdily built. He favored marine blue blazers and his close cropped curly brown hair was always carefully groomed. Dan Schulman was big and fat with bulging jowls and sad hound dog eyes. He was also very rich. Well into his fifties and recently divorced from Cynthia Hall, he was comfortably single. As a consolation prize, he had a mega-yacht built that he called "Kitten."

Jack's eyes were fixed on Doreen who sat next to Fred. Her betrayal was a blow to the ego; he loved the woman and she was bearing his progeny. But being done in by Fred was an ego and body blow, barely softened by the fact that Fred never got Doreen pregnant.

Doreen looked good. She wore a tight red cocktail dress and her hair was done up in a bun over her head. She certainly did not look pregnant. She avoided making eye contact, but gave Jack nervously coy sideways smiles, almost as if she had a few regrets and to suggest that he could always check her out from time to time.

Fred Hawk cleared his throat and spoke directly to Jack.

"We're staking you to an abandoned marine engine repair shop on land owned by Louie Gold in the Bahamas," Fred said.

Jack was shocked and could only ask, "How is Louie in the picture?"

"I was going to expand my business and Fred was going to work it, but it never happened," answered Dan. "Louie owns the land and holds the paper on the place as he does in Boynton Beach. If you ever hit the big one, you can try buying him out. And good luck. Louie never lets go for anything unless he gets his price."

"How come Fred didn't get to work the business?" Jack asked.

"Louie was my backer," replied Dan, speaking slowly in a thick heavy voice. "I needed him back then and he never liked Fred. He didn't want him involved in any of his properties, including the one he leased to you and Bob Byrne. I once leased the Agnes Town boatyard from Louie and he is now agreeable to re-leasing it to you. It has brand new equipment ready to go." Dan took a deep breath. "He likes you, Jake, and that's good for you. You're in and I'm out. And that's good for me and Fred."

"That's right, Dan made me a better offer," bragged Fred. "He gave me a raise and the Bahamas as a sales territory."

Jack ignored Fred, addressing Dan directly, "What's your pitch, Dan?"

"I'm signing the repair shop over to you. The lease is good for five years. The rest is up to you and Louie. With the fine references provided by Bob Byrne and Larry Fisher, the court is giving you traveling rights between the Bahamas and Florida. That will make it possible for you to run the two locations. Just make sure to check in periodically with Bob and Larry for the court stuff. You'll also need to do some deals with them."

"I can't do that directly, Dan; they're government people."

"I know that. I want you to go through Ned Baron."

"That's mighty generous of you, Dan."

Fred threw Jack a disarming smile.

"This is a great thing for you, Jake. I've always made a good living as a sales rep. That's what I do best, and you should do what you do best, Jake."

"You need focus in your life," continued Dan. "And fixing boats is what you're good at. White collar and executive stuff isn't for people like you. One boat yard is good, but two are better, and if you play your cards right, you'll make a fortune in both places, and you don't need much of a brain. Just stay out of trouble."

And of course Fred would have Doreen all to himself, Jack thought.

"Fred is right," Dan went on. "This Borders thing can be a gold mine. And it can be good for us. You'll meet new friends and make new contacts. Some of them can become Fred's customers. Besides, you're washed up as a big ship skipper here."

"They're right," chimed in Doreen. "You can make a fresh start, Shelly. It will be good for all of us."

Jack could only watch helplessly as Fred put his arms around Doreen who was not shy about snuggling up to him while Dan Schulman's ponderously sonorous voice echoed through Jack's ears.

"You'll end up thanking me, Jake. Believe me. You can't go wrong. If you stay off the juice and work hard, you'll make money. Five years will go fast, and when it's over, you'll have your captain's license back and then you'll be able to write your own ticket."

Fred slapped him on the back on the way out.

It was more like a slap in the face. His entire body smarted.

Six months later, Doreen had twins, a boy and girl, Jack's kids. Jack sighed. Dan was right in a way. He was successful at last. While they were waiting for Clarence to show, Reggie was on his ham radio, trying to reach anyone, anywhere in the world.

"I have Woody in South Africa," he yelled.

"Who's Woody?"

"He's my friend in Johannesburg."

A thin voice with a clear Afrikaans accent came through the static, but the tone of the exchange suggested that something was wrong.

Reggie signed off and stared at the open companionway.

"A jet blew up," said Reggie. "Woody's brother was on the flight."

"Maybe he survived," Jack suggested hopefully.

Reggie shrugged his shoulders.

"Hardly; Woody says everyone was dead before the jet came down."

Wednesday, the twenty-fourth of May was drawing to a close.

14

The Salvage

The crowning glory for Jack had nothing to do with money. It came when he and Tom were able to afford equipping Archangel with a pair of high powered diesel engines, a central air conditioning unit that could run off either land or battery power and a brand new suit of sails. The transformation made it a fast bird of prey that was favored by Bahamian marine authorities in their drug boat pursuits thinly disguised as salvages. With ten percent of a salvage's assessed value going into his pockets virtually tax free, he had plenty of money to pass around and still have more than enough for himself. The real bounty was in the interception of drug traffickers en route to Florida. A quid-pro-quo existed here. Some drug boats were taken by force; some were found adrift, apparently left by traffickers as a sacrifice or donation of sorts to Jack and other pursuers. Even Hugo Johnson joined in the game with the understanding that Jack would be selective and not undermine his entire operation.

On Thursday, May the twenty fifth, the air was still and the sea was dead, and the horizon was lost behind a blinding glare. Time and motion stood still, and beads of perspiration crept down itchy cheeks and chins. Jack was studying marine charts spread over the table in the main cabin and listening to news from around the world slowly squeaking and squawking its way through Archangel's short wave radio. Reggie chatted with ham operators in Europe and Asia on Louie's radio and Chico scowled. It was same bad news all over.

People were falling ill and dying, some within hours and some within days and it was getting worse. A pundit demanded that Mexico, China and India be nuked and a talk show host argued in prerecorded messages that immigration was the cause of the outbreak. His audience was invited to his blog, but the problem was that he had already died.

Bermuda announced that its population was being successfully inoculated with a vaccine but gave no details. Reggie kept trying to receive news from Nassau but all he could hear were hymns, sermons and commercials for Bahamas Air which was no longer running. "If you have time to spare, fly Bahamas Air," went the jingle.

Jack decided it was time for action. He jumped to his feet, ordered Reggie to turn off the radios and Chico to check the engines. Reggie did as requested because the news was too distressing to bear. Chico also wanted to ignore the news. There was a tidbit about the epidemic in Santo Domingo, but his family lived in the hills and he hoped they were safe. Besides, he truly believed that Jack always made the right decisions.

Good old Chico Gomez. The only thing more loyal than Chico was a pet dog. He promptly disappeared below to make sure Archangel would be ready on command. The catamaran was a big powerful vessel, fast under sail or power and Chico was a skilled engine man. The cat list slightly and then straightened out. It was Chico scurrying about on the port hull. Jack ran out and to have a look where Chico was leaning over the life lines with a boat hook.

"Something is in the water, boss."

He stuck his head over the side and laughed, saying, "It looks like a dead cat."

Moving with the current was a soaked blob of fur. Chico was disappointed.

"Leave it alone," Jack said. "Let's go below and finish up."

A stir in the water created ripples followed by a small splash. In less than the blink of an eye the furry carcass was gone.

"Cat die and fish eat," Chico noted with a grin.

Minutes later Clarence appeared with his charges and asked about Satan's Rock. It was a cue, and Jack had the usual sling bag filled with cash. He casually handed it to Clarence who slung it over his shoulder without a word.

Jack smiled at the clean cut young man with the light curly hair in the tan suit and figured he was the new covering doctor. The other passenger was no stranger; it was Malcolm Harding, the medical examiner. It was important to be on friendly terms with Malcolm, just as Jack courted Lance's favor. Malcolm doubled as the Bahamian Air and Sea Rescue Association commander, and he fed Jack and Lance the location of abandoned vessels in return for the usual kickbacks. It was all part of that quid pro quo that stretched the outer limits of legality and morality and kept the islands humming. The BDF and BASRA provided a good part of Jack's bread and butter.

The doctor was a landlubber and Clarence had to help him aboard, but Malcolm Harding had no trouble jumping on board. The commander was a bit shorter than Jack and more heavily built. He wore no hat over his white, short sleeve uniform and his thin graying blond hair was slicked down with pomade. Only a small brass name tag pinned to his left shirt pocket revealed his name and rank.

"Jack Shelby Sloane at your service," Jack said with a mock hand flourish.

Clarence was humorless.

"This isn't funny, Jake. It's too early and too hot. This is Doctor Sinclair, Dennis Sinclair. And Dennis, this is Jake, Reggie and Chico."

Handshakes were exchanged and Chico showed them into the starboard cabin where they lay down their duffels.

"Are we ready?" Clarence asked.

"Loaded for bear," Jack noted.

"We have a small job to do on the way," Malcolm informed him.

"What's that?"

"Coop says an abandoned speedboat was reported near Satan's Rock."

Reggie made a face, saying, "We were there to pick up that yacht; we didn't see anything else."

Malcolm waved away the comment with his hand.

"It may have drifted. Anyway, it's there. Old man Graves says it may be carrying drugs. It needs to be salvaged. It shouldn't take us long."

Jack understood what they were up to. A more than decent salvage was waiting out there. Graves knew about it; word had leaked out, and Clarence and Malcolm wanted a piece of Jack's action.

"Are you guys up to this? There might be action out there, said Jack."

Clarence bristled.

"Are you calling us cowards? Besides, Graves says the boat is abandoned."

"That's what he said," confirmed Malcolm. "Let's share and share alike, Jake."

Jack smirked. The mutual understanding was that whoever crewed with Jack on a salvage shared in the spoils.

"A go-fast drug boat, abandoned? Bullshit," he muttered under his breath.

Without further ado, he took the helm inside the wheelhouse and with the dock lines off, they set sail with the sun over their heads and the trade winds pushing them west at twenty knots with the added thrust of the husky diesels. He had all but forgotten about the South African air disaster until Reggie came up to replace him at the helm.

Jack was about to say something when Reggie spotted the boat, a candy apple red racer bobbing in the water in the distance. The sails were furled, the engines turned on and with Jack at the helm, Chico and Reggie set the boarding tackle on the after-deck. The others huddled in the cabin below as the cat pulled up alongside the sleek long nosed racer.

"This can be good for us," Clarence shouted. "So, don't get us killed."

Jack ignored him, preferring to speak with the young physician who came up on deck, scared and out of sorts.

"How long have you been practicing?" The doctor held up five fingers.

"Five years. That's good. Married?"

Dennis shook his head.

"What about you?"

"I'm in between wives."

Clarence and Malcolm came up behind him, and Clarence coughed, changing the subject. "Dennis may stay on to help Henry if he likes it here..."

Malcolm interrupted him.

"Save the thought, Clarence." He pointed into the distance; two yachts were racing towards them on a collision course.

Jack looked at Malcolm who studied the yachts carefully through his binoculars.

"Did you know about this, Malcolm?" Jack asked.

The BASRA officer shook his head.

"Perhaps we should leave," Clarence suggested meekly.

"Do you have a contingency plan?" Malcolm asked.

"Yeah; you guys go below."

Clarence, the doctor and Malcolm retreated to the cabin, being passed by Reggie and Chico who were running in the opposite direction. Reggie had two rockets in his hands and Chico balanced a rocket launcher on his shoulder. He had a big grin on his face and patted the weapon lovingly with his free hand.

"It is rock and roll time, amigos."

Jack drew a cigarette, lit it, inhaled deeply, and watched Chico take a position in the after cockpit with the launcher.

"Are you sure we should stick around for this?" Clarence yelled from below.

"You need to fight for food, guys," said Jack. "If you want a share of the bounty, you need to be up here."

"Keep the bounty," the medical examiner howled from the companionway. "Just don't get us killed."

The two yachts were now close enough for Chico to fire a warning shot.

There was a "whoosh" and the rocket passed across the bow of one of the vessels and exploded harmlessly in the sea next to the other.

It was enough. The yachts turned tail and everyone applauded except the young doctor. Dennis went to the rail and threw up.

Jack brought the cat closer to the speedboat and Chico threw a tow line over its stern cockpit. He jumped over the side, landed on top of the racer and tethered it to the cat. The boat was smaller than Archangel but it was still a good fifty feet long. It had a shiny deep-V hull and was built for speed.

Malcolm climbed on after Chico and followed him down into the forward cabin. In less than a minute, Chico came out.

"You have to see this, boss. Maybe the doc should have a look also."

Jack and Dennis climbed aboard and went below where Malcolm cowered in a corner of the darkened cabin.

Sprawled over turned crates and boxes filled with all sorts of guns, ammunition, explosives and drugs were two men whose half naked bodies were covered with gaping reddish sores and boils.

"Out of curiosity, Malcolm, how did Alexandra's parents die?" Jack asked. "You must have examined the bodies when you arrived."

"Similar symptoms," the medical examiner mumbled.

Chico was about to go rummaging through the boxes and crates when Jack held him back, yelling, "Don't touch!"

Chico stopped in his tracks while Dennis took a closer look at the bodies.

"They weren't shot; that's for sure," he said. "I read about this in medical school. It was called the Red Death in the Dark Ages. It's a deadly form of bubonic plague that killed almost everyone it struck, but we'll know more after an autopsy."

Jack had a sudden change of mind.

"Chico," he said. "Take your knife and open one of the boxes. Tell us what you find. Don't touch anything and leave the knife in the box."

Chico dutifully cut a box open and peered inside, saying, "It is heroin, boss."

"No cocaine?"

They left the bodies on the racer and began towing it back to Hole-in-the-Wall. Then, by chance, Clarence borrowed Jack's glasses and panned the horizon.

"What's that I see over there?"

"Satan's Rock," Malcolm answered.

"No," said Clarence. "I'm looking at a ship."

"Oh, that's an old freighter called the Comfort. It ran aground years ago."

"That's a strange name for a freighter," Jack commented.

Malcolm anticipated the next question.

"It's empty," he said. "It's been stripped bare."

Meanwhile, Clarence and Malcolm were busy figuring out how much they made on this short outing. Back at Hole-in-the-Wall, Lance was having problems of his own. He found out that the power failure was due to the fact that the two men who were supposed to operate the power plant never showed up for their shift. A visit to their homes found them dead.

Lance was in the office when Jack walked in with his crew and passengers. He was standing at a plain metal table and behind him on the wall was a framed print of Jesus Christ. The commander was explaining the time he had getting back from the States and almost broke down when Clarence told him that Cyrus had been killed. He somehow managed to swallow his grief and to carry on with a straight face.

"We chartered a chopper out of Miami," he was telling his staff.

"No commercial flights?"

Lance shook his head, saying, "Nothing is flying except birds. I don't even know how I'm going to get my brother's body home."

He stopped to draw his breath.

"It's too bad," said Reggie. "He was a good man."

"Yes," Jack added. "We'd like to extend our condolences, if that means anything at this point."

Lance's eyes grew moist. "Thank you, gentlemen," he said. "We must also send condolences to Gordon Tully and his family for the untimely loss of his son."

"You heard?"

Lance nodded.

"Clarence told me and I got word out to Tully. He and his wife now have time to prepare for the mass funeral my dad is planning. We have many souls to send on their way and it has to be done fast."

"We should rev up our medical facilities," Jack suggested.

"You're right, Jake" Lance agreed. "That's why Malcolm and Dennis are here. They'll help Henry. I'm sure he's going to have quite a caseload."

The BDF commander was tall, thin and very official in his starched dress whites. Colorless, frizzled hair, thin nose, pursed mouth and beady eyes added a mood of imperiousness to his stern countenance and puritan demeanor. He communicated a stern impression that his orders were not to be ignored.

"Now my friend, it is payday," said Lance. "There was heroin, arms, ammunition and explosives on that boat. We believe the wholesale value to be a million dollars. Your share is ten percent. How do we divvy it up?"

"What about the boat?" Jack asked. "It should bring over five hundred thousand dollars at auction."

"It's off limits," Lance replied dryly. "The commissioner wants it for his son as a twenty-first birthday present. You get twenty five thousand as a consolation prize."

Dennis Sinclair threw up his hands in protest.

"Count me out," he said. "I want no part of this blood money. It's tainted."

Malcolm turned to Dennis, complimenting him, "You're a good man, doctor."

"Let's split the take three ways," recommended Jack. "A third for Archangel and Clarence and Malcolm can split the balance. Is that fair?"

"Done," declared Lance.

He turned to Manny who proceeded to remove stacks of hundred dollar bills in U.S. currency from a large bag. He was placing them on the table in three stacks when a tremor shook the room, paling the hungry faces of the men gathered around him. It lasted less than a second but it was sufficiently strong to knock the picture of Jesus Christ off center. Lance turned and righted the picture, his lips curling into a thin smile.

"This may be a message, Jake" he said. "This business has made you rich, and I trust you will step up to bat when needed."

Jack's only response was, "I'll be here."

He waited until all the money was in his hands before asking, "Hiram asked me to pick something up for him. Do you have it?"

Lance took a large, bulky box from a shelf behind him and gave it to him.

"This is important, Jake," he said gravely. "I'm stuck here for a few days. You'll be in Agnes Town before me. Please make sure he personally gets it."

"What's in the box? Jack asked. "
Lance hesitated a moment.
"The packing slip says the box contains prayer books."
Jack grunted and gave it to Reggie to carry back to the boat. The box was bulky but Reggie noted that it seemed too light to be filled with books.
"Great haul," Malcolm commented later on the catamaran. "You are a gentleman and a good friend."
""I'll second that," said Clarence. "Jake will always come through for us."
Malcolm laughed.
"Not bad for a day's work."
"Damn! I just remembered. What about the two bodies on the boat?"
"Why? Do you want to claim them?"
"Not exactly," Jack replied.
"I took a closer look at them," said Malcolm. But we don't have facilities to do a proper autopsy here. The bodies will have to go to Nassau."

"That's the other thing, Malcolm," Jack went on. "The bodies in North Border were in about the same shape as these dudes. Do you think there's a connection?"
"Clarence told me. We're lost without an autopsy."
"And then there's the girl, Alexandra, You must have seen their parents. How did they die?"
"We have no idea. We'll have specimens sent to the CDC for analysis."
Their eyes met in silence.
By early evening, Archangel quietly slipped away from the dock and made open water. With sails unfurled, it glided gracefully like a giant bird over the darkening sea on a broad reach north for the Borders. When night fell, Jack turned on the auto pilot and joined his passengers in the coziness of the cabin where Chico prepared dinner and uncorked several bottles of wine.
"There is nothing better than a boring night at sea," exclaimed Clarence.
"I'll drink to that," agreed Malcolm. "We love, dull, uneventful voyages."

"Amen," said Dennis, raising his glass.

Later, over cigars and cognac that he doled out to everyone, Clarence asked Jack about Ginny.

"I'll probably propose marriage," answered Jack. Turning to Malcolm, he asked, "What about you, doctor, you're still married, aren't you?"

Malcolm nodded.

"Three kids in school and a wife who shops. There isn't a boutique in Nassau or Paradise Island she hasn't blessed, not to mention her trips to Miami."

He looked intently at Jack.

"Don't go for it unless you can stand long term aggravation."

Jack stared up at the cabin ceiling and sighed.

"Aggravation beats boredom. But kids scare me. What the hell am I going to do with more kids at my age and in my line of work?"

Clarence rolled his eyes.

"You raise them, Jake," he said. "That's what my wife and I do."

"You have a point. What about you Dennis. You're single."

Dennis smiled and nodded.

"It's easier this way," he said. I need to get my practice started first. That's why I'm here. But this isn't the only reason I'm here. I hear geysers shoot up now and again around Hermit Cay. My hunch is that they're from an underwater volcano."

"The geysers, we know," said Clarence. "They'd be a tourist attraction if only they shot up on schedule. I haven't heard anything about a volcano."

"When do you think it's going to blow?" Malcolm asked.

"Maybe now; maybe in a million years," Dennis answered.

"Great. You had us worried for a moment. But if it ever blows, Jake will get us out. He's good at these things."

"Well, I'm glad I'm here," Jack acknowledged.

"So am I," said Malcolm.

"You were a medical doctor in your old life, weren't you?" Jack asked Malcolm.

"That was in the States, a long time ago. I was a terminal care doctor at a hospice where I took care of the dying until one day I left and never looked back."

He swallowed hard in front of his unbelieving listeners.

"Do you understand the meaning of the word, compassion?" Malcolm asked.

"I think so."

"It's from the Latin, 'compassio.' It means to suffer with. One needs 'compassio' to comfort the dying." Malcolm blew circles with his cigar and said, "Somewhere along the way I lost my 'compassio' and I could no longer care for the dying. It got to me. That's why I quit, moved here, married, raised a family and made a new life to which I devoted much energy but little compassion."

Archangel raced on into the black night where sea and sky were one.

15

The Return

There was another story about Malcolm that floated silently over the Borders. It was that he often frequented Cheetah's where he would meet up with Vernon and Terrence, ostensibly to meet women that Ginny procured for them. However, they never did pick up anyone but they did leave together. But that was none of Jack's business and he ignored the story. Archangel was on autopilot, Chico was on watch and Jack slept soundly with thoughts of Ginny on his mind.

He liked Ginny Malone just fine. It wasn't that she was beautiful, but there was something sensual about her that attracted him. It was her father, Kyle, who turned him off and prevented him from popping the marriage question directly to Ginny.

Kyle was friendly with Vernon and Fred and Jack could never understand that at first. Vernon's Pharmacy in Junction Village was one of Fred's major customers. Despite the fact that it was the only one in the Borders, the business should have been too small to deserve special attention. Something else had to be going on to make Fred's monthly trips worthwhile and Kyle and Dale Malone were players.

It was a barter arrangement. Dale shipped rum to South Florida Pharmaceuticals who sold it private label in Florida in exchange for time-expired pharmaceuticals and over-the-counter pills sent to Pirates' Cove Marina for resale through Vernon. Hugo's boats hauled the freight both ways and Hugo coordinated the trade deals at Kyle's docks and Fred got his commission. Kyle got his cut and all monies made by Fred and Dan were deposited at Jonathan's Island Trust.

It was probably more to this arrangement but it was all that Ginny Malone would divulge to Jack in a moment of passion in the aftermath of one of their first sexual encounters which was in the bathroom of Bea's diner. He was sure that Bea Norris noticed, and as a result he rarely went to the eatery.

"Maybe, this can be the start of something good for us," she said later. "Don't you think I'm a better fuck than the other women you've had?"

Jack shook his head. Ginny was too direct and outspoken. This was not a way to start a romance. He was still shaking his head when he woke up, but Ginny was no longer on his mind. A new question gnawed at his innards; what kind of stuff was Vernon sending Doreen anyway? Why was she so sick?

Hiram would have answered the question by saying that it was the Lord's work. Hiram always believed that God was the beginning and end of all things and made sure that everyone understood his position. At one of his meetings, he brought up a basic question raised by a philosophy scholar and presumed acquaintance of his named Richard Allen. Hiram wanted to show that the origin of the Universe began with God and asked, as Jack now recalled, "What is the source of all things?" And he went on to offer an answer, saying, "If all things have a source, then the source of all things is one thing. And that one thing must be God because only God has the power and knowledge to create the Universe and all things within it."

It was not that Jack bought into Hiram's explanation, but it made him wonder if the current outbreak could not have had a single point of origin in time and place. But how does one go from a local health disaster to a deadly global epidemic in such a short time?

Jack's mind was still drifting when Chico shook him to say that Archangel was east of Sanctuary Bay and about to run aground. Jack could hear but not see the inbound waves breaking over the reefs; he rushed to the wheelhouse and threw the diesels into reverse. The engines roared. The cat slowed and everyone woke up. He grinned at Chico and guided the cat the rest of the way through the zigzag channel to Buccaneer Point and Agnes Town. The day promised to be sunny and cool and Jack began thinking that life in Borders might not be bad after all. He could marry Ginny, settle down, have more kids, raise a family, and like everyone else in the Borders, be content with the status quo.

The islands were in a time warp and change was hardly ever welcome. This was sensed by outside investors who occasionally tested the waters so to speak and left without leaving a penny. The few cruise ships that visited anchored off the beach in Canal Pond by the Ocean View on South

Border. The last time a cruise ship visited was in April and more visitations were not encouraged. People were happy with things as they were. The islands were entrenched in the past and were in no rush to embrace the future. Besides, why make problems when there were none to begin with?

Even Hiram Cooper agreed with that assessment, and he stuck fast to his vision of ultimately turning the two islands into a quiet, peaceful and devoutly Christian community. It began to appear that he was now more determined than ever to see that happen. He was gradually becoming increasingly consumed by an evangelical zeal in his view of the world.

A rising wave of religious and secular conservatism engulfed the islands. There were no water treatment systems, drinking water was untreated, and open sewers were the rule, creating a potential public health hazard. Equally serious was the fuel situation; ship and air traffic to the Borders carried just enough fuel for their return to Marsh Harbor where a larger tank farm was eventually built. Marsh Harbor grew while the Borders languished happily in a phony paradise. The real estate market too was immobile. Everyone thought their land was priceless and refused to sell.

The governing council did grant Jonathan Hall's request to allow one cruise ship from the Holiday Line, Princess of the Seas, to drop anchor in Canal Pond's deep water near his hotel as part of its cruise around the Bahamas. The Princess of the Seas was a thousand foot behemoth with twenty six hundred passengers and a crew of eight hundred. It paid for the right to drop anchor as part of its itinerary around the Bahamas from Florida. Ship tenders ferried passengers to the beaches around Canal Pond. That generated business for the Ocean View's restaurants, bars and souvenir shop and for the shops of Junction City and Agnes Town.

The Holiday Line deal worked well for the Borders' isolationist spirit. The ship arrived early and was gone by sundown, its passengers leaving their cash ashore. The smell of foreign involvement in local affairs was absent; the cash would stay without the smell. It also made Dan Schulman happy since he was one of its major stockholders. This self-delusional self sufficiency was the Borders' driving force and its prosperity hummed along on booze, drugs and illegal trade. And just about everyone had a boat, and that was good for Jack. Saint Augustine would have been hard pressed to find one person in the Borders worthy of Heaven.

Jack threaded Archangel through the channel until he saw the Church of Christ spire in the morning haze. He was also able to make out the outlines of two vessels at Pirates' Cove: End Run and Kitten. Fred Hawk and Dan Schulman were in. And as Agnes Town hove into view so did the seaplane landing tarmac. It was deserted except for a family of wandering pigs and goats.

Archangel made a left turn at the seaplane ramp and headed for its Pirates' Cove berth. Mel Stoop was on hand and helped cleat the dock lines. At the ferry landing, a few people were waiting for a water taxi. It was good to be back.

Clarence, Malcolm, Dennis and Reggie took their gear and jumped off the cat to catch the ferry, leaving Chico and Jack to clean up. When they were done, Jack left Archangel to go find Ginny. He found an old leaflet from the Princess of the Seas nailed to a tree. It was intended for the local residents informing them that the big cruise ship was due to drop anchor in Canal Pond in April. Jack happened to be in the Borders when it arrived and had gone to one of Hiram's meetings shortly after the Princess of the Seas weighed anchor. The subject was Judgment Day and Jack recalled that Hiram was uncharacteristically moody.

The reverend took several old leather bound books from the library shelves and laid them on the table, opening them to pages he must have consulted earlier. Why he picked the Judgment Day and the coming Rapture was anyone's guess. "The Judgment Day is coming," Hiram said calmly as he leaned back in his chair and puffed on a cigar with a snifter of cognac in his hand. "It will be the Rapture and the faithful will experience the ecstasy of meeting Christ the Lord. There will be joy and delight when the City of Man is devoured by the flames of Hell."

"Who will be saved?" Clarence asked.

"True believers," replied Hiram. "They are blessed. They will be saved in the end-days and will meet Jesus Christ on the way to life eternal in Heaven."

"What will the Judgment Day look like?"

"Ah. That is the beauty and wonder of it all," Hiram said, smacking his lips.

"The coming is a mystery. It will be an apocalyptic event. It can be over in a flash or it can take years. It can take different forms, like the four horsemen of the apocalypse, Death, Famine, Pestilence and War."

"I thought the four horsemen were Conquest, War, Famine and Death," said Jack.

Hiram took a sip of cognac and watched the smoke rise from his cigar.

"No matter; it is the pale horse we must watch for, the horse without rider that gallops over the plains and mountains and casts no shadow but leaves death in its wake."

He looked around the room.

"We will not see it, gentlemen. But we will feel and know its presence."

Jack thought Hiram might have had too much to drink that evening and was glad to leave. The reverend was a compelling speaker, but sometimes he was a heavy trip.

Jack was thinking about Hiram's words about a pale horse as he went off to see Ginny. A pale horse! That was what Reggie had mentioned after they had sailed past the infant with the red pail. Now, Jack was not the superstitious type, but he had a healthy fear of the unknown and death. His mood improved when he found her at a picnic table with her dad and two couples.

Kyle Malone, unshaven and grizzled, was so engrossed in conversation that he hardly noticed Jack who sidled up to Ginny and kissed her. Jack was overjoyed at seeing her and pleased to see that she had put on weight but not too much. She was just right. Not having to worry about his business which was now in his daughter's hands, Kyle reinvented himself as an exterminator and devoted himself to helping mariners and residents solve bug problems. He even took on a new moniker: Bug Man.

And that was what was troubling the two couples. Their boat had bugs. Kyle saw Jack and gave him a wave.

"Hey, Jake, have a beer," he said in a thick honey drawl. "These here folks have a problem; they sailed in from Haiti and have serious stowaways on their yacht."

"What kind of serious stowaways?" Jack asked.

One of the two women in the foursome replied, waving her hands and fingers frantically.

"It's the creepy, crawly kind. And they're black and huge!"

"We were anchored at Man-O-War Cay," continued one of the men who looked as if he might be the woman's boy friend or husband, "and I was climbing into the dink to motor around the harbor when one of those bugs crawled up from under the floor boards. It was big, black and ugly and had wings. It was one big mother...! I kept hitting it with an oar but it wouldn't die."

"Well, we finally killed the thing," said the second man. "But it was messy and ugly as sin. We had a can of insecticide stowed away in the bilge under the cabin floor boards and I sent my wife below to get it..."

The second woman shivered.

"I raised the hatch cover to get the can and the bilge was filled with those huge bugs crawling all over the place," she said. "I could swear they were even hissing at me."

"Some of those bugs may be from Africa," Jack suggested. "They're like tanks, multi-legged bastards and have things like snapping mandibles.

They can leave you with a nasty bite. Some can even kill with their bite and poison. And then there are the giant wasps; they are really dangerous. They make their nests in folded up sails and sail bags and get mighty pissed when disturbed."

Jack was waving his arms and becoming more animated as he spoke, and Ginny broke out in a broad smile. Jack was actually promoting her dad's business.

"The ones here are water bugs," she added, cringing. "They're big, black, ugly cockroaches. I hate them."

Jack turned to the two unhappy couples and said authoritatively, "What you guys need are several canisters of Bug Man's magic potion. What do you think, Ginny?"

Ginny nodded.

"We use that around here all the time. Bug Man here will sell it to you."

Kyle beamed.

"What's more," he volunteered, "If you buy a supply, I'll personally go on your boat and fumigate it myself."

The couple agreed and happily left with Kyle following them with his gear.

Ginny got up after her father was gone and gave Jack a big hug and kiss.

"How's my favorite ten percent man?"

It was a signal. He dug into his pocket, took out a wad of bills and placed it in her open hand.

"Twenty-five hundred for you," he replied. "That takes care of me for rest of the year."

She took the money and tucked it into a pocket of her dress.

"What happened on your trip?"

"Strange things, Ginny; a little girl was playing on the beach at Hole-in-the-Wall. It turns out that her mom and dad died in a rental cottage. The little girl's name is Alexandra and her folks were from the States."

"Who is she with now?"

"She's with Lance until the next of kin are contacted. The kid being orphaned is bad enough, but I need to know what the parents died of. They were too young to die of natural causes. I think Malcolm probably knows but he's not talking. And we've had other situations."

He went on to tell her about the yacht, the go-fast boat and about the abandoned ship they saw at Satan's Rock.

"The crew was dead?"

Jack nodded, saying, "The crew on the yacht put up a fight and so we had to kill them, but the two guys on the racer were already dead. Their bodies were covered with boils and they were covered with dry blood. I'm no doctor but it seemed like they hemorrhaged or bled to death."

He stared inquisitively at Ginny.

"Come to think of it, the bodies on the boat were in about the shape as the ones at Bitter End."

"I heard that one of them was Tully's son," said Ginny. "They were covered with blisters or boils or something like that, I heard."

"That's right. I saw them myself. But there's something odd about the boats we found. They carried heroin but no cocaine. And then there's the Nassau Clipper. It's way overdue."

"My uncle said it should be arriving soon. But what about the boat you towed in? Do you have salvage rights?"

Jack shook his head ruefully.

"Graves took it for his son and I'm not arguing. I need his protection or I'm out of business. The problem is that here I need everybody's protection."

Ginny commiserated with him.

"Don't we all?"

"I guess," nodded Jack. "But what happened in Jamaica? I missed you, damn it."

He leaned over and gave her another kiss on the lips which she did not resist.

"My club needs new girls," she said. "I found blacks and mulattoes but no white ones. And you know how guys are. White guys want black meat and the others like white meat. But the problem is that I landed in Kingston in the middle of a measles or small pox epidemic that was killing people in droves. All the girls I saw looked too sick to travel and so I came back empty. I have a fucking mess at Cheetah's and I'm done if I can't find fresh meat for the club. But I'm not the only one with trouble. People say it's all over the world. It doesn't look good, does it, Shelly?"

Jack put his head down in his hands.

"No, it doesn't. But let's talk about Cheetah's. What are you going to use as an opening night gimmick if you're short of girls?"

Ginny looked mischievously at Jack, replying, "It's going to be a costume party."

"You mean like a masquerade?"

"Exactly; everyone will wear a costume and mask; it's going to be great. How are you going to come?"

Jack pondered the questions for a few moments and replied, "I'll wear my blazer and come as yachtsman, now that I'm rich; how about you?"

Ginny giggled, saying, "I'll dress up as a baroness, if I can find the outfit."

She leaned forward an exposed a bit of breast.

"You're tired, Shelly. And so am I. Maybe we need some R and R."

Jack looked up.

"I sure could use a bit."

Ginny laughed.

"I'm always open to suggestions," she said.

Jack grinned.

"What about a night of heavy sex? I'll make dinner."

"You're a good salesman, Shelly. But come over after dinner. I need to get dad squared away first."

Jack looked around.

"How's Kyle taking retirement?"

"Oh, dad's ok. Retirement is only a state of mind for him. He pretty much runs the tank farm and everything else except the marina and Cheetah's."

"Talking about the marina, I see that End Run and Kitten pulled in," Jack noted.

Ginny nodded.

"That's right. They came in yesterday evening. Dan is good but Fred looks like shit. I think he lost weight. He can't run his own boat. He's pale, thin and losing his hair."

"Like me?" Jack laughed.

"No, silly; your hair has life and his doesn't. Women see those things."

Jack placed his arm around Ginny's waist and asked, "That's good; I don't need no competition."

Ginny snuggled over to him and said, "You'll have no competition so long as you stay away from other women."

"What about Bea Norris?"

"Damn you, Shelly," replied Ginny with fake indignation. "She's a whale. If you take up with her, I'll cut your balls off."

Jack sighed.

"Well, Terrence can take care of her."

Ginny threw him a sly grin, saying, "I hear he doesn't do that too well either."   "Where did you hear that?"

"Dad went over to the diner the other day and she invited him over for the night. He still has what it takes, but I think that's how he caught his cold."

"Kyle did sound nasal. But I didn't know that sex brings on a cold."

"Well, he may have caught it when he went with Mel to bring in the life boat from that ship in the Sargasso. But he'll be fine. What's your next gig?"

Jack threw up his hands in despair.

"The airline strike is killing me," he said. "I have to take Milton to Hope Town and ferry Henry around. Do you hear anything about it ending?"

"Don't know. I hear it has already spread to the birds."

"What was that?"

"It's a joke around here," Ginny said. "Birds disappear ahead of a storm but it's too early for hurricanes and we're getting no rain."

Jack looked up at the empty sky where rain clouds were beginning to form.

"Weird," he said. "I'm sure there's a reason. In the meantime," he continued. "A new doctor is here. Call Clarence and he'll send him over. Maybe he can give your dad a shot or pills."

"I'll do that, Shelly," Ginny nodded, adding, "Dad says we have a funeral to go on Sunday. I'm going. Will you go with me?" Dad may not be over his cold and I don't want to go alone."

"Not a problem. But I will see you after our rectory meeting tonight."

Jack gave her a light kiss and walked back to Archangel. He had things to do but he did manage to send Chico away on some flimsy pretext.

"Come back with Mel tomorrow morning," said Jack. "I need to inspect that life boat he found."

"Sure, boss."

Jack wanted to speak with Kyle and went back ashore to find him. Ginny had left for her club and Kyle was finished with fumigating his customers' sailboat. He had wanted to suggest that since everyone's insurance policies were cancelled, he and Kyle should work together to find another carrier. Kyle listened closely but he was less than receptive.

"I don't care what you say, young feller," he drawled in between a great deal of wheezing, sneezing and coughing. "You're a fake, a phony and a fraud, and you're after my daughter. You're not with any insurance company; you're nothing but a bounty hunter with the FBI or CIA and I'm not going to let you ruin my business or anything else around here."

"It don't matter what you think about me," Jack said. "You can hear it from me or from Jonathan or Ned. You decide, old buddy."

"You're full of shit," the old man snarled. "And what's more, I want you to stay away from my daughter. We were doing fine until you landed here five years ago. And what's more, I happen to know that all this bullshit about some sort of disease in these islands is just what it is, bullshit. If I had my say, I'd have you run out of these islands." His coughing and wheezing continued.

Jack saw his opening.

"Listen," he said. "My thing with your daughter is none of your business unless we decide to get married. And then we'd ask for your permission."

Kyle's eyes opened wide.

"You would?"

"You're damn right. And about why I'm in the islands; I make a living like you, your daughter and your brother Dale. As a matter of fact, with Hugo and Eldridge, Virgil and Clovis, we probably have the most successful businesses around while the locals sit around with their thumbs up their asses. But they outnumber us and they want our land and our businesses. And now we have this thing dealing death in the islands and throughout the world. You may think it is all bullshit, Kyle, but it's here and on a killing spree and pretty soon the locals are going to be looking for scapegoats, and that means they'll be gunning for us. That means you and me and Ginny."

Jack's tirade shook Kyle up and he sat up straight with a broad smile filling his face. The hint from Jack that marriage to Ginny might be in the air and that Jack would even consider asking his permission changed his frame of mind and made him to forget whatever else he was talking about.

"If you marry Ginny, I won't have to buy you out," said Kyle gleefully.

"I'm glad," Jack responded. "I hate family fights. But we have something more important to deal with right now, Kyle. People are dying and you know that. I'm not into booze or drugs and I don't understand medical stuff but my hunch is that this heroin that's suddenly showing up is bad and may be causing the trouble."

"What do you want me to do?" Kyle asked.

"Just stay away from the stuff until we have it figured out. After all, I don't want to lose a father-in-law before the wedding."

Kyle was beaming and Jack smiled. He had gained a convert but had also made a commitment. It was an indirect marriage proposal if there ever was one. Jack left Kyle in a happy frame of mind and returned to Archangel where he found Chico waiting for him. He was eager to leave the cat to see his latest flame at Sanctuary Village and wanted to make sure Jack knew.

A shadow covered the boat as Chico was about to leave. Jack looked up and saw a cloud hide the sun. Thunder rumbled in the distance. It was going to rain.

16

The Pale Horse

Jack was happy about one thing. He avoided a confrontation with Kyle, but at the same time he was worried about that cold the old man had caught. It wasn't that he really cared if Kyle lived or died; he had never cared much for him. The problem was that his death would complicate Ginny and Jack's personal and business relations. True, Ginny would inherit his estate, clearing the way for them to get married without any backtracking from Kyle, and that was good. However, he was sure that Dale would somehow force himself into the picture as was the custom with many families with siblings. There were also Kyle's tangled dealings with Hugo, Vernon and Dale and just about everyone else. How would these pan out? In the final analysis, Jack concluded that he was better off if Kyle lived. It probably did not matter in the end game. Death or life was no longer a matter of personal choice; their strings were pulled by forces beyond the control of mere humans. There could be a pale horse riding yet.

Jack had briefly run into Milton back in April and now recalled that the subject of the four horsemen of the apocalypse came up in their conversation. It was one of Hiram's favorite topics but Jack had the horsemen confused with Notre Dame's legendary football players. Milton explained that the horsemen were mentioned in the Book of Revelation and were often referred to in biblical literature as specific metaphors for the different disasters of life. Collectively, they represented war, famine, conquest and death. But, there were several interpretations of what they stood for. The first horse was white, and it wielded power through fear, coercion deceit and dissension. Its rider carried a bow and a quiver of arrows that had no arrow heads. The second horse was red and stood for conquest. Its rider rode naked and wore a full helmet with slits for eyeholes and wielded a broad sword in one hand and a double-ended battle ax in the other hand, cutting a swath of destruction as it galloped over the land. The third horse was black, representing famine and pestilence. It too had a rider who wore a mask and threw poisoned seed as it rode, laying land to waste on its forays around the world. The fourth was a pale horse called Death. Its rider wore a hooded cape and carried a long scythe and a pair of scales in some versions. But more often the pale horse had no rider. It galloped back and forth around the world, leaving death in its wake. In other legends, it had a rider named Plague. Dennis had thought that the men on the red racer had died of another form of Plague called the Red Death, and of course Reggie had pointedly told Jack at Satan's Rock that the pale horse had no rider; it rode alone.

Well, Jack had more current and pressing issues to resolve. He looked up again and the entire sky was dark. He had just enough time to duck into the boat before torrents of rain began falling, rattling the catamaran's decks and cabin top. In the midst of this rainstorm, the VHF phone buzzed. It was Gordon Tully.

Gordon's voice was subdued, the depth of his loss and grief behind a façade of good natured humor. It was almost as if he had come to accept life's grim fatalism. He first chided Jack for being too chicken to call on his own behalf.

"I'm sorry, Tully," Jack said. "I'm deeply sorry. I'm just no damn good at these things."

"Let me ask you this, Jake. If you wanted to propose marriage to Ginny, would you propose to Kyle or to Ginny?"

Jack almost dropped the receiver.

"That's what I did, Tully," he admitted. "I proposed first to Kyle."

"I thought so," continued Gordon. "You're a great guy, Jake, but you're a damn low down chicken shit."

That broke the ice and they began talking.

"How is your wife taking it?" Jack asked.

"She's wiped out, and so am I. The only thing that keeps me going is work. I hear you made out well at Hole-in-the-Wall."

"It wasn't bad, Tully, except that Coop stole part of my bounty."

He heard Tully laugh.

"Clarence told me. Graves is going to give the boat to his kid. But don't worry. He'll make it up to you. What else is new?"

"You know what I know," said Jack. "I think we have a problem but I can't put a finger on it. What's happening in Marsh Harbor?"

"People are dying, but it's not as bad as here. I checked in at the barracks and the icehouse is overflowing with the dead. It's going to be one big funeral on Sunday."

"Would you know if Doreen ever got to Marsh Harbor," Jack asked.

"I spoke to Cynthia who said her sister just flew in from Florida."

"That's crazy, Tully. Who flew her in?"

"The story is that Bob Byrne put up the money and made it happen."

"She's supposed to be sick," said Jack.

"I heard that too," said Gordon. "Cynthia took her to her condo on Treasure Cay. I think she goes to that holistic clinic nearby for treatment. Anyway, I'm going to Marsh Harbor tomorrow and I'll tell Doreen you asked for her. You should call her, Jake."

Jack sighed.

"I'll do that, Tully."

"Good. Now, I suppose you know that Dan and Fred are here. I ran into them at Vernon's store. Dan is full of shit as usual, and Fred looks like shit. They're down at the Ocean View talking money with Jonathan."

"Why? Does he have any?"

"Beats me; I followed your advice and never banked with him. And oh, people are yapping about the power outage in Hole-in-the-Wall."

"People are always talking. So what finally happened down there?"

"Two guys who were supposed to be on shift died. Two more guys were brought in. The shift supervisor's log reported that they looked sick but he let them work anyway and he went home. When the power went, he came back to see what was going on and found them dead too."

"I kind of hoped that it was a bad rumor," said Jack.

"No, it's bad news," continued Gordon. "What's more; whatever they had is spreading. Ten more people down there died."

"We need to take a closer look at the Angelina in the Sargasso and the Comfort over at Satan's Rock," said Jack.

"Lance is going to do just that," said Gordon. "By the way, did you see Henry?"

"He high tailed it out of here," answered Jack.

Gordon's voice expressed concern.

"That's weird. Henry usually doesn't run from trouble."

"Clarence and I never got the chance to ask him anything," Jack went on.

"Well, I'm sure he knows more than we do, but he may be scared. He may open up when you see him in Hope Town. He trusts you more than any of us. I would stop at his place but one of Clarence's guys is taking me directly to Marsh Harbor Sunday after the funeral. Is anything else going on?"

"Nothing really," said Jack. "But there is one thing. How come heroin is showing up instead of cocaine?"

"Hugo might have the answer," said Gordon. "He sells the stuff. Maybe we'll see him at the funeral Sunday. Let's stay in touch."

Jack needed to deliver Lance's parcel to Hiram despite the rain. He put on a pair of slickers and borrowed one of Kyle's power skiffs. He thought the parcel was too light for prayer books but never brought it up with Hiram when he caught up with him at the rectory.

Jack thought that Hiram would be in mourning over his son Cyrus's death but he seemed unconcerned and strangely serene when Jack extended his condolences and expressed his concern for the sudden wave of deaths sweeping the islands. Instead, Hiram was fixated on the box that Jack had brought and mumbled how the box was going to save lives. What a weird bird the man was turning into, thought Jack.

The rain never stopped. He spent the night with Ginny, sleeping late on Saturday. The rain kept falling and they spent most of the day listening to the news from the outside world on the short wave radio. Most of it was bad. Port-of-Prince in Haiti and Santo Domingo in the Dominican Republic were reporting street riots and fires when the funeral homes and churches ran out of coffins and burial space. The news from Florida was no better. People died where they fell, government broke down and civil order disappeared under the onslaught of rampaging mobs. The radio was suddenly jammed by static and music came on. The radio finally cut out altogether.

Jack hit it and it started working again. But this time only music came through. He tried stations in Nassau and Freeport and got more static and then more music. Giving up, he shut it down and turned his attention to Ginny.

Her easy nature and pleasant smile were gone. Her lips were pursed and she bit them repeatedly, revealing her angst and the raw ends of her nerves. Her father was sick and she feared for his life and she feared the future. And so, her sole defense was to cling to Jack as if he was the only man who could save her, her father and the world she knew.

"What should we do?" she asked, pressing her body against his. "What is going to happen if dad dies?"

"He's not going to die," Jack said firmly.

"Will you take care of me?"

Jack swallowed hard.

"Of course," he replied.

"What's going to happen to us?"

"Your guess is as good as mine," he replied glumly.

"I have money in a Florida bank. Maybe we should leave," she suggested.

Jack shook his head.

"There's no hiding. It's here and in Florida. We'll need to see it through."

"You didn't have to come back to the Borders, you know," said Ginny.

Jack smiled in acknowledgement.

"True, but my business is here and you're here."

"They say rain is good," Ginny commented hopefully. "Maybe it will take this thing away."

Sunday, the twenty-eighth of May, came and the rain stopped for a while. But the sky stayed gray, and people shivered in the bone chilling dampness. An overflow crowd filled the Church of Christ and many mourners and worshippers were left to assemble in the street. Hiram Cooper was at the pulpit. He slowly called out the names of those who had died while a funeral cortege assembled outside the police barracks. It was almost as if he was reading an honor roll for fallen warriors. And when he was done, he said, "Satan has challenged us to mortal combat; let us meet this challenge and drive Satan back to Hell."

It was short, brief and effective and it galvanized his listeners to dry their tears and square their shoulders as if they were about to march off into battle. He gave them a surface bravado that at least temporarily dampened their fear of what was happening to them. They listened politely to his few words and then filed silently out of the church and joined the ever lengthening procession at the barracks.

Many piled into jeeps, cars and trucks, but many walked, and as they walked, they were joined by others falling in line as the cortege slowly made its way north through Patrick City to the cemetery at Sanctuary Village. It crawled at a snail's pace behind the Castaways that seemed to struggle with its instruments in the gray dampness of the morning. Bringing up the rear in an old panel truck with the sign Avalon on its doors, was Virgil with Clovis and Winthrop sitting in the open back.

Jack was no stranger to funerals in the Borders. He played trumpet and usually marched with the band in front of the horse drawn caisson. But this was different. Jack's buddy, Tom Kennedy was in one of those caskets, and the horn was given to another player. It was a very long procession line, a measure of losses suffered in just a few short weeks, and grieving families marched behind each of the many caissons in the procession.

Jack drove Kyle's pickup with Ginny at his side and squeezed in front of Virgil's truck to stay behind Gordon's entourage. He noted that Gordon's wife was absent. Hiram and his two sons, Lance and Milton, and close family members rode in a school bus but most everyone else walked. Hugo and Eldridge walked with the Castaways, drawing many Dominicans and Haitians between Patrick City and Sanctuary Village with them as the cortege slowly made its way to the cemetery.

Rain began falling again and Jack turned on the wipers and closed the windows. It was cool, but the drizzle added to the general discomfort as they trudged into Sanctuary Village. When the procession reached the cemetery near the beach, the Castaways lightened up and let loose with a medley of cheerier tunes at a faster but respectful beat and Jack looked forward to the band climaxing with the 'When the Saints Come Marching In' theme after the funeral.

Father Francois Honoree was standing in front of All Souls to preside over the funeral rites but he was largely ignored. The turnout was huge and everyone who was well enough to ride or walk was present, even Fred Hawk, Dan Schulman and Martin Wilson who was with Jane Nigel.

Behind Dan, hidden by his bulk, was Larry Fisher. That was a surprise. Ginny, in a plain black and white print cotton dress, stayed close to Jack. Jack looked over to where Martin Wilson was standing and saw a piece of paper drop out of his pocket. He walked over to greet Dan and picked it up. He was about to return it to Martin when the rain picked up and forced him back. A canopy of black umbrellas opened suddenly and the rain bounced harmlessly to the ground.

"Dad was hallucinating when I left him and was saying something about a pale horse," whispered Ginny when Jack ducked under her umbrella. "Is that from one of Hiram's sermons? I never heard that one before."

"Your dad isn't going nuts," Jack responded. "The line is from Revelation and he probably got it from Hiram who's big on that stuff. It goes something like this:

'And I looked, and beheld a pale horse: and the name of he who sat on him was Death, and Hell followed. And power was given unto them over the fourth part of the earth, to kill with sword, hunger, death, and the beasts of the earth.

'And they rode and they rode, until they laid waste to the land, and it lay barren, and all things died under their galloping hooves. But Death was invisible and the pale horse rode alone without its rider, with its nostrils filled with flame and steam, leaving thunder and dust in its wake over the lifeless world.'

"I picked up those lines from Milton," said Jack in a whisper.

The skies turned darker and Ginny drew closer to Jack.

"It sounds like prophesy."

It was so crowded along the narrow beach in front of the cemetery that Jack found himself almost shoulder to shoulder with Dan and Fred, both of whom nodded solemnly. Ginny and Gordon were right. Dan was fine but Fred was pale and drawn.

"We need a meeting," said Dan. "Jonathan says you might be able to help us with this outbreak."

"Yes," Fred echoed. "We can get enough serum to inoculate the entire population against this thing."

"That would be great," agreed Jack. You should speak to Malcolm."

"This could be a nice action for all of us," added Jonathan. "You might want to be included. But you need to put up some money, just some loose change…."

Jack was not listening. His eyes were fixed on a big black dot on the horizon. The wind picked up, the rain fell harder and Ginny shivered under the umbrella.

Pretty soon, everyone was seeing what he saw and a silence fell over the cemetery. It was a ship heaving in the swells, clearly in view and moving fast. It was out of control and heading for the beach.

Screams and howls rose from the crowd as the ship barreled through the surf and its hull ground over rocks and sand with ear splitting creaks, groans and screeches. Huge breakers lifted the bow out of water with a thunderous roar and heaved the floundering ship sideways into the shallow water with one final deafening roar in front of the stunned mourners on the rain soaked beach.

No one moved at first as the stricken vessel came to rest on its side, a gargantuan monster of rusted iron and steel, fire, steam and smoke hissing and belching out of its broken body. It was the Nassau Clipper.

Several bodies hurled themselves overboard to be gobbled up by the turbulent waters but one seaman made it to the beach. He was soaked, his eyes were red and wild and angry sores covered his bare legs and arms. Unsure of where he was, he looked around dazed until he saw human forms quickly giving ground as he stumbled about in the wet sand and begged for help, blood leaving his nose and mouth with every gasp for air.

"Please," the seaman cried. "Help me. Don't let me die. Help me."

His pleas were ignored. People ran from the sight of the ailing mariner and he was given a wide berth. Some hid behind gravestones, fled back to the road or took refuge inside All Souls, bolting shut the door behind them. Those who stayed on the beach formed a moving circle that surged in an out as the sailor staggered and thrashed bout until he fell face down in the sand and lay still. Jack left Ginny by the gravesite and followed Jane and Dennis who ran over to the seaman and took his pulse. They bent over him and the young doctor shook his head sadly, pointing to the boils and sores on the man's body. "Red Death," he said.

"You mentioned Red Death once before, doctor," Jack whispered. "What the hell is it?"

"It's Bubonic Plague," said Dennis, making sure he was not overheard. "Black Death and Red Death are cousins. Each is a variation of the plague and each is a killer; but the Red death kills more people faster."

17

A Yacht Adrift

Sunday, the twenty-eighth of May had been a terrible day. The cemetery was left deserted and the seaman's body was left to rot in the rain and to be eaten by animals during the night. Hugo and a few men returned much later and had the remains cremated and given to Virgil for burial at sea. One would have thought that the funeral and Nassau Clipper incident would have been enough to bring the people of the Borders together. Unfortunately, that never happened. Some families were so scared that they attempted to leave the islands on their private planes and yachts that very night.

That was a big mistake. One family flew out of the airstrip on South Border. . Their plane was seen being hit by some sort of rocket west of the Abaco islands and disintegrated over the sea according to local fishermen in the area. Another family left on a yacht and radio contact was lost an hour later. A Bermuda ham radio operator in contact with the vessel reported hearing heavy weapons fire before the radio fell silent. When word spread that escape routes were blocked, efforts to leave ceased as suddenly as they started.

Dennis Sinclair stayed up all night trying to convince Clarence that this was a severe health emergency and that martial law should be declared. But Clarence would do nothing on his own and called Gordon who personally called Hamilton Graves for help while Jack agreed to meet with Dan and Fred who claimed at the funeral that they could get their hands on cure-all serum. Jack also tried calling Bob Byrne in Florida but was unable to reach anyone.

Sunday faded into Monday, the twenty ninth of May, and rain grudgingly gave way to a cheerless cover of dull gray clouds. Kyle was sick but he was hanging in and not getting worse. That was good news. There were also interesting bits of information emerging about the Nassau Clipper. Lancelot Cooper acknowledged receiving a distress signal from the ship but that it was subsequently cancelled. He also confirmed that a search of the beached vessel found several dead crew and quantities of semi-processed heroin in cases bearing the Angelina's angel wing markings.

And then there was a reply from Hamilton's office. His young son had fallen ill and the commissioner was not returning any calls. That was not good news, but it was up-staged by a fisherman's urgent radio message that a yacht with several people on board was adrift between Hermit Cay and Bitter End.

Jack and Ginny found Clovis manning the jitney ferry between Buccaneer Point and Agnes Town Monday morning. The regular ferryman was out sick, Clovis was explaining and Virgil was hauling more dead bodies out to sea. Jack spent the rest of the morning at his boatyard while Ginny began cleaning up Cheetah's for what she hoped would be its grand re-opening. Several younger women from Freeport and unable to leave the Borders found themselves broke and decided to pay their bills by selling their bodies at Cheetah's. They seemed clean and Ginny hired them as prostitutes on the spot.

At lunchtime, Jack and Ginny returned to Pirates' Cove. Ginny went to see how her father was doing and Jack called Doreen from his boat.

"It's so sweet of you to call," said Doreen with the usual affectation in her voice. "How did you know I was here?"

"This place is too small for secrets," Jack said. "How are you doing?"

"I'm coping, Shelly. I still have a bad cold, but I found a doctor here in Treasure Cay and I think I'm getting better."

Jack tried not to sound concerned.

"That's good," he said. "But, what brings you to this neck of the woods in the wonderfully cool month of May?"

"Vacation, Shelly. It was my idea. Fred is on his monthly trip to the Borders and I thought we'd get some quality time together. Besides, Fred thought it would be safer in the Bahamas. He spoke to Bob Byrne who got me on a special flight to Marsh Harbor. Isn't that neat?"

"That's good, Doreen. Maybe we can get together."

"Are you coming over?"

"Yes. I'll be heading over to Marsh Harbor in a few days. I can call you when I arrive."

There was a pause at Doreen's end.

"I know it's crazy," she said, "but I'd love to see you. Why don't you stay at the Grand Bay in Marsh Harbor and call me from the hotel. I'll come down."

"It sounds like a plan. Did you speak to Fred?"

Doreen giggled.

"Why be shy, Shelly? We were once married, you know."

"You're right. I'll call from the hotel."

"Shelly?"

"Yes?"

"Cynthia tells me you now own your businesses outright. Is that so?"

"It was not my doing," said Jack.

"That's what Bob Byrne says. But did you know that if you and I die, he gets to manage your estate until our kids become adults?"

"That's what you and I agreed to," Jack reminded his ex-wife. "Actually, it was s what you wanted. I had no choice so I went along with the flow."

"Well, we should talk about it anyway. You're doing well now, Shelley, and maybe we don't need Bob as executor anymore. Besides, you make enough money now to take better care of me and the kids. I'm sure he wouldn't mind if you begin taking charge of your life. And you don't drink anymore," she added.

"I've become a saint," said Jack sarcastically.

"What are you going to do when you get your captain's license back?"

"I'll worry about it when it comes," he replied. "But we should get together and talk about the kids."

He ended the conversation on that note and lay down for a nap. That was the way it was with Doreen and it was hard to tell what her true intentions were. She made sense however. This was a time of crisis and it seemed wrong to him that families should be physically apart when they should be united. Doreen may have been entertaining the same ideas. At least Jack hoped so. He fell asleep thinking about Bob continuing generosity and involvement in his life and began wondering if he might not have one or more ulterior motives. In the moment before he dozed off, he thought about his children so far away with his parents and prayed they were safe.

When he awoke, the afternoon was over and he suddenly remembered that he was to spend the night with Ginny. But colds usually made Kyle restless, and Jack feared he would still be up. However, Kyle filled up with hot tea and rum and was soon several sheets to the wind. Dennis came to see him early in the evening. He wasn't sure what he had but as a precaution he gave him a shot and a mix of assorted antibiotics. After another cup of tea and rum, Kyle was out like a light.

Later, Jack walked over to the two trailers behind the marina office. Kyle lived in one and Ginny in the other. Differentiating one from the other was easy. One was bare. The other had an awning over the front door and was surrounded by a white picket fence and was fully landscaped with shrubs, flowers and a palm tree under which a small clearing was filled with cheap white patio furniture. It was her way of creating a homey atmosphere.

Ginny was in a cotton work dress with flower prints, the kind with buttons down the front, and was wearing sneakers and white socks when she greeted him at her trailer.

"I'm glad you're still here," she said. "I hear many families are trying to leave."

"Leave, and go where?"

A sudden tremor buckled their feet but it faded in seconds. Moments later Ginny tripped over something and fell against Jack's chest.

It was the rotting carcass of a dead rat. Jack gave it a kick and it went flying out of the way.

Ginny made no effort to draw away. Instead, she placed her arms around his neck while he held her across the small of her back. He let one hand slip slightly lower and she pressed her body into his groin while he gave her a lingering kiss.

"Have you had dinner?" Ginny asked. "Dad is asleep. I can make you a bite to eat inside, if you wish."

Jack followed her into the trailer and waited by the door while she turned on a light. Ginny wore a heavy perfume and he liked the way she threw her head back and to the side, sweeping through her long hair with her hand. But it was her sensuous surface coarseness that attracted him. She was not very beautiful but she was sexy, and he had long found more than a grain of truth to the old adage about 'last call' at bars: 'Everyone is beautiful at closing time.'

However, Ginny's sexual resources had merits of their own. Her bedroom eyes and pleasingly plump body and voluptuous breasts were irresistible. He could see that her stockings were tied to a garter belt and that she wore no bra and no panties. Resisting her overtures was pointless as usual. Every time he saw her and laid his eyes on her, he felt himself drawn to her.

Ginny gave him a seductively wicked smile.

"Would you like to take care of me tonight?"

Ginny undressed and climbed into bed.

"What do you think?" she asked later when they were done. "We make great lovers, don't we?"

Jack smiled.

"I noticed that."

"I bet you're going to see Doreen the first chance you get," she said accusingly."

"That's a sure bet," Jack replied. "I spoke to her this afternoon. We need to talk about our kids. It's important."

"No sex?"

"No sex. I'm going to be a monk."

"What about other women?"

"It depends on who you bring over to your club."

"You lead a boring life, Shelly. But I'd like to be your steady. I could even be your wife."

Jack sat up straight as if he had been electrocuted. She was much too direct.

"That's serious talk, Ginny."

"Well, I don't want a local. They're too inbred and give me the creeps. Look, I know you're thinking of selling your business. It's a gold mine like my marina. If we married, our properties merge and we'd be the richest couple in the Borders. And if we sell, we'd have more than enough money to start over in another place. I think dad would like that."

"I've thought of that."

"We can try living together for a while. No strings attached."

"What about Kyle?"

"Dad doesn't want to leave but he will if I leave. What do you think, Shelly?"

There was a note of quiet desperation in her voice.

"I tell you what," Jack said. "Let's try to solve our problems right here today. Once we do that, we'll worry about tomorrow and get married. I did tell your dad that we'd ask his permission."

Ginny dressed and followed Jack to his boat and kissed him on the dock.

"I'm going to make you mine yet."

They stood there, holding hands in silence, watching the darkness of the night turn gray to usher in a new day, Tuesday, May 30. After a while, he returned to Archangel.

What would Kyle do if he knew what his daughter was doing? What would any father do? Of course fathers always knew what their daughters were doing but they never said anything.

Jack was alone. He napped for a few hours before getting up again to shower and shave. He skipped coffee since no one was not around to make it, and then jumped off the boat to re-set the dock lines. Stepping back to admire his handiwork, he felt something mushy give way under his feet. Looking down, he saw a dead rat. What the hell was going on?

He jumped away, sat down at the edge of the dock and dipped his boat shoes into the water in an effort to rid them of any real or imagined contamination.

A buzz from the VHF radio inside Archangel announced an incoming call and he rushed into the vessel to answer it. Chancing to look back, he saw a cat jump out of the brush and drag the rat's fresh carcass away.

Reggie was on the line and his voice was urgent.

"I'm at the dock at Nigel's hotel. You need to come over, Jake."

Jack took one of the marina's tenders and left for the hotel docks. He powered up to the dock where he found Reggie helping Clarence and Gordon secure a yacht at a slip behind the hotel after a police launch had pushed it over from the middle of the harbor.

"What's up?" Jack asked, scampering up to the dock.

"Someone's on board," Gordon said. "We heard something."

Clarence pointed to one of the portholes.

"I saw something move inside."

They boarded the yacht and made so much noise with their yelling and banging that hotel guests came out to see what the commotion was about. Jane Baron and Martin Wilson happened to be on the dock to see Dale Malone who was about to go fishing with Marvell Sullivan and Winslow Bates when the yacht was boarded.

Heavy breathing could be heard from below decks but there was otherwise no response to their persistent calling and banging on the yacht's sides. Jack took one look at the vessel and immediately recognized it as did Jane.

"That's my dad's boat," she shrieked.

And she started running to the yacht.

"Keep her away!" Jack yelled.

Martin tried to restrain her but without success. Nigel was also on the dock and saw his brother's boat. He bounded past Jane and jumped aboard and disappeared inside the cabin with Jack and Clarence on his tail.

Fortunately, Dennis also appeared on the dock, his ever-present medical bag in hand. Marvel and Winslow wrestled Jane to the ground and held her until Dennis was able to give her shot that put her asleep. Making sure she was safe, he boarded the yacht and went below to join the others.

Nigel was on the floor holding his brother Ned in his arms, and four more bodies, two adults and two children, lay nearby. They were Emile Honoree, his wife Juliet and their two children.

"Don't get close to him!" Dennis yelled, waving away the others.

Jack stayed with the young doctor but Clarence stood numb in a corner, leaving Gordon to pull Jack away.

"Don't go near him," Dennis warned. "He's dying and you don't want to catch what he has."

"He's my brother!" Nigel screamed. "Do something!"

Ned Baron raised an infected arm.

"Water," he gasped. "I need water."

Dennis pulled out a small plastic bottle of water from his medical bag and threw it to Nigel who twisted off the cap and held the bottle to Ned's blistered lips. He tore the bottle away from Nigel and began guzzling.

"Where's my daughter Angela?" Nigel asked as Ned fought to get some water into his parched mouth.

But the effort was futile. The water mixed with blood and spilled out of his mouth as he struggled to say, "She stayed behind. She's with Frank Doyle."

"What happened?" Dennis asked Ned. "How did you get here?"

"It's over, Ned," said Jack quietly, "You need to tell us what happened."

Ned heard Jack's voice and turned his head.

"That job I gave you, Jake," he gasped. "We knew an epidemic was coming and had to cancel insurance policies before claims started pouring in. We didn't want anyone to know so we tried to keep things quiet."

"Who is 'we' old buddy?"

Ned began choking before he could reply.

"What's happening in Florida?" Nigel asked.

"My wife died. Dead bodies are everywhere...Too many to pick up," answered Ned, coughing up more blood. "That's why I tried to run. Emile knew the way so I took him and his family. I didn't know they were sick."

He went into convulsions and grabbed Nigel's arm so tightly that his fingernails broke his brother's skin.

"But that thing didn't start there," he panted. "It started here."

Those were Ned's last words.

"The guy on the Clipper had Plague," said Dennis, "and Plague killed these poor folks. It's the Red Death variant. You catch cold at dawn and die at dusk."

It was still May 29 and Jack had been in the Borders eleven days. The Red Death was spreading, and somewhere far away Jack could hear that pale horse galloping, its thundering hooves spreading death clouds in its wake.

18

Cheetah's

Life's biggest fear is death when its certainty strikes with random selectivity. If ten people live on an island and it is certain that every day ten percent of the population will be killed at random, how many people will be left in ten days? How long will it take for just one person to be left? And what will the survivors do to stay alive even knowing that their efforts are to no avail? Whatever the answers, Jack knew that fear begot violence and that both were magnified by the shrinking pool of survivors.

Dinner Monday night was at Ginny's trailer and Jack had asked Milton to join them. It was a solemn affair and the table talk was all about survival. Milton had an interesting view of the subject and spoke of Tamerlane who carved an empire from China to the eastern Mediterranean. At Damascus he ordered built a high pyramid of one hundred thousand skulls. Now, it was said that Tamerlane had a personal physician who had never harmed a fly. When Damascus fell he was given fifteen prisoners as slaves. But Tamerlane's men were required to each execute fifteen prisoners to meet his quota of skulls or they themselves would face execution. It was kill or be killed.

"What do you think the doctor did?" Milton asked over dessert.

Neither Jack nor Ginny had an answer.

"The doctor ordered his slaves killed to meet Tamerlane's demand," said Milton, leaning forward over the small kitchen table. "You see," he explained. "The good doctor was following God's advice. God helps those who help themselves and God saves those who save themselves."

Milton smiled smugly, leaned back and finished his dessert

"How come you never became a priest or reverend like your dad? Jack asked.

Milton shrugged his shoulders and replied, "Oh, my dad is fine but he can be a heavy trip. That's why Cyrus left for the States; he actually ran away from home.

And Lance, he's a good guy and loves dad, but he keep his distance, if you know what I mean. As for me, I always liked numbers and accounting, and I like what I'm doing; it keeps me moving, and as they say, a moving target is hard to hit."

There was a family resemblance in the small hook nose but it ended there. Milton was hawk faced, round eyed and square with thin arms too long for his short body, and he combed his light hair from side to side to cover a large bald spot.

Kyle was feeling better and joined them for coffee. He too said little except to mumble that they had to find a way of this mess.

Dinner was done, the dishes washed and it began raining again. The rain fell on the trailer's roof and poured down the sides of the thin walls, forming dark muddy puddles on the soft ground. Jack found the noise deafening and the sound of heavy raindrops splashing the puddles made him feel as if he was drowning and heading for a watery death. He finished drying the dishes, kissed Ginny, bade Milton and Kyle a good night and left for his boat.

He sank into a deep sleep that lasted into the next morning, Tuesday, May 30, and when he awoke the sun was shining brightly and all signs of rain were gone. He never knew that in the middle of night a band of doped up vandals crept into the cemetery and set a fire that spread to All Souls. A bucket brigade saved the church, but the fire consumed the Nassau Clipper, leaving a smoldering hulk on the beach. The vandals escaped undetected, leaving used needles behind them.

He went to the barracks early that morning to see Clarence and found him having coffee with Dan Schulman and Fred Hawk who looked better than at the funeral.

Clarence was telling them about the grand re-opening gala at Cheetah's coming up soon.

"It's going to be a costume party," he was saying, "something like a masked ball or masquerade. It'll be a real swinging affair, and everyone's going to be there. I hope you guys can make it."

"We'll certainly try," said Dan. He nodded to Jack as he entered. "It's good to see you again, Jake. I see that prosperity has not passed you by."

Jack nonchalantly shook his and Fred's hands.

"How are you doing, guys? Have a good trip in?"

Dan rubbed his fat belly.

"It was rough, but don't ask me, Jake. I hate boats and I hate water. Larry Fisher drove my boat. I slept."

Fred laughed.

"Don't mind Dan," he said. "He likes things that don't move. I single handed my boat, but let me tell you, it was fierce out there."

Poor Fred; he was the eternal braggart and showoff, and always at the expense of the truth. Jack did not try to remind him that it was Otis who had gone to Nassau to skipper his yacht and bring him back to the Borders.

"I can imagine," replied Jack. "I hate heavy weather myself. Where's Larry? I saw him at the funeral."

Dan dismissed the question lightly.

"Oh, I gave him a few days off. I bet he flew down to Nassau to get laid."

Clarence's eyes narrowed but Jack did not comment

"Well, you look great, Jake," said Fred quickly. "How are things?"

"I can't complain, old buddy. Incidentally, I spoke to Doreen. I told her I'd like to come over and see her, if it's all right with you."

Fred gave him a reassuring smile.

"You don't have to ask, Jake. You're family. But call ahead of time."

"I'll do that, Fred. Now, what brings you and Dan to the Borders?"

Dan cleared his throat.

"Two things, Jake." he looked at Clarence. "Want to tell him?"

The police chief sighed.

"You know the Princess of the Seas, don't you, Jake? Well, Dan tells me that he owns stock in the cruise line and wants to grow its business. He wants to tow the Angelina to our docks and have it refitted as a floating hotel. Fred is angling for a piece of that action too. I said they would have to speak to Lance."

"I can't speak for Lance," said Jack. "But who's fronting the money?"

"We have great plans for the Borders, Jake," said Dan. "And we'd like to include you. Fred and I want to build a cruise ship terminal, with long piers and a shopping complex in Agnes Town, just like in many other islands. And for that we're going to need financing and waterfront space, like all the land from Nigel's hotel to Cross Island Air. Let me tell you. We're going to put the Borders on the map."

"It sounds great, Dan," said Jack. "Where's the money coming from?"

"Island Trust will take care of that, Jake. Jonathan says it's not a problem."

"This sounds good, Dan. You're need a half mile of land facing deep water, a lot of waterfront when you figure those long piers will be perpendicular to the land. You'll also need local approval and approval from Nassau."

Clarence made a face, saying, "I hadn't thought of all that."

"No problem, Jake," went on Fred, taking over for Dan. "That's the second thing. We need the land on which your business and Cheetah's sits. It's going to be a new pharmaceutical plant. We know we need to work directly with Ginny Malone, but we have a great deal for you."

"I thought Dale Malone was doing some production for you," Clarence broke in.

"He is," replied Dan. "But he's squeezed for space and we'll have more facilities here. Of course, he'll have the option of buying into our new venture."

"How come you can't keep supplying the islands from Florida?" Jack asked.

Dan smiled benignly.

"Import taxes, Jake. The Bahamian government is promoting local industry and is giving big tax incentives. We want to cash in on them, and you must have heard, Jake..."

He was talking fast now.

"We have enough inventory of a special antibiotic serum to protect the Borders from this epidemic. We have enough for thirteen thousand people. We can produce enough here to ship out to other countries and save the world."

"I thought you'd be interested in this," said Clarence.

"I am," Jack responded. "But how do you know what's ailing us?"

"Could it be anything but the bubonic plague?" Dan asked.

"Probably not; anyway, what's the pitch?"

"It's simple," Fred answered. "South Florida Pharmaceuticals currently sells the serum at a thousand dollars a shot in the States and in Bermuda. If you sell us your land for which we're prepared to offer $1 million, we'll offer the Borders our stock of serum for a flat $10 million, payable in cash. We can start using the money to buy more land."

Jack smiled.

"That's mighty generous, but I'll make you a better deal. Milt Cooper assessed my land for $3.5 million. I'll sell you my land and business for one dollar and leave the islands forever if you give away the stuff. Think of it; you get the whole works for free. It's the same deal you gave me give years ago. I'd go for it if I were you. You'll recoup the cost of the shots in less than a year if you work the business right, and you'll be swimming in cash in a couple of years.

The veins in Fred's neck swelled slightly.

"We need cash now to show the Holiday Line earnest money. We can't afford to give away the serum."

"I imagine that's where Jonathan can help," said Jack.

Fred could not respond but Dan did his best to smile and field Jack's comment.

"He will later when his bank is not so heavily invested. But say, how come you never banked at Island Trust."

Jack could not resist a dig at this point.

"It's because my mom and dad raise a fool, Dan."

It was now time for a counter offer.

"Tell you what, guys. Ginny and I are thinking of getting hitched. If we do, she might give up Cheetah's. That land has also been appraised by Milton for the same $3.5 million as mine. My land and her land are worth a cool $7 million. That's a fair trade for the serum; our land for the serum. You'd be doing a good deed and so would we, and you'd also end up with the land you want. Of course, I need to talk to Ginny and see how she feels, but I'm sure she'll go for it. How about it, guys?"

Fatigue settled into Dan's face, and Fred turned haggard and began panting. His hand reached into a pocket filled with loose pills. He took some out and popped them into his mouth.

There was a sudden short crack in the air and the floor jarred under their feet. Dan grabbed the edge of Clarence's desk for support and Fred looked around nervously. But the disturbance lasted less than a second and both Clarence and Jack laughed.

"This might be a great attraction for your business," said Clarence by way of a joke.

Dan did not find his humor funny.

"Do these things happen often?" he asked.

"Not too often," replied Jack. "But they do happen."

Dan put on a brave face.

"This project needs seed money; so we can't let the serum go for nothing."

"Yes," Fred added. "You should not pass up this investment opportunity."

They hurried out, testing the ground under them with their feet as they left.

"What do you think, Jake?" Clarence asked after they had gone. "Are they phony or what? But say, would you really give away your business?"

Jack nodded.

"You bet, if it's going to save lives. Why don't you call Bermuda and see if that serum works?"

Clarence grinned.

"I'm quicker than you think, Jake," he replied. "I did that yesterday. People are dying there now just like elsewhere in the world."

"I thought you wanted to return to the States," Clarence reminded him.

"I may do so some day, old buddy, but right now, we have a bigger issue. The Angelina is carrying bad heroin, and we need to get people to stop using it."

"Do you know that for sure?"

"No, but the heroin we've been finding was from boats with dead bugs and rats."

"So?"

"Boats have live bugs and rats, not dead ones."

Clarence walked over to the window. The rain was falling again.

"Avalon must be on the move again," he said. "I see Virgil's truck heading down to Winthrop's place, and he's short on lumber I hear," Clarence added. "It's going to get worse if Hugo can't get his boats in and out of the islands"

"Things are going to get real bad if he can't get us fuel," said Jack.

Virgil was getting ready for another mass funeral scheduled for noon in front of Hiram's church where crowds, bigger than ever, were gathering. The only person missing was Nigel Baron and Jane explained that he was nursing a bad cold. It was also true that lumber was in short supply. Dale Malone sent Marvel Sullivan and Winslow Bates with a truck full and they stayed on to help with the carpentry.

The atmosphere was subdued and even the sendoff provided by the Castaways and Jack with his trumpet was brief, and when Avalon finally pushed away from the dock, the skies darkened and a heavy rain began falling on this, Wednesday, the thirty first of May. Jack had now been in the Borders a full two weeks.

Ginny went to Cheetah's to ready the club for the evening and Jack went to his boatyard to help Otis and Mel with two police launches. Jack's timing was off and had to keep looking at his watch. It did not take long for him to realize that Cross Island Air was no longer flying, and without the roar of the seaplane engines he could not tell the exact time of day without consulting his watch.

That afternoon he took a break and dropped over at Madame Lamar's across the street to see how Gladys was. She was sweeping the wooden walkway in front of her door. On one of the windows behind her was a long line from which many crystal chimes were dangling.

"Good to see you, Shelly. What's up?"

"Not too much, Gladys. What's with the chimes?"

The old woman rested an elbow on her broom.

"It's for the number of folks who died here since you returned," she cackled.

At a loss for words, Jack went back to work. Later that afternoon, he received an unexpected visit from Dennis Sinclair who was carrying a large box in his arms.

It was the same box had delivered to Hiram.

"Hiram gave me this box," said Dennis. "And you'll never guess what's in it."

Jack put down his work and smiled.

"Are we talking about lightweight bibles?"

Dennis burst out laughing.

"No; it's something better," he explained. "Hiram told me the story. Cyrus had developed an anti-plague serum years ago for the CDC and kept several lots in his office. That's what he sent to Lance in one box, serum, syringes, everything, and claimed it was filled with bibles."

"I'm not following."

"Bibles are books, and books are duty free," said Dennis. "Pharmaceuticals and medicines require permits and licenses and can be subject to duties. That wastes a lot of time. Besides, no one would seize a bunch of bibles; prescription medicines are another issue."

The young physician patted the box lovingly.

"We have enough in here for a thousand shots," he announced jubilantly.

"Is it any good?" Jack asked.

"It should be," answered Dennis. "It's been approved by the CDC and has been used in the States for years whenever a case shows up here and there."

"That's great," said Jack. "But how did Cyrus or anyone know that this bubonic plague was going to break out here or anyplace else?"

"That's beyond me," replied Dennis. "Right now, I need a cool, secure place." He looked around to make sure that Melvin and Otis were not within earshot.

"Jack took a key from his pocket, walked over to a wall closet and unlocked the door, saying, "This paint room is insulated and cool, and I have the two keys."

They placed the box on a shelf and Jack gave Dennis one of the keys.

"Now," he said. "When will you be giving the shots?"

"I was going to start tomorrow," answered the doctor. "But the more important question is who gets the shots and who doesn't."

Jack shook his head.

"I'm not going to touch that one. Someone else needs to call that one. All the big

"Will you be there?"

"It's the opening night. The whole world will be there."

Jack groped in his pocket for his cigarettes while he walked Dennis to the door. Instead of cigarettes he found the piece of paper Martin Wilson had dropped at the first mass funeral. A list of names was handwritten on the wrinkled sheet and he had to squint to understand the writing.

Dennis was about to leave when Jack said, "Hang on a minute, doc. This may be interesting."

"What is it?"

"Take a look at these names. Martin Wilson dropped this piece of paper at the funeral last Sunday." And he read off the names. "Cyrus Cooper, Hiram Cooper, Malcolm Harding, Eldridge and Hugo Johnson, Vernon Peters, Jonathan Hall, Nigel Baron, Ned Baron, Kyle Malone, Dale Malone, Henry Alden and Louie Gold."

"Louie Gold?" Dennis asked. "Why would Louie Gold's name be on a list like this? He's dead."

"And there's a line across Cyrus's name," said Jack. "If I didn't know better, I'd say that this is either a wedding list or a hit list."

He showed the list to Dennis who did a double take. "Clarence or Tully needs to see this," Dennis declared.

Dennis left and Jack worked at the boatyard though the afternoon and into the evening before changing into his costume for the function, a clean blue blazer and a pressed shirt and tie. Cheetah's was humming when he arrived and was amazed at the size of the crowd waiting to enter. The pink neon sign on the roof lit up the street where men and women of all ages in all imaginable types of costumes and masks rocked to the catchy reggae beat of the Castaways performing inside.

Jack found Reggie on patrol with two officers in a police jeep parked outside the club. They were reinforced by a half dozen Jamaicans on loan from the Zebra, two of whom stood at Cheetah's entrance as bouncers. He went over to the jeep and handed out cigarettes. It was small gestures such as these that made him popular.

Jack had to speak loudly to compete with the band's noisy music.

"Expecting a busy night?"

"It has the making of one, Jake," Reggie replied. "This is real tossed salad. You know what I mean. We have men seeking women; women seeking men; women seeking women and men seeking men, and everyone seeking drugs. You know what I mean." He made an obscene flourish of the hand. "A true mélange," he said in an affected French accent.

Jack could see Hugo lurking in the shadows with another bunch of Jamaicans making their drug deals with customers who he recognized as local merchants or their employees. It was business as usual.

"Who's inside the club?"

"The same old faces," answered Reggie. "Vernon is at the bar, trying to put the make on Ginny."

Jack laughed.

"What else is new?"

Outside, drug deals were being made. Gordon and Clarence showed up to meet with Jack and Dennis as did Jonathan to discuss the distribution of the anti-plague shots and were about the only ones not in costume for the opening. Transvestites in extravagant feather lines outfits showed up at the door and Jack followed them into the noisy smoke filled club where the dance floor was full and the Castaways were and their calypso music were making the club shimmy and shake.

The side bars were three deep with customers of all sexual persuasions and men who wanted sex with women waited anxiously outside back rooms. Jack circled around the dance floor until he saw Vernon chatting with Ginny who was working behind the main bar. Melvin Stoop was tending a side bar and Eldridge and Milton were working the other bars. Vernon had on a pirate's outfit and even Jack had to admit that he looked his swashbuckling best. He cut through the dance floor to the bar where Ginny leaned over and gave him a kiss in front of Vernon.

"Hi," she said. "Vernon here wants to marry me and take me away from all this. Don't you, Vernon?"

Vernon nodded and gave Jack a dirty look.

"What the hell, Ginny," exclaimed Jack. "That's not good. I'll go one better; I'll take you away from all this and you don't need to marry me."

Ginny almost dropped the cocktail mixer she was holding.

"Is that the best you can do?"

"Okay," Jack said. "If I can't take you away from all this, will you marry me?"

He yanked the signet ring off his finger and placed on hers while she still had a hand on the counter.

"This will keep you until we get a real engagement ring," he said.

His proposal left Ginny speechless. All she could do was to stand open mouthed, staring happily at the ring on her finger. But Vernon was fuming and his comment was understandably testy.

"Why don't you sell me your business and go back to Florida? You don't belong here. We never had a problem until you returned."

He smelled from liquor and had obviously started his drinking early.

I'll keep that under advisement, Vernon," said Jack. "But if you want to buy me out, come see me when you get enough money to buy a pot to piss in, you hear?"

As he did once before, he brushed off an imaginary speck from Vernon's coat collar and gave Ginny a long, languorous kiss. They were fortuitously interrupted by Dennis who came over and tugged at Jack's arm.

"Eldridge says he has a room for us."

Vernon slinked away quietly, leaving Jack to follow Dennis through a side door to a small, dimly lit room where Clarence, Gordon and Jonathan were sitting at a small table. He noted mentally that Nigel, Hiram and Malcolm were not present.

No explanation for the absences of Hiram and Malcolm was given but Jonathan placed his hands on the table and stared at them when Nigel's name came up.

"He died an hour ago, Jake. I was at his bedside with his wife and niece. He may have caught what his brother had. The last thing he said was about drawing lots by family when I told him about the stock of antidote."

Gordon rose to his feet and began pacing around the room.

"You could call an emergency meeting of the Borders' governing council," Jack suggested. "It should weigh in on this thing."

"You're assuming of course that the antidote works," said Gordon.

"It works!" Dennis declared.

"What's the difference?" Jack went on. "If it works, we're good; if it doesn't work, we die; and if we do nothing, we still die."

"What happens to you?" Jonathan asked. "You have no family."

Jack chuckled.

"I guess I'm the odd man out," he said. "And that's fine with me. I'll take my chances. What do you guys plan to do?"

A long moment of silence followed his question. Finally, Clarence responded, speaking for Gordon and Jonathan.

"We want to do the right thing, Jake," he said. "But we have families to protect and you don't. We think a lottery is the best way to go and we want to be in it."

"I don't blame you," smiled Jack. "I'd be in that lottery too if I had a family. I'd want to protect the next generation."

The consensus was that Jonathan would call a council meeting to be held as soon as possible to present the proposal of having at least part of the Borders' general population inoculated with the antidote.

"There's one more thing," said Dennis. "Jake picked up a list dropped by Martin Wilson at last Sunday's funeral. Tell them about it, Jake."

Jack retrieved the piece of paper from his pocket and gave it to Clarence who read it and passed it to Gordon who read it carefully and gave it to Jonathan. His eyes narrowed when he came to his name on the list.

"Who is this Wilson guy, anyway?" Jonathan asked.

"We'll have to ask him or Jane," said Jack. "Martin keeps telling everyone that he works for the government."

"This may or may not be a hit list," concluded Gordon, "We need to know who Martin really is and why he had this list."

The meeting over, they re-entered the club's noisy main room where music from the Castaways wafted loudly above the din of the crowd.

Vernon was back at the bar and was now joined by Terrence Moore. Ginny was visibly annoyed but she kept her cool and focused on other customers and their pickups milling at the bar. Jack was about to return to the bar when a tall shapely

red-haired and slightly tipsy woman with heavy white facial makeup staggered over, placing an arm around Vernon's shoulders.

"Vernon darling," cooed the newcomer. "What happened? You never showed up at my place. I was hoping you would bring my pills."

Both Vernon and Terrence swung around on their barstools and glared.

"You sick freak," screamed Vernon. "Get the hell out of here before you kill us all."

He socked the redhead in the face and Terrence followed up with a viscous kick to the groin. The woman doubled up and collapsed on the busy dance floor. The skirt hiked up and the red hairpiece toppled off.

"Damn. It's Malcolm!" Jack muttered half aloud.

Not only was it Malcolm Harding; the medical examiner's exposed limbs were covered with angry sores and the heavy white makeup could barely hide the ugly open lesions on his face. Blood began oozing from his nose, ears and mouth.

Jack, Clarence and Gordon rushed forward to help the medical examiner only to back off when they saw his physical condition. Eldridge and Milton bounded over their bar counters, drawing weapons to keep everyone at bay.

It was unnecessary. The crowd stampeded and ran for the exits, spilling drinks, toppling stools, chairs and tables and leaving Malcolm to struggle under the glare of the lights. He staggered to the dance floor and, blinded by the blood in his eyes, thrashed about trying to grab moving shadows in the blurry light.

"Do it," he screamed hoarsely. "Do it! I'm dead. Do it now! "

Milton moved out of reflex, not even realizing that he had never fired a weapon let alone killed a man. The pistol he had borrowed from Clarence for the evening slipped into his hand and he walked over to Malcolm. His hand was trembling as he jammed the gun muzzle into the medical examiner's mouth and squeezed the trigger. The crack of the shot echoed loudly, announcing to whoever heard it that the party was over.

19

Canal Pond

The one good thing about Cheetah's aborted grand reopening party was Jack's marriage proposal to Ginny. She had snagged herself a husband which was what she wanted, and as for Jack, although he didn't know it yet, that day was the turning point of his life. It was also the day he had his last cigarette.

"This is not a good time for the Bahamas," observed Eldridge when the club had emptied.

"This is not a good time for the world, Eldridge," said Jack.

"This is a bad time for Cheetah's," remarked Ginny, fighting back tears.

Milton looked at Ginny sympathetically.

"Shit happens," he said. "Your customers will be back. Heaven needs a little bit of hell to keep us from going crazy and Cheetah's is the thing that keeps us tight assed, God fearing folks sane."

"Thanks," said Ginny. "But what do I do right now? What do I do for the girls on my payroll? They can't make a living unless I have customers."

"Send them to the Zebra," Eldridge offered. "It's a hard drinking pickup joint at night and my brother Hugo will take care of them and make sure they get paying customers that won't get drunk and hurt them."

"What about your Jamaican guys?" Jack asked.

"The girls are off limits unless our guys want to pay the price" said Eldridge with a knowing grin. He walked over to the front door with Milton.

"Listen," he continued, looking back. "These are tough times and worse are on the way. We need to stick together."

"Count me in too," said Milton. "Things will work out somehow; they always do."

Jack seemed more skeptical.

"I hope Hugo is on the sane page you are."

"I'm glad you brought him up, Jake," Eldridge responded. "Hugo and I need to talk to you about that incident at Satan's Rock. We were out there when you got that red go-fast boat and fired a warning shot. My brother is pissed and wants to talk to you about it. You should drop over at the Zebra."

"Not a problem," agreed Jack. "I'll be over in the next day or so."

Jack was now alone with Ginny in the deserted club and together under dimmed lights and eerie silence they surveyed the damage in the bar and dance hall areas.

There wasn't much to see. Despite the up-turned furniture and broken glass, it was in good shape. They found a table under a slow moving ceiling fan at the edge of the dance floor and sat down.

Jack was beginning to notice even more how well built and pretty Ginny was. She was slightly hippy but that went well with the fullness of her breasts. There was a sturdy, barnyard beauty about her that was both sensual and potentially maternal, and that appealed to him. The slinky black cocktail dress with a slit down the side that she wore at Cheetah's accentuated her shapely legs, meaty thighs and a trim waistline kept under control through constant dieting.

"I missed you while you were away," she whispered. "What kept you away so long? You were going to return in a few weeks, and when you got back, we only had time for a little sex. Do you love me?"

"Yes. Now tell me, what happened in Nassau?"

Ginny threw Jack a sly smile and answered, "I went to see a doctor."

"Are you sick?"

"She laughed.

"No. I'm pregnant."

"You're kidding."

"No, silly; I'm very pregnant. Five months pregnant."

Jack seemed stunned and then took a closer look at her belly. Damn, he said to himself; she was indeed beginning to show.

"Are you sure?"

"Of course you fool. I haven't been with another man since you moved here. I can even tell you exactly where were when it happened. Do I look pregnant? Dad doesn't know yet."

Jack blushed and agreed that he would not have guessed, not yet anyway.

"Okay, okay," he said. "Any idea what it's going to be?"

"It's a boy."

"How do you know?"

"You know, there are pediatric services in the Bahamas, Shelly."

"Come to think of it," Jack said. "There's that two year old little girl who was orphaned at Hole-in-the-Wall. She's being cared for by Lance Cooper's guys but sooner or later she'll need a doctor, for check-ups and shots and that sort of thing."

"We could adopt her," Ginny suggested hopefully.

"We should get married first," Jack said.

Ginny grinned and waved Jack's signet ring in his face.

"I have the ring," she said. "All we need is a time and place, and that can be arranged. Hiram is a regular at Cheetah's, and he owes me."

"What do you mean a regular?"

"He's a back-door customer," she answered. "He's been a customer for years."

"Isn't he too old for that kind of stuff?"

"Why, were you ever too young for sex?"

"No."

"Well, you can never be too old."

"Damn, damn, damn. Nature does find a way, doesn't it?"

Thursday, the first day of June, was the start of Ginny's sixth month. The sun was out; it was breezy and not too hot. Malcolm was dead, Vernon and Terrence stayed out of sight, Jonathan could not be reached and Clarence waited in vain for instructions to make funeral arrangements for Malcolm. It was hopeless. No one could be reached. Since the medical examiner was Catholic and his family was in Nassau and could not be reached, his body was trucked to All Souls for a funeral service and then delivered to Virgil's death ship which was now going out daily.

In the meantime, Jack and Ginny broke the news of their engagement to Kyle who was still under the weather. They went to sleep on Archangel that night and awoke the following morning, Friday, the second of June, to find Kitten gone. End Run was still in its slip.

However, their real concern was for Kyle Malone's health. They had no need to worry. They found him at one of the picnic tables with Reggie under the shade of a palm tree. Kyle was in excellent spirits, relieved that Ginny had at last landed a husband. He was telling Reggie how he looked forward to being a grandfather and to Jack and Ginny merging their businesses and raising a family. Reggie of course was an inveterate gossip and would undoubtedly spread the news to the far corners of the islands.

However, Kyle's joy was short lived when he found out that Dan Schulman and Fred Hawk skipped out on Kitten without paying its fuel bill.

"That ain't the first time they done that," he admitted." But I've got Fred's boat and I siphoned its fuel. I'm short anyway. And I'm placing a mechanic's lien on that tub and I'm going to keep it until I get paid, with interest."

"You can also take the fuel from Louie Gold's plane," said Reggie. "Jake owns the paper on that thing now that Louie is dead and I won't be using it for a while.

You don't mind, do you, Jake?"

Jack agreed.

"Be my guest," he said. "None of us are going anywhere these days."

Somewhat mollified, Kyle turned to the subject of matrimony.

"Now, you say you're getting married? That's good, but are you sure you know what you're in for? A man and wife are stuck to each other like pieces of paper glued together." He seemed proud to have asked and answered the question.

"That's interesting, Kyle, talking about paper" Jack remarked. "Martin Wilson accidentally dropped a piece of paper with a bunch of names on it the other day, including yours and your brother's. It looks like a hit list to me. Why would you be in anyone's cross hairs?"

"I wouldn't worry about it, young feller. It's only Satan who has come for his due. We'll be ok if we stick together."

"I don't follow."

"You will," said Kyle. "You will. But right now, welcome to the family; and you two stay lucky, you hear."

Jack had no idea where he and Ginny were going to live, let alone how, where and when they were going to be married. But at least they were engaged and that was progress.

He excused himself and returned to Archangel where he ran into Otis Foote and Melvin Stoop.

"We heard you wanted to see us?" Melvin said, speaking in a monotone voice.

"Is something wrong, boss?" Otis asked.

"No," Jack said. "I just wanted to make sure that you guys were still working for me. I wanted to speak to you guys about something, but where's Chico?"

"He's at the shop in case something comes up."

Melvin stood impassively and announced gravely, "We found two boats, Jake. Want to see them?"

Mel's face was slightly flushed and there was a nasal quality to his voice. Jack thought he had a cold.

"Is that right? We're going to end up with a fleet if we don't watch out. What, when and where?"

"It's an old freighter and a lifeboat. We left the freighter alone and took the other to Canal Pond. You were away when we found them. I have my motor scooter. We can go now and see the lifeboat if you want."

"What was on it?"

"Dead bugs, rats and heroin, the same what was on the Angelina."

"What happened to the heroin?

"We sold it to Hugo."

Jack began cursing so loud that he scared Melvin.

"Did I do something wrong, boss?"

There was such a naive sincerity in Mel's voice that made up for his slow mind and flawed sense of judgment that it was impossible to be angry at him. Jack told Otis and Melvin to get over to the boatyard and help Chico.

"Where are you going, boss?" Otis asked.

"I'm going to pay Hugo a visit."

Archangel's dinghy happened to be in the water behind the cat. Jack jumped into it and powered across to Agnes Town's public dock where he thought Clarence might be hanging around with his jeep. He found the jeep but not Clarence. It was Milton Cooper who was at the wheel. He had borrowed the jeep from Clarence to visit homes and businesses in town whose property values and tax rates needed to be re-assessed.

"I need a ride to the Zebra," said Jack.

Milton invited him to hop in and asked, "What are we doing?"

"Melvin sold Hugo some tainted heroin. We need to get it back."

The tax assessor shook his head.

"This seems so pointless, all this work and now this," he said. "I did assessments at Hole-in-the-Wall and most of the homeowners either died or left and the place is gone. And now this, and then I still need to get to Hope Town and Marsh Harbor. I should quit before I get killed."

"Quit and do what?" Jack asked. Then he added. "Archangel is ready when you are. We can catch the ebb tide at dawn tomorrow if you can get up early enough."

"Dawn is good," Milton said. "I haven't slept well since I shot Malcolm anyway. On top of everything, I'm a killer."

"You're no killer, Milt. You did what had to be done and it was the right thing to do. There comes a time when each of us must take a turn at bat."

"I can see that, Jake, but why now, and why us?"

"It's because we're here, Milton. There's no one else here but us. And now we need to see Hugo."

Hugo was at one end of the bar when they arrived, speaking to one of his men, and about a dozen Jamaicans were sitting at tables in front of the dance floor and stage. The place fell silent when Jack walked in with Milton. Leaving him at the door, he wedged himself between Hugo and his companion. Eldridge was behind the bar.

"I want to talk to you, Jake," Hugo said gruffly.

"Same here," Jack replied quietly.

"Your man sold me bad stuff," Hugo began. "My guys are getting sick and a few have died."

The man behind Jack went for a gun that was hidden inside his shirt.

Jack raised his hands high, saying, "I'm unarmed."

Milton still had the pistol he had borrowed for the party at Cheetah's. He drew it and took aim.

"But I have a gun," he said. "Be stupid and I'll be at your funeral, young man."

The man wavered. Finally, he backed off and moved over to one of the tables. "I think we should put away the hardware and talk," said Eldridge from behind the bar.

But one of Hugo's men at one of the tables had different ideas. He pulled a knife but a shot from the batwing doors nicked his elbow. The man dropped the knife and grabbed at his wounded arm. Melvin Stoop stepped inside holding a carbine.

"Eldridge is right," Jack said. "We should talk."

And then he turned his attention to Hugo.

"We don't need more trouble," he explained. And I'm sorry about that bad stuff, Cap. But we're not here to pick a fight. What can we do to make things right?"

"You tell me, man."

"First, you tell me what else is bothering you, Cap."

"That red go-fast boat at Satan's Rock was a plant and you were in on it, Jake."

"I don't follow," said Jack.

"Then, you're real stupid, boy," went on Hugo. "We found out that Terrence and Manny worked a deal with Graves to steal our business. They picked up the racer in Nassau, stuffed two bodies and some heroin in it and towed it to Satan's Rock, but we only found out about it after you guys got there when we caught a BASRA chase boat that was following the operation and they spilled the beans when we tickled them a bit." He laughed hoarsely. "That's when we learned that you guys were supposed to blow us out of the water. With us gone, Graves and his gang would take over our routes."

"It wasn't my doing," Jack protested. "I thought it was a salvage bounty."

"You're lying," said Hugo.

"No way," replied Jack softly. "And if it makes you feel better, Graves grabbed the red boat for his son. The kid took the thing out, and got sick and died."

"What about the Angelina in the Sargasso? It's loaded with heroin."

"How would you know?"

"I skippered that tub five years ago when you got busted and I saw what was in it. It was part of a three ship convoy that sailed from Beirut filled with heroin. I was there and helped load the stuff myself."

"How do you mean?" Jack asked.

"Louie Gold bought it at salvage with Dan Schulman and Fred Hawk and leased it to the Bahamian government who sublet it to the U.S. Navy through Bob Byrne to ship bodies of soldiers killed in the Middle East to the States for burial. Louie wanted you as skipper but Bob Byrne had you framed on a drug and manslaughter rap. Hell, man, you must have figured it out by now."

"Figure what out," Jack retorted. "It was a fight gone bad."

"Fight, my ass," Hugo chortled. "The fight was the icing on the cake. The drug rap would have been enough to put you away for years. Louie pulled some strings and made deals all over the place to keep you out of prison. That guy really must have liked you. Anyway, I got the gig instead of you."

Jack's mouth dropped.

"But why would Byrne go to all that trouble?"

Hugo stared at him in disbelief.

"Shit man, you're dumb. Byrne hated you for marrying Doreen; you showed him up. And he hated Louie who disowned him. So, when Doreen was making it with your buddy Fred, he decided to screw you good. He never expected you to bounce back. But it was good for me. Byrne sent word to Dale Malone who asked me if I wanted a short clean job that paid cash, and when I said ok he sent me to Malcolm Harding who hired me and my guys to sail the Angelina to Lebanon. My brother and I got a hundred thousand grand each and the crew got twenty five thousand grand up front."

Jack whistled.

"That was chicken shit," countered Hugo, "The heroin was worth millions. Two short tons were loaded on the Angelina; another two tons went on the Comfort and a ton went on the third ship. The Angelina's cargo was to be off-loaded at Hermit Cay before taking the bodies the rest of the way to Florida."

"Do you know how much money we're talking about?" Eldridge interrupted on behalf of his brother. Jack shook his head.

"I'll spell it out and you do the math," said Eldridge. "Refined cocaine or heroin goes on the street for about a thousand dollars an ounce or sixteen thousand dollars a pound or more in their many boutique variations. We usually wholesale the stuff out for twelve grand per kilo or about five grand per pound. At those prices, that would have come out to ten million dollars per short ton per ship or fifty million dollars for the five tons of heroin in the three ships."

"You and Hugo should have become millionaires many times over," said Jack.

Hugo sighed.

"You'd think," he moaned. "We were at the eastern edge of the Sargasso when the Angelina lost power, forcing us to ditch it. We planned to return but the ship drifted west and we never found it until this year."

"So, who made out on this junket?" Jack asked.

Eldridge answered with a shrug of his shoulders,

"Who knows; we made out because we got paid up front and we've been taking heroin off the Comfort, and I always figured that Louie lifted the heroin from the third ship. I spoke to Dale but he told us to forget the whole thing. If he and Byrne were planning to deal drugs, it never happened."

"That's right," growled Hugo. "We do the trafficking in these parts, and we don't need competition. And now that the Angelina has been found, we want in. Where is it?"

The drug crazed Jamaican who was nursing his flesh wound yelled to the others in the room.

"Let's take these bastards. They can't kill us all!"

On cue, a dozen guns and knives flashed and Mel began to edge forward.

Eldridge produced a long barreled rifle, Melvin and Milton leveled their weapons and they all fired into the ceiling simultaneously.

"Gentlemen," said Eldridge. "Let's discuss this in a civilized manner."

Jack grinned broadly.

"Sounds good to me," he said.

He waved his gun in the air and then placed it on the bar counter.

"Mel, Milt," he said. "Put your guns away. They can kill you if we have some sort of misunderstanding."

"Are you sure, boss?"

"Positive."

They put away their weapons and waited.

With an uneasy truce being maintained by Eldridge, Jack began, "I'm trying to clear things up in my mind. "What happened when you abandoned the Angelina?"

"I had a crew of six and my brother. I left four and took off with two guys and my brother. We went back later but never found the ship. That was five years ago. The crew left on board must have gone for the lifeboats when we never returned."

Hugo shook his head from side to side and took a deep breath.

"Those poor bastards never made it. One lifeboat ended up between Bitter End and Hermit's Cay with two of my crew. That's the one that found by Tully's kid and one of my men. I don't know what happened to the other.

"By then the guys on the boat were long dead," Hugo was saying. "Tully's kid and my guy must have died on the way back to Bitter End. That's when Otis and me found them. I got scared and ran off but Otis called Clarence. We came back later and burned the bodies."

Hugo looked down at his big hands, broke down and began sobbing.

"This is bad, Jake. I don't know what's going down."

"It's not that bad, buddy," said Jack, trying to sooth his nerves. "We'll figure it out. Tell me about the rest of the convoy."

"The second vessel in our group was a hospital ship, the S.S. Comfort. It too was supposed to head for the States but it must have gone off course and was marooned at Satan's Rock. Everyone aboard was dead when we found it. We looted it for the heroin."

Jack dreaded his response to the next question.

"What about the third ship in the convoy?

Hugo looked up.

"Oh, that was a pocket destroyer escort ship, the HMS Leeds. I don't know what happened to it."

Jack guessed that the Leeds was the vessel newscasts reported as a terrorist ship blown up off the coast of Florida by the Coast Guard. Its crew had probably died, leaving it to drift aimlessly westward over the years.

"Let me bring you up to date, Hugo," said Jack. "Lance sank the Angelina, and I'm sure the Comfort will also be sunk. Now, tell me about the Nassau Clipper."

"I know nothing about it. Dale Malone chartered that freighter to bring sugarcane to his factory but all it did was to take heroin off the Comfort."

Jack took a deep breath.

"Well Hugo, that leaves the stash from the life boat that Mel found. It's bad and we need it back."

The man who had stood behind Jack spoke up for the first time.

"We sold some of it and used some of it," he stated.

"We'll take what's left but we'll pay for the whole thing," Jack said.

"What's wrong with it?" Hugo asked.

Jack shrugged his shoulders.

"Don't know, Cap. It's a killer; that's all I can say."

Hugo frowned suspiciously.

"And you're paying us for the entire lot? What's the catch?"

"I need the names of the people to whom you sold the heroin, the names of your buddies who used it, and I need you to return what's left. Then I need your guys to reinforce Lance's security details around here. He doesn't have enough men to do the job."

"We're being deputized? How are you going to fix that with Clarence?"

The Jamaicans in the bar burst out in laughter and Jack laughed with them.

"Oh, I'll fix it with him. You wait and see."

"The living we've made wasn't always very legal. What about the law?"

"I'll fix that too," replied Jack.

"Jack can fix anything," Mel exclaimed happily, overjoyed that the confrontation had been diffused.

There was a noise outside the bar and all eyes turned to the door. Clarence was at the door with Reggie Mayhew and Clifford Mills.

"Melvin called us for backup. Is everything under control?" Clarence inquired.

"It was a misunderstanding," said Jack. "Everything's cool; right, Hugo?"

"Yeah," Hugo agreed. "Everything's cool."

The encounter ended with Mel suddenly breaking into an uncontrollable sneezing and coughing fit. His legs gave way and he had to be helped out of the Zebra Club. Jack and Clarence drove him quickly back to the boatyard in Agnes Town where he crawled into his cot and covered himself with an old tarp. His coughing started up again.

"I'm sorry for the trouble I made, Jake" he said. "I'm sorry. It will never happen again."

"You did right and we need you," responded Jack. "You get better, you hear."

20

Hope Town

Jack was supposed to have set sail for Hope Town on Friday, the second of June but he delayed his departure to marry Ginny that weekend. That gave Milton, a compulsive bean counter by his own admission, to make a mental tally of Jack's newly acquired assets now that Tom, Louie and the Honoree family were gone. He found out from Father Francois Honoree to whom Emile had earlier mailed his last will and testament that essentially left everything to Jack in the event the priest died. The priest immediately surrendered his claim to the Honoree estate in deference to Jack who he thought was better qualified than he was in managing business matters. That meant that Jack now had a controlling interest in the Boynton Beach boatyard, or at least in what was left of i.

Milton rushed to Pirates' Cove to give Jack the news. He was even more elated when told by Jack that he was to be in the wedding party. That afternoon, Jack and Ginny were married by Hiram Cooper at the Church of Christ rectory with Milton, Kyle, Dale, Clarence, Eldridge and Hugo as guests and witnesses. At the ceremony and hanging on tight to Lance's hand was Alexandra Cole. The BDF commander had arranged with his father to have the infant adopted by Jack and Ginny. Alexandra was in a party dress and a bit bewildered but she bravely kept from crying; and when the ceremony was over, Hiram turned the toddler over to Ginny who pacified her with cookies she had baked earlier.

Jack and Ginny, now Mr. and Mrs. Jack and Ginger Sloane, also had their first postnuptial fight. Jack wanted to stay on his catamaran but Ginny argued that her trailer had more space. They compromised in favor of a vacant cottage that was furnished and equipped with window air conditioners. It had a small living room, two bedrooms, a bathroom and a stand-alone kitchen, and both Jack and Ginny agreed it would do as a starter home. That same evening, Ginny prepared her first dinner in her new home for Jack, Kyle and Alexandra. They were about to dine when Clarence called to say that Melvin Stoop had passed away.

The grim business of dying was hitting home and dovetailing with public health concerns. Right after the wedding, Lance and Jonathan prevailed on the governing council to require the dead to be buried immediately in the waters between Bitter End and Hermit Cay and set up a budget for families unable to afford the funeral expenses. Money was also allocated for body bags. It was a nice gesture but Hugo donated his entire inventory and Virgil offered his burial ship for nothing, stating that Avalon would go out on demand every day for the Border and Abaco islands so long as fuel was available.

Later that night, Milton and Chico joined Virgil and Clovis on Avalon with the bodies of Melvin Stoop and others who had died in the past couple of days. They powered in silence to a point where they were joined by Lance, Hiram, Francois Honoree and Dennis in a BDF launch. After a short prayer, the black bags were gently eased overboard where they sank quietly into the deep. On a sandy bluff at Bitter End, the Castaways, with Jack on his trumpet, played Amazing Grace, its haunting tune reaching across the dark still waters.

Marriage in a way was for Jack an escape from the quickening pace of life and death in the Borders. The duties of his newly found fatherhood kept him busy the better part of Saturday morning, June the third. Diapers needed to be changed and washed and Alexandra had to be played with. Well wishers showed up with baby gifts and toys and Hugo, Eldridge and Clarence arrived with paint and wallpaper for Alexandra's room and went to work making the place cozy and cuddly.

But things were happening elsewhere in the world. Reggie dropped over with a doll for Alexandra and informed Jack the latest developments. The South African airline disaster had triggered a lethal epidemic that brought South Africa to its knees, and its domino effect had paralyzed the entire African continent. Most of the world was under martial law with shoot-to-kill curfews, and sports stadiums, public parks and concert arenas in cities were turned into hospitals to which the sick were taken in trucks, buses and trains. Once there, they received injections of whatever antidote was on hand. But more often than not, nothing was available and people who were ill often died.

The problem was not the efficacy of the vaccine or of any of the other standard antibiotic treatments used for different strains of the epidemic. The issue was that the world was caught short with not enough to go around and facilities for the sick and dying were under-staffed. Widespread breakdowns in handling the dead also existed. Individual burials were out of the question and open dump trucks prowled city streets, going house-to-house picking up bodies and carting them to collection points for incineration at sanitation department crematoriums. Since there was no longer any way to claim the ashes of loved ones, they invariably ended up in land fills.

Sunday, the fourth of June, was gray and wet, and church attendance was down. Perhaps this was a stay-at-home day in the hope that bad news would not breach the walls of domestic tranquility. If so, it was an exercise in futility because Plague struck several families in Agnes Town and more people died. Dennis had his hands full, leaving Jack to fight the temptation of raiding the vaccine stocks that he had sworn to keep under lock and key.

Dennis came over that evening with Clarence and Jonathan and their wives. The young physician made up a medical kit and stethoscope that Alexandra used on herself and on everyone else in the room. Clarence gave her a red pull cart and Jonathan brought her a small wooden rocking horse. It was a nice evening and for a while festering disagreements and the issues of the day were set aside.

Hiram came later with Lance and Milton, bringing with them a bottle of cognac and box of cigars. He was in an evangelical mood that evening and when asked by Ginny whether Plague was Satan's work, he replied, "No; Satan does God's work and Plague is his knife that cuts the damned from the blessed. But you and Jake, my dear, have every opportunity now to be saved."

The next morning, Monday, June the fifth, was dry and cool and Archangel eased away from Pirates' Cove with Jack, Chico and Milton. Ginny stood at the dock and blew him a kiss as he sailed away. The catamaran raced through the cut and once in open water, it raised its sails and headed due west for the Abaco islands.

"I bet real estate tax revenues are getting mighty slim these days," said Jack in an effort to make small talk and break the monotony of the trip.

"It's bad, Jake," Milton replied. "People stop paying in anticipation of dying."

"How much value do you figure finding in Hope Town?"

The tax assessor made a face.

"It's not that bad," said Milton. "Marsh Harbor is better because it's bigger."

Milton squinted at the late afternoon sun.

"I'd leave this place if I could," he said suddenly. "What about you?"

"It's no option anymore. What else is bothering you?"

"It's a feeling," answered Milton. The entire family came down with a case of sniffles this morning as I was leaving and I'm scared of what may happen to them.

I'm hoping not to get a call on your VHF. You're lucky in a way. You can leave anytime for Florida, but I'm stuck here."

"Oh, I don't think I'm going to leave anytime soon now that I have a family. I don't even know if I have a business left in Florida. Besides, Ginny won't leave without Kyle and he's not sold on going anywhere. But tell me, Milt, why are you thinking of leaving? You're basically a decent guy with a steady income and a nice family. If your dad is right, you'll be among those who are saved. To me, it means you probably won't get sick."

Milton scoffed at Jack's suggestion.

"Dad means well," he said, "and he's a true believer. But he's way off base. I did a lot of reading about different people, different cultures, different religions, and I believe that God is a metaphysical fiction, a figment of our imagination."

"Are you saying that God is created in our image?"

"I'm going further. What I'm saying that God is created in the image of Man, a male, heterosexual male."

"How do you figure that?" Jack asked.

"It's simple," answered Milton. "We don't worship God as a woman. Nor is God a Black, Indian or Asian man. God is a White man; he has a long white beard and wears a white robe. I'll also bet that God is an Englishman who speaks English."

Jack could not dispute that image because it was his as well.

"What else do you have under your thinking cap, Milt?"

Milton laughed and stared at Jack with a strange intensity.

"Say it, Jake. You think I'm crazy."

"No, no," Jack protested. "You're not crazy; you're just weird."

"My ideas may be strange, but I'm not weird, If God is Man's creation, so is heaven and hell. There is only one place and it is ruled by God. When one dies, the soul presents itself to God who then decides upon discussion with the soul where it is to go and it is supposed to do when it gets there. It's kind of a game of 'let's make a deal.' For example, a man kills someone and subsequently dies. His soul goes before God and says that his only sin was to commit murder once when he was alive. What's the worst that can happen? God will probably order him to take an anger management course before being mainstreamed in heaven, if indeed there is one.

Jack smiled.

"Are you questioning the existence of heaven?"

Milton shook his head.

"I can't answer that. Louie Gold showed me a prayer book once, and I can still recite some of the lines. Birth is a beginning and life is a journey, and death is a destination, an undiscovered territory, a land without report. That's what I believe, Jake. We don't know what happens after death, if anything happens at all."

"Well, I have a secret and it's going to make me rich. That will be my passport out of here with my family."

"What's that?"

"I wrote the beginning of a poem and it's going to be in my book. Do you want to hear it?"

"Why not," Jack replied. "Fire away."

"It goes like this, Jake. Plagues and famines come and go, and nuclear war will set the world aglow. But I'll be yours through thick and thin, I, your conscience from within."

"That's a great start," commented Jack. "Now what's the book about?"

"I can't tell you."

"What about a hint?"

"Well, you know those warm water spouts near North Border?"

"You mean the geysers?"

"Right; I went fishing out there and I saw them again. I'm doing a book about a volcano that rises from the sea and destroys these islands. It's going to be a best seller and my exit visa."

"Sounds cool, Milton. Do you have an alternative story line in the event that one doesn't fly?"

"I do," Milton replied. "It's about a cruise ship that leaves here with passengers afflicted with a fatal illness. When it returns to its home port, an epidemic is set off that infects the entire world. Is that a better plot, Jake? Maybe I can combine the two story lines."

Jack almost lost control of the helm.

Let's talk about that last story line," he said. "It sounds good.

"Jake?"

"Yes?"

"I've been thinking. Someone needs to keep this tax assessment business going if something happens to me. I spoke to Charleen a few weeks ago and she said she'll help me if I ever got sick or something like that. Do you think it's a good idea?"

"It is a good idea, Milton. But you're not dead yet."

"I don't know," said the tax assessor. "I was only thinking."

Archangel arrived at Hope Town's public dock inside Elbow Cay's lagoon under the shadow of the island's s red striped lighthouse before noon. Milton thanked Jack and went off, briefcase in hand, to find a room at a local inn before going out to assess the private homes and businesses on the cay.

Elbow Cay was small and hilly, and Hope Town was a tiny village of pink and white homes with green shutters and flowering gardens spread around the lagoon inside the cay. The air was breezy and puffy clouds driven by trade winds moved briskly over the island. Chico was looking up at the sky when he finished securing the lines and drew Jack's attention.

"Nice," he said after trying to see whatever it was that Chico was staring at. "Am I missing something?"

"That's it," Chico replied. "Listen. What do you hear?"

Jack strained his ears.

"Nothing."

"And what do you see?"

"Sky. Clouds. Nothing else."

"Si. No birds. Birds always fly and make much noise. I no see the birds."

Chico stopped to slap a fly that had landed on his bare arm.

"Do you think a storm is brewing?"

"No se, boss. No se."

Jack was temporarily at a loss for words.

"Let's settle in," he said at last. "We'll pick the doctor up in the morning."

"Are we going home tomorrow?"

"No. We're stopping in Marsh Harbor. But while we're here, call Tully and ask him if he's free for lunch Wednesday or Thursday." As an after thought he added. "Check the weather channel and see if your hunch is correct."

Early the next morning, Tuesday, the sixth of June, Jack went to Henry's Alden's home, leaving Chico on the boat with a bad cold. Henry's home was near the docks and faced the light house across the lagoon. Finding the doctor's front door open, he entered and found him filling his pipe in the kitchen.

"Am I glad to see you," he exclaimed. He stopped, put his unlit pipe on the kitchen table and gave Jack a vigorous hand shake.

Noticing that Jack was eying the clock on the wall, he asked, "Are we in a rush?"

"We are," replied Jack. "But that's not why I'm staring. Your clock stopped." "The clock is fine," said Henry. "It stopped five years ago when my brother died and I never rewound it. Now, what's our schedule?"

"I'm stopping in Marsh Harbor," Jack replied. "And you're needed back in the Borders."

Henry's smile evaporated.

"May I ask why?"

"People are falling sick and dying in droves, and the situation may be similar in Marsh Harbor," said Jack.

"It's probably a good idea," said Henry. "I want to see my wife and check on my hotel. I might need a few days. How are things at your end?"

"Not good," replied Jack, getting right to the point. "Listen, Henry, I'm no doctor but something god awful is killing us. Dennis calls it Red Death."

"I'm worried too, Jake." Henry relit his pipe and began puffing away. "Dennis has it right, Jake. We are seeing an outbreak of Plague. Let me elaborate. There are three types of Plague, pneumonic and bubonic Plague. The first is viral; the second is bacterial. Both are deadly. Sometimes, the two strains combine with the Ebola virus and strike with horrific lethal impact. That's the third type and people call it the Red Death.

"The body is literally eaten alive by the germs and the victim dies of external and internal hemorrhaging from sores created by the devouring invaders. I believe such an epidemic hit Europe in the middle ages and killed off half of its population."

"That's fierce, Henry. Is there any treatment?"

Henry blew smoke into the air.

"The good news is that the infection can be stopped with proper medication if it's caught early enough. The bad news is that by the time the real symptoms show up, it's usually too late. The disease starts with a cold or flu, a headache or a cough or even a mild case of measles. They can last a few hours or a week before the main disease strikes. Then come chills, fever, vomiting, diarrhea and tell-tale hacking tubercular bloody cough. The lymph nodes swell and form buboes that burst and tear open the flesh as the blood vessels rupture. In the last stage, blood dries under the skin and turns it black. That's how Bubonic Plague earned its nickname, Black Death or Black Plague. It turns into the Red Death when the Ebola virus joins the invasion and massive bleeding boils and lesions form from flesh inside and outside the body being quickly eaten away. It's a horribly painful way to die.

"That's what we're facing, Jake. It's the Red Death. It starts the same way, with a common cold. But everything happens internally, inside the body. The internal organs are attacked. Boils form inside, causing massive hemorrhaging when they break and the body bleeds from the inside in sheer agony. On the outside we see the terrible blisters and sores, the shakes, uncontrollable contortions, high fever and bleeding from the mouth, nose, ears and eyes. It's hard to diagnose until it's too late, and like the rest, it's contagious and fatal. Plague germs ride piggyback on bacteria carried by fleas that travel on the skin of any rodent like animal. When rats get close to humans or other animals, the fleas and germs leapfrog to humans and other animals and go on a killing spree. It's that simple. Proper public hygiene can control the plague; if we don't have that, we need to get everyone immunized."

21

Marsh Harbor

Archangel was originally scheduled to leave Hope Town for Marsh Harbor the next day. In fact, it did not leave until Thursday, the eighth of June. Henry was too busy with patients complaining of all sorts of ailments from upset stomachs, colds to allergies. It was just as well. Jack wanted to relax and think over his new life with Ginny and wanted to fix a few odds and ends on his boat. Luckily, the thousand or so residents who called Hope Town home seemed remarkably happy and healthy and showed no signs of Plague. It also turned out that the old doctor had several protracted radio conversations with his wife Cynthia who was at his hotel in Marsh Harbor. There had been rumors that she wanted a divorce and in fact she had been pushing for a separation. He managed to convince her to hold off until they met and tried to reconcile their differences. With that issue under control, he was now ready to leave.

The old physician arrived at the dock with two duffels at the appointed departure hour and was helped on board Archangel by Jack. He set his bag down on deck and wiped off his spectacles.

"How is Cynthia?" Jack asked who was already privy to his domestic problems.

"Oh, she never changes. I bet you wonder how an old man like me ended up with a young wife."

"Tell me your secret," Jack grinned.

"Marriage was her idea. She was married before to Dan Schulman, you know. It was a nasty divorce and she returned to the Bahamas to start a new life. We met and I let her manage the Grand Bay. That's what my first wife did until she died. I loved my first wife, but this is a marriage of convenience. I'm much too old for kids, as you can see."

"About this plague," Jack asked. "You said there was a treatment?"

"Yes. It's a special cocktail of conventional antibiotics that can be delivered with a shot or orally. It's no big secret and it's available, but not in great quantities since Plague hasn't been a problem for a long time. I got together with Cyrus in Florida a few months ago and made up a batch of vaccine that he and my brother developed more than five years ago when they suspected that a plague epidemic might occur."

"How come they suspected that might happen?"

Henry avoided Jack's eyes.

"I never asked Cyrus, and my brother worked in the States those days."

"But you and Cyrus must have had a more recent hunch if you helped him."

"It was a feeling," said the physician. "A cruise ship pulled into South Bay for a two-day stay in April and let its passengers ashore. Some of them fell ill before the end of the first day and one of them died on the beach in front of the Ocean View hotel. I took one look at the body and knew right away it was the Red Death.

"I told Jonathan and we met with the ship's captain. I urged them to report the incident and quarantine the ship. The skipper called Dan who was a big shot at the cruise ship company and he decided to send it on to the States where he said better medical facilities were available. It was a bad idea," continued Henry. "I knew that wherever passengers left the ship, death would follow. I even called Bob Byrne who said he would take care of the matter, but I guess he never did."

"Is that when you and Cyrus decided to make up your own vaccine?"

Henry nodded.

"We had no choice. We made enough for the patients in his practice and another batch for my patients. We also made an extra thousand cocktails that was supposed to have been taken to the Borders by Lance when he came to see Cyrus. I don't know if that happened."

"It did," said Jack. "Lance gave me the package and I gave it to Hiram who gave it to Dennis. It's in a safe place, I guarantee it."

"That's good," smiled Henry. "I have the formula and can make more, but I don't have the ingredients. How many people do we have in the Borders these days?"

"We had thirteen thousand," Jack answered. "What about here?"

Henry Alden shrugged.

"We have twenty thousand people in Marsh Harbor, Treasure Cay, Dundee and Hole-in-the-Wall, and maybe another five thousand in the outlying cays."

"You can forget about Hole-in-the-Wall," said Jack. "That place is gone."

Henry wiped his glasses.

"That's too bad. But we still have the rest of the country. The population of the entire Bahamas stands at around three hundred thousand. We can make enough stuff to cover everyone if we can get the ingredients. We're not primitive, you know."

"Who makes all that stuff?"

"South Florida Pharmaceuticals," replied Henry. "I spoke with Dan but he wants too much."

"How much is he asking?"

"I don't care. I wouldn't give him a dime. He's the one behind all this misery. He is the one who helped bankroll that shipment of tainted heroin to the islands from the Middle East five years ago and he's the one who approved the departure of that damn cruise ship from South Border."

Jack suddenly recalled that he too had advised Jonathan to allow the ship to sail on to the States.

"That's one hell of an accusation," he said. "But that was then and this is now. You'll need to prove those charges in a court of law, Henry."

"We have no time for legal games," said the doctor. "You don't fight Plague in the courts. You fight it hard and fast in the streets with proper hygiene. That's how we do it here in Hopetown. Our water is heavily treated; we incinerate waste and garbage daily and we exterminate rats and bugs vigorously. But if people want to live with blinders, then we need the plague vaccine. If we don't get enough stock soon, most of us will die. Now, let's get out of here."

Archangel was barely a half hour out of Hope Town when he suddenly blurted out, "I'm afraid Dan is going to try to shut me up," said Henry.

"What makes you say that?" asked Milton who was listening.

"I know too much."

Jack felt it was time to tell Henry about Martin Wilson's list.

"You're part of an endangered species, Henry, if this is a hit list and this Wilson guy is a hired gun, all of you must have done something real interesting to deserve that distinction whether or not Schulman is involved."

"You don't know half of it," said Henry. "But I don't want to die over anything I may or may not have done."

He pointed to one of the two duffels on deck.

"Make sure Cynthia is safe and that if something does happen to me, it happens fast. That bag will save your life and those of the ones you love."

Jack understood. To save himself and his family, he was now Henry's watchdog. He took the duffel and secured it below.

The sail to the Grand Bay hotel docks in the bight of Marsh Harbor took less than an hour downwind, but the sky, which had been bright and blue was now overcast and rain began falling. They all donned slickers and huddled in the wheelhouse as Archangel entered the bight of Marsh Harbor.

Jack pointed a finger at the sky.

"See, Chico?" Rain; now we know why the birds flew away."

Chico mumbled something under his breath and was bringing the catamaran to a bulkhead slip when someone on land jumped out of a clump of bushes and began running along the embankment firing an automatic weapon.

A bullet whizzed through Henry's slickers and he ducked. Chico turned the cat about and threw Milton a revolver. He squeezed off a round at the same time that two more shots came from another point on shore.

The shooter with the automatic weapon staggered and spun around to return fire but he was too late. Milton's round found its mark as did the others and he fell into the water.

Archangel made a full circle and brought itself parallel to a pedestrian path on the embankment that connected a coffee shop and fuel pump to a path leading to the Grand Bay's sprawling back porch. Far to the right, the hotel with its striped green and white window and porch awnings came into view, and a sign on a piling announced, "Welcome to Marsh Harbor."

The cat was moving at a slow crawl when more small arms fire crackled in the air. Two men jumped out of the brush only to fall to the ground. Jack glared down at Henry who sat quietly on the deck, examining the hole in his slicker. Milton was shaken but otherwise unscathed, aware only that he had scored a hit.

"Were you expecting company, doctor?"

He took the wheel from Chico and guided the vessel the last hundred yards to a vacant bulkhead space. By the time the vessel came to a stop a wailing siren and screeching tires announced the arrival of police. Two jeeps pulled up in the parking area behind the coffee shop and several uniformed officers jumped out with their weapons drawn, trying to figure out what was happening. In the meantime, the rain slowed to a drizzle and Gordon Tully and Cynthia Alden appeared on the dock.

The police inspector had a smoking revolver in one hand and a golf umbrella in the other which he held over Cynthia's head. Holstering the weapon, he let Cynthia hold the umbrella so that he could help secure the catamaran.

Henry was stoic about the entire affair.

"At least, the rain stopped," he said.

Leaving Chico on board, Jack followed Milton and Henry off Archangel. Henry immediately sought out his wife and kissed her on the cheek while Gordon took Milton aside and whispered something into his ear. Whatever it was he said was enough for Milton to sit down on a nearby bench and start crying.

Gordon motioned to a couple of officers who came over to stay with Milton as he went to greet Jack who asked Cynthia if she had a room at the hotel.

"How many rooms do you want?" asked Cynthia sarcastically. "The tourists are gone for the season. You can have the entire hotel for yourself."

Jack pointed to Milton, still crying on the bench.

"What's the trouble with him?"

"I had to tell him that Lance called to say that his entire family died of Plague earlier today. Hiram ordered their cremation and their remains will be taken out on Avalon when it returns."

"Damn. Where's Avalon now?"

"It's on funeral duty here. We have the same problems you have. Who fired the shot from Archangel?"

"Milton did," replied Jack. "I didn't know he was a good shot."

"He's a fighter, Jake," replied Gordon. He doesn't want trouble, but he'll fight it when it comes."

Milton raised his head and asked, tears rolling down his eyes, "Does the police need a statement from me?"

Gordon gave the tax assessor a pat on the back.

"We'll get you settled first at the hotel, Milt."

Milton mumbled his thanks and took off stoop shoulders with the two officers while Jack gave Cynthia a friendly kiss on the cheek.

"Anyway, it's great to see you and I hope you don't mind my bringing back your husband alive and well."

Henry's wife laughed.

"I wouldn't expect you to deliver him any other way."

Henry winked at Jack and kissed his wife again.

"Don't hit me; I'm here under a flag of truce."

"I think we can reach an understanding," said Cynthia.

They exchanged more hugs and kisses, and Gordon, satisfied that they were at least not feuding, suggested that they wait with the bags at the coffee shop.

"Jake and I need to take care of some business," he explained.

Cynthia nodded and led her still somewhat dazed husband away.

"I received your message, Jake" said Gordon once Cynthia and Henry were gone. "But I didn't exactly know when you were arriving. But here I am."

"Well, thanks anyway for my welcoming reception."

"It's was the least I could do to celebrate your marriage," said Gordon. "Clarence called and told me about it. How do you like married life?"

"It's great, but I've had prior experience so I'm better at dealing with things."

"I bet, but say, have you picked up enemies since the last time we met?"

Jack shook his head and said, "I'm telling you. That shot was for Henry."

"Who is after him?"

"He keeps raving about Dan having it in for him," answered Jack. He stopped talking when a police officer came up.

"We have three bodies, sir, two on land and one we're fishing out of the water. What happened?"

"They popped out of nowhere," Gordon explained, and he ordered him to have men cordon off the area. "Shall we have a look at our sharpshooters?"

The police placed the three dead men shoulder to shoulder on the ground.

Jack did a double take when he saw the bodies.

"That's Manny Sylvester," said Gordon. "I know the other guy too. It's Martin Wilson, Jane Baron's fiancé. And the third shooter is Larry Fisher. He heads up the marine police up in Palm Beach County around your way, Jake. But that's not all."

"I don't follow," said Jack.

"When Fisher went through customs with Dan and Fred, Clarence asked Lance to do a background check on him since he has good internet access on his cutter. It seems that our three dead friends are old buddies and worked on and off with your buddy Bob Byrne and were CIA contractors. They also belong to an outfit calling itself Sidewinder. Does that ring a bell?"

"Bob Byrne tried to recruit me for that group," replied Jack.

"So, what do we have, Jake?"

"I call that a conspiracy."

Gordon's smile faded.

"I'll buy that, but it's a conspiracy to do what?"

"It's about that hit list I picked up that Martin Wilson dropped. Remember?"

Jack proceeded to give Gordon a rendition Hugo's and Henry's stories.

"I can buy into Hugo's and Henry's stories. Here's my take. The names on that list were involved in a drug deal that went bad and has to do with the Angelina."

"Are you saying these three dead dudes here were hired to kill a whole bunch of people to keep a drug deal quiet?" Gordon asked.

"Yes, but it is part of a larger scheme," answered Jack. "Whoever put together the deal found out that the heroin was infected with Plague and kept it quiet. It is ass saving time now that the epidemic has gone global. That person put together the hit list and hired our three guys to get rid of everyone who might have had a hand one way or another with the outbreak."

Jack's reasoning had Gordon partially convinced but he tried once more to poke a hole in his conspiracy theory, asking, "How can a single incident trigger a world wide epidemic?"

Jack kicked some stones on the ground.

"Isn't that how AIDS started? I read somewhere that one infected immigrant to the States from Haiti started the whole epidemic. But here I say there were several totally unrelated triggering mechanisms. Look, it's like three dudes at the edge of a lake tossing stones, trying to have them skim across the water. The first throws a stone, and it hits the top of a small rock in the water before skimming over the water. But the rock is the head of a sleeping alligator that is roused but doesn't stir. The second throws a rock and the same thing happens again. Now, the critter is up. The third throws a rock and the 'gator is pissed and takes off after them.

"It sounds good, Jake," Gordon said. "The only two things missing to back your theory are suspects and evidence."

Jack smiled.

"I'm working on that. In the meantime, how do you like your job in Abaco?"

"I hate it," said Gordon. "I don't know anyone."

"What about Cynthia? I thought you were tapping her behind Henry's back."

"Not on your life, Jake. I wouldn't touch her with a tent pole. She's been fooling around with too many guys, including Fred, and he's sick. I think he's dying."

"How do you know that?" Jack asked.

"I'm a cop," replied Gordon.

"Too bad you're a cop," Jack quipped. "Or else you might have been a nice guy."

He took Gordon by the arm, saying, "The bottom like is that Henry thinks this is an epidemic that's going to kill most of us unless we practice better public hygiene or get people inoculated or both."

Gordon looked back at the bodies.

"I'll buy that," he said. "Most of our losses here are among the poor. And right now we have another sick dude in Dundee north of here that Henry needs to see. It's a kitchen worker at the Grand Bay."

"We'll get Henry to do that, but right now, tell me about Fred."

Gordon turned to face Jack squarely.

"Your problem, Jake, is that you're too straight to read people right."

"What do you mean?"

"Fred is a flamer in a macho male body who hits it big with women. That's how he got Doreen. The trouble is that his pecker is limp as a noodle and doesn't work with women. It works better with guys like Malcolm, Vernon and Terrence.

"That's what he really did in the Bahamas. He could never make money selling pharmaceuticals here; the market was too small. His thing was meeting up with young boys and men. The only way he made a living was to buy drugs from Hugo for Dan Schulman and run them to Florida by boat. That's how you got snagged five years ago. Fred was running the stuff on your boat. That part of Hugo's story was right on."

Gordon stopped talking when a public affairs officer came up.

"Inspector, our local paper wants to report this incident. What do we say?"

The inspector shrugged his shoulders.

"Explain that there was a fight and that we're looking for suspects. There are too many shootings in the islands," he mumbled out loud. "It's called progress."

The police left, leaving the van with two officers to tape off the area with yellow crime scene tape to keep bystanders away. The rain picked up again and the small crowd of onlookers quietly dispersed. The town's only reporter from the town's only newspaper arrived. Sensing no cooperation and no story from anyone he left.

"I spoke to Clarence and Lancelot last night," said Gordon when they were alone once again. "And you're confirming just about everything they said. Am I missing anything?"

"No," answered Jack, "We need to speak to Henry and then to Dan and Fred."

"I think so too," said Gordon. "Now, did Henry ever tell you about his brother, Benjamin?"

"You mean Ben, the crazy bio-chemist?"

"That's him. Henry told me the story once but I never paid much attention to it. The way it goes is that Ben Alden was working on a bio terrorism program that killed a bunch of other scientists. The last thing I heard was that Ben went to the Middle East to run a field test. It was successful but it killed him. That was five years ago. He wrote to Henry about it before he died but I never saw the letter. Now Henry was afraid for his life and came to see me because he thought Ben may have told his story to someone else. I thought he was over reacting. Maybe I was wrong."

They stopped at the coffee shop where they found Cynthia and Henry.

"It's good to have him back," she commented. "He can help me with Doreen."

"How is she?" Jack asked.

"Not well," replied Cynthia. "But she's hanging in."

This gave Jack an opening.

"What about Dan and Fred?"

"They're on Kitten," she answered, fighting back tears. "The clinic treating Doreen has been sending its doctors to help Dan with Fred. I think he's dying. But

I'm more worried about Doreen. You should go see her, Shelly."

"Cynthia is right," said Gordon. We've secured Kitten at the dock in Avalon's spot. It's not leaving anytime soon."

"Dan should drop dead," Cynthia commented. "Henry gave up half his equity in the hotel and willed the other half to Dan upon his death in exchange for financing about three years ago. I'm sure Dan has a contract on Henry so he can inherit the place. Henry and I have been fighting over this ever since."

"We discussed it before I made the deal," argued Henry. "And you agreed."

"The hotel was broke," Cynthia retorted, her voice rising. "What did I know?"

"You knew everything," Henry shot back. "You married me because your dad told you the hotel was a gold mine."

"And why did you marry me, for sex? You could have asked my dad for money."

"I did; he refused. But you could have asked Fred, since he was screwing you."

"You dirty old bastard!"

"You're lucky he didn't give you AIDS."

"And you're lucky you were too impotent for me to pass it on to you."

"Guys, guys," interrupted Gordon. "Let's not fight here."

Gordon gave Cynthia the doctor's gear and she and Henry stalked away.

"Too bad those birds can't fly well together," said Jack.

"Speaking of birds," asked Gordon. "When will our planes be flying again?"

"Never," answered Jack. "Lance says we're on our own. If we want to leave, we should try swimming."

PART THREE

Final Reckoning

22

Henry's Confession

The real or imagined reasons for the matrimonial spat between Cynthia and Henry were inconsequential in the grand scheme of things and Gordon and Jack knew that and therefore preferred not to make a big deal over it. They were all caught up in the same mess and like Dan, Fred and Doreen they were hemmed in with no way out. Only Milton, alone with his grief, got drunk that night and resolved to leave the Bahamas and never return.

Cynthia called Archangel later and invited Jack to the hotel to have dinner with her and Henry but he turned her down, saying he repairs to do. Gordon invited him but Jack demurred again, explaining that he wanted to stay with Chico who was not feeling well. Furthermore, he had promised Ginny he would call that evening.

An old joke kept running through his mind. "When you and your buddy are in the woods and a bear is chasing you, what do you do? Do you try to outrun the bear or do you need to outrun your buddy?"

Jack had another reason for staying on board. He gave himself an injection of the vaccine from the bag Henry had left with him. He offered to give Chico a shot but the deckhand refused.

With little else to do, they busied themselves with cleaning the weapons they had on hand until late in the evening. It was feel-good work if nothing else and it kept more serious problems away. When he called Ginny on the VHF before turning in, he aired his suspicions and told her about the shootings.

"Henry must have a guilty conscience," she said. "Be careful, hon. Fred may be out of the picture, but Dan can be dangerous if he's cornered."

Jack woke up early on Friday, the ninth of June, to a strange stillness in the air. He got up, dressed and listened to Chico's snores and coughing in the main cabin. There was no sense waking him. Jack stepped off the boat and strolled to the coffee shop where he found Gordon.

"What's up?" Jack asked.

"I'm waiting for Henry," he said. "I'm taking him to his patients. Are you going to see Doreen?"

"I was thinking about it. But I want to see Dan and Fred first."

"They'll keep," said Gordon. "We have problems in Dundee and I want to see first hand what's going on. Why don't you tag along with us? We can grab a bite at the hotel."

"Sounds good to me," said Jack.

"Cynthia and Henry came by last night for dinner," said Gordon. "I think they've resolved their differences and were even talking about buying you out if you and Ginny plan to move to Florida."

"I don't know if that sterile partnership of theirs is going to last."

"You don't seem impressed."

"I am, Gordon. I am. But selling out is not on my mind right now."

Gordon was nonplused by his friend's indifference.

"I thought you might be slightly more excited, Jake."

Jack stared at the police inspector.

"I'll leave when I'm ready, Gordon. I'm not ready yet. Shall we go?"

Gordon backed off.

"Okay, okay, Jake. Let's do breakfast."

Jack had not been to the Grand Bay in months. The hotel's stucco walls and its striped green and white awnings over its windows and doors kept the inside cool even in the warmest weather. Its front livery entrance faced the road leading to town. Its canopied rear entrance through which Gordon and Jack entered faced the docks and led to the lobby and reception counter through a narrow hallway with terra cotta floors and walls. The business offices were directly inside the entrance on the left near a stairway to the second floor. An old elevator used by guests stood idle across the hall from the stairs. Another entryway led to the lobby from a lush   tropical garden and café halfway between the hotel's front and rear wings.

The executive office door was ajar and they walked in to find Cynthia at her desk reviewing the receipts of the previous day with Henry. The physician seemed to be happy and relaxed and fully recovered from his ordeal and fight with his wife.

"Nothing like a good night's sleep," he clucked happily.

Cynthia got up and gave him a kiss.

"You look terrific, dear. I have some work to do. Why don't you three go to the café? We'll get together later."

Jack, Gordon and Henry left Cynthia with her paperwork and went through the lobby to the outdoor café. They were in the process of ordering breakfast when an agitated waiter ran to their table.

"I'm sorry, but we need you in Dundee right away, Dr. Alden. I've bought your medical bag." And he pointed to the black bag in his hand.

"What's happening?" Henry asked.

"It's that hotel kitchen worker. He's getting worse. And on top of that, we have four, maybe five more very sick people. You need to go now, doctor."

Dundee was ten miles north of Marsh Harbor halfway to Treasure Cay on a pot holed single lane road. The town lay on a narrow slice of land joining the southern half of Abaco Island with its northern half. The bumpy drive lasted a half hour and it took another half hour to find the right address in the jumble of shacks hugging the road. Gordon left the car in front of a hut whose front door was open. If it was hot outside, inside the airless one room house it was stifling.

In one corner was a stove on which a pot of water was boiling. In another, a man lay shaking on a cot. His eyes were bulging and blood oozed out of his mouth and nose. A very nervous woman and two small children stood by helplessly and they had to be drawn away to allow Henry to make his examination.

Henry struggled to check the trembling patient's vital signs but it was too late. The man grabbed his arm in a death grip. He made one final retching sound and then fell back, his arm dropping to his side like a broken clock hand. Questioning the woman and the children was futile. They spoke no English and were hysterical. The only thing they knew was that he went fishing and that he and his men fell ill upon their return.

Clement Lloyd, the Grand Bay chef who had called Gordon to bring a doctor to Dundee, showed up at the door. He too looked sick but still seemed to be in control of his senses.

"What happened, Clement?" Henry asked.

"Everyone on my boat is sick," he cried. "I see Satan in the water. He poisons the fish we catch for the Grand Bay. We are going to die!"

Henry stared coldly at the chef over his spectacles.

"I can't speak for the others, Clement, but you will certainly die unless you raise your arm and let me give you a shot."

Clement stopped talking long enough to allow Henry to pull a vial and syringe from his medical bag. He held up his arm and winced as the needle broke his skin.

Gordon peered over his shoulder.

"What is it?"

"It's a cocktail against Plague."

"I hope it works, doctor."

"I hope so. It's all I have in my bag of tricks,"

He gave Clement a small packet of pills.

"You need to take two pills now and one each day for five days."

To Gordon and Jack he said, "Let's go see the others."

Clement took them from house to house until they had seen all the stricken crew members. One more died before they reached him but the doctor was able to give shots to the rest.

"How do we stand?" Gordon asked when they started back to Marsh Harbor.

"We have forty percent mortality on Clement Lloyd's boat," Henry replied. "We could really use the real anti-plague serum."

Later, at the Grand Bay, Jack brought up the issue of bio-terrorism as they sat at a table on one of the verandas.

"Henry. You need to tell us about your brother so we know what we're fighting."

"It started over five years ago with Ben's experiments," began Henry.

"Did he work with anyone else?"

"Yes. He did research with Cyrus and worked on a secret germ warfare project with Vernon Peters who was doing a stint as a pharmacist with your Navy. He said that before going to the Middle East he was commissioned to do field experiments with a bubonic plague germ that was genetically engineered and could be spread to enemy forces in an aerosol propellant. In addition to the usual symptoms, it caused internal blisters and boils that invariably broke and bled. Once the bleeding began, the process was almost irreversible. It was a mutant form of Red Death and victims died within hours or lasted at most a couple of days."

"If your brother developed the germ, he must have thought of an antidote," Jack said.

"Oh, it's the standard antidote or treatment for Plague. It's been around for years, and Ben and Cyrus perfected it, but it's best when the disease is caught in its early stages. The mutant Ben developed is lethal and cheaper than any weapon. It's the ultimate weapon to wipe out an enemy or the world without destroying buildings.

Ben didn't know much about it but thought that the best way to see how it worked was to get it battle tested. That was why Ben and Vernon ended up with a Marine contingent in some fortified town near Damascus.

Ben kept a journal and when he was dying, he sent it to Hiram who gave it to me. I was to keep it a secret."

"What happened to the Marines?"

"They were under siege by a fundamentalist sect and the consensus was that even with reinforcements they would lose. That's when a decision was made to try out the germ, but no propellant was on hand. So injected rats were stuffed into plastic canisters and flown over enemy positions in unmanned gliders that were shot down by the besiegers. A few rats must have survived because the fundamentalists began dying within days.

"Ben wrote in his journal that the attackers called off the siege and took off. But he grew suspicious when they left their dead and dying behind. Against his advice, the Marines retrieved them for examination and treatment. That's when the plague began spreading. Unfortunately, the Marines were unprepared to deal with it. They had no supplies and medics had no bunny suits. Sick Marines had to be evacuated, but the only vessel in the harbor back in Beirut was the research vessel that Ben worked in which was once a hospital ship."

"Was that the USS Comfort?"

"Yes. But they needed a second ship. That was the Angelina whose real job was to pick up heroin that Dan and Vernon had bought in exchange for antibiotics and other medicinal compounds. It was the ideal setup and many of us bought into the scheme. The Comfort, the steamer and a British escort destroyer called the HMS Leeds was loaded with the sick and the heroin."

"I was supposed to sail the Angelina," said Jack. "Who was the original owner?"

"It belonged to the Holiday Line, and Dan got it for us. It was in disrepair and was not Coast Guard certified. Dan got together with Bob Byrne, who was with the Coast Guard at the time and offered him a piece of the action in return for having it certified. A whole bunch of us met once we learned that Dan had made a deal for the boat and had Jonathan form a dummy corporation. It was the classic sale and leaseback deal. Dan sold the boat to Hamilton Graves and Malcolm Harding who leased it back to our dummy firm that negotiated a transport contract with the U.S. Navy. Each of us invested one hundred thousand dollars in the venture, including myself."

Gordon's mouth dropped.

"You?"

Henry looked at his hands.

"Yes. We made some conservative estimates and calculated that each of us would earn at least one million dollars after all expenses were discharged.

I didn't have enough cash to make the investment, so Island Trust gave me a mortgage and Dan took a fifty percent stake in my hotel. We did make money at first, but never came close to recouping our initial investment. That's how the Angelina officially ended up in the eastern Mediterranean to carry wounded soldiers back to Nassau and the States as part of a three ship flotilla. It was really a flotilla of drug ships but we never knew the heroin was tainted.

Henry took a deep breath before continuing.

"Safeguarding the heroin on the three ships was no longer a priority. Plague was running havoc and the focus was on troop evacuation. The ships were loaded up with the healthy, the sick and dying, and raced out to sea. In the rush to leave, a Comfort's life boat was placed on the Angelina. Ben was on the Angelina...."

"What about Vernon?"

"He flew to Nassau in a private plane. Technically, he deserted; but Dan had pull in Washington through Bob Byrne and arranged to have Vernon receive a general discharge. That's how Vernon settled in the Borders with a clean bill of health."

"What happened to the ships?"

"Word spread and every European port denied the vessels access. A thousand men started the voyage, including my brother. By the time they got to Gibraltar, less than a hundred were left. The Brits allowed those healthy enough to go into quarantine on their escort frigate, the HMS Leeds. The rest were left to cope on their own on the Angelina and Comfort.

"The ships had short crews by then, and when they reached the Bahamas, only Hugo and Eldridge and a few of his men and my brother were left alive on the Angelina. It made it to Nassau where my brother was taken off but it was never allowed to stay. The ship was finally ditched in the Sargasso and you know the rest. The Comfort limped on to Satan's Rock where it went aground."

"If this was an American mission, why involve the Bahamas in the first place?" Jack asked.

"It was logical. The Bahamas was an ally and Washington and the Navy wanted to keep the affair quiet and contain the Plague. It's easy to lose and hide the largest ships among the hundreds of Bahamian islands. Satan's Rock was chosen for the Comfort because it's outside the shipping lanes and isn't on any nautical charts.   "What's more, if Plague did break out in the islands, Washington felt there would be no problem in isolating the country. If things went real bad, the Bahamas would be the world's sacrificial lamb.

"A burial unit from Puerto Rico was airlifted to handle the bodies on board the Comfort which were supposed to be burned, but the bunny suits got sick and left. The Comfort is probably still filled with bodies. The HMS Leeds also ended up at Satan's Rock, but it must have broken its mooring and drifted west to the Florida Straits where I hear it was sunk by the Navy or Coast Guard."

"What about Hugo and Eldridge? They were on the Angelina."

Henry's face became animated.

"Ah. Here's the clincher. I learned from Lance that they were paid more than a million dollars and given immunity from prosecution by Hamilton Graves so long as they kept his mouth shut. Lance was furious when he heard the news. He wanted to resign his commission but Hiram convinced him to stay with the BDF. Hiram told his son God needed good foot soldiers for the Judgment Day. But you can't fault only Hugo or Eldridge. There's enough blame to go around. The way we got our investment back was through Hugo's kickbacks. I suppose in a sense we all profited from the heroin he siphoned off those ships over the years."

Gordon stared dumbfounded at the doctor.

"You're sure of your facts?"

"Positive. The bottom line is that the money we made was blood money."

"If you knew," asked Jack. "Why did you keep silent?"

"I always thought you had a hand in some of these things or at least knew what was going on, Jake. After all, you were supposed to be the captain of the Angelina. Bob Byrne was your friend and you did build a nice bounty business with our help and cooperation."

Jack looked at Gordon, asking, "Did you know, Tully? I knew money was being laundered but never over this."

Gordon gulped hard, shaking his head, "Most of this is news to me." He looked at Henry. "How bad can it get, doctor?" Gordon asked.

"This strain kills everything: bugs, fleas, rats, cats, birds, fish and people. It kills anything and everything, anyone and everyone. If an infected bug or flea touches a rat, the rat dies; if a cat catches the rat, the cat dies; if fish touch a dead rat or cat, the fish die; if a bird catches the fish, the bird dies; and if a man eats the fish or the bird, he dies. The Red Death is a non discriminatory, equal opportunity killer. It strikes rich and poor and all colors alike. It is Nature's great equalizer."

"Tell us. How long does this epidemic last?"

"Up to two years. We'll be dead by then."

23

Death Ship

Jack was reminded of being invited to a Passover dinner at Louie Gold's home many years ago. At the end of the dinner young children were asked to recite a limerick and Jack remembered some of the words. "I had one kid, one kid, which my father bought for two zuzim, one kid, one kid. And the cat came and killed the kid which my father bought for two zuzim, one kid one kid. And the hyena came and killed the cat that killed the kid which my father bought for two zuzim, one kid one kid. And the lion came and killed the hyena that killed the cat that killed the kid which my father bought for two zuzim, one kid, one kid. And the hunter came and killed the lion that killed the hyena that killed the cat that killed the kid which my father bought for two zuzim, one kid one kid. And the angel of death came and killed the lion that killed the hyena that that killed the cat that killed the kid which my father bought for two zuzim, one kid, one kid." Those weren't the exact words but they seemed to work in his mind.

Later that afternoon a police officer came to the Grand Bay to tell Gordon that Dan Schulman was threatening to blow up his yacht in the harbor and all the other boats alongside. They wanted to leave Marsh Harbor, explained the officer.

Gordon held his head in his hands.

"I don't need this crap," he complained. "I have an epidemic and now this." He looked up at the deputy and asked, "Is Avalon back?"

"It's due soon. It needs to collect the bodies of the children who died in the last couple of days. It will bury them at sea on its way back to the Borders."

Gordon turned to Jack. "This is a bad time, Jake. Will you join me?"

The skies turned ashen again and a drenching rain started up. The deputy had spare slickers in his jeep that they put on as they sped away to the harbor. He also had an extra pistol in the glove compartment but Jack declined to take it.

"We don't need to add to the death rate," he said.

A short while later they were parked at the marina where big and small boats rocked at their slips or moorings in the wind driven rain and chop. Visibility was poor and it was dark when they reached the long dock at the far end of the marina where Kitten was tied to pilings about halfway down. Two police launches were rafted against the big yacht with grappling lines and hooks against its hull to block its exit.

Vague shadows of family members whose children had died moved about at the end of the dock, mourning over small body bags and waiting for the return of the death ship. The gloom of night was setting in.

Dan's yacht dwarfed the other boats at the sprawling marina, and Jack speculated that it could have easily rammed the police launches had Dan really wanted to do so. But he was basically a landlubber and was helpless without a crew. He could blow up the yacht but Jack could not imagine that Dan and Fred came all the way from Florida to blow themselves up.

Gordon grabbed a megaphone from the jeep and they trotted down the dock until they were alongside the towering yacht. The rain eased but a fog set in that made it difficult to see if anyone was on deck or on the bridge. Jack took the megaphone from him and aimed it at the deck above.

"Permission to come aboard, Cap," he called out.

A strange silence filled the air that was only occasionally broken by the mournful wail of the Avalon's horn announcing its approach.

"Permission to come aboard, Cap."

They heard a movement on the deck above them.

Jack returned the megaphone to Gordon and yelled.

"Dan, it's me, Jake. Tully and I want to speak to you."

A thick, gravelly voice responded.

"What the hell are you doing here, Jake?"

"We need to speak to you and Fred."

"What the hell for?"

"We need to talk."

"What's that ruckus at the end of the dock?"

"Families are waiting for Avalon to pick up their dead kids," Jack answered.

A long pause, and then....

"Now, that's a damn shame, Jake, a damn shame, but I got nothing to talk about. You get Tully's boats out of here or this ship goes up with everything around it."

They could see from the dock that he was carrying a shotgun.

"Why Dan," said Jack with sarcasm dripping from his voice. "You came all the way from Florida to blow yourself up?"

"I came here to get my money from Jonathan Hall," Dan responded gruffly. "I struck out, so I want to go home. Fred wants to die in Florida. So do I."

"I can't let you do that, Dan," interrupted Gordon through the megaphone.

"I know you want me and Fred. That's not going to happen," Dan retorted.

"You're not going to be arrested," Jack responded. "We have nothing against you and we're not going to harm Fred."

"Then, what do you want?"

"We need your help, Dan, and you need our help; and Henry Alden has stuff for Fred that will make him better."

"What kind of help are you talking about? Fred doesn't have Plague."

"That could be, but folks here are dying of Plague, and if we can't find a way to fight it, most of them are going to die. Henry has some real medicine that can help Fred live longer, and we need what you have to keep us alive."

"Are you armed?"

Gordon drew his pistol, waved it in the air and placed it carefully on the ground while Jack turned his pockets inside out and drew up his trouser legs to show that he was unarmed.

"Please let us come aboard, Dan. We don't have guns and you're not going to be arrested. I promise," said Gordon. "You can keep that shotgun of yours on us while we're on board. At the very least, you owe us a hearing, and we need your help."

"You wait there," said Dan. "I'll lower a gangplank at the center deck."

They waited a few minutes until they heard creaking chains as the long gang plank slid down and hit the dock with a clang.

"Do you want me to come up with you?" The deputy asked.

"No," said Gordon. "Get some backup and wait for us at the jeep."

They climbed the gangplank to the deck where Dan was waiting, double barreled shotgun in his hands.

Dan Schulman seemed larger than life in the half light.

His meaty hands gripped the shotgun tightly, relaxing their hold when he saw that they were unarmed. He led them into the main cabin behind the bridge, turned on a few lights and pointed to a round table where they sat down.

Dan kept the shotgun at his side and carefully eyed his guests to make sure they made no sudden moves.

"Now that you're here, what do you want to talk about?"

"I'm curious, Dan," Jack started. "How come you decided to come here at this time all the way from Florida with Fred?"

"Looking back, it was a bad move, Jake," admitted Dan. "I needed to personally speak to Jonathan about my money and Fred wanted to see Doreen and ask her to forgive him."

"Doreen is sick too, you know," said Gordon. "Why did you bother?"

"I know that, and Fred knows that. But that's what he wanted to do and for his sake I had to take him here. Besides I have medicine that may help her. I did it out of pity. It was the right thing."

"What's this about your money?" Jack asked.

"I've banked at Island Trust for years, just like most of us."

Jack shook his head.

"Not me. I go direct deposit to Florida through Chase in Nassau."

"That exposes you to U.S. taxation, doesn't it?"

"It sure does, Dan, but it's safer that way."

The short sharp hoot of a ship's siren outside broke up their conversation. Dan looked up and grabbed his shotgun.

"What's that?" he asked.

"Avalon has arrived," replied Gordon.

Dan nodded and put down his gun as Jack asked, "What's Jonathan's story?"

"Jonathan is broke. He emptied his bank had and lost it gambling in Nassau and Puerto Rico and on the ponies in Florida. My company was registered in Nassau to avoid stateside taxes so banking at Island Trust made sense. I knew it was bust but I figured Jonathan socked away enough cash so that if I saw him personally I could shake him down."

"We thought you're here because you and Cynthia were getting back together."

"I had a great time with her and I wish her luck but she's history."

"Henry thinks you're out to get him," said Jack.

"I heard," replied Dan. "He's a total asshole. I don't give a shit if he lives or dies. He never put up a fucking dime and made big bucks off us. He was in as deep as all of us in this mess."

Dan put down the shotgun, folded his hands on the table and stared at them.

"I guess I should tell you that I'm the guy that started it all once Fred and Bob Byrne came up with the Angelina caper. I put up the earnest money."

"Did anyone really make out on the deal?" Gordon asked.

Dan shook his head.

"Some petty cash changed hands, but no big bucks. The plague broke out on the ship and we were never able to unload the cargo like we wanted. We never counted on this plague thing. But Fred and Bob made out. The only problem is that Doreen made Fred give his cut to Bob and forced Bob to use it in keeping you solvent and out of prison. That and Louie Gold's help kept you afloat until you could swim."

Jack could not believe his ears.

"Why the hell would she do that, Dan? She shit canned me."

Dan looked up, surprised at Jack's question.

"I thought you knew. Man, you're thick. Doreen wasn't doing for you. She had something on Bob and blackmailed him through Fred who was proving to be no bargain either. Bob Byrne was forced to keep you above water. That was Doreen's guarantee that she would keep receiving alimony and child support checks from your business. Bob Byrne subsidized you and you paid the bills. You got back on your feet and then some but she's the one who really made out."

Dan burst out laughing and then muttered under his breath, "Damn woman!"

Frank Doyle's words aboard Ned Baron's yacht were now coming back to Jack.

He had told Jack then that Doreen was behind Bob's largesse. But Frank never mentioned the reason beyond the generosity. Maybe de didn't know. Or maybe, she still harbored a soft spot for Jack. This was all too much for Gordon who wanted to stick to the Angelina issue. He pressed on.

"Why did you bother getting into the Angelina business in the first place? We thought you made your fortune in pharmaceuticals."

Dale snickered.

"I wish. South Florida Pharmaceuticals was a front. I sold cocaine in Florida that I bought from Hugo," he said. "It came from South America, but when he told me early this year that he found the Comfort stranded at Satan's Rock, I switched to heroin because the price was better. At last I thought I'd make my money back on that Angelina fiasco.

"Hugo took it in small lots to Dale Malone's plant in Hermit Cay for processing, but when we learned the cay sat on top of a volcano, the operation was moved to his factory in North Border. We never knew the stuff was bad until people began dying and Bob Byrne tipped us off when he came for his piece of the action. By then, the Angelina had been found and Bob wanted us to shut down the operation."

"You're kidding."

"No. I'm dead serious. But the feds knew also. They sent some guy I never saw before who tried pushing me for information."

"Was that Martin Wilson?"

"Yeah, he claimed he was a consultant for the government and was friendly with Larry Fisher who skippered this boat when he was off duty. Frankly, I think he was a phony and his story was full of shit. I think Bob Byrne fished him out of a sewer and put him on to me.

"He must have gotten engaged to Ned Baron's daughter to get closer to our drug trafficking business and probably never really intended to marry her. He promised me immunity from prosecution for tax evasion in exchange for the names of all my partners in the drug scheme. I believed him at first and gave him names, and then I found out that he gave the list to Byrne."

"Bob Byrne is supposed to be a friend of mine," said Jack. "He's the executor of my estate."

Dan's laugh was more like a bellow.

"I realize that, Jake. You're dumb for a smart guy and you need better friends. Here, let me spell it out for you. If Washington wanted to keep its role quiet in a bio warfare experiment gone so bad that it caused a global epidemic, all involved parties would need to be killed. Bob Byrne is Washington's point man to make sure the people on the list were killed. By giving Martin Wilson names, I bought time for me and Fred."

"How come Tully, Clarence and I never made the list?" Jack asked.

Again, there was that fat belly laugh.

"Too straight and stupid," guffawed Dan. Then he continued, "Listen, Jake. You need to understand that Byrne believes that with your five years in the Borders you knew what was going on from the start and that you were in on part of the heroin take. That means he feels that you're wise to his action. You may not be on that list, but sure as hell, you're in his short hairs. One more thing: with you out of the way, and if Fred and Doreen die, he gets your businesses, your assets, cash and all the other shit you own."

Gordon looked at Jack.

"That makes sense, Jake."

"What about my folks and kids?"

Again, Dan guffawed.

"You're here and they're holed up in West Virginia. He'll have them picked off one by one once you're gone."

"That makes even more sense," said Gordon.

"You're damn right it makes sense," insisted Dan. "Furthermore, what you hear about airline slowdowns and strikes is sheer bullshit. Washington has closed your borders. The feds are willing to kill 300,000 people to save 320 million, and you can bet that Nassau is in on the conspiracy. Nothing gets in or out. I'd have to run a blockade to leave the islands. If Martin Wilson is still around, he's stuck too. The bottom line, when you get right down to it, is that I'm done. I played my best card, Jake, but it was only a three of clubs."

Dan sighed, picked up his shotgun and laid it down on the table.

"Martin Wilson was a hit man and he's dead," said Jack. "He had those names you gave him on a list we found when he dropped it accidentally. Manny and Larry are dead too."

Dan nodded.

"That must be why Larry dropped out of sight when we got here."

"Where did Larry go when you guys got to the Borders?" Gordon asked.

"He holed up on Kitten," replied Dan. "He said he wasn't feeling well."

Gordon threw him a cheesy smile, saying, "For a smart guy, Dan, you're pretty thick too. Do you really believe those hit men wouldn't have come for you and Fred after they finished the others?"

Dan began sobbing quietly.

"It doesn't matter anymore. I fucked up and in doing so I fucked up the world. If you're here for help, I have enough vaccine in the freezer for a thousand shots and you can have it. I should have given it to Henry free. I also have stuff for Doreen; make sure she takes it. It will save her life."

"What does she have anyway?"

"Cyrus Cooper examined her before he died," replied Dan. "She has a chronic bronchial condition that was never treated. It turned into a chronic pneumonia, something like a walking pneumonia. Doreen thought she had AIDS and didn't believe him. She walked out and refused regular medical attention. Now, if you want to see Fred, he's in the master suite."

Dan rose to his feet, took his shotgun and led the way to the large suite in the center of the vessel. The door to the opulent quarters was open and inside the drawn scarecrow of a man in oversized pajamas lay on bare sheets on an oversized bed. It was Fred Hawk.

A wake from the Avalon swept under Kitten as it braced itself against the dock as the dead were being lifted aboard and they had to steady themselves for a few seconds. They could hear a dog barking, and Jack guessed it was Styx.

Fred's eyes were sunken and his cheeks were hollow. Lesions lined his face and arms and his emaciated body shook each he coughed. He was moaning and barely aware of anyone in his presence and just kept crying about wanting to see his wife.

"Do you still want to move him off the boat?" Dan asked in a whisper.

Gordon glanced at Jack who shook his head.

"It seems pointless," replied Gordon. "He's going to die, isn't he?"

"He has a few hours, maybe a day or so. What do you want me to do?"

Dan sounded finally as if life had caught up and defeated him.

"It's your move," Jack answered. "Let's see if that scattergun works." He took the weapon from Dan's limp hands and cocked it. Returning it, he said, "Now, you do the right thing, Dan, you hear?" Then to Gordon he added, "We're done, Tully. Let's go."

They turned and left, stopping long enough in the galley freezer to take the bag of Plague antidote before leaving the yacht. They were back on the dock when they heard a shot. It was followed moments later by another.

Gordon spoke to one of the deputies who came running down the dock.

"It's over. Is Virgil ready?"

"He's casting off with the tide in a half hour."

"Good; tell him we have two more bodies for Avalon."

24

Doreen

So that was that. Dan Schulman and Fred Hawk were history and the plague raged on in the gloom of night. It was time for making cool moves. Jack enjoyed brief moment of grim satisfaction, but he also needed to see Doreen before her condition worsened.

It was late that evening when Gordon left Jack off where Archangel was docked. Jack hoped to find Chico on board but the deckhand was apparently gone for the night. That was fine for Jack. He was tired and wanted to get some sleep. He called Ginny and told her that Dan and Fred were dead, and she replied that Gordon had already called Clarence who called her. But there was something else, she said. Hamilton Graves and his entire crew had died of Plague on his yacht. The vessel was bound for Marsh Harbor when the incident happened. One of Lance's cutters found the vessel towed it out to sea to be destroyed after siphoning its tanks.

"Shelly?"

"Yes?"

"I think we really need to leave the islands, at least for a while."

"I think so too."

Jack went to sleep and awoke at dawn on Saturday, the tenth of June. Chico was still away. He washed, shaved, dressed, waited a half hour and then walked over to the marina cantina. He had just poured himself coffee into a Styrofoam cup when Milton showed up sobbing.

At first, Jack thought he was still grief stricken by the loss of his family, and he probably was, but now to add to his distress, he had more bad news to convey.

"Chico is dead," he said, choking on his words; and he went on to explain as best as he could that Chico had fallen ill, wandered in a delirium about Marsh Harbor until he finally fell and died.

"I was there, and I did nothing, Jake. I stood there and watched him die. And I kept standing there when a mob poured fuel over his body and torched it on the spot."

Gordon showed up as Milton was talking and reconfirmed his story. "There was nothing that could be done, Jake, nothing."

Jack crushed the Styrofoam coffee cup in his hand and looked up at the clear blue sky.

"I spoke to Ginny last night," he said. "She told me Hamilton Graves is gone."

"She's right," Gordon confirmed. "He's dead and Lance is doubling as acting commissioner," Gordon answered.

"What about BASRA? Who is taking over for Malcolm Harding?"

"Lance has Reggie Mayhew standing in for him." replied Gordon. "I also spoke to Clarence. He needs to deputize every able bodied person in the Borders to keep the peace and essential services going."

Jack sighed.

"When does this thing end? What the hell are we going to do?"

"We have Schulman's Plague vaccine," said Gordon. "I'm going to inoculate every kid here, and I'm going to ask Clarence to call a meeting in the Borders to make a decision on the shots there."

"Well, you do that, Tully. I'm going to see Doreen," Jack declared suddenly. "Do you have that medicine Dan gave us that's supposed to make her better?"

"I gave it to Henry," answered Gordon. "He wants to examine her. Can you get her to leave her condo?"

"I'm going to do that." Turning to Milton, Jack asked, "Care to join me? I could use help on Archangel."

They were well on their way to Treasure Cay a half hour later, passing Dundee to their left. Milton knew boats as well if not better than Jack who was comfortable with the accountant at the helm. Archangel picked up the wind and it was soon barreling north over the flat water to cover the twenty miles or so to Treasure Cay.

"I'm scared, Jake," Milton said suddenly out of the blue.

"Try the power of prayer," Jack suggested. "Your dad believes in it."

"It's not about me," he continued. "Avalon will be busy in the Borders, so Tully impounded Dan's yacht and asked me to run bodies out to sea on it. I don't mind pitching in for a while, but I don't want to die here, Jake. You need to help me."

"I've got Ginny with one kid and another cooking," said Jack. "And I can't make a move without taking them along, aside from the fact that we would probably be shot out of the sea or air if we tried to escape. Do you have any great ideas?"

"I'm thinking of trying to make a run on Kitten if I can get it fueled up," Milton suggested. "I can make it in less than two days; I know I can."

"Good luck," said Jack. "You're gutsier than I am. Maybe you can work a deal with Bob Byrne to let you get through the blockade."

"How am I going to do that?"

"I can give you his secure call numbers. Tell him that you have a shipload of heroin. He may be greedy enough to let you through,"

"That might work," Milton acknowledged. "How long will we be in Treasure Cay?"

Jack was not listening. He was thinking about Doreen and how things could have been different had he tried harder to be a better husband when the ancient legend of Gilgamesh's and Ishtar's love affair flashed across his mind. It was the part where the goddess offered herself in marriage to Gilgamesh who refused her advances.

"Be my lover, be my husband," said Ishtar to Gilgamesh. "Give me the seed of your body and abundance will follow with riches beyond riches."

To which Gilgamesh replied, "What could I offer the queen of love, who lacks nothing at all? I have nothing to give to her who lacks nothing at all. You are the door through which the cold gets in. You are the fire that goes out. You are the pitch that sticks to the hands of the one who carries the bucket. You are the house that falls down. You are the shoe that pinches the foot of the wearer. You are the ill-made wall that buckles when time has gone by. You are the leaky water skin soaking the water skin carrier. You are the feast that turns to famine and the rain that brings the storm. You are the breeze that brings disease, killing all it touches.

Where are your husbands, your bridegrooms and your lovers? They moan and wail as they walk in the land of the dead, as soon will I if I stay with you. Why should I eat rotten food when wholesome food beckons? Why should I live with you in fear and sorrow if I can laugh and live without you?"

In retrospect, this was no way to treat or to talk to a woman.

Treasure Cay lay on a flat spit of land. It had a hotel, a marina, a tiny strip mall with an ice cream parlor, a telephone center, a health clinic and a row of condos along the beach. It was close to sundown when Archangel tied up at the marina.

Jack called Doreen. He detected a slight hoarseness in her voice but otherwise she sounded delighted to hear from him.

"Come on over," she said lightly. "It's the duplex at the end of the point."

Jack hung up and walked over to her development and found her standing at the open door in a house dress. The sun was setting and it was dark inside the condo. Doreen had not yet turned on the lights and he sensed that something was not right.

If she expected a passionate embrace, all she received was a peck on the forehead. One thing had changed for sure. The long hair was gone in favor of a short page boy cut. But it was thinning, brown and highlighted with artificial color to cover splotches of gray. He did not recognize the statuesque blonde with the dancer's legs who was once his wife.

"It's my matronly mature look," she explained.

"Nice digs," Jack observed. "You must be rich."

Doreen laughed.

"It's a struggle, but I manage. How are you doing, Shelly?" She always called him by his middle name.

"Taking time off from work," he replied.

"You never took time off from work in the old days."

Doreen invited Jack into the condo and he took time to have a look around in the dim light. The furnishings were not cheap. They were not the usual mass produced south Florida rooms-to-go reproductions, the ones found in so many homes. These were high end European imports that screamed money to the world and were paid for by Fred in his better days, or so Jack thought.

"Are you staying a while?" Doreen asked.

"Only for a while," answered Jack. "We have problems in Marsh Harbor and in the Borders. But we could have dinner. I was thinking of Touch-of-Class. It's just on the other side of the bridge. It has good food and a calypso band."

"Touch-of-Class it is," she agreed. She called a cab which arrived a few minutes later and took them to the restaurant. She seemed weak-kneed and Jack had to help her in and out of the car.

The food and drink was always good at the local dining and watering hole. It was a popular with locals and tourists even though the fare was not very gourmet. The restaurant did offer a few vintage champagnes and wines and some fancy fish and meat dishes but most of the menu items featured local conch dishes and lobster favorites. The menu did show steak, but Jack knew it was imported from the States and frozen.

"Green meat, the locals call it," he said.

"I hear you're doing well," Doreen remarked as they were led to their table.

For some reason she had never changed from her house dress before leaving the condo. She looked haggard and seemed to have lost weight.

"I make out," he responded. "I'm getting used to living here, but I'm looking to get back to the States."

"And do what?"

He avoided her eyes and watched some couples moving to the band music on the small dance floor. Finally he shrugged his shoulders.

"I don't know. Maybe I'll run my business in Boynton Beach. Or maybe I'll just stay here. I haven't made up my mind. What about you?"

"I'm doing fine, and I have two beautiful kids nice and safe in West Virginia."

She placed his hands in hers.

"Don't you smoke anymore?"

"I went cold turkey a few days ago, and I can't figure out why. I guess it just happened."

"You could have fought harder to keep me, you know."

Jack bristled.

"What were my options? I was too broke to fight a murder rap and you wanted a divorce, and it was tough to compete against Fred, what with my drinking and all."

"You never tried, Shelly. You never even tried to keep in touch after you went off. I never saw you again until tonight. I was here every winter. You could have come by. You didn't have to give me a cold shoulder. I didn't divorce you because I didn't love you. I divorced you because of your drinking and your lousy temper. You should have called."

Jack sounded resigned.

"You went your way and I went mine; I thought that was what you wanted."

"Anyway, tell me about Ginny Malone."

His jaw tightened.

"We're married."

"That's convenient. Do you love her?"

"I suppose so. We have one child and another on the way."

They ordered a local fish dish for the both of them and a drink for Doreen who declined it. As a matter of fact, she began complaining of a headache and wanted to return to the condo. Jack left money for the dinner they never finished and took her back in the same cab that drove them to the restaurant.

"What else is new, Shelly?" Doreen asked when they were in the condo. "You don't drink and smoke anymore and neither do I."

"How come you're not drinking?"

"The doctor said I have some sort of infection. Drinking and medication doesn't mix well," Doreen answered, sitting down on the sofa.

"Well, you'll be back to your old self soon," said Jack, taking a seat on a chair next to the sofa. "As for me, I'm working on my first million." He did not care to elaborate. "Let's talk about you," he suggested instead. "You're more interesting."

"What do you want to know?"

"Did you leave Florida for health reasons?"

"That epidemic scared me. That's why I sent the kids to stay."

"What about Fred?"

"The bastard got himself sick. He came down with AIDS. He's the other reason I'm here. I had to get away from him. But he came here anyway."

"You don't have to run anymore, Doreen," said Jack. "He's dead."

"Oh my God!"

"And so is Dan Schulman. It was a murder-suicide. Dan shot Fred and then killed himself. It happened last night in Marsh Harbor."

"Shit! They're dead; dad is bankrupt and I don't have enough money to pay my bills. I need cash. What am I going to do for money? How am I going to pay for my treatments?"

"I'm footing the bills now," said Jack.

Doreen smiled weakly.

"You are?"

"Yes, and you should have pity on Fred, Doreen, He was dying and Dan did him a favor. Dan brought Fred here so he could ask for your forgiveness."

Jack got up to stretch his legs and walked over to the sliding glass door leading to the patio. The night sky was bright with stars and a beckoning moon.

"That's bull shit, Shelly. Fred never loved me. He married me to screw you in the face because you were such a big ass know-it-all drunk that could fuck any female alive. He couldn't put his pecker through a doughnut. He was just like Bob Byrne before him. They were only good with boys. What a total pisser! I jumped from a fag to a drunk and then to another fag!"

"Damn!"

"What? You didn't know? I blackmailed those bastards so that they would keep you afloat."

"Why?"

"Because I loved you."

"I thought it was about the alimony and child support."

"Of course it was about the alimony and child support, you big jerk. But I still loved you. But love alone couldn't carry us. Love is nothing without money. How dumb are you anyway?"

"I was dumb enough to marry you," said Jack, his voice rising. "I'm not here to beg for forgiveness, Doreen. I know I did you wrong, and I wish I could turn back the clock and change the past, but I can't; and I wish I could change the present but I can't. I came here to talk to you about our being friends and maybe sharing in the raising of our kids, and I came here for Fred."

Doreen laughed hoarsely.

"Fred wasn't here for me, and I knew he was dying. He was a patient at the same clinic that takes care of me. It's going to cure me, you know. It would have cured Fred had he made it to the clinic. I'm glad that cocksucker died. He deserved it."

"You're dreaming. Doreen," said Jack, turning to face her. "That clinic of yours sells quack cures. You need a real doctor with real medicine if you're going to get a chance to see our kids and live to old age. What you have isn't fatal, and you can be cured, but not at this clinic and not in the Bahamas, at least not now."

"I thought I would have been safer in the Bahamas."

"And how would you have known that, Doreen?"

"Dad warned me. It had something to do with the passengers that got sick when a cruise ship stopped in Canal Pond. He also told Cyrus, my doctor in Florida, but I refused his treatment. I thought it could complicate my condition."

"What about the kids?"

"I let Cyrus give them shots even though I didn't think they needed any."

"It's good they got vaccinated, Doreen," said Jack. "That epidemic in Florida is Plague, and that's what we have here now."

"No!"

"It's no joke. But you don't have Plague and you don't have AIDS, if that's what you're thinking," said Jack.

Doreen stared defiantly at him, saying, "How the hell do you know what I have?"

"Listen, Doreen. I'm not going to argue. Right now, you need real treatment by real doctors. You need to let me get you to Henry Alden."

Doreen began crying. The bathroom door next to the living room was ajar and on the sink, Jack saw needles and other drug paraphernalia used for shooting up.

"What the hell am I going to do?" Doreen cried. "I need money. Get the hell out of here until you get me some money."

Her tears dissolved the makeup on her face and Jack now saw for the first time how sick she was. He gasped and dug a hand into one of his trouser pockets.

"Listen," he said, taking out a wad of bills. "I'll get out of here. Here's money to tide you over. It's yours, so hang on to it. I'm going to spend the night on the boat, but you call me on my radio if you need me. I'll get you out of here first thing in the morning if you're still interested."

Jack placed the money on the coffee table but Doreen kept crying.

"I thought we might make a fresh start," she said. "We can make a fresh start, can't we, Shelly, just you and me?" She looked up at Jack imploringly.

Jack was weakening.

"Do you want me to spend the night with you? I will, you know."

"No," replied Doreen, sobbing. "I don't want to kill the father of my children."

"Then, we'll make a fresh start together, but we need to get you well first," he said. "Right now, try to get some sleep. Tomorrow morning, pack a bag and I'll take you to see Tully and Henry. That will be the first step. I loved you once, I love you now and I'll love you always."

Jack took her in his arms and tenderly embraced her. Kissing her softly on the head he was shocked to find his lips touching a bald spot. He summoned all his energy to keep from breaking down. He wanted to cry but he controlled his tears and said nothing. He kissed Doreen on the lips, slowly let her go and walked out of the condo and into the night, leaving Doreen to collapse on the sofa and stare at the cash on the coffee table. What was he going to tell Ginny? He leaned against a tree for support, burst out crying and smacked his head against the tree trunk.

Later, on Archangel where he found Milton waiting, he told him of his evening with Doreen. He further explained that they had to leave at first light to get her to Marsh Harbor. If he expected any back-talk from Milton, there was none. Neither did he say anything about Jack's bruised head.

"I'll call Tully to give him a head's up," Milton said.

A blinding sun greeted Jack the next morning. He went back to the condo to pick up Doreen and found a police van parked nearby. She was gone and someone said that she had wandered off during the night and that she might have died. One of the police officers recognized Jack and let him into the condo. The money he had left was still on the coffee table. He stuffed it back into his pocket and left. Back at the boat, he took out his horn and played 'Amazing Grace.'

25

The Omens

Doreen was gone, but Ginny Malone was alive; Jack was now married to her; they had one child and another on the way. He had feelings of guilt and obligations that hung like weights from his neck but deep inside he knew that his life in the islands was coming to an end. After all was said and done the central question was how he and his new family to leave the Borders alive. Signs of disaster were everywhere and it was time to leave.

Milton never sailed back to the Borders with Jack. Gordon appeared moments before Archangel was leaving with a duffel slung over his shoulder and instructed Milton to drive back to Marsh Harbor in his jeep to operate Kitten and do whatever he could to help maintain public order.

He had already been forewarned about Doreen's disappearance and told Jack that she had not yet been found but that his men would continue searching.

"That's all we can do" he said. "Milton will keep us posted. Right now, we need to return to the Borders and be at the governing council meeting on Tuesday, and Archangel is the only available transportation. You and I also need to talk about the future."

But they had no appetite for conversation at the moment and they set sail in silence. It was Sunday morning, the eleventh of June, almost a month since Jack left Florida for the islands. He concentrated on navigating the cat through shallows as it passed Dundee on their right where he saw thin lines of smoke rising high into the sky and heard church bells mix with police and fire fighter sirens.

"We're having trouble delivering essential services," he said. "Some government workers aren't showing up for work."

"Don't forget that today is Sunday," Jack noted. "Many folks are off and many more are in church. What counts is who shows up for work tomorrow."

"That will be Milton's turf tomorrow," said Gordon. He happened to glance at Jack's forehead and asked, "What happened to you?"

"I had a fight with a tree," answered Jack.

"Have you started drinking again, Jake?"

Jack shook his head and replied, "I should start drinking, Tully. I really should."

Gordon only words were to briefly explain that he and many other people too were now quite familiar with grief.

"I understand," said Jack. "Who is holding the fort while you're away besides Milton?"

"I asked Cynthia to help run things with Milton, and I've deputized Clement Lloyd, and I'm hoping for the best."

"It sounds as if you're setting up your succession," Jack noted.

"What other options do I have?"

They were about an hour under sail when Gordon broke the silence in the wheelhouse.

"I guess Doreen must be a really special woman."

Jack sighed.

"I'm upset," he said. "And I'm not upset. I was no angel and she put up with me, at least for a while. We had great times while it lasted, but she did give me a lot of grief. Still, I never wished her dead and I would never have wanted her to go the way she did. She deserved better. I let her down."

"What about Dan and Fred?"

"They played the wrong cards, Tully. They lost and then kept losing until it was too late. I have no regrets, but in a way I did like them; they had guts and were risk takers. But it's over. My concern now is to help control this damn epidemic."

"Henry and every available medical and nursing person are giving children shots at the Grand Bay as we speak," said Gordon. "Cynthia and her staff are lending a hand and Clement Lloyd will be taking over that clinic in Treasure Cay for the same purpose. All children will be inoculated in the next forty eight hours. At least that's supposed to be the plan and I hope its happening. And I want to make sure that the same thing happens in the Borders."

Jack grew pensive.

"It might be easier to get people to cooperate in Marsh Harbor than back home," he opined.

"What makes you say that?"

"There's a power vacuum in Marsh Harbor and you don't have much opposition. The Borders are different. We have many chiefs and few Indians. We're a feudal communal cooperative with total power sharing, Tully. Everyone has an opinion, even Hugo and Eldridge."

Gordon grimaced.

"At least, you and I should be reading from the same page at that meeting on Tuesday," said Gordon.

"We'll be on the same page," Jack assured him. "But there'll be many big egos jockeying for those shots."

"I'll bet. But, tell me honestly, Jake. Did Henry or Dennis give you a shot?"

"I got a shot; so did Ginny and Alexandra."

"I had Henry give me a shot," Gordon confessed. "I have one left for my wife."

"God helps those who help themselves, I hear," said Jack.

Gordon mulled over Jack's words for a few minutes and then began talking about a strategy for the Tuesday meeting.

"We need a strikeout pitch at the outset," he said.

"You and I need more than that, Tully. We need an escape plan."

"Do we ignore the blockade?" Gordon asked.

"We can run the blockade," answered Jack. "

"And where do we run?"

"We go home to the States, Tully."

Gordon's jaw dropped.

"Am I hearing you right, Jake? You're saying that we should leave our homes, our livelihoods and friends and everything we've ever built for ourselves behind and run like thieves in the night?"

"You got that right, Tully."

In one last attempt to poke a hole into Jack's idea of leaving the Borders, Gordon brought up the issue of Bob Byrne.

"Do you think he's going to let us into the States alive?"

"We won't ask him for permission," replied Jack.

A call came in on the cat's VHF radio and Gordon picked it up. He mumbled a few words into the transmitter and then slapped the radio several times and cursed.

"It's Milton," Gordon informed Jack with a sideways glance. "He called to say that the police found Doreen, and then static broke us up. The VHF frequencies are being jammed."

"Doesn't anyone on Marsh Harbor have a ham radio?" Jack asked.

"Not that I know of," replied Gordon. "People have CB radios, but they're only good on a line of sight and we're out of range."

Jack gritted his teeth and said nothing.

The wind was blowing from the southeast and it blew Archangel slightly off its course to the cut between North and South Border. Three hours into their trip they found themselves peering through their binoculars at the All Souls church spire on Sanctuary Village.

"We turn right and run south along the coast," said Jack, adjusting course.

But it wasn't the spire that caught their eyes. It was the ribbons of black smoke spiraling up along the coastline from Sanctuary Village south to Agnes Town.

The wind turned and the acrid smell of smoke stung at their nostrils.

"Maybe it is time for us to quit these islands," Gordon mumbled half aloud.

Jack radioed Pirates' Cove to say that Archangel was at Buccaneer Point and turning into the cut. Kyle took the call without comment. Something indeed was wrong and Jack's first thought was that something had happened to Alexandra or to Ginny.

Archangel dropped its sails, powered through the cut against the tide and made a sharp turn into Pirates' Cove where Ginny and Otis Foote were at the dock. Jack could tell from the anxious expressions on their faces as they helped secure the cat that things were not well. Ginny usually kept Alexandra close to her and she was nowhere in sight.

Ginny had a bad cold but was otherwise seemed none the worse for wear, but her lips were pinched and her face was pale. And Otis was sullen and had little to say.

Jack nevertheless gave her a kiss and gave Otis a hearty slap on the back and asked about Alexandra and Kyle.

"Dad is babysitting Alexandra," she answered in between sniffles. "And I caught a cold. Dennis says it's a reaction to the shot he gave me. He gave Alexandra a shot too and she's doing fine."

Jack and Gordon exchanged sidelong glances and for the first time Ginny noticed the bruise on her husband's head. She gasped and pointed to it, but seeing no point of going into details, he decided to lie.

"Archangel's mast swung around on a jibe and grazed me," he explained

"What about Chico?"

"Dead," replied Jack. Again, there was no need to explain. Everyone knew.

Ginny tried again, asking, "And did you see Doreen?"

Jack did his best to keep a straight face, saying. "She's gone too."

"What's happening here?" Gordon broke in. "We saw smoke on the way in."

"Nothing good," replied Otis. "Rioting broke out in Patrick City last night when its power was shut down for a few hours."

"How did that happen?" Jack asked.

"Lance says we need to save energy," answered Otis. "So his men took over the fuel tanks and the power generators by the seaplane landing. If they shut down, the juice goes off everywhere in North Border unless some folks have their own fuel source and generators. It sucks," continued Otis. "Power is cut off when we need it most, from noon to midnight. Who needs power from midnight to noon? It's cool at night. I can't do a full day's work at your place in the heat."

"We'll just have to get used to your working half a day," Jack said, suppressing a smirk.

"That sucks," repeated Otis. "The police barracks are air conditioned. So is the rectory and Lance's ships. Many places are air conditioned. So is Cheetah's and the Zebra. So is your boat. What the hell, Jake. You're rich. That Jew, Louie Gold, let it happen by leaving everything to you when he died. What the hell did he ever do for about the rest of us who are Christian, God fearing folks?"

Jack was speechless but Ginny gave Otis a dirty look and shot back.

"That's unfair, Otis," she said. "Many places have their own their generators and tanks and generators and paid through the nose to install backup systems years ago, and they're not Jewish."

"I can swear to you, Otis," said Gordon. "Louie Gold was the only Jewish person in the islands, and he's dead. Why pick on him?"

"He and Louie made a deal with Satan," declared Otis. "That's why the rich are making out and the poor suffer. It's Satan's plan. You call that fair?"

"Okay, okay," interrupted Jack. "Let's not argue over what's done and who's to blame. When did the power outages begin?"

"Lance is rationing power," said Otis. "He can do that. He hangs out at the air conditioned barracks or on his air conditioned cutter. He's in bed with the devil too."

"Are there any other news?"

Otis looked at Jack.

"Are you sure you want to hear this?"

"Go ahead," said Jack. "We need to know what's going on."

Otis began trembling and tried to avoid speaking directly to Gordon.

"It's Mrs. Tully," he said in a low voice. "She got sick and died."

Gordon heard Otis all too clearly. Out of sheer impulse, he clenched his fist and hit Otis so hard in the face that he fell to the ground. In a moment he was on top of Otis, pounding him with his fists.

Jack jumped on his back but Gordon threw him off. Kyle came out of his trailer waving a shotgun and little Alexandra trailing behind and ran over to help Jack. He fired into the air that stopped Gordon cold. Alexandra jumped into Ginny's arms as Kyle reloaded and planted the weapon against Gordon's head.

"The next one is for you, young feller. You decide, you hear?"

Gordon fell to his knees next to Otis and pounded the ground with his fists until they bled.

"My wife; my son, my life is over! Oh my God! What have I done?"

He started bawling like a child while Otis, who was dazed but unhurt, struggled to his feet. His nose was bleeding and his chin was cut.

"You've got no call doing this, man," he said, mopping the blood from his nose with his shirt sleeve. He picked himself up off the ground and backed away. "Who the hell are you anyway? My mom says you don't belong here. You're not one of us. You're like Jake and them other rich folks. You own everything while we pay with our lives. That's why my dad died."

Gordon looked up.

"Winthrop?"

"Two days ago. No one came to help him."

Otis waved an accusing finger at Gordon.

"And the old Johnson couple with that farm near Bitter End, they caught the bug too," he blurted out. "They're dead also. They died alone. That's your fault."

"The smoke from the boat," said Jack, helping Gordon up. "Was it from Patrick City?"

Otis nodded.

"Those are bodies being burned," explained Otis.

"And houses set on fire from the riots last night," said Ginny with Alexandra in her arms and Kyle at her side. "Fires were set from Bitter End to Sanctuary Village and Patrick City."

"There's more," Kyle went on, lowering his shotgun. "A mob looted Vernon's store and burned it down. They were looking for antibiotics. When they finished with his place, they set homes on fire all to way to Jonathan's hotel and when they got there, they torched it. Clarence showed up with Hugo and some Jamaicans and drove away the mob. But Jonathan must be hurting. His hotel is gone and his bank is wiped out. I'm sure glad Dale and me kept most of our cash is in the States."

Otis pointed an old revolver he had tucked into his belt.

"Jonathan can stop worrying from now on," he said bravely. "I'm going to make sure that nothing more ever happens to him."

"That's good, Otis," said Kyle. "But a gun isn't going to help him or us."

Gordon wiped himself off, made sure that his pistol was securely holstered and slowly recovered his senses.

"I don't know what came over me," he groaned.

"You'll get over it," said Kyle. "Hugo was the same way when he heard that his folks died. But he came along. We're all in the same boat."

"You should all rot in Hell," said Otis, walking away.

Alexandra had stopped crying and wanted to be held by Jack who took her gently in his arms and gave her a sweet he happened to have in his pocket.

They were distracted by the sound of a dog barking dog at the ferry dock where Jack happened to notice that the jitney ferry was parked at a vacant slip and in its place was Avalon. It had obviously returned from its run to Marsh Harbor, but it usually picked up the dead at Agnes Town and rarely stopped at Buccaneer Point.

Clovis was at the helm and Virgil was helping the Castaways band members load five body bags on board the death ship. Virgil's black hound dog was barking at Jonathan Hall who was arguing with Clovis.

Virgil caught Ginny's eye, waved and came over. A thin smile sneaked across his bony face.

"Good afternoon, gentlemen, fair lady."

He looked directly at Gordon.

"My condolences, sir; we are giving your wife a right proper burial at sea later today if you wish to join us, sir."

"Yes, yes, of course," Gordon stammered.

Virgil turned to Jack.

"We can use your horn, Jake. The Castaways need you."

Jack nodded silently as Virgil continued, "I must also apologize for Styx and Mr. Hall. His Honor wishes to go to Agnes Town and Clovis is explaining that he must wait until our work is done." He drew a deep breath to control his temper. "What a pity we must keep meeting under these circumstances." And to Jack and Ginny, he added. "My brother and I pray you may you enjoy a long, healthy life."

"Thanks," said Jack. "Let's keep the accent on healthy."

"Oh, it's so sad, Shelly" said Ginny, her voice quivering. "Remember the two couples with the bug problem? They died of Plague last night."

Jack cradled her in one arm and held Alexandra in the other.

"It's all right," he said. "We'll get through this. I guarantee it."

"Jake is right, little lady," agreed Virgil. "This will pass."

He turned to Gordon.

"It's good to see you back, chief. Are you here to stay?"

Gordon shook his head, saying, "It's that meeting tomorrow. I can't miss it."

"Meetings are good," Virgil nodded. "But fuel is better."

"I don't follow your meaning," said Gordon.

"It goes like this, chief," continued Virgil. "I'm short. Avalon cannot move without fuel even if our services are free."

"That's mighty generous of you," said Ginny, drying her tears. "And you're more than welcome to our fuel, but we don't have much left either.

Just then Jonathan Hall staggered over, reeking of liquor.

"Ah, I see you're back, Jake. How's Doreen?"

Jack cringed, replying as best he could, "We don't know, Jonathan."

Gordon jumped to Jack's rescue and explained as briefly and calmly as possible the events of the last few days, but his surface calmness only enraged Jonathan.

"Jake is alive and Doreen is dead. How does that work?"

"You're wrong," Gordon replied. "We don't know if she's dead or alive. But if she is dead, we are dreadfully sorry. She was a good woman. And if it makes you feel better, Dan and Fred are also dead."

Jonathan was seething and turned to Jack.

"How come people die when you're around, Jake? You're to blame for all this, you and Louie Gold. You probably killed Dan and Fred too. And I bet you had a hand in burning down my hotel."

"You're out of line, Jonathan," said Gordon. "You're pissed because you lost your hotel. But you'll recoup. You must be insured."

"My insurance was cancelled," Jonathan snapped back. He gave Gordon a dirty look. "Are you challenging my authority?"

"No sir; I'm simply citing some facts. Your daughter was very ill and wandered off alone in the middle of the night. And Jake was not present when Dan shot Fred and then shot himself. He was with me."

"We'll see about that at the meeting," Jonathan warned. "We don't need his sort here. We were fine without him and we'll be fine when he leaves. I hear you're going to talk about your killer bugs."

Jack and Gordon said nothing.

"I know what you're up to," Jonathan ranted, "You and Jake. "You're spreading a rumor about a bunch of bugs running around killing people to force people to sell their homes on the cheap."

Gordon tried to calm Jonathan but it was in vain. Jonathan teetered back to the ferry dock, and at that instant the earth under their feet.

"What's that?" Gordon asked.

"It is an omen telling us to find a new home," replied Virgil.

26

Deadly Encounter

One would have assumed that Milton, left pretty much to his own devices by Gordon, would have tried to make a run for the States. He didn't. It may have been because he had accepted his father's belief that there needed to be a basic order to society if it was to function at all. He did his job and dutifully stayed in radio contact with the Borders until the very day that even satellite transmitted signals were cut off.

Sunday was turning out to be a long hot day. Church services were cancelled without notice. The source of the decision was unclear and Hiram was nowhere to be found. The only prayer service was on Avalon where the Castaways and Virgil did the honors as bodies were gently eased overboard to their watery graves to the slow wail of Amazing Grace from Jack's horn.

They returned that evening where Ginny whipped up a sandwich and lemonade picnic dinner served outdoors. If anyone at all was happy, it was Alexandra who played and basked in the company around her despite the dour circumstances. They would have ordinarily dined indoors but the power was turned off and that meant there was no air conditioning. But even under the stars, the air was stifling.

A routine was slowly shaping up. Alexandra was getting used to the ongoing tumult around her and seemed comfortable with it and the company of different people showing up unexpectedly. She was acquiring a vocabulary, words like mommy and daddy and pappy, uncle and aunty. Jack was daddy and Ginny was mommy; Kyle was Pappy. Dennis, a frequent visitor, was Uncle, and Jane Baron, who often came with Dennis, was Aunty. Dennis came alone that evening and Alexandra asked for Aunty Jane.

"Aunty?" she cooed. "Aunty?"

Dennis smiled.

"Aunty is working," the young doctor explained.

"Everyone works," added Kyle who sat down with them.

"Work?" Alexendra repeated.

"Are you and Jane becoming an item?" Jack asked.

"Shelly, that's not a fair question," Ginny admonished.

"Just wondering," said Jack.

"It's all right," Dennis nodded. "I'm stuck here so I thought to make the best of things. Jane is single and so am I, and we have mutual interests."

"Oh yeah, what are they?"

Ginny shook her finger playfully at Jack.

"Shelly is such a pig."

Jack laughed and asked why no butter was on his bread. Alexandra took his cue and tapped the table with a spoon.

"Bread and butter," she echoed with a self-satisfied giggle.

"No butter," Ginny told her sternly. "You may have bread and jelly."

"No butter?" Jack repeated.

"No butter," insisted his wife. "No refrigeration, no ice and no butter."

"Isn't this stuff produced in the Borders?" Dennis asked.

Jack shook his head.

"Nothing grows well in the islands," he explained. "We have a few cows, pigs, goats and chickens but not nearly enough to feed us. Everything we have comes from Canada, the States or Europe, and veggies come from South America. The only thing we make here is rum."

Having no way to get back to Agnes Town that evening, Dennis spent the night sleeping on the couch in the living room. The next morning, being Monday, the twelfth day of June, he hitched a ride after breakfast with Jack on one of the idle dinghies at the marina and they powered across the cut to North Border. On the way Jack told Dennis about the spare vials of antidote he and Gordon had.

"I had a couple for Ginny and Alexandra, and Gordon had one for his wife," he said. "My guess is that you gave my wife and daughter their shots while I was gone and Gordon won't need his spare shot."

Dennis nodded.

"That's right. Alexandra is the next generation and Ginny must be around to raise her and so should you."

"I've taken my shot," said Jack.

"Great. Then why don't you and Gordon save those extra shots for people who deserve them most? I've already given Jane a shot."

"I'm not good at playing God," said Jack.

"God doesn't decide who lives or dies," Dennis argued. "He only decides who goes to Heaven or Hell, and even there, I'm not positive."

They tied the dink at the public dock and walked over to Madame Lamar's store. It was a strange feeling. The customs office was closed, Cheetah's was shuttered, the seaplane tarmac was deserted and the streets, normally filled with families walking about after Sunday services, were empty. The store, however, was open and Gladys Lamar was there, sweeping the porch as she always did, almost as if nothing at all had happened. She was humming some vague tune, had little to say and seemed quite resigned about Winthrop's death.

"His time was up," she said. "It's that life line, you see. All of us have one, and it is cut at different lengths long before we're born."

"Well," said Jack. "I'm sorry just the same. Winthrop was a good man."

"He sure was," agreed Gladys. "And he was a better man than you. He was a true God fearing man. He'd still be alive were it not for you and your foreign friends."

She kept sweeping and humming and staring at the deserted seaplane tarmac on the other side of the dusty road.

"It's that string of life. That's what Hiram Cooper calls it, a string of life. You have one too, Shelly, and you too, doctor. How long is your string of life?"

Dennis held out an open hand.

"You mean my lifeline, the one in the palm of my hand?"

"No, young man," she cackled. "That means nothing. The string is the one you have in your soul when you're born. It determines how long you live."

"Can the string be broken?"

"Yes."

They wished her well and left. On the dock, they saw Clarence and Lance jump out of a police launch that had pulled up at the public dock. With them were about a dozen heavily armed men, half being Hugo's Jamaicans.

Lance, reserved as usual, greeted Jack politely.

"It's nice to have you back," said Lance with the hint of a smile on his lips.

"Yes," echoed Clarence. "We need you. Things are bad."

"Do you have new troops?" Jack asked.

The BDF commander made a wry face.

"I've declared martial law in the Abaco and Border islands and deputized every able bodied male around. I found these guys at the Zebra and Hugo loaned them to me. They report to Eldridge."

"Where are Hugo and Eldridge?"

"They're at a memorial service that Francois Honoree is running for their folks at All Souls," Clarence answered, wiping his brow.

"I hate doing this," said Lance, "but unless we maintain order, this place is going to collapse."

"What about Gordon Tully?"

"We'll use him here," said Clarence. "And you too, doctor."

"Not a problem," said Jack. "You can count on us. So, what do you need?"

"We need you to keep things under control in South Border," said Lance.

"You can have Otis," offered Clarence. "I'll also send Eldridge, Winslow Bates and ten Jamaicans. I'll keep Marvell Sullivan here in Agnes Town."

"What about the other Jamaicans?" Jack asked.

"You're looking at them," replied Lance. The rest either died or skipped, I'm not sure. But I need these men here. They're going to keep the peace with Clarence and with what's left of his police in North Border. I have another twenty men on my cutter in Sanctuary Bay and that will be the command center. It will monitor things and will be in constant radio contact with you and dispatch reinforcements if needed."

"I'm going to Sanctuary Village to pay the Johnson brothers a visit," Jack said.

Clarence pointed to three jeeps parked near Cheetah's.

"I can drive you," he offered. "I'm heading there to position my men along the way. Doctor, do you wish to be dropped off at the hotel?"

Lance returned to the launch with two men, leaving the rest to pile into the jeeps with Clarence, Dennis and Jack and head up Queen's Road. They made a pit stop at Church of Christ to drop off two Jamaicans to protect Hiram in response to death threats he was receiving. Further up at the barracks they saw Winslow and Marvel, armed with pistols, waiting for them. Dale Malone's men knew the Jamaicans in the jeeps by name and greeted each one before taking them inside to await orders.

"We'll cover the infirmary, Bea's Market Diner and the hotel from the barracks," said Clarence when Marvel and Winslow came out again. "Marvel, you'll be my backup here, and Winslow, you'll work with Jake at Pirates' Cove. That will be my command post on South Border."

"What do we do if someone tries to loot the diner? Marvel asked.

"Shoot to kill," replied Clarence, looking at his watch. "Those are Lance's orders and we'll be announcing a dusk-to-dawn curfew soon on the VHF, We'll also use word of mouth and flyers. No one stays out after dark without official permission."

Dennis was dropped off at the North Border hotel where Jane stood outside with a worried look on her face. It turned to all smiles when she saw Dennis. She waved at the jeep and Clarence and Jack waved back as they sped away, calling Hugo on the jeep radio to say that they were coming over.

From the junction where Queen's Road and King's Highway merged into West Leg Road, Clarence and Jack saw smoke in the distance coming from Patrick City. They followed it until they reached the town's smoldering outskirts and drove on to the main square. The buildings around it looked as if they had been fire bombed.

Groups of people spilled out of their burnt out dwellings and almost immediately began screaming, cursing and throwing bricks and stones at the jeep as it bumped along the street around the square. An angry mob encircled it and it was forced to stop.

Clarence was in uniform and well known to residents, but it made no difference. The crowd had been whipped to frenzy and it surged forth in a murderous mood. Bats, clubs, pitch forks, crowbars and knives appeared and the rioters banged on the jeep's sides, leaning hard against it on all sides in attempts to tip it over.

Jack grabbed a shotgun from under his seat and used it as a club to hold the mob at bay while Clarence kept calling the barracks for backup on the jeep radio. Two men jumped into the jeep but were thrown off by a swing of Jack's shotgun. In the melee one of them fired a gun. The bullet grazed Jack's head and dropped him to his knees. Guns now popped up everywhere and bullets flew every which way.

Without thinking, Jack discharged the shotgun's both barrels into the mob and it fell away, leaving four bodies on the dusty road behind the jeep. Clarence tossed a spare pistol to Jack and drew his own service pistol, and within seconds, they were firing point blank into the attacking mob until they heard the short, staccato blasts of automatic weapons coming from the sides of the square. Fearing that a general gunfight had erupted, they emptied their guns, reloaded, and fired again into the mob that was suddenly breaking apart.

Bodies fell where they stood and screams and moans filled the air. More shots rang out and more bodies folded to the ground and the marauding crowd, faced with greater fire power from all sides, scattered and ran for cover.

When the shooting stopped, a ragtag band of Jamaicans waving automatic rifles appeared, led by Hugo and Eldridge. They waded through the carnage and formed a protective gauntlet around the jeep.

Clarence sat dazed in the jeep, pistol still in hand but was otherwise unhurt. Jack wiped the blood off his brow, made sure that Clarence was not hit and sighed with relief when he saw the Johnson brothers.

"We came to pay our respects," he said. "This welcome was unexpected."

"Thanks for the thought, Jake," said Eldridge. "But you made a mistake coming here. We got your message but we're holed up at the Zebra and had to shoot our way out. Mobs control most of the island. Even Dale Malone had to shut down his plant and is stuck with his family and a few workers in his warehouse."

"That's right," Hugo continued. "Folks here are pissed. They think they're being screwed over and not getting the medicine they need. They're also short on fixes."

Clarence put away his pistol and handed Jack alcohol and a bandage from a first aid kit in the glove compartment.

"What do you mean, 'short on fixes.' What sort of fixes?"

"Heroin or cocaine, you fool," cried Hugo. "I can't get any because of the damn blockade and Jake here says that what we have on hand is bad stuff and killing us. What the hell am I going to do? If we do drugs, we die; if we don't, we go crazy and die. If we don't go crazy and die, we die from Plague; and if we don't die of Plague, we die killing each other."

Eldridge put his arm around his brother's shoulder.

"What Hugo is trying to say," Eldridge explained, "is that we need a meeting to discuss our next moves. Sooner or later, we're going to run out of bullets, or out of people."

"We're having one to do just that at Bea's," said Clarence. "You and Hugo need to be there."

Hugo cursed and looked at the dead and wounded.

"We know all about that, chief. Now, are you going to keep yapping away or are you going to help us clean up?"

The dead were brought to local church for family members to claim. Those with superficial wounds or bruises were let go; those with minor gunshot wounds were treated on the spot with first aid supplies from Clarence's jeep and by an EMS van from the infirmary in Agnes Town and released. The more seriously wounded were taken in two jeeps to the infirmary. "Ten dead and fifteen wounded," Clarence said when it was over. "And we don't know how many went down at the Zebra."

"We have one more problem," added Hugo. "Charleen lived near our club with her kids and she died of Plague this morning. We took her kids in, but they need a regular home and family to look after them."

Eldridge nodded.

"I was at her bedside," he said. "She gave me a set of books from Island Trust and I sent them to you early this morning, Clarence. You still have them?"

"They're in my safe," Clarence assured him.

"I hope they help you out," said Eldridge. "She died real hard."

"That's what Lance wants to discuss at Bea's," said Clarence. "We want to keep more people from dying that way. We have medicine for a thousand people and we need to decide who gets it."

"That should be an interesting meeting," Eldridge noted. "We'll be there,"

27

Original Sin

Hiram Cooper often discussed Original Sin with Father Francois Honoree and they could never agree. What is Original Sin? Is it an act that causes a sequence of events that leads to chaos and destruction? Is Original Sin a despicable act at the beginning of the chain or is it defined by the entire events chain culminating in one horrific act? A serpent tempted Eve with an apple and Eve offered Adam a bite, and that started a mess as everyone knows. But suppose the apple had been offered by a fuzzy rabbit or a small monkey? Would that have been wrong? And what's so bad about giving a woman an apple? And why pick on poor old Eve? Maybe the serpent gave Adam the apple first and Adam gave it to Eve as a way to get into her pants. Of course, he need not have bothered since she was naked.

How can a snake, which has no arms or legs, offer anyone an apple? Could the snake be Satan? Why? A meek little rabbit passing for Satan is hard to sell. Maybe that's why. But why would Satan take the form of a snake? Would it not be smarter for Satan to be disguised as a rabbit, monkey, pussycat or penguin? They are warm, cuddly creatures.

Now about that first sin: it may be that it has a domino effect and is defined by the final act. That is causation. So now it can be asked: how did matters get so far out of hand?

The bullet that grazed Jack left barely a nick and he was none the worse for wear. But the bleeding was stubborn and a bandage around his head was needed. He had no need to worry. News of the shootout preceded their return and a medical team assembled by Dennis was on hand and Jack was the first patient. Dennis took over the infirmary and he was now at the barracks barking orders as the wounded began filling the makeshift cots.

Jane became his chief nurse. Lance also showed up with a detachment of men to support Hugo's Jamaicans and Clarence's meager police reserves.

Jonathan Hall, who had stayed at the barracks since his home was uninhabitable, took a jaundiced view of the presence of so many armed men. He took exception to the Patrick City confrontation in the first place and threatened to raise the issue at the forthcoming meeting. But Clarence ignored him, being more interested in the reason why there had been no response to his call for help.

"I had to defer to the acting mayor," replied Marvel Sullivan when Jonathan was out of earshot. "He ordered me not to answer your distress call. That's why I called Hugo and asked him for help. When the mayor found out, he went ballistic and fired me. Am I fired, chief?"

Clarence patted Marvel on the back.

"No. You work for me. He went to his back office desk, pulled a deputy's badge from a drawer and pinned it on Marvel's shirt pocket. "Here, that makes it official. You still need to be nice to Jonathan because he's been having a bad time but you don't take his orders. You work for me," he repeated. "Now, divide the Jamaicans in teams of two. They'll patrol the town and keep people off the streets tonight. I also want you to get a shot of antidote from Dennis."

That won't be necessary," said Marvel. "Lance took care of us."

Later, when things had quieted down, Clarence invited Jack and Winslow to his office where he removed the Island Trust books from the safe and laid them out on his desk. Inside the ledger folders were sandwiched a collection of documents and statements chronicling the bank's financial history. Deposits, withdrawals, loans, repayments, credits and debits were all meticulously recorded with pen and ink by Milton Cooper in an easy-to-read book keeping format.

What struck both Clarence and Jack was the appearance of Hiram Cooper's name and signature as bank founder and principal stockholder, a position he relinquished one year later to Jonathan Hall for $10 million, half of which was deposited to the Church of Christ account and half to Hiram's personal account. There were more surprises. Dan Schulman, Henry Alden. Hugo Johnson, Vernon Peters, Dale and Kyle Malone, Malcolm Harding, Hamilton Graves, Fred Hawk and Bob Byrne were also depositors and shareholders from the very beginning. Bob Byrne? So, the Navy man was a player after all.

They flipped through six years of records, from the Angelina deals, the mortgage transactions for the Grand Bay, North Border and Ocean View hotels, to the more recent expansion of the North Border Treacle factory. The most fascinating feature in the ledgers was the special fees. A two percent surcharge was added by the bank on transactions, cash in or cash out, with the charges credited in equal amounts to the accounts of Jonathan Hall, Hamilton Graves, Hiram Cooper and Bob Byrne.

Bob Byrne again? Milton had carefully recorded that he had received half of the two percent surcharge. It was clear. Bob Byrne was running a protection racket and his piece of the action was a cut of every operation whose cash flows went through Island Trust. His end of the bargain was to keep the Coast Guard and Navy cutters under his command away on short leashes.

And of course, most of the income generating cash flow came from Cheetah's, the Zebra and Hugo. Even Ned Baron's phony insurance policies were recorded. Insurance premiums went to Ned from fictitious clients in the Borders in return for payments made by Ned's principals on fake claims in the same islands. It was a clever circular money laundering scheme in which all concerned, including Ned, took a cut.

The insurers and underwriters hardly paid much attention because the Borders were hardly a blip in their global operations. They panicked and pulled the plug only when the CDC raised the red flag on the bubonic plague. The Angelina affair was also chronicled through monetary outflows and inflows in the ledgers and confirmed all that Jack had learned and/or suspected. And what about Hiram Cooper? He was in just as deeply as Bob Byrne.

This was a shock to Clarence and his hands shook as he turned and examined each sheet of paper.

"I can't believe this," he stated bravely. "These are leading citizens, and Hiram is our spiritual leader. His family has lived here for centuries. Did you suspect any of this?"

Jack shook his head.

"I played the game with everyone, just like I did with you; it was a quid pro quo. I never realized a much larger game was going on. Not until I got here. I told Tully and he was just as clueless as you."

"This is one lousy surprise, Jake. Lance must have known. He's Hiram's son."

"I don't think he ever thought of anything except to do his job, Clarence."

"I'm mortified. What about Milton? He kept these books. They're damning."

"Milton is a question mark," answered Jack. "He may have known but kept quiet to protect his dad. Long story short, it was a convergence of random events with , unrelated human actions with totally different intentions. Ben Alden created the Red Death for patriotic reasons; Bob

Byrne was the architect and mastermind of an international conspiracy to sell drugs and everyone else fell in line to make a buck and then cover up when it was clear that their collective actions unleashed a global plague epidemic. That's the short and long of it, Clarence. Shall we close the books on this one?""

Clarence closed the ledgers.

"We need to speak to Hiram," he said. But it was all too much. He broke down at the barracks as they were about to leave for Pirates' Cove with Winslow Bates.

"Do you know that I never killed a human being until I shot Malcolm Harding at Cheetah's? I stay up nights thinking about it. Today, I shot and killed a bunch of people and became a mass murderer. On top of that, I'm a lousy cop."

"You're not a mass murderer," said Winslow. "You did what you had to do. You and Jake did just fine. I would have done the same thing."

"Still, I feel terrible," the police chief insisted. "I'm not a killer. I'm not even a good cop. What the hell am I going to do about Jonathan and Hiram?"

"You're a great cop," said Jack. "You're a great law enforcement officer, and besides, you're the only top cop we have in the Borders."

Clarence looked at Jack.

"Do you really believe that?"

Jack grinned.

"You're the man, old buddy."

Winslow nodded.

"Jake is right, chief. You're the man."

Clarence smiled. He was reassured.

A recorded message announcing a dusk-to-dawn curfew was broadcast from the barracks every few minutes and an armed detail from Lance Cooper's cutter and a Jamaican cohort began fanning out throughout the two islands with posters and flyers to make sure the message was communicated.

"Let's stop at the rectory," said Clarence. "I want to speak to Hiram."

"Should I wait outside?" Winslow asked.

Clarence sighed and looked at Jack.

"You might as well join us," he responded. "The time for secrets is over."

The two Jamaicans on guard duty were outside the rectory and one of them went inside to inform Hiram that he had company. He came out, tall and straight as an arrow, as he always was, and invited Clarence, Jack and Winthrop into his study. It was the first time that Winthrop set foot in the rectory and he stared open mouthed at what must have struck him as opulent quarters accentuated by the gentle hum of the air conditioning.

Hiram wore his usual ascot and silk smoking jacket, the one with a shawl collar, and that too upset Winthrop who had never seen him at services in anything but his simple black frock. Hiram was cordial but he was slightly tipsy and his speech was slurred. It was hard to tell if he had been sleeping or drinking or both. In any case, he appeared disinterested when told of the events around him. What irked Clarence was the air conditioning. It was on and was supposed to be off.

"Drink, gentlemen?" Hiram offered.

They declined his offer.

"We'd love to, but we're on duty," said Winslow.

Hiram went straight to an open bottle of cognac and poured himself a shot.

"What can I do for you, gentlemen?"

"I'm a little slow," said Jack. "So, you have to help me out."

Hiram took a sip of cognac.

"I'll help all I can."

"Charleen died of Plague as you know. But before she died she gave Eldridge the Island Trust books she was auditing for Milton."

"That is much like giving a bible to Satan," Hiram noted.

"Yes, but Eldridge gave them to me for safekeeping," said Clarence, "We took a look at them and your name shows up as the founder of Island Trust."

"It's an obvious forgery," Hiram stated without blinking an eyelash. "My church has an account with Island Trust; that is true."

"Well, it's not so important now," Jack added. "I'm more curious about the stock of antidote Cyrus gave Lance for delivery to you. It seems to me that Cyrus knew a plague epidemic was coming. How did he know?"

Hiram struggled for an answer.

"He may have learned about it from Ben or Henry Alden. Once he knew, he told me that we may have a problem in the Bahamas."

"But how would anyone know the Bahamas might be in danger unless it was known that the Angelina was carrying contaminated cargo?" Clarence asked.

Hiram had no response.

"Then what I don't understand is how you thought a thousand shots of antidote would have been enough," Clarence went on.

"It wasn't enough. I was hoping for a miracle."

"But hear me out. If you knew we were in for this kind of trouble ahead of time, you could have said something. An orderly evacuation could have been arranged."

Hiram laughed sarcastically.

"Where would you have wanted that orderly evacuation to go? It was April when I thought we had a problem and I had no idea how bad it was going to be. It began with that cruise ship in South Border when some of the passengers took sick and died when they got home. That's where it started. My son Cyrus was at the CDC and told me that Washington suspected a plague epidemic was imminent and had redlined the Bahamas. The American Embassy in Nassau closed its visa office in late April and followed up with this blockade."

Clarence was dumbfounded.

"Are you blaming the plague on Washington, reverend?"

"Of course not," Hiram snapped back. "Washington has over 300 million people to protect. We are less than 300,000 in the Bahamas. Who do you think should be sacrificed: the many or the few?"

"But we'd have cut our losses with advance warning," sputtered Clarence. "If an evacuation was out, we could have taken other measures. Besides, you knew that we might have a problem five years ago."

Hiram Cooper stood up and curled his lips.

"Yes, I knew. I knew that God was planning to punish us for our transgressions. All efforts to fight his will would have been futile. Plague is God's way to punish sinners by using Satan and his disciples to bring death. My regret is that I could not reach the sinners in my flock that started this mess. They were seduced by Louie Gold and his friends and must take the blame, but the Lord will decide if they are to be damned to Hell."

Winslow, who had kept his peace all this time, spoke up.

"Shifting blame and finding fault isn't going to solve our problem, reverend."

"You are right, my young friend," agreed Hiram. "We made all our money from the drug trade. But I had no idea that the heroin coming in here was contaminated until it was too late. We were all caught short, gentlemen, and it has cost me the lives of two of my sons and the family of another son."

"But that doesn't make sense," said Clarence. "Damn it, Hiram. This could have been avoided."

"In retrospect, we could have been more transparent." Hiram laughed nervously and then recovered his nerve. "Mistakes were made but it doesn't matter anymore.

Do you believe in original sin?"

"I don't follow," said Winslow.

Hiram gripped the edge of a table for support and leaned forward to explain in a voice that was now thick and slurred.

"Original sin was committed when the plot to bring that tainted heroin here from the Middle East, gentlemen. It was all about greed; and whoever was directly or indirectly or even circumspectly involved must pay the consequences. Whatever has happened or whatever is happening and whatever will happen is God's will and punishment.. In the end, on the Judgment Day, true believers will be saved and all sinners will go to straight to Hell. The quantity of available antidote is therefore irrelevant. Everything is irrelevant now."

"What happened to the drug money received by this church, reverend?"

"It went into my account and into the church bank account at Island Trust."

Hiram ranting was becoming incoherent.

"Jonathan was tempted by Satan. Our ancestors left Sodom and Gomorrah for a better life and never looked back; but Satan made Jonathan look back and we must pay. Jonathan cannot be blamed for Satan's work."

As if to punctuate his words, a tremor shook the rectory. Hiram's glass dropped off the table and broke into pieces on the floor, spilling its contents over the rug.

It was a long day, and Jack heaved a huge sigh of relief when he finally got home to Pirates' Cove.

"We're at a crossroads," he concluded grimly after dinner.

"What do you mean?" Ginny asked.

"I think we've gone about as far as we can," he explained. "We must leave."

Looking directly into his eyes, she said, "Yes; we have to think of Alexandra and our unborn child." Tears rolled down her cheeks. "But it's hard, Shelly. This is our home and life is good here. Where are we going to find this kind of life, and what about the blockade?" Ginny asked, drying her tears.

"Archangel can get out of here if we have a decoy to draw fire."

"You've been planning," she said.

"I guess so," he admitted.

28

The Meeting

Contrary to what Gordon may have been thinking, Jack did not entertain high hopes for the coming meeting and dreaded going. The air was too charged and poisoned for it to have a positive outcome. He resolved to attend if for no other reason than to support his few friends and allies and out of a sense of obligation to Lance Cooper who was supposedly going to preside over the meeting.

The long awaited meeting set for Tuesday, the thirteenth of June, needed to be put off for logistical reasons. Too many people were sick and many of them were dying. Conditions were bordering on anarchy. A new date was set for Saturday, the seventeenth of June. Jack had now been in the Borders one month. Virgil did some figuring and estimated three hundred bodies were taken by Avalon to their watery graves, an average of ten bodies daily. He calculated further that for every body taken out to sea, ten or more died where they stood and were disposed of on the spot. If he was right, it meant that the Red Death had claimed the lives of about three thousand residents of the Borders in that one month. These were men, women and children of all ages and from all walks of life. Jack did the math. The islands' population had fallen from thirteen thousand in May to ten thousand in June. That was a twenty three percent drop in one month.

A tenuous peace prevailed over the Borders, although it was broken occasionally by the sound of gunfire in outlying areas. Winslow and the Jamaicans kept order on South Border, and no news was good news in North Border where Marvel was in control in Agnes Town. The Johnson brothers and their small band maintained order from Patrick City to Dale Malone's factory while the Castaways reggae band took up arms alongside their musical instruments and joined the Johnson brothers.

On Tuesday, Dennis and Jane jumped into dinghy with their belongings and went over to Pirates' Cove. They were scared of staying alone at the hotel and asked to spend a few days in one of the empty yachts at the marina. They were joined later by Gordon who was alone at his home and asked Jack to stay on Archangel. End Run lay unoccupied at another slip but no one wanted to stay on it.

That night, over a picnic dinner under the stars, Dennis brought up the subject of the tremors that were increasing in intensity and frequency.

"We felt the shakes here," said Kyle, "It broke one of my fuel pumps."

Ginny put her arm around Alexandra and looked at Jack.

"Do we add that to our worries?"

Jack shrugged his shoulders and kept picking at his plate. Turning to Dennis, he asked, "What do you think, doctor?"

"It's that underground volcano at Hermit Cay," he answered. "I went over there with Hugo the other day with some instruments. That thing is going to blow soon." "Maybe we should plan to leave," said Gordon.

"If you guys are going to cut out," Jane added. "Dennis and I want to tag along."

Kyle Malone sighed with resignation.

"I'm in," he said. "I've done enough damage here to last several lifetimes."

"What about Dale?" Ginny asked.

"I spoke to my brother," Kyle replied. "He's out of business. We all are. He'll leave if we leave. Luckily, we have most of our money in the States. He's ready to take a chance with the blockade. We're ready to move on with our lives."

All eyes turned to Jack.

"We can start by getting some of our things together," he suggested.

Saturday brought more heat than usual. A tremor shook the Borders shortly after dawn and added a note of urgency to the meeting at Bea's diner.

Bea Norris and Terrence Moore were up early, pushing tables aside and lining up the chairs in the main dining area. Bea was a big fat woman with a babushka on her head and an apron around her ample waist. Her roots went back to the slave days and she often gave Jack a recitation of events in the lives of her ancestors whenever he stopped in. Her most vivid accounts were of the deadly epidemics that had swept the islands and she now added historical perspective to the Borders' current situation as guests began arriving.

There was an outbreak of Plague several hundred years ago, she said as Terrance dutifully began serving coffee, tea and biscuits. Cholera struck the

Bahamas in the early 1800's, she related. That was followed by outbreaks of Yellow Fever, Malaria and other diseases like Small Pox and Influenza. Entire communities were literally wiped out but somehow the islanders survived.

"How about what's happening now?" Clarence asked. "Aren't you scared?"

Bea laughed and her blubbery body shook.

"No. This is God's way of clearing the world of dying leaves, dead wood and fallen down sinners. I have no fear because I believe in the Lord, Jesus Christ. He will provide and I will be saved!"

"That's right," Terrence chimed in. "We will be saved because we believe in the Lord. We're not foreigners like you who have snuck into our land to steal from our people. We believe!"

"Amen to that," said Hiram Cooper who had just arrived with his son, Lance.

Encouraged by Hiram's words, Terrence pressed his point.

"This sad state of affairs is the fault of foreigners whose evil ways have brought us death and destruction."

Vernon, who walked in and overheard the conversation, added, "We must get rid of these people before they get rid of us."

Of course, the bigger problem was that due to the ravages of the plague and the embargo, most businesses, including Bea's Market Diner and Vernon's store were on their backs. The Borders lay in economic paralysis. In an effort to raise cash, Bea tried to sell the huge antique crystal chandelier that hung down from the high ceiling in front of the restaurant's walkup counter, but there were no takers. No one knew where it came from or how it ended up at the diner but it was a curiosity and local attraction and was considered by many as a good luck symbol.

Under the chandelier's dominating glare, people drifted in and out; tables were pushed aside to make room for rows of chairs in front of the counter behind which Lance now stood, ready to preside over the meeting. He was as personable as was possible for a change.

Ginny stayed at the marina with Alexandra but Kyle showed up with his brother Dale. Clarence stood with Gordon behind the counter with Lance in their freshly cleaned and pressed uniforms.

Jane came with Dennis and sat in the first row with Father Francois Honoree and Virgil and Clovis. Behind them sat Reggie, Hugo and Eldridge. Jack sat in the last row, pretty much alone. In the row directly in front of Jack sat Jonathan, Gladys Lamar, Otis and Vernon who would from time to time turn their heads and glare at him. Hiram took a seat next to them. The space between the last row of chairs and the door was crowded with standees who seemed to be Hiram's parishioners.

Once the guests were seated Lance returned to his usual grim self and barely a smile ever left his lips when he spoke. He was not at his best as a public speaker and there were no protocols for the rules of order so he started the meeting and tried to be brief and to the point. He spoke about the plague without fanfare and emotion and went over the emergency measures he had enacted as the region's acting commissioner.

"They are just and necessary to preserve out lives as long as possible," he said in conclusion.

Everyone listened politely with scarcely a murmur until he came to the subject of the plague antidote. Pulling up a box from under his feet he put it on the counter. It was the box that Jack and Dennis had given him at the start of the meeting.

"We have a thousand units of antidote," Lance declared. "It is enough to keep a thousand people from falling ill and dying. Our purpose here is to decide on a fair and equitable allocation system."

Virgil raised his hand in a request to say something and was acknowledged by Lance. Virgil was brief.

Three thousand of our people have been lost since May," he started. "At this rate the Borders will be zeroed out by the year's end."

Jonathan rose to his feet and demanded to be heard. Without ever bothering to be acknowledged by Lance he began by questioning the very existence of a plague epidemic in the islands.

"My family has lived here for generations," he said. "We have suffered the wrath of the Lord many times and have survived. No one lives forever and we must die someday, but those of us who are true believers will have eternal life in Heaven."

"I agree completely," said Lance. "But why die now if we can die later? We have the antidote to stop this plague from killing a thousand people."

"These germs," continued Jonathan with a sneer. "Why can't they be seen?"

"They're microscopic bugs, Jonathan," Dennis interrupted. "Plague is caused by a bacterium and virus. It's ugly and has killed many people here so far and it has killed millions throughout history. Tetracycline and other antibiotics mixed with flu shots work. Doctors have no problem diagnosing the disease and neither do I. I even have some of the cocktail antidote, and so does Henry. I gave it on Kyle and he lived."

"Oh. They're not big bugs, you say. They're small bugs. They're so small that they can't be seen. They're invisible."

"That's right," Dennis confirmed.

Jonathan's eyes narrowed.

"So I can't see them."

"That's right," said Jack. "It's like a virus or bacteria."

Jonathan turned to face him.

"Oh, so now you're a doctor. Maybe a scientist too, you say? You and this young punk who says he's a doctor? Well, we know nothing about him. And Jake, he's a murderer. He murdered my daughter Doreen and he shot and killed Dan Schulman and Fred Hawk. He should be arrested and tried for murder."

Gordon protested.

"You're wrong, Jonathan," he said. "We have no idea what happened to Doreen; she may be alive for all we know. And I was with Jake when Fred and Dan died. Fred died of AIDS; Dan shot him and then himself."

Jonathan was defiant and refused to believe Gordon.

"Oh yeah, where is Henry? He'll set things straight."

"Henry is in Marsh Harbor with Cynthia treating Plague victims," said Gordon.

Jonathan pressed on.

"So you say. How do we know you're telling the truth? Milton will know; we'll get him to testify."

Gordon shook his head.

"Milton stayed on in Marsh Harbor with Henry and Cynthia."

"You're lying," Jonathan yelled. "Milton is probably dead, and now you say that invisible bugs are killing people? If you ask me, I say that you're the ones trying to kill us."

Gladys Lamar took over where Jonathan left off.

"We were doing fine until foreigners took over our lives. They should leave."

Otis Foote agreed.

"Our troubles started with Louie Gold, the Jew who brought all these foreigners to our land. He did Satan's work and these foreigners are his legions. They patrol the streets of our towns and spread death disguised as Plague.

"There is no real plague. We're dying because they're poisoning our food and water. They should be driven out. And that antidote we're talking about? I know for a fact that the box on the counter has over twenty thousand needles. And I know for a fact that they're filled with deadly poison."

"These damn foreigners are going to kill us all if we don't stop them," Vernon s yelled in turn. "Kill them and the dying will stop!"

Terrence Moore jumped up.

"Let's get rid of them now!"

Jonathan waved one hand at Lance and pointed to Jack with the other.

"As the mayor of South Border and the acting mayor of North Border, I demand that Jake Sloane be arrested for murder," he screamed.

"I'll second that," said Vernon. "Chief Cox must arrest him now."

He rose to his feet and produced a parchment document from the inside of his jacket and waved it in the air.

"I hold in my hands," he said triumphantly, "the original charter granted to the settlers of these islands by the English Parliament and the King three centuries ago. It grants exclusive land rights to the Borders' original settlers and their descendents forever. This means that we own this land in fee simple absolute. It also means that people here who are not direct descendents of the first settlers are guests with no rights except as tenants at will. These tenancies can be revoked. These interlopers should be rounded up, arrested and either executed or deported!"

Vernon's neck veins swelled and his face turned beet red as his tirade was met with wild applause and cheers. Jack finally knew why Vernon wanted to position himself as an old line family descendent. The document he waved in the air must have been the one Father Honoree gave him, a copy of a royal land grant, and he intended to make it a centerpiece to legally evict the newer residents from their freeholds. Plague aside, if Vernon's arguments succeeded, the wealth and income of the Borders could change hands and he, Jack, would lose his business without ever receiving a dime for it.

Clarence looked nervously at Lance who banged on the counter.

"Relax. No one is going to arrest anyone, gentlemen," Lance said. "No one is going to be rounded up and no one is going to be deported. We have courts who can rule on land claims and other such weighty issues in due course. But as of now, the rights of landowners are not in issue, and I endorse Chief Tully's testimony.

"What's more, we happen to have more than enough evidence that indicates that both Fred Hawk was sick with AIDS for more than a year. As for Dan Schulman, it is very unfortunate, but I suspect he took his own life because he lost all his money when Island Trust went bankrupt."

"That's not true," Jonathan snapped back in his own defense. "There was nothing wrong with Island Trust. It was sabotaged by insufficient deposits from these damn foreigners running our businesses and our government. They withdrew their money from Island Trust, convinced their friends to do the same and deposited their funds in Jewish owned banks. I know that for a fact."

"Can you explain that statement, Jonathan?" Clarence asked.

"Very easily," responded the mayor. "Let's talk about you. You weren't born in the Bahamas."

Boos came from the onlookers standing behind the last row of chairs.

"I'm a Bahamian citizen, like you," protested the police chief.

"You're an interloper, like the rest of them," Jonathan insisted. "You came from the States because you couldn't make a living there. That's the only reason you're here. We pay you to protect us and all you do is take our money. It used to be that you deposited your money at Island Trust. You don't even do that anymore. Matter of fact, you closed your account with us."

"I did the same," said Gordon, in support of Clarence. "Your bank had too many risky investments." He was politely referring to the mayor's gambling addiction at the gaming tables of Nassau with his bank depositors' money.

Hiram came to Jonathan's defense.

"I encouraged Jonathan to make those investments in the name of the Lord. Satan is responsible for the bank's losses. Gambling, unless it is sanctioned by God, is a sin. I plan to circulate a petition making all sin a crime punishable by law. I hope to have your support."

The crowd stood up and cheered loudly, shouting, "Hear, Hear!"

Reggie could not believe his ears.

"Are you saying that any sin is a crime?"

"All sins are crimes," yelled Hiram. "The wage of sin is death."

"Amen," screamed the crowd.

Jonathan continued his tirade.

"Who convinced Chief Cox to close his account with Island Trust? Who talked Gordon Tully into canceling his account with us? It was Louie Gold and Jake who came here to make money out of our blood and never banked at Island Trust. And look at Dale Malone. He's not a Bahamian; he's from Georgia. He took his money out of Island Trust. So did his brother, Kyle. I tell you, they drove our bank under, as did the Johnson brothers, the Zebra, Cheetah's and Ginny Malone. She is a real Jezebel and Bathsheba. They are traitors and should be run out!"

The "Amens" changed into boos and catcalls.

"Island Trust is the pride and joy of these islands," Jonathan stated proudly. "It is the symbol of our strength and our belief in the Lord. These foreigners and their kind do not believe in the Lord. They do not believe in our land. They have come here to milk it dry with their Dominican, Haitian and Jamaican slaves who must also be driven out.

"They are Satan's servants and have conspired against us. They took our money and now they want to steal our lives and our souls. Drive them out of the islands, I say. This so-called epidemic is a hoax. Our food and water are being poisoned by these foreigners to force the sale of our land and businesses so that they can take over everything we own and hold dear. We must get rid of these foreign devils."

Father Francis Honoree could not contain himself and felt compelled to speak.

"We are all foreigners," he reminded everyone in his lyrical Haitian accent. But his words fell on deaf ears, received only with more boos and catcalls.

"In the beginning, Indians inhabited this land until Europeans came and killed them. Some of us are here longer than others, but we are all from other places. We have recent immigrants, like Jamaicans, Dominicans and Haitians, and we have immigrants like Jake and the Malone brothers and the Johnson family. It is these recent arrivals who have made the Borders rich and what is it today. If we blame them for our misery, we must also credit them for our prosperity."

Someone from the back yelled that he should go back to Africa and the remark was followed by hoots, catcalls and taunts. And object flew through the air and hit the priest in the back of his head but he was unharmed. Hugo wanted to jump into the standing crowd but was restrained by his brother.

Hiram took this opportunity to rise to his feet and the diner fell silent.

"My son Lancelot means well but he is terribly misguided, and I happen to like Francois Honoree, but he leads a fallen religion and his lips are moved by Satan. The Judgment Day is upon us and sinners will go to Hell and the blessed will go to Heaven. We must fight to restore our Christian values. It is that simple."

The crowd roared and turned violent. Hands grabbed Jack's shoulders. Their grip tightened and he would have been in trouble had not a severe jolt shaken the diner at that moment. It was followed by loud tremors that rocked the diner and began cracking its floor, ceiling and walls. One tremor split the rafters supporting the chandelier and it came crashing to the floor. Its crystals smashed on contact and an explosion sent chards of glass flying through the air like shrapnel. It was enough to clear the diner in less than a minute.

Jack never budged from his seat. He sat there, arms outstretched over the tops of the chairs around him, grinning at the faces of those who had stayed behind.

"You are the true believers," he said admiringly. "Are you ready for a fight?"

29

Life Carries On

Lancelot Cooper was not an ideologue and he could only watch with dismay as the meeting disintegrated into a near riot that ended only when the earth tremor nearly shook the diner apart. He was more of an idealist whose goal was to be a good naval officer, an effective commander and preserver of public order and last but not least a good Christian. Doing the right thing was important to him. But he was also a realist like Jack. Neither men were fools and knew they had to protect themselves and their families. Faced with the facts that the islands were falling into anarchy and that their existence was threatened by the frequency of ever more violent quakes, plague or no plague, they each concluded in their own way that it was time to go.

Nothing came of Jonathan's outburst. The quake that ended the meeting at Bea's brought spread fear among the residents. Jonathan and his friends retreated to their homes and shelters to regroup and ponder their next move. It was abundantly clear that their jaundiced view of the more recent arrivals to the Borders was a festering sore that was about to burst open into organized violence. Vernon had identified the targets as everyone not born and bred in the Borders. They were the interloping foreigners and the cause of all that was evil.

These old line families accounted for about half of the population and could trace their ancestry at least to the Civil War era in the States when many southerners left the States migrated to the Bahamas. Some families even tracked their beginnings to the Tories who fled to the Bahamas during the American Revolution. A few, like Hiram Cooper, Jonathan Hall and Gladys Lamar had an even longer pedigree and bragged about being descended from English settlers who had lived in the islands since the seventeenth and eighteenth centuries. Why they felt threatened now was anyone's guess.

Jane Baron, despite her deep roots in the Bahamas, was an outsider because she had left her homeland as a child. Perhaps that was the reason she was drawn to Dennis Sinclair, the newest arrival, who by now was also eager to leave for good.

Ginny Malone had greater acceptance issues stemming revolving around her night club. Indeed, Cheetah's, where many adult residents went for sex, was the crux of the problem. Her well frequented establishment was seen as a necessary evil. But necessary evils are held in low esteem and are often considered dispensable in trying times. Thus Cheetah's was the first casualty after the failed meeting. A mob led by Otis and egged on by Jonathan marched on Cheetah's and burned it to the ground. Ginny was now out of business.

Nor did the old line families accept Clarence, Gordon, Virgil and Clovis who had come to the Borders in their younger years. They worked hard, enjoyed their new Bahamian skins and were fiercely independent and unwilling to be pushed around by anyone. They were thus resented for their success and their perceived greed for not wanting to share or sell their going businesses. The Malone brothers, Dale and Kyle, were despised for similar reasons. They had built their enterprises from the ground up, were major employers and were therefore eyed with envy. They were tolerated but never accepted.

Most successful of all was Jack Sloane, and probably for that reason, he was the most hated person in the islands, at least behind his back. That dislike extended to the Johnson brothers and their Jamaicans. They were drug traffickers, another one of those necessary evils, and too much successful for local wags to swallow.

And then there were the Dominicans and Haitians. They did the menial work and were otherwise ignored. Father Francois Honoree had a good following among the Haitians but that was the limit of his influence. The Haitians hated the Dominicans and conversely. They nurtured this mutual hatred, retreated to the relative safety of their respective ghettos from where they launched raiding parties and began setting fire to adjoining neighborhoods.

To make matter worse, everyone was armed, shootings were commonplace and it was hard to tell if people died more often from random killings than from the Red Death. The old line families fared well. They were better organized and well dug in. They called themselves Patriots, formed militias and soon controlled South Border except for Pirates' Cove. This meant that they held the airstrip where Jack had his plane.

North Border was an anarchical mess and under no control by anyone. Warring factions fought for turf, having long forgotten why they were fighting. The island slid into a deadly 'no-go' bombed out war zone with fires raging in Agnes Town, Patrick City and Sanctuary Village.

Indeed, Pirates' Cove was the only foothold Lance could claim, turning him and people like Jack and his rag tag followers, none of whom he really liked or trusted, into default allies. To add to his grief, he felt betrayed by his father who sided with the Patriots and refused to speak with them on any and all matters. He made up his mind never see any of them again.

Jack quickly saw that they were outnumbered and outgunned. The saving grace was that the Patriots were basically leaderless. Otis was long on action but short on brains, Jonathan and Hiram were habitually drunk, Terrence, Bea and Gladys had no action plan and Vernon was a coward.

Plague was another constraint on the Patriots. Many fully armed families turned their homes into mini-fortresses to ward off any and all uninvited guests, including the Patriots. Most of them were more concerned with staying alive than in waging civil war and refused to be drawn into the struggle.

One day, Otis and his mob went to All Saints Church at Sanctuary Village and set it on fire. Francois Honoree stood his ground and confronted the arsonists in front of the church, giving his parishioners a chance to escape. He was stoned and went up the bell tower where he was seen spreading his arms out in prayer for his tormentors when it was engulfed in flames. His incinerated body was found later in the charred remains of church.

The mob's next stop was the Zebra Club but it was too fiercely defended by the Jamaicans who held fast. They routed the attackers, killing half of them. The mob regrouped, stole several skiffs, and sailed down Sanctuary Bay to Agnes Town where it gathered at Jack's boat yard. The buildings were torched and destroyed, but the mob found itself facing a machine gun nest in the customs hut that Lance and his men had installed ahead of time. The machine gun opened fire and in less than a minute the mob dissolved, leaving its wounded, dead and dying behind.

A separate group headed across Sanctuary Bay in skiffs to Dan Malone's factory and set it ablaze. It was another tactical blunder. Word of the pending attack leaked out and the Castaways, armed with automatic weapons, were lying in wait.

Dale, concluding that his days in the Borders were numbered, wanted to destroy the plant and this gave him the opportunity. The band waited until the factory was burning before opening fire. Most of the attackers were killed as they tried to make it back to their skiffs.

Realizing the futility of hanging on to the Zebra, the Jamaicans burned it down, took to their boats, made a pit stop at the Barracks to pick up Clarence, his wife, Winslow Bates and a few men, and fought their way through hostile fire across the cut to Pirates' Cove where Lance welcomed them like long lost friends. Their first order of business was to put up Contadina wire barricades and a stockade around the marina on the land side to keep outsiders at bay.

It was time to retaliate. Jack dispatched Hugo's Jamaicans late one night to North Border where they burned down Bea's Market Diner, the barracks, infirmary and telephone center. By morning, and for weeks to come, fires raged, smoke filled the otherwise cloudless skies and gunfire filled the air. The islands fell into a frenzy of burning and killing, the anarchy and annihilation lasting the entire summer. In the end, the bloodbath was too costly for the Patriots and they were eventually forced to withdraw to their encampments on South Border.

This is not to say that the epidemic took a holiday. It didn't. The body count on both islands rose. Schools and churches were empty and children were rarely seen. Shortages worsened, air conditioning was a distant memory and rationing a way of life. Philosophical differences mattered little to an equal opportunity killer like the bubonic plague. It struck everyone, rich or poor, young or old, good or bad. Death cast a shadow that was almost taken for granted as part of ordinary life. Husbands and wives, sons and daughters, aunts, uncles, cousins, neighbors, friends and foes fell ill and died, and by September, no family was untouched and more than half of the Borders' population was gone.

Jack often wondered through it all what was happening elsewhere. The naval and air blockade had the Bahamas in a death grip that crippled communications to and from the Borders, and despite his daily efforts he was never able to reach anyone outside the islands on any of his radios. Virgil and Clovis were also curious about what was happening in the outside world, but were too busy with their mournful trade to pay much attention. Fuel was all but gone, so they teamed up with Jack to cart the dead or their ashes out to sea on Archangel.

The marina doubled as a crematorium, and even the Patriots sent their dead to Pirates' Cove under a flag of truce. After a while, Avalon was retrofitted with a makeshift mast and a set of sails made of discarded clothes stitched together by hand, enabling it to use wind power.

And then the suffocating heat and humidity of summer set in and the tremors increased in intensity and frequency. The air was stifling hot but there was no rain. Palm trees wilted and the few fresh water wells on the islands began running dry. Pirates' Cove had a deep well, creating a constant fear of a possible Patriot assault on the enclave.

Quite amazingly, people began showing up under white flags to receive shots of the antidote. Not too many adults came to see Dennis and Lance who had set up an emergency clinic at Pirates' Cove. However, they did send their children and soon it was understood that adults would stand aside to make sure that the children were cared for. The adult population was at war with itself but determined to keep the children alive.

It was similarly important to keep essential services and communications going. The meager clinics and infirmaries that existed were staffed by volunteers; when they died, they were immediately replaced by others. Communications too were maintained by a network of volunteer messengers making their rounds under truce flags, each one being replaced by another when struck out by the plague. Fish was the major food source and there was no shortage of people to go out every day at dawn to harvest local waters.

Despite the reality of the American quarantine of the Bahamas with a naval and aerial blockade, it did not impact free movement within the Bahamian islands. Jack often eavesdropped on his ham radio to exchanges between Reggie and other ham radio operators reporting on SOS signals from small craft and planes shot at trying to leave the perimeter around the Bahamas. These reports dropped in number over time.

One day, at a meeting with Reggie and Lance to set up a maintenance schedule at the marina for the three operational cutters left in the BDF fleet, Jack asked Reggie about the blockade. Reggie demurred to allow Lance to respond.

"We were thinking the same thing, Jake," replied Lance. "You need to keep this quiet, but I was supposed to rendezvous with a American destroyer north of here that was going to bring us enough serum for our entire population. I went to meet the vessel on our BDF flagship and found it adrift outside the Sargasso.

"We radioed the bridge but received no answer. So we sent out our launch with a squad of men and boarded the destroyer. Everyone including the captain was dead. We think the plague was to blame. We sent the launch out again, this time with a detail of men in hazmat suits to look for the antibiotics."

"Did you find any?" Jack asked.

"Not really," replied Lance. "The infirmary had been broken into and ransacked. The crew must have taken anything it felt could have helped. Anything we found left was spoiled and useless. Those poor bastards must have mutinied and raided the infirmary to try saving their own lives. The captain was shot and killed in the process."

"What Lance is suggesting is that this plague may have spread to those trying to enforce the blockade," Reggie added. "That's why we're not getting many distress signals from people hop scotching out of here. Some of them are getting through."

"We'd like to learn what they're finding once they make it to the States," said Lance. "We get lots of round-the-clock music but little news."

"What about the destroyer?" Jack asked. "Where is it now?"

"It's new, in perfect shape and loaded with fuel and guns," bragged Reggie. "We put a crew on board and anchored it in the bay. It's our new headquarters."

"That's our way out of here," Lance confided. "You, Ginny and Alexandra can have free tickets if you're interested, Jake."

Jack grinned.

"Is that with or without the dead bodies already on the destroyer, commander?"

"That's what we want you and Virgil to handle," said Reggie. "We need to dump them overboard."

"We can do that," Jack agreed. "And we'll also keep your cutters running, but we need oil and fuel to do that."

And so, Lance Cooper had snagged himself a U.S. destroyer and was going to cut and run with a chosen crew and a select list of passengers. Jack never bothered his disgust when they left. Here was good old Lance, the son of a holy man and a wannabe Noah with an Arc that he stole but never built. Did he truly think that like Noah he would live to a ripe old age or be granted eternal life like the other Great Flood mythical heroes?

Back on Archangel Jack tried once more to reach Frank Doyle in Florida. He was lucky this time.

"Jake! It's great to hear your voice. Where are you calling from?"

"The Borders," replied Jack. "What's up in Florida?" How's Pattie?"

"The tide is coming in from the inlet so she went fishing. If we don't fish, we don't eat. This place is a mess, but I think the worse is over."

"Is Bob Byrne still hanging around Florida?" He asked.

"He still runs the show, but his command center was moved to Washington. But he calls every day as if he owns the place, and he keeps saying that you're never coming back. As a matter of fact, he called yesterday. Unfortunately, he had bad news, Jake. Bob says your kids died last week. So did your folks."

There was a long moment of silence.

"Jake?"

"Yeah; I hear you."

"I was going to call you, but I didn't know what to say. I'm sorry, Jake."

Jack's voice choked and his trembling hands almost dropped the transmitter.

"Jake? Jake? It's a bad time to ask, but how are things at your end?"

"Lousy," Jack blurted out. "We're dying and can't get out."

"That's what I hear. I clear Lance Cooper's messages for Bob Byrne."

"How did that happen?"

"Bob got me into the loop after the two guys ahead of him died."

"Well, you stay alive, you hear," said Jack. "I'm going to need you again."

"Thanks. That will be fine because I think this epidemic is running out of steam."

"Does that mean the blockade will be lifted?"

"It will be, soon, but don't make a move until then. Central Command wants Bob to run the show when the blockade is over and things settle down."

"That's ok. How's the boatyard? Is my equipment still there?"

"Everything is pretty much the way you left it. The grounds are a bit overgrown and all the boats were stolen but they weren't yours anyway. The business should have no problem getting back on its feet once we're back to normal. "By the way, Jake," Frank went on. "Experts are detecting strong seismic shocks in your neck of the woods. They say an underwater volcano is about to blow its cork."

"That's why I'm calling, Frank. I need to get my pregnant wife and our baby girl out of the Borders. How do I do that?"

"That's going to be difficult. Our systems pick up everything but dead wood."

"I can't wait, man."

"Then try swimming or paddling a wooden raft."

"That's not funny, Frank."

"I'm not being funny. Whatever you do, don't hitch a ride on the destroyer you guys stole from us."

"We didn't steal it," said Jack. Its captain and crew were dead."

"It doesn't matter. It will be blown up if it moves," Frank warned. "Bob says he wants to keep the wrong people from using the ship to get back here."

"I understand," said Jack.

"On the subject of wood, do you remember that old Bahamian skiff you sailed back from the Bahamas two years ago?" Frank asked. "It's made of wood."

"So?"

"I'm fixing it up. Most of the wood is good and I can replace the bad stuff from other pieces that float in with the tide. Do you mind? It's good busy work."

Jack shrugged.

"Have fun," he said, switching off the ham radio.

The news about the twins and his parents left him so despondent that refused to leave Archangel and holed up inside the cat for days, refusing to see anyone. He even turned Ginny away. A week passed and finally Gordon took matters into his own hands and boarded Archangel late one evening when he saw a light flickering through a porthole in the main cabin. It came from a candle in a whisky bottle on the table, and that was where he found Jack, unshaven, unwashed, and sitting in the semi-darkness staring into space.

"What's eating you, Jake?" Gordon asked. "We're falling apart and all you can do is sit and act funny. Ginny is worried sick and so are we. Aren't you with us anymore?"

"I don't want to be with anyone anymore," replied Jack.

"That's not like you, Jake. What the hell happened?"

Jack looked up at Gordon, tears rolling down his cheeks.

"The twins died," he answered in a low, steady voice. "My folks died too."

Gordon sat down next to Jack and stayed there for several minutes, hands folded, saying nothing and leaving it to Jack to break the silence.

"What's wrong, Tully?" Jack asked suddenly. "The cat got your tongue?"

Gordon shook his head.

"Sorrow can't be shared, Jake. What's yours is yours, and what's mine is mine."

"I know, Tully. You've lost your wife and kids. I know how you feel. I just never thought personal losses could hit so hard."

"Well, at least, you have a wife, a daughter and a baby on the way."

"I guess so," said Jack. "But my daughter is adopted; I have no idea whether our unborn child will be a girl or a boy, and I would have never married Ginny had I been able to get back together with Doreen."

"Why? Did you love her?"

Jack pounded on the table with his fists.

"Did I love her? I adored her," he cried out. "And I still love her. She was my life and I let her down. I didn't need to get drunk. I didn't need to get into fights and I didn't need to kill anyone. It was my fault that she ended up with Fred Hawk. That sleaze bag married her to cover up for being a fag. Damn! Damn! Damn! How could I have let things go so far? And now I've got Ginny; we're married and she's pregnant. How the hell am I going to spend the rest of my life with her? And that other sleaze bag, Bob Byrne. He wants to steal my business. Louie and my old man were wise to that guy. That son-of-a-bitch, that motherfucker was supposed to be a friend, the executor of my estate. Tully, I swear on everything holy or unholy, if I ever live to survive this, I'm personally going to kill him."

He rose to his feet and started pacing like an angry tiger.

Gordon slapped his thighs and got up.

"Terrific. Now, shave, wash up, put on fresh clothes and get out there. You love your wife and family and they're waiting for you. We have more important things to do than listen to you whine. Besides, Ginny is in labor."

And so, on a bright sunny day in the middle of September Ginny gave birth to a screaming, healthy baby girl who weighed in at six pounds with Dennis and Jane doing the honors with the delivery. She was given the name Rebecca.

Life had a way of carrying on, no matter what.

30

End Days

Gordon and Jack were furiously hatching escape plans, and everyone else at Pirates' Cove was also floating ideas on leaving the Borders sooner rather than later. Individually and collectively, the decision to leave had become a foregone conclusion. The only questions left to be debated were: how and when?

Rebecca's birth was the thing that brought Jack about. He became once again the loving father and Ginny was relieved to see him back to normal. Even Alexandra accepted her violent surroundings and was especially kind and attentive to her new baby sister. She learned to play in the tumult as opposing sides suddenly revved up the tempo of the fighting, running bloody forays night and day.

Dominicans in Patrick City accused the Haitians of using Voodoo and witchcraft to spread death. In turn, the Haitians blamed the Dominicans of practicing Santeria and sending death curses. The arguments turned violent and boiled over into armed attacks by all sides that daily grew worse. Soon, fires raged once again in Patrick City and Sanctuary Village, and before long they, already pretty well gutted, were totally leveled with people forced to live in the ruins of homes and shops.

Adding to the desolation were the frequent quakes that made movement difficult and dangerous. Sometimes the ground separated underfoot and people dropped into sinkholes and were crushed when the ground closed over them. Nothing seemed to matter. Death and desolation were everywhere.

The news from Marsh Harbor was spotty, being reported by area fishermen and by Hugo's remaining Jamaicans who still ventured out in their skiffs. The quakes were lighter but the disease was hitting hard. Henry

Alden had a heart attack and died; Cynthia and Milton were reported gone with Clement Lloyd on Kitten, their destination unknown. There was no word one way or another about Doreen.

Hiram did not take the news about Milton well. One evening, he drank too much and accidentally set fire to the rectory. It spread to the church, and soon flames lit up the night sky. Hiram's remains were found the next morning. The Borders had lost its religious leader and Jonathan lost his best backer.

Jonathan had become an evangelic zealot but he not a charismatic public speaker and was often too drunk to make any sense. Otis stood behind Jonathan but Jack's former mechanic had no vision or strategy to address the malaise of the islands. He was content as leader of the Patriots to lead raiding parties against everyone and anyone. This left Vernon as Jonathan's only ally and friend when they were not too drunk to get together and hatch plots.

One late night shortly before dawn, they stumbled drunk to Jack's plane at the airstrip in South Border and took off. Their destination was a question mark. The plane's range on a full tank was two hundred miles. The problem was that its tank was almost empty. The craft took off and flew west. It flew over Marsh Harbor and made it to the open sea. But it ran out of fuel and dive bombed into the sea. A local fisherman later reported seeing it blown up by something that looked like a rocket before it hit the sea. No bodies were recovered.

"How many people do you think we lost?" Jack asked Virgil as they returned on Archangel with Gordon from a day of unloading body ashes in the waters between North Border and Hermit Cay.

"Hard to tell," Virgil replied. "What do you think, Tully?"

"We're easily down more than half," said Gordon. "And I have no idea how many have been lost in the Abaco islands."

"Hugo says that Marsh Harbor lost half of its population so far," Virgil said.

"How would he know?" Gordon asked.

"He sends Eldridge over by boat now and then. The blockade and air surveillance circles the Bahamas but doesn't bother with local traffic."

"Where does Eldridge get the fuel?"

Jack shrugged his shoulders.

"He probably siphons it from the tanks of other boats. That's what Hugo says. He brings in rum and cocaine from Abaco for sale here now we're out of stock."

Gordon's arched his eyebrows.

"Cocaine?"

"Yep," said Jack. "It's cocaine from Jamaica brought in on old wooden sail boats that the feds cannot detect."

He felt compelled now to tell them about his meeting with Lance and Reggie a while ago and their plans to leave the Borders on the American war ship that they found drifting crewless.

Virgil was livid.

Those bastards are going to leave us high and dry," Gordon snarled.

"Let them," said Jack. "I called an old buddy of mine in Florida on my sideband. He works for Bob Byrne in a naval intelligence unit for ships patrolling the waters around the Bahamas and knows what happened to the destroyer. He says that the Navy has orders to blow it up if it pops ever pops up in open water."

"Should we tell Lance?"

Jack shook his head.

"Let's wait. Maybe he's all talk."

"What about Clarence?"

"Let's find out what he knows first," said Jack.

"By the way, your boat is made of wood, isn't it, Jake?" Gordon noted.

Jack nodded.

"Well, the feds won't be looking to blow up wooden flotsam," said Virgil. Too much of that crap coming loose from the Sargasso is lying in the ocean between here and Florida. This boat may be your ticket back to the States."

"I've been thinking about that," Jack nodded. "That's assuming anything is left there. Avalon is made of wood too, isn't it, Virgil? And it has a mast and sail now, doesn't it?"

"It sure does," said Virgil. "If you cut out, we're cutting out, and I wouldn't be surprised if Hugo and his Jamaicans follow on their schooner. It's also is made of wood."

An explosion rattled their ears. They looked in the direction of Hermit Cay and saw a fire ball rise into the sky. Moments later, the early evening light was dimmed by a descending blanket of hot, gray ash that covered the vessel with a coating of dust coating speckled with glowing embers.

A red hot rock grazed the sail and it caught fire. Luckily, a rain cloud formed. It released a downpour that doused the flames, reducing the ash on deck to wet silt.

"It's that volcano," yelled Jack. "It's for real. Let's get the hell out of here!"

The rain followed them all the way back to Pirates' Cove, and that was good. The islands were parched and needed a good soaking. Ginny was standing at the dock with her father and Clarence when Archangel pulled up. In an open shed near the trailers, Jack could see Winslow Bates and Marvell Sullivan huddling with Alexandra and baby Rebecca, trying to keep them dry and waiting apprehensively for the cat to return.

The explosion at Hermit's Cay had been heard throughout the Borders, Ginny said later when they were drying out in Kyle's trailer. First it was the blast and then several minutes it was the ash shower followed by the rain. And finally the tremors came.

They were not the light jabs they had come to know. These were short, sharp rib jarring jolts followed by a deluge of ash and red hot pumice rock. And every time the earth trembled, Alexandra screamed, visibly upsetting Ginny who went off to boil water for tea and coffee for the men. Interestingly, the noise and shocks never seemed to disturb Rebecca who cried only when she was hungry or about to make. But it was no longer safe to let Alexandra run loose at the marina and Rebecca too needed to be protected. Kyle had to keep them indoors in the stifling heat, adding to everyone's misery. Ginny nerves were frazzled and she was running short on patience.

Jack looked at her toiling over the stove. She was still beautiful, her thick brown hair slightly mussed, but she was clearly tired. There was another aftershock and Alexandra cried. She ran, first to Kyle, then to Jack and then to her mother. A call on Jack's VHF came in. It was Dennis who was with Jane in Agnes Town tending to patients at a new makeshift infirmary near the ferry dock. It was an "I told you so" call, but he was also inquiring if everyone was all right.

They talked briefly before Jack hung up.

"What did he say?" Clarence asked.

Jack looked at everyone around him in the crowded trailer.

"He says it's time to go. They're coming over."

The absence of air conditioning and scarcity of electrical power meant no relief from the oppressive heat and humidity and no hiding from bugs, biting mosquitoes and all sorts of mean spirited flying insects that hissed and buzzed every time the earth shook with the volcanic pyrotechnics from Hermit Cay. And then there were almost daily assaults by Patriot gangs and the constant sniper fire. They produced no casualties but since they were a constant nuisance, Hugo and his men rolled out more rows of Contadina wire around the stockade and barricades. The barbed wire worked with fearful results and attacks came to a halt when bodies began piling up, impaled on the barbs.

Cooling rains returned and made life slightly more bearable, making it easier to ready Archangel, Avalon and Anvil for departure. While all adults took turns doing guard duty, work crews prepped the vessels around the clock in a race against time. The goal was to leave in when the currents and trade winds would work together in pushing the three boat fleet west over the top of the Bahamas to Florida. The sun was moving south again and that was supposed to be a good omen. The hope was that Hermit Cay would not blow its stack before then or that the Patriots would not breach the compound's defenses. In the meantime, Clarence left suddenly to pay Lance a visit on his newly acquired destroyer.

The vessels were of oak, mahogany and teak. Avalon and Hugo's Anvil had full displacement hulls and were primarily sailboats retrofitted with diesel power, but Archangel was purely a sailing catamaran with a pair of diesels to move it when the wind was dead. All engines had to be removed along with their transmissions, tanks, all fittings, propellers, prop shafts, stuffing boxes, rigging and other metal parts. Wooden blocks and pegs and cotton ropes replaced copper, brass and steel fasteners, and the vessels' wheel and cable steering systems were scuttled for stern mounted wooden tillers using lumber from cottages that had been dismantled for the project. When it was over, a tiny fleet of three vintage vessels that could have jumped out of an old painting was ready to set sail.

The plan was simple. Archangel would carry Jack and his wife, daughters, Kyle and his brother Dale and Gordon. Jane, Dennis, Marvel and Winslow, their wives and kids would sail on Avalon with Virgil and Clovis, leaving room for about a dozen more people. Anvil, being the largest of the three vessels, would carry the twenty or so Jamaicans, the Castaways and Eldridge.

It was not long before Lance learned what they were up to. One morning, he and Clarence paid Pirates' Cove a visit on one of the destroyer's launches. They found Gordon and Jack on Archangel. Gordon was sweeping ash off the deck and Jack was coiling a makeshift depth and anchor line of rope tied to a heavy rock at one end with every yard marked with red ribbon.

"Leaving?" Lance asked.

Jack sighed and Gordon kept on sweeping, saying nothing.

"We're doing what you're doing, Lance," Jack replied. "If the Patriots don't get us, that volcano will get us."

"We can't help you with them, Jake. We don't have the muscle anymore," said Clarence. "However, we do have room for you and your family on the destroyer."

"So, you are splitting," Gordon noted.

Lance blushed slightly but his voice betrayed no emotion.

"If that's what you want to call it, it's fine with me" he said. "Nothing's left here. Either Plague or this mindless killing will destroy us all. My father and brothers are gone. My good friends are gone. The country I knew is gone and the islands I love are about to be blown up. I'm finished here. But our ship has plenty of fuel to get us and a few true believers out and away."

"Where is away?" Gordon asked.

"We have enough fuel to get to Honduras or maybe Belize or Costa Rica. I plan to start a new Christian community. We tried and failed here. We will succeed in another place."

"You're a real fighter and a true believer, Lance," Jack said.

"Thanks, Jake. And that's why we're here," Clarence added. "You have a chance to save yourselves by coming with us."

"Are you going with Lance?" Gordon asked.

Clarence looked down and did not respond.

"Clarence and his family are with me," answered Lance. "But, we do have room for you and your family, Jake. We'd also like you to join us, Tully. You're like family to us," he added quickly.

"What about the others?" Gordon inquired, continuing his sweeping. He went on to give Lance a list of names.

Lance shook his head.

"We're crowded as it is," said Clarence. "We can take Dennis and Jane. We can't take the others, especially Hugo and Eldridge. They're wanted for crimes all over the Caribbean. Moreover, I don't think they could ever share our vision. They were trouble here and they'll be trouble elsewhere."

"That's right," Lance agreed. "They're not right for us."

Gordon stopped sweeping and grinned at Clarence and Lance.

"Well, I guess you've already decided on the guest list," he said. "I'd like to join you guys, but I can't leave my friends behind."

"I wouldn't even leave my enemies behind in this mess," said Jack.

Lance sighed.

"That's too bad. Only true believers can make the cut. Anyway, that's not my call. I'm here to save lives and I'm giving you a chance to save your own. You should come with us. You can't make it on your own."

Jack put down the depth line and rose to his feet.

"How come you're not heading for the States?"

"We could," answered Lance. "That's an option. I haven't yet made up my mind. Things are settling down in Florida where we also could make a fresh start. We have a good chance of getting there on a destroyer. No one is going to fire on an American warship."

"Where is it now?"

Lance pointed to the outline of the destroyer off in the distance. It was hard to see the gray shape in the early morning haze.

"We're ready for a quick exit if necessary. We plan to leave through the cut."

"You'll be blown out of the water," warned Jack.

"You're either crazy or lying," Lance retorted.

"I may be crazy, Lance, but I don't lie. Anyway, we wish you all the best luck in the world, you hear?"

Clarence seemed disappointed with Jack's response.

"Then, you're not coming with us?"

Gordon nodded.

"As Jake says, have a great trip. Hopefully, we'll meet again."

It was a sad parting of the ways, no handshakes and no extended farewells. Deep inside, Jack knew they would never meet again. He went below and wrote a short note that he placed on top of his bunk while Gordon watched the launch lose itself in the mist. He came back on deck to help Gordon review the check list of supplies on board when a loud crack that sounded like a thousand firecrackers exploding at once jarred his ears.

31

Immortality

One of the stories Jack learned in school was the epic of Gilgamesh. It was the passage where Gilgamesh was speaking to the ghost of his friend, Enkido, who had been allowed to rise briefly from the land of the dead, that Jack tried to piece together in words poorly borrowed from the recesses of his memory.

Have you seen down there the man who has six sons? I have seen the man who has six sons. His heart rejoices and he sits on a throne and listens to music as with the gods.

How is it with the man who has five sons? They treat him in the Nether World as if he were a scribe of the court, dispenser of justice.

Have you seen the man down there who has four sons? His heart rejoices as that of a farmer measuring his bounty.

How is it with the man who has three sons? He drinks from the water his sons have brought.

Have you seen down there the man who has two sons? He sits on two bricks and has some bread to eat.

How is it with the man who has one son? I have seen the man. He sits by the wall and weeps.

Have you seen the down there the man who has no son? I have seen the man who has no child to call his name. He wanders alone and wonders how it would be with the man who has six sons.

An English warship heading for the Caribbean from Bermuda was within sight of Hermit Cay when it reported hearing a clap of thunder although the sky was clear and the sun was shining brightly. The thunder was followed by a dark gray haze that filled the horizon and hid the small island from view. The vessel radioed the incident up the chain of command and within seconds all shipping in the area was alerted and diverted. The report also reached Lance on his destroyer and he relayed it to Jack at Pirates' Cove. Messages flew back and forth with each update sent by the British ship.

There was more thunder, and after that came several ear splitting explosions. The warship held its position while officers on the bridge focused on a large cloud that formed over Hermit Cay. The sky darkened and hot ash began falling. The warship stood fast until it was pelted hard by glowing pumice and was forced to withdraw.   It moved a few miles to the north, hove to and kept sending out reports every few minutes. Hermit Cay was breaking up, it radioed. One half hour later, a new radio message indicated that it had disappeared from sight.

Instruments on the bridge recorded a rapid rise in sea level and the commander reported that the sea had turned into a caldron of boiling water bombarded by red hot rocks. It was too dangerous and the warship pulled away beyond the horizon.

By a strange coincidence, Washington had lifted the blockade the night before. It might have been an oversight, but orders to bring down the American destroyer if it left the Borders were not cancelled and the blockade's end was never broadcast. But announcement or no announcement, the race to leave the Borders was on.

A container ship carrying jet engine parts from Brazil to the States was steaming north between the Borders and Abaco when it was caught in a sea surge under dark skies. Fearing a hurricane, it jettisoned containers on the top tiers and moved closer to the Borders' western shore for protection when it too was bombarded by burning rock. The skipper radioed that the bluffs on South and North Border were slowly disintegrating. This observation was confirmed by aerial reconnaissance from a U.S. carrier patrolling the edge of the Sargasso. The airwaves filled with talk about launching a massive sea and air rescue mission but the region was considered too dangerous and unstable.

The explosion at Hermit's Cay brought new downpours of ash and pumice rock to Pirates' Cove. It also brought stronger tremors and more powerful quakes. The dock shook, fissures appeared on the ground and boulder sized red hot rocks began falling like glowing meteorites. Whatever they hit ignited and soon Pirates' Cove was a blazing inferno. The sun was obscured by black clouds, turning midday into nightfall.

Jack was on Archangel when he saw the ground at the picnic area open and the tables and barbeque pits tumble in. The fuel tanks were hit and a fiery blaze began spreading to the ferry dock. The heat and smoke seared Jack's eyes and blurred his vision but he could make out human forms scurrying away from the trailers and the scattered encampments to the three boats. He saw Anvil and Avalon preparing to leave, and at the marina's far end he saw Otis running with Terrence and several men. They had breached the barricades and were making a mad dash for End Run.

Lance's destroyer was also on the move. It had weighed anchor and was making for the cut both sides of which were tumbling into the sea, adding to the mayhem. Churning swells beat against the bluffs, shearing off chunks of land like slices off a loaf of bread. A bellowing roar grew louder and tremors morphed into deafening quakes that tossed people into the air like rag dolls. Gunfire broke out, and Jack knew that Hugo, Eldridge and their Jamaicans were fighting a rear guard action, shooting and running and shooting again, to keep the Patriots at bay, buying time for those making a beeline for the boats.

Ginny, holding Rebecca to her breast, was struggling to get to Archangel with Gordon at her side, carrying Alexandra like a football under his arm. The ground shook under them and Gordon grabbed the infant from Ginny to lighten her load and make it easier for her to run to the boat. But a new tremor under her feet threw her off balance. Gordon made it to Archangel where Jack was waiting on deck and deposited the two girls in the main cabin. Looking out, they saw Ginny still trying to catch up. They jumped off Archangel to give her a hand but they were too late. The earth opened, swallowing her, and then closed. Ginny was gone.

Jack fell to his knees and screamed but Gordon knocked him senseless, threw him over his shoulder and carried him to Archangel where he laid him out on the deck and doused his head with a pail full of water.

Gordon saw Dennis in the smoke and began yelling at the top of his lungs, but the doctor was paying no attention; he was too busy trying to find Jane. He finally gave up and, hoping that she was already on Archangel, ran as fast as he could through the smoke to the boat.

Somewhere behind him were Dale and Kyle Malone. Unfortunately they were too old to run and could only manage a slow walk in the ongoing melee. Dennis made it but the two brothers were too slow. They were caught in a torrent of falling pumice and were killed by the burning rock.

Jane, who had stuck close to Ginny, was alone and blinded by a dust cloud. She screamed, and her cries were heard by Hugo and Eldridge and their Jamaicans. But they were pinned down in a ditch, encircled by a gang of Patriots trying to reach End Run. Fortunately, Clovis was behind, wielding an automatic rifle and fighting his way to Avalon. He fired point blank into the Patriots and they collapsed like a pack of cards.

Only Otis and Terrence made it to End Run, giving the Jamaicans wiggle room. They bolted from the ditch, found Jane and left her with Dennis who by now had scrambled off Archangel to find her.

While the Jamaicans and Clovis took off for their boats, Dennis grabbed her hand and pulled her aboard. He was not a moment too soon. Gordon released the dock lines and the cat drifted away as the dock burst into flames. Archangel turned with the current and began drifting to the cut.

The Jamaicans wasted no time. Running backwards and firing, they fought their way to Anvil where they cut the lines loose and pushed the schooner away into the current.

Virgil and Clovis waited patiently until Marvel, Winslow and their families were safely aboard Avalon and made sure that Hugo, Eldridge and their Jamaicans and the Castaways were aboard Anvil. Clovis counted twenty men.

Virgil shook his head.

"There must have been a hundred of them a year ago," he said.

He had Clovis, Marvel and Winslow used deck poles to push Avalon into open water and then had them raise the vessel's only sail. It caught the wind and current and quickly entered the channel behind Archangel. Archangel and Avalon drifted in tandem, followed by Anvil, gathering speed as the outbound tide surged through the widening cut between North and South Border.

Jack was still groggy but the splash of cold water on his head did its magic and he was conscious of the vessel moving under him. He pulled himself to his feet and saw Gordon at the helm in the wheelhouse struggling to keep Archangel in control. He nodded at Dennis whose face was quite green and was gripping the handrail on deck with one hand and his other hand wrapped around Jane's waist.

"You're going to need to help Tully raise all the sails, doctor, if we're going to get out of here alive."

His words were enough to cure Dennis's sea sickness. The young physician sent Jane below to tend to Rebecca and Alexandra and followed Jack to the helm.

"Let me take over, Tully. We need more speed. I need you and Dennis to unfurl the sails."

"Are you okay now?" Gordon asked.

"I'm fine," replied Jack. "Get the sails and keep an eye on that motorized skiff. It's gaining on us."

The sails went up, and like a signal, the sails on the other two boats were also hoisted to catch the wind. The tiny flotilla picked up momentum and ploughed through the turbulent waters to the broad swells of the open water beyond. Jack looked out at the horizon in front of him. The destroyer, with Lance and Clarence and their families and a few friends aboard, was a speck far to the northwest.

Avalon and Anvil were following in Archangel's wake and way behind them and about to emerge from the haze filled void between North and South Border was End Run. Ash and rock continued falling but it was better in open water than it was closer to land.

End Run was closing fast, but the motorized skiff that was dogging Archangel's wake since leaving Pirates' Cove was a more immediate threat. It was now close enough for Jack and Gordon to make out its occupants. Gladys Lamar was at the tiller and Bea Norris was waving a shotgun. They caught up with the catamaran, came alongside with Bea screaming, "This is the Judgment Day! Praise the Lord!"

Gladys kept exhorting Bea who threw a line over Archangel's gunwales.

"Kill those bastards," Gladys shrieked in her cackling voice. "Kill them all!"

Gordon yelled back, a revolver in each hand leveled at Bea and Gladys.

"You ladies should turn back," he said.

Bea did not budge and began berating Gordon.

"You are Satan incarnate! But I will be saved. We will all be saved but you will rot forever in Hell! I will do the Lord's work!"

She aimed the shotgun at Gordon's head and he was momentarily frozen. He had never shot a woman before. Closing his eyes, he fired blind and emptied his guns into the skiff.

The two women fell bleeding into the water. Gordon loosened the line from the gunwales and it slid off the cleat, leaving the small boat to slowly slip away and start sinking. It disappeared from sight when Avalon ran over it.

The short lived assault by the skiff cost the flotilla precious minutes, giving End Run enough time to catch up. Jack knew that Fred's big yacht was heavily armed and that it could easily overwhelm them unless it could be stopped cold. But he also knew it was short on fuel. He called Gordon and Dennis to the wheelhouse.

"I need you guys to do me a favor," he said, allowing the cat to move faster in the gathering wind gusts. "Ready the inflatable on the davits and get the grenades and grenade launcher that I keep in the banquet locker of the main cabin."

Dennis looked dumbfounded at Gordon.

"What the hell is he saying?"

Gordon stared at Jack.

"Are you sure you want to do this?"

Jack pursed his lips.

"I want to do this," he replied. "Now go!"

Dennis vaguely remembered where Chico used to store the cat's weapons cache and went to fetch the grenades and the launcher and fished out a rifle as well that he loaded and brought out on deck.

"What are you doing?" Jane asked when she saw him carrying the weapons out in his arms.

Dennis shrugged.

"I don't know what I'm doing," he replied. "I think Jake wants to stop that yacht from chasing us."

"I can do it," said Jack. "It's low on fuel. I can blow it up if I get close enough."

He brought the weapons on deck and loaded the rifle and grenade launcher while Gordon loosened the lines on the davits holding the inflatable and made sure that the dinghy's motor was primed and connected to the red fuel tank tucked away in the bow.

Jack turned on the auto helm switch and walked back to the deck.

"Is everything ready?"

Gordon gave a short nod, his face ashen with worry and fright.

"Everything is in the dinghy," said Dennis.

Jack smiled.

"Great. Now, listen up, Tully. Keep going. Head for Florida and don't look back. You'll find a signed note on my bunk. When you reach Florida, go to my Boynton Beach boatyard and square things for me."

"What about Bob Byrne?"

"He's going to be your bag, Tully. Good luck."

Turning to Dennis he said, "You take good care of Jane, you hear."

He shook the doctor's hand and slapped Gordon on the back.

"Cheer up, Tully. This is the only way, you know."

Gordon growled.

"Get into the dink, Jake, you lousy son-of-a-bitch."

They winked at each other and Jack climbed into the inflatable.

Gordon lowered it into the water and ran to the wheelhouse without ever turning his back. Neither did Avalon and Anvil slow down. But Gordon could hear Styx barking as the inflatable passed them on its way to intercept End Run.

All they could hear was a mighty explosion as the two boats collided and were engulfed in a fire ball and a cloud of black smoke. Anvil did stop when the smoke cleared and made a few turns around the floating wreckage. It lingered a while as men on deck scurried about and then resumed its course.

But Gordon was not looking. His eyes were glued on the northern horizon where a Predator Drone in the sky had found the destroyer. It relayed the information to a submerged submarine laying in wait. There was a streak of bright light followed by a brief blinding blaze. It was the end of the destroyer.

A large lump of molten lava hit the water between Archangel and Avalon with a loud hissing sound and a geyser shot up into the air. For a while it was indeed a sail in and out of Hell. Agnes Town was on fire and Buccaneer Point was dropping into the sea piece by piece.

But the three vessels pressed on and slowly left the inferno behind. Screams and sounds of people dying and land crumbling grew fainter and the sky turned light again and soon there was nothing to hear but silence and nothing to see but the sea and sky. Behind them, way back over the horizon, eruptions and radiating quakes were breaking up the Borders, tumbling large chunks of land into boiling waters. A crack of lightening raced across the sky and the islands imploded and disappeared from sight.

Archangel was sailing westward under a stiff and blustery trade wind a day later when Gordon saw a speck on the horizon. It grew larger as the cat approached and he took a closer look through the binoculars. There was no doubt about its size and shape; it was Kitten and it was floating aimlessly in the broad swells.

Archangel pulled up an hour later and Gordon called everyone up from below to see the yacht. They counted four people on the deck. The catamaran was alongside Kitten in minutes and two men threw down lines and rope ladders.

"Milt Cooper and Clement Lloyd," yelled Gordon. And then he noticed the two women next to them. "What the hell; Cynthia and Doreen!"

"We had our own issues after we lost contact with the Borders," said Milton when they were reunited on Archangel. "Doreen was alive but we couldn't get word to you. She was in a coma and we took her to Henry who found that she was slowly being poisoned. When he asked her about it, she pointed the finger at Bob Byrne who she said was supplying her with prescription drugs. It turns out that the stuff he was giving her was slowly killing her. Anyway, she got better and we decided to make a run for it. I contacted Bob Byrne and said I was coming in with Clement Lloyd with a ton of gold bars that we found hidden on the Angelina. I think he thought that Dan and Fred were holding out on him and so his ships never came close to us. But now we're stuck. We have no fuel." He added sheepishly.

"Where's Shelly?" Doreen asked, looking anxiously around Archangel for him. Her tenor of her voice rose when he failed to appear. "Where's my husband?"

"He didn't make it; He stayed behind to save us." Gordon's eyes filled with tears. "Neither did Ginny; but they left you with two healthy baby girls."

Doreen began crying and looked out at sea.

"I have loved him once," she sobbed. "And I have lost him twice."

Kitten's stock of food and water was loaded aboard Archangel and it continued on its course following the setting sun to Florida.

That evening, Gordon found the note that Jack had left on top of his bunk.

"Dear Tully," it read. "Take care of my kids. And if anything is left of my estate, divide it evenly among all the good people on Archangel, Anvil and Avalon. I wish I could have been a better husband, a better father and a better man." It was signed, "Your friend, Jake."

32

Final Curtain

All was quiet in the hospital waiting room when Milton finished his story and looked impassively at his audience who continued to sit in total silence. The young FBI agent seemed riveted by the story and sat ever closer to Alexandra who quietly slipped her arm over his and took his hand.

"Was that the engraving from Hiram Cooper's rectory?" Ron asked, referring to the Yin and Yang picture in the Sloane home.

"Yes," said Eldridge. "It's from the ruins of the Church of Christ rectory and we took it to Florida."

"It's a great symbol," the FBI man noted. "What does it really represent?"

"Life," said Eldridge. "It has a dark side and a light side. We're now on the light side. Some would say that's why we survived and did well over the years, but you never know. The final chapter hasn't been written yet. I just don't know who'll be around to write it."

"But Uncle Milt, how did you finally end up in Florida?" Alexandra asked.

Milton cleared his throat to answer.

"We abandoned Kitten and went on Archangel."

"What happened to the gold?" Alexandra asked.

"There was no gold," laughed Milton. "It was a ruse to keep us from being blown out of the water. It worked. But you know, the luckiest guy of all was Jake."

"How were you able to pluck him out of the sea?"

Eldridge looked intently at the younger man.

"Do you believe in fate?"

Ron shook his head.

"Man makes his own luck," he declared.

"Sometimes, I guess," agreed Eldridge. "But this had nothing to with luck. It was simply not Jake's time to die. We saw him pass us in the inflatable and head right into End Run, and then we heard the explosion. We figured he was gone. End Run sank on the spot. We searched the area for a while and were about to leave when we saw Jake hanging on some debris. We fished him out and followed Archangel and Avalon to Florida."

He took a deep breath.

"Frank Doyle is the real hero," said Eldridge. "It was the story about the wooden skiff that he wanted to restore that tipped off Jake when he realized that wooden boats with no metal parts had the best chance of evading detection."

"Why do you think Bob Byrne had it in for both Doreen and Jack?" Alexandra asked. "Did it have anything to do with the Angelina or with Jake's businesses?"

Milton shook his head.

"Yes, but it was more personal than that. He believed they knew he was gay and therefore they were a threat to his career," answered Milton. "Bob Byrne could not afford to be known as gay in the Navy. He needed to protect his reputation and that fear of exposure made him paranoid and drove him crazy."

"Did Jack follow through with his threat to kill Bob Byrne?"

Eldridge's eyes narrowed.

"I never followed the story closely, but my guess is that Bob felt guilty. That may be why he took his own life."

In fact, Eldridge knew what happened to Bob Byrne.

*   *   *

It was snowing, and snow in Washington D.C. was rare, even in winter. But this was more than a snowfall; it was a blizzard and the snow was high and piled up in drifts. That hardly ever happened in the capital city. The deep freeze was not only in Washington and the Northeast; it extended to Florida and covered much of the state with a frost that destroyed palm trees, ruined the citrus crop and brought the Red Death to an end.

A freeze in Florida was unusual. Jack remembered that the last time cold and ice came to south Florida was when he was in his early twenties. He was doing a yacht delivery from the Bahamas to Fort Lauderdale in and the temperature gauge on the vessel registered below freezing. It also ruined the state's citrus crop and forced the rich to spend small fortunes on restoring the landscaping to their properties.

The rich always made out. Whenever hurricanes and other cataclysmic acts of nature struck, the poor would somehow disappear under the guise of gentrification and their places taken over by high end digs. The same was happening now. There were fewer people, less crowding and more opportunities, especially in cities like Washington where tall buildings around Union Station were anchored on land once occupied by slums. Plague had rid the area of the poor.

Bob Byrne had a condo in one of those fancy high rises near Union Station and Jack needed to see him. Bob was still the executor of Jack's estate and that needed to be changed. Moreover, he was threatening to contest Louie Gold's will making Jack his sole beneficiary. That too was unacceptable.

Luckily, it was Monday night and holiday decorations blinked brightly over the empty snow filled streets. The snow began falling days before and never stopped. By the time Jack got off the train that night, mountains of soft white fluff was piled high over cars left at curbs that glistened under the glow of streetlights.

Jack did not know the building. Bob Byrne had a penthouse apartment on the top floor, and Jack's friends had cased the high rise thoroughly. Gordon Tully diverted the doorman's attention with a request for directions while Jack snuck into an alley at the side of the building where he met Virgil by an emergency door that had been jimmied open and its alarm neutralized.

Virgil pressed a loaded revolver into his hand.

"This is yours. I found it on Archangel. I don't know if it still works. Try not to use it," he warned. "Things could get messy if you do."

Jack grinned and replied, "I won't fire a shot."

He found the fire stairs and slowly climbed to the top floor where he stopped to check his watch when he reached the last landing. The late evening news would be starting and Bob Byrne would be stretched out on his favorite sofa, the TV on and a drink on the coffee table waiting to be consumed. It was probably a martini.

Jack listened closely. The TV could be heard through the walls. He smiled and made his way down a rear corridor to a door opening into the penthouse kitchen. It was unlocked and opened effortlessly. Clovis had taken care of that.

He took off his loafers, left them at the door, put on a pair of surgical gloves and walked in. Sounds he might have made were drowned by the TV noise. The news began and peeking in from the kitchen, he saw Bob on the sofa in the living room. An empty martini glass stood on the coffee table next to a stack of magazines. Good. He had already started on his nightcaps. A leather armchair stood next to the sofa and on the far wall was a large sliding glass door to a terrace overlooking the snow bound street.

Jack eased himself into the living room.

"How are you doing, Robert?"

Caught by surprise, Bob Byrne froze in place. And when he tried to get up, Jack pushed him down and drew his revolver.

"You're alive!"

"I think so," snickered Jack. "But you never know. I might be a ghost."

"But Frank swore you were dead."

Jack grinned.

"He told a fib, Robert."

"Please don't kill me," begged Bob Byrne. "I never meant any harm. I was just doing what I was told. I was following orders."

"I'm sure you were, but that's all in the past. So, you sit quietly, Robert, you hear. I just wanted to wish you a Merry Christmas and ask you a few questions. Then I'll be out of your way forever."

Bob began to sweat.

"You're not going to shoot me?"

Jack smiled and shook his head.

"Not unless you want me to," he replied, sitting down on the armchair. Keeping the pistol ready, he asked gently, "What's your rank, Robert?"

"I just made rear admiral."

"That's a good rank," Jack noted. "You can retire on that."

"I did that last week," Bob acknowledged.

"Well, that's great," said Jack. "Tell me, I spoke to Frank when I got back. Why did you tell him my folks and kids were dead when they weren't?"

Bob Byrne was perspiring profusely by now.

"It was for your protection, Jake," he stammered. "I didn't want you to leave the Borders and get yourself blown up in the blockade. You must also understand that my bosses thought you knew too much and wanted you killed, just like the others."

He was talking fast.

"It was all I could do to convince them that you were re-marrying and staying in the Borders. You would have been killed if you returned to Florida. Someone had to protect your business and look after your kids in the event you died. It was a bad time for all of us, Jake. Your ex wife was ill, her husband was nowhere and your folks were old…"

"Talking about my ex-wife, Robert; she's alive."

"No!" Bob Byrne screamed. "No!"

Jack slapped his temple with the revolver butt to quiet him down.

"There's no need to get uptight, Robert, I just thought you'd like to know, and I won't ask you why you wanted Doreen dead; it doesn't matter anymore."

"She was up to no good, Jake. She tried to blackmail me, and..."

"I appreciate your concern, Robert," interrupted Jack. "For a moment I thought you were planning on getting your hands on my business. But I was wrong. And I do want to express my gratitude for how you looked after everything while I was gone. I'm grateful. I truly am."

"How did you get back?" Bob asked.

"On Archangel."

"I thought you were on that destroyer."

"No," replied Jack. "Lance Cooper and many good friends were on it when it was blown up. They never made it, Robert."

"But how did Archangel make it?"

"It's made of wood, you know," smiled Jack. "That makes me real lucky."

"It is lucky," Bob echoed.

"A blessing, I'm sure," Jack agreed. "But what I really want to know, old buddy, to whom did you report and why did they want me dead?"

Bob Byrne struggled to find an appropriate answer but was taking too long.

"I think you were working for yourself and with some other folks here and in the Bahamas," said Jack. "But that's an old story, Robert. They're all dead and can't testify for or against you. Now, tell me about your thing with Louie Gold."

Bob Byrne broke down.

"He and his wife adopted me as an infant and tried to raise me Jewish. But that wasn't the real problem. I grew up as a gay man and Louie would not accept me. He even wrote me out of his will when he made you his beneficiary. That was the last straw."

He started to sob.

Jack shook his head in sympathy.

"Is that why you married Doreen and hooked up with Fred Hawk? He too was gay."

"It was important to my career," cried Bob. "The Navy doesn't accept gay men. Doreen gave me the cover I needed and Fred Hawk turned out to be a good buddy.

He too needed a woman to appear straight."

Bob began crying uncontrollably.

"It was never about you, Jake. I had to prove myself and in doing so, I thought I could have it all, power, money and influence and in doing so I brought ruin on much of the world and on people close to me and to you. I must have been crazy and out of my mind. Oh, what nightmares we make when we bend reality!"

Jack got up and pointed to the terrace with the revolver.

"Is this the final curtain?" Bob asked.

"You're sweating, Robert. Let's go out and get some air."

"It's snowing," said Bob.

"That's ok," replied Jack. "I want to breathe in the clean fresh winter air."

He nudged Bob up and prodded him to walk to the terrace door. Bob shivered as he opened the sliding door and stepped out into the wintry night, and never knew what hit him when the gun butt swung across the back of his head.

Jack caught him as he fell, carried him to the terrace ledge and threw him over, accidentally letting the revolver drop with the body. Oh well. Let them trace it back to him. Moreover, it might never be found. Tomorrow would be Christmas and there would be no sanitation trucks to clear the streets and collect the garbage. Bob Byrne's body would keep well, buried under piles of snow in the freezing weather. The terrace too would fill with snow and the footprints would disappear.

Jack left the sliding glass door open and made his way back to the kitchen past the flickering shadows from the TV dancing on the walls. Behind him he heard the announcer say that snow would fall for a few more days before the weather cleared in time to bring in the New Year. He found his shoes in the doorway, slipped into them, closed the door behind him and left. Bad weather, good weather; bad times, good times; it didn't matter. Life had a way of carrying on. Jack smiled and left.

*   *   *

The midnight hour was approaching and Jack was still in surgery. Ron seemed confused by what he had heard and was deep in thought. Eldridge, Milton and Gordon now sat quietly, watching the hour and minute hands slowly move on the wall clock and paying Alexandra and the young FBI man no mind as they drew closer to each other.

"You never told me your name," said Alexandra.

"Oh, I'm so sorry. I'm John Wales, and I've never met your dad. It was my father who knew him. His name was James Wales. People called him Jimmy Wales"

"Was, called…?"

"Yes. My dad retired from the Washington DC police a few years ago. He died a month ago and gave me this to return to Bob Byrne's next of kin. I thought your dad might know if Bob had any living relatives."

He placed his attaché case on the table and opened it. Inside, packed in bubble wrap was the revolver that had dropped into the street with Bob's body.

"My dad returned it twenty years ago on a fishing trip. He wanted to give it to Bob but he was busy so he left it with Jack who I assume gave it back to Bob at the end of the trip. The weapon was recovered when Byrne killed himself and my dad wanted to make sure that it went back to its rightful owner. That's why I'm here."

It was a minute before midnight and from where they sat they could see the door to the operating room far down the corridor opening. The surgeon stepped out to speak with Dennis and Doreen who had emerged from the adjoining room.

Everyone stood up, trying in vain to hear the muffled words or catch a clue from the surgeon's body language and his listeners' subdued reactions. Meanwhile, it was midnight and the fireworks over Palm Beach began. When they were over and everyone had gone back into the Sloane home for a final toast to the New Year, the Christmas tree lights in the living room shorted out and a small fire broke out. The blaze spread and the house was consumed by flames that could be seen for miles around. Firefighters arrived and rescued everyone except a young child who was already dead and whose body was covered with sores. An autopsy indicated that the child had died of bubonic plague.

END